Born in 1951, Petra Hammesfahr wrote her first novel at the age of seventeen. She has written over twenty crime and suspense novels and also writes scripts for television and film. Her book *The Quiet Mr Genardy* was her first bestseller and was made into a film. It was soon followed by *The Sinner*, also published by Bitter Lemon Press and her first novel to be available in English. She has won numerous literary prizes, including the Crime Prize of Wiesbaden and the Rhineland Literary Prize, and lives near Cologne.

THE LIE

Petra Hammesfahr

Translated from the German
by Mike Mitchell

BITTER LEMON PRESS
LONDON

BITTER LEMON PRESS

First published in the United Kingdom in 2009 by

Bitter Lemon Press, 37 Arundel Gardens, London W11 2LW

www.bitterlemonpress.com

First published in German as *Die Lüge* by
Wunderlich, Rowohlt Verlag GmbH,
Reinbek bei Hamburg, 2003

Bitter Lemon Press gratefully acknowledges the financial
assistance of the Arts Council of England

A CIP record for this book is available
from the British Library

ISBN 978-1-904738-42-8

Typeset by Alma Books Ltd
Printed and bound by CPI Cox & Wyman,
Reading, Berkshire

The Lie

Prologue

It was a horrible sight, even for the boy who, at fourteen, had already witnessed much barbarity, though not in this country. People didn't get their hands chopped off here because they'd stolen something, nor women their fingers because they'd painted their nails. Nor were women here in danger of being buried up to the waist and stoned. And children could play without losing their legs or even their lives. The boy thought that was good, he liked living here. His sisters could go to school and he could too, of course. And after school he could be what he was: a young boy who liked playing football.

On that Sunday at the end of November 2002 he left the little flat his family had been allocated with a ball under his arm and a bag full of rubbish in his hand. He was to put the rubbish in one of the bins beside the house. Then he was going to see if he could find a few other boys who'd play with him. But that was quickly forgotten.

He pushed back the lid of the bin and saw the bundle of humanity lying among the refuse – filthy, scorched, covered in blood, dumped like garbage. A woman, he saw that straight away, even though she was wearing a suit like a man. They'd been here a long time now and his elder sister had started wearing trousers and painting her fingernails.

The nails of the woman in the bin were black, both her hands had been burned black, her head was deformed and encrusted with blood, as if she'd been stoned. For a few seconds the boy stared at her. He tried to scream but couldn't. He dropped his ball and the sack of refuse, ran back into the house and told his mother what he'd seen. She came out with him to check before she called over a neighbour who informed the police.

The boy never found out who the woman in the bin was and why she'd been killed. The police thought they had, but they were wrong.

Part One

It all started one Thursday at the end of July 2002, one of those summer days in this part of the world that are only tolerable with an ice-cool drink in the shade. Susanne Lasko was standing, sweaty and nervous, by one of the four lifts in the air-conditioned entrance hall of Gerler House, a large office block. The lift arrived, the door slid open and Susanne Lasko found herself walking towards herself.

In her external appearance the young woman who suddenly appeared before her was not identical with her. She was her height and had her figure, her eyes, her mouth. And it was her face – but with perfect make-up and framed by fashionably styled hair. The woman's hair was a rich brown and considerably shorter than the sun-bleached mop coming down to her shoulders. Her double was wearing a light-grey, pinstripe suit with a white blouse.

A boring colour combination, Susanne thought. But the suit and blouse were impeccable and looked as crisp as if they'd just been ironed. The handbag that was swinging from her right shoulder must have cost a fortune; a document case was tucked under her left arm. Never before had Susanne felt so shabbily dressed, so pathetic, so wretched, old and worn out.

She was wearing a suit as well, the green one she'd bought ten years ago. She'd last worn it three years previously, when she got divorced from Dieter Lasko. It may well have been right for that, it was less so for a job interview with a superior estate agent's. But she'd found nothing better in her wardrobe that morning.

At the time of that first encounter with Nadia Trenkler she had two euros sixty-two cents in her purse. She'd checked before setting out to get her life going again. She'd lost her last job in January. It hadn't been a proper job, so she couldn't claim the dole and she was too proud to apply for supplementary benefit. She was also afraid they might draw her divorced husband's attention to her situation or even approach her mother, who had a little money tucked away. But her mother needed that for her old age and, anyway, Susanne wanted to keep her ignorant of her only daughter's predicament.

During February and March she'd written countless job applications and used up all her savings. Since April her mother had been supporting her – unsuspectingly. Agnes Runge didn't trust strangers and was no longer capable of looking after her accounts. Because she was afraid of injections, her diabetes had gone untreated for years and had resulted in blindness.

When her husband died, Agnes Runge had been left financially secure. She had received a considerable sum from his life insurance policy, sold the house where Susanne had grown up and taken a room in a comfortable old people's home, where she enjoyed the best of care – for three thousand euros a month. The management of her finances, which were to pay for this, she had entrusted to her daughter, happy in the belief that Susanne's clever investments would guarantee her an old age free from worry.

Instead, she was helping herself. Not to huge sums, no. And she was going to pay everything back as soon as she was in a position to do so. So far she'd taken sixteen hundred euros, four hundred a month. After deducting three hundred for the rent and other costs that came with the flat, she was left with a hundred for food and other necessities such as writing paper, large envelopes, photocopying and postage. She lived mainly on noodles and had to think very carefully before making more than a short journey on the tram. She had gone to Behringer and Partners on foot.

Four and a half miles in the heat and exhaust fumes. Her mouth was dry and her body soaked in sweat, her blouse was sticking to her sides and her feet aching a little in her black court shoes. But it was bearable, she was hardly conscious of it. Until the moment when the lift doors slid open she was completely occupied with her great hope. A personal interview! Only someone who has gone six months without a wage coming in and two and a half years without health insurance, without pension contributions, only someone whose every job application has been returned with a curt letter of rejection, or not at all, can appreciate what that meant.

"Are you young, dynamic, motivated?" Behringer and Partners had asked in their advert, declaring, "Then you are the person we are looking for. We can offer... We expect..." At thirty-seven Susanne Lasko didn't feel old. Her dynamism had probably suffered a little during the last few months, but she was certainly motivated – and she was willing to learn.

She was a quick learner and she would definitely even be able to cope with a computer as long as she was allowed to get on with it in peace. In her last regular job – three weeks with an insurance company – she'd failed miserably with the word-processing package, because a young colleague had insisted on giving her jokey tips instead of a handbook.

And foreign languages. At school one of the teachers had realized she had an exceptional gift for languages. They just had to put her next to the child of an Italian immigrant for half an hour and she was speaking the same broken German as if she'd been doing it all her life. Naturally that wasn't sufficient for business use, nor the little English she'd learned at school either. And apart from a few expressions, she had no knowledge of French at all, which Behringer and Partners also required.

And that is what she had told them in a detailed, not to say brutally frank application – not, it has to be said, with any great expectations. That they were interviewing her despite that surely justified her great hopes. All the way there she had worked out what she must say to the personnel manager, if there was one. Then for the next few minutes she completely forgot everything she'd prepared.

She stared at the woman in the pinstripe suit who, for her part, looked her up and down in stunned astonishment. People pushed past them, grumbling or with irritated expressions because they were in the way. No one seemed to notice that by the lift two women were facing each other who looked more alike than some pairs of identical twins. Perhaps the difference in the way they were turned out meant it wasn't so obvious to others as it was to them.

For, despite her painful experiences, Susanne well remembered the way she had looked when she had still been in regular employment, suitably dressed with unobtrusive make-up. And presumably Nadia Trenkler would have seen her own face in the mirror when she was going through a bad time herself.

Nadia was the first to recover her composure. With an exclamation of disbelief and a muttered, "That's impossible," she introduced herself and said, smiling, "We must have a coffee and find out which of our fathers is responsible."

Susanne couldn't imagine her father doing anything wrong. He'd been a decent, honest man right up to his sudden and too-early death. She didn't know Nadia Trenkler's father, of course, but she did know her own mother very well. For Agnes Runge marital fidelity was an article of faith and what the woman with her face was suggesting was out of the question.

And she didn't want to discuss it with Nadia Trenkler. In those first minutes she genuinely didn't. It had nothing to do with some premonition, it was just the general situation. Nadia Trenkler was clearly at the top of the ladder, of which she desperately needed to clamber onto the bottom rung, if she was to get out of the poverty trap.

"I'm in a hurry," she said. "I've got a job interview." This last statement slipped out against her will, perhaps because she had such little opportunity to talk to other people.

"At Behringer's?" Nadia asked, surprised.

Not for one second did Susanne wonder how her double had come to make such an accurate guess. She nodded automatically.

"It won't go on for ever," said Nadia. "I'll wait."

Now Susanne shook her head vigorously. "I don't want you to wait. I don't want to have a coffee with you, nor to talk about my father or yours. I don't want to know who you are. Can't you understand? It's enough for me to know who I am."

And that was something that was crystal clear to her. If she didn't get the job as secretary with Behringer and Partners it was more or less the end of the line for her. All that was left for a woman of her age and with her background was hope and the determination not to let herself be ground down. Only unfortunately there was very little in the way of job opportunities.

The day was coming when she would be compelled to resort to the small ads in the vacancies section of the Saturday paper if she wasn't going to ruin her mother completely. Cleaner wanted – three hours per week. Waitress required – temporary, two evenings. And that would be the end. It was a matter of simple arithmetic. To keep body and soul together and at least be able to afford health insurance again, she would need several such jobs. That would scarcely leave her any time at all to write applications and go to job interviews. Ignoring Nadia Trenkler, she went to the next lift. The one they were standing by had long since departed.

"Pity," she heard the woman with her face say.

* * *

She went up to Behringer's on the fifth floor, still feeling shabbily dressed, wretched, old and worn-out. A deep-pile carpet, even in the lobby – on it an acrylic-glass desk and behind that a young woman looking like a catalogue illustration for correct business dress. She didn't look particularly dynamic, in fact she was clearly struggling with the problem of how to explain to someone of Susanne's appearance that Behringer's didn't do properties in the lower price range. The receptionist's tentative smile froze when Susanne told her she had not come for help in finding an apartment.

She was still feeling churned-up inside from the brief encounter with her spitting image and the light in which it had made her see herself. She was almost grateful that she was made to wait. It was a good quarter of an hour before she was shown in to see the office manager. He was called Reincke, a pleasant young man with a thin moustache who had familiarized himself with the details of her situation.

After they had talked about her lack of foreign languages and computer skills, he leaned forwards and lowered his voice. "I don't want to anticipate any decision the management might come to, Frau Lasko, but what I can say is that we have already discussed your application. There are four others, all from ladies who are younger and —" He broke off, suddenly embarrassed. "We're looking for someone who will not leave after a short time for family reasons, if you understand what I'm getting at. That does not seem to be a danger in your case. If, then, you were prepared to give up your time during the initial period to acquire the necessary skills... There are, for example, courses in foreign languages in which right from the beginning not a word of German is spoken; you learn very quickly. Naturally we would bear the costs."

If was practically a job offer, she thought, hastening to assure him that she would be delighted to devote all her spare time to acquiring the necessary skills. With a pleased smile, Herr Reincke accompanied her to the door of his office. "You'll be hearing from us very soon," he promised.

She was walking on air as she crossed the lobby. The smile she gave the young woman behind the desk was one for a colleague and friend.

She looked round, feeling almost as if she belonged there already. The telephone on the acrylic-glass desk rang and one of the office doors opened. Automatically she halted and looked back. The receptionist picked up the receiver and said, "Behringer and Partners. Luici speaking." A man appeared in the doorway.

She smiled at him, hoping to catch his eye and thus influence the senior management in her favour. His imposing appearance alone suggested he was important. He was six foot tall, with receding hair. His bulky physique hid most of the luxurious interior of his office and the two visitors sitting at a coffee table. She merited nothing more than an uninterested glance as he turned to the receptionist.

Frau Luici was saying, "Herr Behringer is in a meeting at the moment, could you try again later?" The tall man asked who it was. Putting her hand over the receiver, Frau Luici whispered, "Hardenberg."

"I'll take it," said the man, clearly Behringer himself. He positively grabbed the receiver from Frau Luici and asked in effusive tones, "Hi, Philip, what is it?", in the same breath telling the receptionist to get drinks for his visitors. Frau Luici leaped up and hurried into an adjacent room, presumably a small kitchen.

Susanne kept her eyes fixed on the giant at the telephone and saw him give a gasp of surprise. Frowning, he gave her a quick look, as if he were surprised she hadn't moved. "By what devious route did that come to your ears?" he asked, adding, "May I know why you're so interested in this property?"

Then he listened, gave a short laugh and said, "That could be done, assuming an appropriate quid pro quo. There are other offers on the table and there's been water damage recently." As he listened, he finally gave her a smile. She nodded to him and went to the door, breathing a sigh of relief.

Out in the street she felt a slight regret that she'd rejected her double's offer. In her euphoria she felt there'd have been nothing to lose in having a coffee with Nadia Trenkler, perhaps an iced coffee. This heat! Her mouth was still dry, only now did she notice it again. She'd presumably not have had to worry about the fact that she only had a few coppers in her purse. Nadia Trenkler would surely have insisted on paying and might even have driven her home. She wouldn't have had to inflict another four miles' wear and tear on her old court shoes.

It was early evening by the time she reached her dilapidated flat in Kettlerstrasse. One and a half rooms – she'd managed to squeeze a narrow bed and a similar wardrobe into the "half room" – plus a mini-kitchen with a mini-balcony, a mini-bathroom with shower and the one square yard behind the door that the lease dignified with the name of "vestibule". A local train rattled past outside. Once the noise had died away, she flung open the window, went into the kitchen and drank two glasses of water.

At seven she cooked her daily ration of noodles and carefully brushed her teeth as soon as she'd finished: without health insurance, cleaning her teeth was an absolute must. At eight she switched on the TV, stretched out on the couch and dreamed of her future. Once she had a regular income again, had plugged the hole in her mother's nest egg and put away a little for a rainy day, the first thing she'd do would be to buy a new fridge, then look for a larger, above all quieter flat, perhaps even go away on holiday.

On Friday she bumped into Heller by the apartment letter boxes. She only knew his surname and he was the only person she was at all acquainted with in the tenement apart from her immediate neighbour, Jasmin Toppler. She got on well with Jasmin, they said hello and exchanged a few words whenever they happened to meet on the stairs. Jasmin Toppler was in her late twenties, an energetic but friendly woman. Heller, on the other hand, was an obnoxious type, whom she tried to avoid. He grasped any opportunity to shower her with abuse. He was about the same age as her and had the front second-floor flat. It was rumoured that he had several convictions for car theft, grievous bodily harm, attempted rape and other offences.

When she came down the stairs to check her mail, he was standing by the open door, a can of beer in his hand. He heard her footsteps and turned round. He gestured towards the street with his free hand. "One fucking hot motor," he said. She had no idea what he was talking about and since he regularly applied expressions like "hot" and all variants of "fucking" to her, she ignored him. "An MG," he declared. "Saw it from the window. The third time it's driven past. And slowly, as if he was looking for something."

He took a step out into the street. "Now he's stopping," he told her, almost dislocating his neck. He was presumably talking about a car that had stopped a little way from the tenement.

She was relieved to see him occupied with watching the car instead of subjecting her to his usual volley of obscene remarks. Her letter box was empty; naturally it was too early for a response from Behringer's. She hurried back up to her flat before Heller's interest in the car waned and turned to her.

A little later there was a knock at the door. It wasn't Heller, as she feared, but a young man who claimed to be doing a survey on unemployment. Heller was on the landing, gawping at them. She asked the young man in simply in order to get away from Heller's glassy stare.

Without being asked, the young man sat down on the couch and asked for a glass of water. Friday was as hot as Thursday had been, so there was nothing odd about his request. After she had brought him a glass, he noted her answers on a questionnaire and took down – "Just for the statistical evaluation, you understand, it's completely anonymous," – some personal details: date of birth, place of birth, marital status, children, school, professional qualifications, dates of birth and, if applicable, death of her parents and any siblings etc., etc.

Naturally she didn't tell him the truth. For the last two years she hadn't even been telling that to her mother. Agnes Runge thought she had a well-paid position with a small firm. To the alleged pollster she claimed she worked as a secretary with a well-known estate agent's. It wasn't, she told herself, really a lie, just a little premature, given what nice Herr Reincke had hinted at the previous day. When the young man responded with a sceptical look round the room, she told him she was obliged to pay maintenance to her divorced husband, besides which she was also making a small contribution towards her mother's upkeep, so that there wasn't much left for herself.

As if to punish her for her lies, the letter box wasn't empty on Saturday morning. One of her own large envelopes was in it. Her fingers were already trembling as she took it out of the box and recognized the company stamp. As she went up the stairs her knees were trembling as well. There was something raging inside her for which disappointment was too mild an expression.

After two days her documents had been returned with kind regards from Behringer and Partners. They were pleased to have met her but unfortunately had to inform her that they had given preference to another candidate and wished her all the best for the future. She couldn't understand it. Hadn't Herr Reincke indicated her appointment was as good as settled? She spent the rest of the day staring at the TV. She had intended to go for a walk, but she felt she would burst into tears sooner or later and she didn't want to do that out in the street.

On Sunday she went to see her mother. The old folks' home was twenty-five miles away and Johannes Herzog drove her there. His grandmother had a room next to her mother's and at some point or other Johannes had offered to drive her home. Since then he had been coming to pick her up punctually at two o'clock every second Sunday, as long as he didn't have a problem with the car.

Johannes was in his mid-twenties. He was studying – sporadically – some technical/scientific subject, but most of the time he was working as a stuntman for a TV series consisting mainly of wild car chases and crashes. It showed in the way he drove his car, an old BMW. She often felt carsick. But going with Johannes cost nothing.

She was still smarting from the disappointment with Behringer's. Despite that, the usual fictions flowed from her lips while she was with her mother: the stress at work, going to see a play with her friend Jasmin Toppler. And that nice Herr Heller from the second floor had invited her out to dinner next Saturday. Specially for her mother she had endowed the obnoxious Heller with a lucrative profession, perfect manners and a pleasant appearance. But she wasn't sure whether she'd go out with him, she said. She still hadn't come to terms emotionally with her failed marriage.

That corresponded to the facts. There were moments when she felt a burning hatred of Lasko. He had made a name for himself as a freelance journalist and at the same time had been successful as a writer of books on current events. While she, three years after their divorce, was at her wits' end as to how to survive, he was working on a book about the background to the conflict in Palestine. His previous book, about the operations of the UN forces in Bosnia, had been in the best-seller lists for ten weeks and must have earned him a tidy sum.

There was no contact between them. Despite that, she knew exactly how her ex was doing. Sometimes she saw him on television, sometimes she read an interview or report by him in the weekend edition of the paper, which she bought regularly for the vacancies section. Perhaps he would have helped her get back on her feet. When they got divorced he'd said, "If you ever need help..." But she had her pride.

She preferred to continue her monthly visits to the bank, and on the Monday she nervously filled out the slip to transfer four hundred euros from her mother's account to her own. A hundred of that she took out straight away. On Tuesday she went for a long walk and concentrated all her hope on the next vacancies section. Then on Wednesday she found the slim white envelope in her letter box.

Her name and address had been handwritten in capital letters. There was no indication of the sender's address. The stamp had a local postmark. She couldn't wait till she was back in her flat but tore the envelope open on the stairs. As she went up, she unfolded a printed letter and read:

Dear Susanne Lasko,

You said no. I attribute that to your surprise and the fact that you were understandably in a hurry. But I refuse to accept it. If Nature can play a trick like that, then surely we must give ourselves the chance to laugh at it together, at least just once. On Friday at three I'll be on the balcony of the Opera Café and I'd be delighted if you could find the time to come for a coffee. Even if you don't want to know who I am, I'd like to know who you are and what kind of life you lead. Not the best, was my impression. Perhaps I can do something to change that.

With best wishes,

Nadia Trenkler

It was obvious where Nadia Trenkler had got her name and address. There was only one possibility: Behringer and Partners. From her appearance she could even have a business of her own in the building, so knew Herr Reincke, Frau Luici, possibly even Behringer himself, had made enquiries and discovered that her double had not got the job. Perhaps she was desperately searching for a reliable secretary herself.

Friday started with vain attempts to moderate her wild hopes. She spent half an hour reviewing the meagre contents of her wardrobe, eventually deciding on a cotton skirt and a T-shirt. They gave her a fresh, summery look, she felt, not too poverty-stricken.

She set off at two, her head full to bursting with crazy hopes for some kind of miracle. She reached the Opera Café punctually at three and scanned the balcony. No sign of Nadia Trenkler. Most of the tables were occupied by middle-aged ladies. She sat down at one that was free. The waitress scurried over, but she told her she was meeting someone and would order when she arrived.

Nadia Trenkler was half an hour late. Despite the blazing sun, she was in a grey trouser suit with a bulging document case under her arm, as if she were coming from a meeting that had gone on longer than expected. She seemed slightly out of breath and excused her lateness with the traffic in the city centre and the time it took to find a parking place. She sat down and smiled. "I'm glad you waited."

The waitress came. Nadia ordered two pots of coffee and two slices of fruit flan. "Sorry I didn't ask, but what else can one eat when it's so hot?"

Susanne nodded. They sat there in silence.

"Well now," said Nadia after a while, stretching out the words, "where shall we start? I told you my name, wrote it in the letter too, and I've found out what you're called. You don't want to know anything more about me, but we can still be on first-name terms, can't we?"

Susanne nodded again. The coffee and cake arrived. The flan was covered with a thick layer of fruit – juicy peach halves, cherries, slices of banana and green grapes. She cut off a piece with her fork, trying not to bolt it down, and waited to hear what Nadia could do for her. But for the moment the woman with her face showed no sign of coming up with an offer. She didn't like to ask straight out, and no harmless topic of conversation occurred to her.

As Nadia was putting the second piece of cake into her mouth, Susanne noticed her wedding ring. It was slim and almost invisible below a second ring with a showy blue stone that sparkled in the sun. "You're married, er… Nadia?" she asked hesitantly.

Nadia was chewing and just nodded.

"I'm divorced," Susanne explained. "Have been for three years now. He married again right away and had a daughter."

She hadn't meant to tell her that, just to mention the divorce to make her situation clear, but not that festering wound. His daughter! Dieter had announced the birth of his child with a half-page spread – and a bombastic message: "In a time when hope has all but vanished, we are delighted to have brought a little ray of sunshine into the world: a child's smile." It had sounded as if she were being blamed for failing to bear him the expected messiah – when she would have loved to have a child while she was still married.

"How long were you married, Susanne?" Nadia asked. The name came quite naturally.

"Seven years."

"That's too long just to smile and say thank you for a kick up the backside," Nadia declared. "But some men are desperate to become fathers and if you don't go along with it, or can't, they give you the heave-ho."

Susanne said nothing to disabuse Nadia of her belief that her cupboard was bare. Perhaps it was. Since the divorce her periods had been very irregular. Often there was nothing for months. But without a husband there was no point in worrying about it, and without health insurance nothing she could do about it anyway.

Nadia explained briefly that she had been more fortunate in her husband. He wasn't interested in having a family. With that she passed on to the next topic and asked Susanne about her parents. It was, she said, making a joke of it, to rule out the possibility that they were related after all, even if at twenty-seven removes. Their excavations got them as far as their great-grandparents. All Susanne knew of hers was that they were honest, respectable people. She had no uncles and aunts at all.

The conversation was taking a course that was unlikely to fulfil her expectations. Bearing in mind Susanne's declaration that she didn't want to know who she was, Nadia told her neither with whom or how long she'd been married, nor where she lived or what her work was.

It must have been lucrative. Everything about Nadia screamed money. The ostentatious ring, the gold lighter and the cigarette case she held out to her when they'd finished their cake. She declined.

"So you don't smoke then," Nadia observed, almost with a note of envy. "How do you do it? Lord knows how often I've tried to give it up."

"By never starting," she said.

Nadia smoked three cigarettes with her second cup of coffee. Then she waved the waitress over, paid and left a generous tip. For a few seconds the sight of her bulging wallet left Susanne floundering in a welter of contradictory emotions, a revolting mixture of greed, envy and shame.

"You've still got some time, I hope?" Nadia asked. "I thought we'd go for a little drive in the country. We can talk without being overheard there." She sketched a nod in the direction of two old ladies who appeared to be holding a whispered conversation about them. Time was the one thing Susanne had plenty of. A drive in the country sounded nice. And to talk without being overheard sounded promising.

The car for which Nadia had spent so long finding a parking place turned out to be an extremely manoeuvrable vehicle that could squeeze into small spaces: a white Porsche. Susanne settled as comfortably as she could into the passenger seat and scrutinized Nadia's face with surreptitious sidelong glances. It was a strange feeling, as if she were sitting beside herself. She hadn't felt it so strongly in the café. In the confines of the car it became overpowering and oppressive.

Stuck to the dashboard was a tiny frame with the photo of a man's face. He was laughing. A nice guy, in his mid-twenties, Susanne guessed. Blond hair blowing in the wind, a straight nose, thin lips. The photo was too small to make out any more details.

"Your husband?" she asked, assuming it was an old photo.

And Nadia said, "Who else? It was taken two months ago, since then he's had his hair cut. He only goes round with a mop like that during the holidays. Do you like sailing?"

Susanne shrugged her shoulders and swallowed. Two months ago, on a sailing boat! A sailing boat?! A boat wasn't Nadia Trenkler's style. A white yacht, that was it, with Nadia lying on the deck and the man oiling her back.

After a good hour's drive they stopped at a little car park where a path led off into the woods. Nadia picked up her handbag and document case from the back seat and took both on the walk with her.

Then they strolled through green-filtered shade. Bit by bit Susanne spread out her whole life along the dry pathway, adopting Nadia's tone of voice, though without noticing it herself. Her initial monosyllabic answers soon gave way to fluent candour. At the back of her mind she was still hoping for a job offer, but apart from that it did her good, after all the lies of the previous months, to talk to someone about the way things really were.

* * *

She'd had a good start in life: loving parents, good marks at school, good reports during training as a bank clerk and during her first years at work. Her father was proud of her and already saw her as a branch manager. Now and then she dreamed of getting married and having children.

She'd not been short of admirers. At twenty-four she met Dieter Lasko. He was working for the local paper and hardly earning enough to pay for more than the bare necessities. When they went out together she'd picked up the tab. Three years later they got married, moving in with his mother. And that was the beginning of the end.

Naturally it wasn't all Dieter's fault. A year after they were married she gave up her job after a bank robbery, which, it turned out, had been carried out with a toy gun. It would have been the right time to have a child. But it was not to be. Her mother-in-law became bedridden following a stroke and, shortly afterwards, Dieter started going to international trouble spots as a freelance journalist. It was probably preferable to the running battles at home.

For six years she'd looked after the house and garden, and taken her mother-in-law on fictional journeys to the castles of princes who regularly fell in love with their chambermaids. Dieter, meanwhile, had seen a war-torn world from the front line, and on his rare trips home he found she was becoming more and more of a cabbage.

By the time his mother died, they had nothing to say to each other. Dieter had found another woman in one of the trouble spots: Ramie, a translator, twenty-four and already pregnant with his child when he brought her home. Susanne was thirty-four, without children and convinced that after six years she'd fully got over the trauma of the bank robbery.

At this point Nadia gave a snort of contempt and said, "Parasites, that's what they are. Let their wife finance them while they launch themselves on a high-flying career, then take her for every penny."

"No, it wasn't like that," Susanne protested.

"But you said he was a freelance journalist," Nadia insisted. "You had to support him financially when he wasn't working."

"No," she said. She'd told the man doing the opinion poll something like that but had forgotten it by now. "For a start I had no income of my own. He even voluntarily paid a lump sum so I could get a flat in the city and furnish it."

"He did, did he?" said Nadia. "And you haven't seen him since your divorce?"

She shook her head.

"No other contact? Not even an occasional telephone call?"

"I haven't got a telephone. And we wouldn't have any more to say to each other than we did three years ago."

Nadia nodded thoughtfully but said nothing more. After a few seconds Susanne went on with her story. After the divorce she'd applied for a job with her former employer – with her heart in her mouth and a shot of schnapps in her belly. Her father had sworn by schnapps in stressful situations. It worked for her as well. She was taken on – for three months.

The first month was taken up with familiarizing herself with the changes that had taken place over the years. Everything in the bank was done by computer now, but she could cope with that – more or less. In the second month she was already working at the counter. At times she was nervous, watching the door rather than what she was doing. Twice some money was missing at the end of the day. The second time it was a significant sum.

The manager agreed with her that the five thousand marks she'd recorded as paid in must in fact have been a withdrawal. She'd presumably pressed the wrong key. They relied on the honesty of the customer, unfortunately in vain. She'd had to make good the loss. The money was to be deducted in three instalments from her salary. But it never came to that.

She was transferred from the counter to the customer-service desk. One Thursday she went down to the basement with a middle-aged man called Schrag. He came regularly on Thursdays in the late afternoon to deposit something or take something out.

Herr Schrag ran a small electrical business from which he barely made a living. His accounts made grim reading. Whether things looked any better in his deposit box, no one knew. On that particular Thursday he came back from his deposit box with a brown envelope, which he put in his inside jacket pocket. Then he followed her up into the main hall.

Pale-faced, the cashier was emptying the tills. The manager and two of her colleagues were standing by their desks, hands raised, and beside the manager stood a figure like the one who'd put the fear of death into her all those years ago with a plastic toy. She wasn't going to put up with that again.

Herr Schrag stared at the masked man and opened his mouth, but all that came out was a groan as he clasped his hands to the left side of his chest. Not for one second did she think of the envelope in his jacket pocket, only of her father's sudden death. Ignoring the gun, which she assumed was as harmless as the previous one, she placed herself in front of Herr Schrag and pushed him backwards to the exit. The masked man waved his gun around wildly. "For God's sake, Frau Lasko," the manager cried, "don't do anything stupid."

"Don't worry," she shouted back, "it's not a real one. I've been here before."

The manager believed her and hit the masked man's outstretched arm. Then everything seemed to happen at once. She heard a bang, saw a red stain appear on the manager's shirt and rapidly spread, heard a piercing cry from the cashier and saw the look of disbelief on the manager's face as he grasped his wounded shoulder. Then the gun was pointing at her. Herr Schrag was uninjured because she fell on top of him when the masked man—

"Don't tell me he shot at you," Nadia broke in, breathless and horrified.

"No." He'd tried, but after the first shot the pistol must have jammed. The masked man had knocked her to the ground with a punch, dragged her along with him, shoved her into a car, drove her to a disused factory, aimed and pressed the trigger twice, to no effect, then in his fury hit her again and again with the butt of the gun, hissing, "If you move, you're dead."

Of course she moved – after he'd gone. For a long time – it was two whole days – she crawled round among rubble and debris with a fractured skull and a raging headache, unable to find a way out. Eventually there was someone bending over her. She thought it was the masked man who'd returned. But it was only a dosser who'd come to spend the night in the disused factory and happened to trip over her. Since then she was incapable of working as a bank clerk; just the thought of having to go into a bank set off palpitations...

What happened next she recounted only reluctantly. It didn't reflect very well on her. She passed over her job with the insurance firm, which she'd messed up because of her lack of IT expertise. It had only lasted three weeks anyway. She went straight on to the two years she'd spent working for Herr Schrag.

The old man felt he owed her something and, on closer inspection, his business turned out to be flourishing. So far his wife had done the office work, but now she had fallen ill and he needed someone he could trust to replace her; the only requirement was the ability to use a typewriter. He didn't give her a contract, they just shook hands on it. There were five others Herr Schrag employed on the same basis; the only ones in regular employment were two electricians.

She got two thousand marks a month, net, cash in hand. When the new currency came in, it was converted exactly into euros. She could survive on that – without health insurance, that would have swallowed up half her income. But apart from a headache following physical exertion she'd felt she was generally in good health and preferred to put something aside for a rainy day.

Given the ailing state of government finances, Herr Schrag felt it made more sense for each individual to take personal responsibility in providing for their old age. Private clients – as most of Herr Schrag's were – could pay in cash and enjoy a discount to the value of the VAT. It was from these cash payments that Susanne and the five other freelancers were paid. What was left disappeared into one of the envelopes for which she had risked her neck.

Herr Schrag had a courier who took each instalment of his retirement fund out of the country. And his trust in her was absolute until the courier turned up in January of that year. His name was Röhrler. How often this Röhrler had appeared at Schrag's on a Thursday evening to pick up an envelope she had no idea. In January he didn't arrive until Friday lunchtime, because his car had broken down.

He gaped when he saw her. "What are you doing here?" he asked, astonished, then a grin spread over his face. "You've come down in the world and no mistake. But that's what happens when you get caught with your fingers in the till. It's the beginning of a slippery slope."

It had never occurred to her that Röhrler could be mistaking her for someone else. It didn't even now, when she told Nadia about it, because she'd got it into her head that he must have read about her in the paper. After the second hold-up, while she was still crawling round in the disused factory, a very unfavourable, almost libellous report about her had appeared in the newspaper – together with a photo. The two times there'd been a deficit in her till were mentioned, together with speculation that she might have been in cahoots with the robber in order to conceal the fact that she had embezzled money. Later they had had to print an apology but probably no one had noticed it. She wanted to explain this to him, but before she had the chance Herr Schrag appeared. And Röhrler told him she'd lined her own pockets while working for the bank.

Nadia stared impassively at the path in front as Susanne repeated Röhrler's words. "It was a simple error," she assured her. "I wouldn't have risked my job for a few thousand marks."

"That's OK," said Nadia soothingly. "You don't have to justify yourself to me. How did Schrag react?"

"He threw me out."

Nadia shook her head, uncomprehending. "And you let him do that to you? In your place I'd have said, 'OK, Herr Schrag, I'm not going to insist on continuing to work for you. From now on I'll get three thousand a month and if you pay up punctually, you'll see how good I am at keeping secrets.' "

Susanne said nothing. The idea of blackmail had never occurred to her. Nadia gave her a thoughtful sidelong glance. "And what have you lived on since then?"

She came close to admitting the truth, but she couldn't bring herself to say, "By stealing from my mother." Instead she said, "I had some money saved up."

Nadia looked up at the treetops. Above them the sky was still a rich, deep blue. "Let's go back," she suggested. She had not said a word about what she could do for Susanne.

Nadia offered to drive her home. Instead, Susanne asked to be taken to a cinema, on the pretext that she wanted to see the late showing. It would have been too embarrassing to have had to ask her, when they reached Kettlerstrasse, "Would you like to come up for a while?"

She got out at the cinema and said, in a voice tinged with disappointment, "It was a nice afternoon."

Nadia was leaning over the passenger seat to see her on the pavement. "Yes, I thought so too." She said nothing about their having to do it again. No "See you soon", just a "Cheerio, then."

Susanne slammed the door shut. The engine roared and the white sports car overtook two others then disappeared from view, as if Nadia couldn't wait to put as much distance as possible between her and her poverty-stricken double. Suddenly she felt ashamed of the openness with which she'd told her life story, of the ravenous way she'd eaten the fruit flan, horribly ashamed of the whole afternoon and her wild hopes.

She took her time going home. It was after midnight when she reached the shabby tenement, which she would have so loved to say goodbye to for good. As usual the main door wasn't locked. Heart-rending groans came from Heller's flat, accompanied by the crack of a whip and coarse male laughter. She shivered as she went past. She hurried up the last few stairs, locked the door behind her, headed straight for the shower, spent minutes cleaning her teeth and climbed into bed wondering if Nadia was also home by now and what her home looked like.

While still awake, she dreamed up a snow-white villa on some coast or other. But the house with the yacht anchored offshore was only her holiday home. For a while she lay on the deck in the sun and got the blond man to rub oil over her, then dived into the sea to cool off. The fact that she couldn't swim was irrelevant as far as her dream-self was concerned.

When she finally got to sleep, she dreamed of her father. They were sitting at the coffee table having a cosy chat. In the middle of a sentence he clasped his chest and the bewildered look appeared in his eyes. Then he fell forward, dead, dead at just fifty-seven. And she screamed and screamed, unable to stop herself.

At once she was wide awake. She heard the old fridge chuntering to itself, the early train rattling past and, inside her head, Nadia's voice. It hurt terribly because it looked as if all Nadia Trenkler had wanted from her had been to amuse herself for a few hours, then perhaps go home to have a good laugh with her husband at the tricks Nature could play.

But she was wrong. Only a few days later a further letter from Nadia arrived. This time she wrote:

Dear Susanne,

I have some things lying around that I don't really need. Please don't get me wrong, it's not jumble. The things are fine, it's just that I don't wear them any more. They should fit you. I don't want to force anything on you and I don't want you to feel you're receiving charity. If you don't want them, all you have to do is say no. Let's meet at the Opera Café again, Friday, 3 o'clock.

Nadia

It was Thursday already, not much time to think it over. Just one night to sleep on it. Did she want Nadia's discarded clothes? No. She wanted Nadia's job, Nadia's car, Nadia's money. Nadia's life.

She spent the afternoon running a scenario though her mind. It started with a walk in the woods and continued with a heavy stick or a stone, a hastily dug grave in the undergrowth followed by an accident with the Porsche. Then she could tell Nadia's husband she was suffering from total amnesia and apply for a divorce soon afterwards. That would kill two birds with one stone: she wouldn't have to spend her life arguing with a husband who didn't want children and she'd have got rid of a car she wasn't happy with. She hadn't been at the wheel of a car for years and a Porsche wasn't the best model to start on.

She was a little late on Friday because Heller intercepted her on the stairs. He stood on the first-floor landing, blocking her way, and asked with a lewd grin on his face whether she didn't fancy a real man after her two toy boys. He insisted on assuming Johannes Herzog was her lover. Watching from his window, he'd often seen her get into his BMW on Sunday afternoons.

She tried to get past. He grabbed her arm, tight, and brought his face close up to hers. As usual he stank of sweat and beer, and hissed his usual obscenities, spraying her cheek with drops of spittle that made her feel sick.

She insisted he let go of her, telling him she had an appointment and was in a hurry. Furious, he told her she was one of those women who went round with their noses in the air, as if they didn't leave the same kind of crap in the shithouse as other people. "I'll have you some day, don't you worry," he said.

After that threat he let go of her arm, jerked his thumb in the direction of the main door and told her to get on her way, the boy had already been waiting a while. "I only came out to congratulate you. Unlike the midget with the clapped-out BMW, the one out there really is something to write home about. But don't let your hopes run away with you. The boy knows you've got two irons in the fire."

She'd no idea which boy he was talking about and told him so. Heller thought for a moment and said it was Friday that he'd seen the young man at her door. She realized he was assuming the man from the opinion poll was her lover. When she explained his mistake he tapped his forehead.

"You can't fool me. Opinion poll my arse! He didn't poll any opinions from me. You were the only one he went to see, and I bet it wasn't the only time. I saw him on Sunday as well. You'd just left with the other guy in the BMW and that's what I told him. Since then the MG's been driving round and round the area all the time."

Before she could reply, a door opened on the third floor and Jasmin Toppler came down the stairs. Heller stepped to one side to let her past and she grasped the opportunity to follow her next-door neighbour to the ground floor.

Heller's claims had disturbed her a little. As casually as she could, she asked Jasmin what an MG looked like and whether she'd also been visited by an opinion pollster. She knew Jasmin had been out on the Friday at the end of July, but if it was an important poll the young man would presumably have come again on the Sunday in order to interview occupants of the tenement who were in employment.

Jasmin explained that she always went out on Sundays and that pollsters didn't come at the weekend. At the door Jasmin stopped. "If you're worried about it, ask around in the building."

She wasn't worried, she said. And it would look ridiculous to go round knocking at the doors of people she didn't know just because of what Heller had said. It would give the impression she had a persecution complex, but for the life of her she couldn't think who might be persecuting her, unless it was Heller himself. With a laugh, Jasmin agreed. There was only one way of dealing with Heller, she said, and that was a quick knee in the groin. With that she went to her motorbike.

She stayed by the front door for a moment and looked along the cars parked on either side of the street. There were quite a lot, most of them fairly old. What an MG would look like she couldn't say, Jasmin hadn't answered that question. But she couldn't see anyone in any of the cars and none started as she set off.

* * *

She hurried off to get to the Opera Café on time. Nadia was already there, but had only been waiting for ten minutes to go by the single cigarette end in the ashtray. This time she was wearing a dark-grey ensemble, which gave the impression she'd just come out of a meeting where a company's turnover at least as high as the defence budget had been discussed. She was clasping her document case and handbag in her lap.

Scarcely had Susanne arrived than Nadia stood up. "Do you mind if we go straight to the car? I haven't much time anyway, and I left my laptop in the boot. Breaking it open's a piece of cake and the data's irreplaceable."

She shook her head and followed Nadia. The Porsche was in a nearby multi-storey car park. There was a suitcase on the passenger seat. Nadia opened it and showed her the things she didn't need any more. The light-grey pinstripe suit wasn't among them, but they were good clothes, expensive clothes in very good condition. Skirts, trousers, blouses, two blazers. All in shades of blue or grey, except one white blouse. If she had Nadia's money, she'd dress quite differently. On the other hand, they were precisely the kind of things a successful businesswoman would wear. She hadn't worn brightly coloured dresses when she'd worked in the bank either. She didn't bother trying them on in the car park, just slipped her feet into the two pairs of shoes Nadia picked up from the floor of the car. They fitted as if they were made to measure. "Thanks," she said, "I'm pleased to have them."

"You don't exactly look pleased," Nadia commented, leaning back against the car and surveying her thoughtfully. "But I can understand that. I've been asking myself what I would feel like in your situation. I almost got kicked out myself after Michael's career took off."

So it was Michael. Susanne glanced at the photo on the dashboard. The photo of the blond man was still there.

Nadia rummaged round in her handbag for her cigarette case. After she'd lighted the cigarette, she went on, hesitantly, as if she wasn't sure whether Susanne wanted to hear more about her life or not. They had a lot more in common than face and figure, Nadia said. "What you told me could have been the story of my life."

Nadia had also trained in banking and until two years ago had worked for a private bank in Düsseldorf. She didn't have a mother-in-law who needed looking after, just a husband who was earning nothing during the first years of their marriage.

"Michael was still a student when we got married," she said. "When he finally graduated, he didn't find the right job immediately. And when he did, I was still earning three times as much as him. Until…"

When Nadia broke off, Susanne completed the sentence for her: "Until there was a hold-up at the bank."

Nadia gave a pained smile. "Nothing so dramatic. I just thought I'd been on the treadmill for long enough. Michael's career was going places and I wanted to take more time for myself and for him. And with more time I quickly found out that he was sleeping with one of his little laboratory mice."

For a brief moment Susanne wondered whether to ask about Nadia's further career. She must have found another job by now – the document case and what she had told her about the laptop with its irreplaceable data indicated that. But she was shocked by what Nadia had said about her husband. She would never have associated the nice holiday face with infidelity.

"But he didn't want to marry her and have a child?" she asked, forcing herself to make a joke of it.

Nadia gave a brief and decidedly unamused laugh. "No idea. If he did want to do that, I managed to talk him out of it. Since then we've been behaving as if I'm the only one he loves, and I'm too busy to get bored in the evenings."

"You think he's still cheating on you?"

Nadia gave another laugh, a mocking laugh this time. "What's this? Suddenly we are interested after all?" She pouted. "But it's not worth talking about. I've stopped letting it bother me. He's not the only attractive man around."

"You're unfaithful to him as well?"

Nadia's shrug of the shoulders said everything. "I'm really short of time today, Susanne. We'll talk another day, OK? Can you manage with the suitcase?"

She nodded. Her thoughts were still on the mutual adultery and the question of why Nadia had not left her unfaithful husband, if she'd found a replacement. Nadia put the clothes, including the shoes, back in the suitcase, and put it down in front of her. She thanked her again.

"Don't mention it," said Nadia. "All you need now is a chic hairstyle. How do you like mine?"

"It's great."

"Good," said Nadia, glancing at her wristwatch. "Hey, I must be off. See you."

Seconds later the Porsche was gone.

Another trip to the old folks' home was scheduled for Sunday. Even as she carried the suitcase back through the streets Susanne was wondering what she could wear. Then she was home and trying the clothes on. Her heart missed a beat when her fingers felt the thin piece of paper in one of the blazer pockets. Two hundred euros. With a handwritten note attached by a paper clip: "For the hairdresser." And she'd assumed it was just a casual remark.

She would certainly have been able to find a hairdresser on the Saturday morning who would have taken her without an appointment, but why spend more money than absolutely necessary? She bought a pair of sharp scissors in the supermarket and some brown tinting lotion. Using the mirror in her tiny bathroom, she first of all cut off most of what she needed to get rid of, then, bending her head as far forward as possible, managed to get a fairly straight edge at the back. Finally she applied the tinting lotion.

At two o'clock on Sunday afternoon she was standing on the edge of the pavement with slightly straggly but dark brown hair. She could hardly wait for Johannes Herzog to arrive, for his look of astonishment and a remark such as, "You're looking very elegant today." She did look very elegant in the white blouse, a narrow, dark-blue skirt, a pair of court shoes and, casually draped over her left arm, the blazer which had contained such a momentarily embarrassing surprise.

At half-past two she was still standing on the pavement. Up above, Heller was leaning out of the window pouring forth speculations as to why her toy boy had stood her up and, with obscene suggestions, volunteering to help her pass the time, even the whole afternoon if necessary, so that she wouldn't know whether she was coming or going. She ignored him, wondering, with a mixture of irritation and concern, where Johannes could be and whether he'd had an accident. The way he drove that wasn't impossible.

After a further ten minutes Heller's abuse was just too much for her. But she wasn't going to abandon the trip to see her mother. Nadia's money gave her other possibilities. She went to the station, took the suburban railway and did the last part by bus. From the bus stop it was only eight hundred yards to the old folks' home.

Agnes Runge was delighted to see her but said it would have been better if she hadn't come. There was flu in the home, half of the inmates were ill and some had even gone into hospital. That was why Johannes Herzog's grandmother had told him not to come. Naturally it had not occurred to Johannes to pop over to Susanne's and tell her. But you couldn't expect a young man to think of that. And since she didn't have a telephone – so as not to be disturbed during her weekends, she claimed – her mother hadn't been able to tell her either. It was easy to lie to Agnes Runge – she wanted to believe all was well with her daughter.

On the way back to the bus stop Susanne was caught in a heavy shower and got soaked to the skin. On the Monday she felt under the weather and spent most of the day in bed, hoping that would nip any flu in the bud. Despite that, she had a cough on Tuesday. It wasn't so bad as to cause concern, it just gave her a headache, as did any physical exertion since her skull had been fractured.

On Wednesday the cough was worse. She bought some bronchial tea from the chemist's, drank two cups and went to bed, sweating profusely. Her poor nourishment over the past few months was taking its toll. Sometimes she was sweating so profusely the sheets stuck to her, at others she was so cold the shivers gave her cramp in all her muscles. Every breath she took was a struggle and set off fits of coughing that made her feel as if her head were about to explode. In the evening she remembered she hadn't checked her post, but she couldn't face the effort of dragging herself down the stairs.

Shortly after two in the morning she woke from a nightmare in which her mother was standing by an open grave, supported by Johannes Herzog, who was reading the inscriptions on the wreaths out to her. As the coffin was lowered, her mother asked through her tears, "Why did she never say anything?" It was a while before she realized she was lying in bed and not in her coffin.

She had a high temperature. With difficulty she managed to stand up and stagger to the bathroom, where she soaked two towels in cold water and wrapped them round her calves. She placed a third damp towel over her head. And since the tiled floor was so lovely and cool, she spent the rest of the night wedged between the shower and the lavatory. Early in the morning she forced herself to go to the kitchen, made another cup of bronchial tea and drank it in little sips, almost coughing up her lungs as she did so.

All was still quiet in the building, it was only just after five. Heller was presumably sleeping off the effects of the previous evening's drink. At least at that time in the morning there was hardly any danger of him popping up and exploiting her pitiful state to abuse her in one way or the other. Really she was in no condition to bother with her post, but she had a feeling that sent her down the stairs. And, indeed, one of the familiar envelopes was in her box.

When she got to the couch and unfolded the letter, the clear print was swimming before her eyes. "Dear Susanne," Nadia wrote, expressing the hope that she had not used the money in the blazer pocket for experiments and reminding her of her first letter and her desire to do something for her. Then came the sentence that suddenly brought everything back into sharp focus: "I may have a job for you. It's only as a stand-in, but we ought to discuss it." She suggested they meet in the multi-storey car park where she'd given her the suitcase. Below were day and time: Friday, five o'clock.

It was Friday. But it was crazy even to think about setting off for the city centre. She'd stumbled over her own feet going down the stairs and just managed to catch onto the wall to stop herself falling. When she tried to get up off the couch to make herself another cup of bronchial tea in the kitchen, the floor and walls started to sway, forcing her to flop back onto the couch.

It was well after midday when she managed to get to her feet again, staggering so much she knocked the little table, sending it skidding across the floor. One of the legs gave way. Something fell on the floor: a thin, elongated object, thicker at one end. Her vision blurred by fever, she assumed it was a screw. It was a self-assembly table and, not having a screwdriver, she'd put it together using a butter knife. It had always been a bit wobbly. She left it where it was and dragged herself to the shower.

The cold water washed the tint out of her hair but cleared her head sufficiently for the idea of taking a taxi to occur to her. She thought she could make it as far as the telephone kiosk. There was one close by, round the corner only fifty yards down Kettlerstrasse. Shortly after four she was standing at her wardrobe on shaky legs. She chose a pair of Nadia's trousers, one of her blouses, the second pair of shoes and the second blazer.

The next fit of coughing came while she was on the stairs. She was close to turning back. But she struggled on determinedly until she reached the street. The humid air made breathing a little easier. She made it as far as the telephone kiosk. Once there, however, she realized that all the effort had been in vain. The receiver had been torn off. It was lying on the metal holders for the phone books, the flex dangling. She leaned against the side of the kiosk and slowly slumped to the floor.

More than half an hour must have gone when a dark-blue Mercedes drove past – as had countless other cars already. In contrast to the others, however, the Mercedes stopped a few yards further on, as if the driver had realized there was a woman squatting on the floor of the kiosk. The Mercedes reversed, stopped. The driver got out, rushed to the kiosk, opened the door, leaned over her and asked, his voice full of concern, "Don't you feel well?"

He must have been in his late forties, early fifties. Of average height and severely overweight, he was wearing an expensive suit and, on his left hand, a showy signet ring. He didn't look like a criminal. He stretched out his right hand to help her up. There was no ring on his right hand.

"I wanted to call a taxi," she mumbled and pointed to the torn-off receiver. "But it's not working." That set her coughing again.

"That's a nasty cold you've got," the man said. "You ought to see the doctor about it."

"That's where I was going," she wheezed as he pulled her up. The man put his hand under her arm to support her.

"I can drive you there," he said as he helped her out of the kiosk. Hesitating, she looked at the Mercedes. It was one of those models that are out of the reach of ordinary mortals. The man gave her an understanding smile and pulled out a mobile. "I could ring for a taxi."

"No need," she whispered, "I'll go with you."

She let him assist her into the passenger seat. He got in behind the wheel and gave her an encouraging smile. They reached the city centre just before five. She got out, thanked him and headed for the pedestrian precinct. There were still a few minutes to go. She felt sick. In the last few days she'd had nothing but bronchial tea. She bought a cherry waffle at a snack bar and wolfed it down. After that she felt a little better. Only it didn't last long.

When she came to she found herself sitting on a concrete slab in a vault, with no idea how she'd got there. At first she thought she was back in the disused factory. It was several minutes before she realized it was just the multi-storey car park. The air was full of exhaust fumes. Her cough got worse. There was a pillar behind the slab of concrete. She leaned back against it and dozed off.

Hours later someone was shaking her shoulder, a hand gave her several gentle slaps. She became aware of a voice. It sounded as if it were coming through cotton wool. "Susanne, for God's sake wake up." Nadia's face, looking worried, appeared in front of her in the murky half-light and didn't go away when she blinked as hard as she could.

Angrily, Nadia said, "Have you gone out of your mind? You look like death warmed up. What are you doing here?"

Her answer was to cough up the cherry waffle over the concrete floor. Nadia prattled on, something about a lorry blocking two lanes, making it impossible for her to be there on time, and something about an acquaintance who was supposed to tell Susanne. That must have been the man in the Mercedes. But he hadn't said Nadia had sent him.

Finally Nadia thought of helping her to her feet. Two minutes later they were sitting in the Porsche. Nadia told her off for being so irresponsible with her health. In between fits of coughing, Susanne explained why she couldn't go to the doctor. At that Nadia gabbled some instructions, finishing with, "That's no problem. I have private insurance."

However, she thought it was too risky to find a doctor in the city who took patients without an appointment. "He'd send you straight to the nearest hospital." What they needed was a good old-fashioned country GP who had confidence in his own skill and knew from experience that there were patients who automatically resisted going into hospital. Nadia knew one like that – she'd last been to see him over a year ago. "He might be a bit offended because I haven't been to him for so long, but we needn't worry about that. We can regard it as a dry run."

Susanne paid no attention to her last remark, she was fully occupied keeping her cough under control, and the dizzy spells, and her stomach, which was rebelling against Nadia's driving. Johannes Herzog would have been delighted with such a journey. After a couple of miles on the autobahn there was a stretch along a narrow, twisty country road, where Nadia removed any remaining doubts that her driving skills might not match Johannes's. Still doing fifty, she roared into a small town, coming screeching to a halt a few yards past a large detached house. A sign beside the door indicated a doctor's surgery. Dr Peter Reusch.

Nadia took a powder compact and a folding brush out of her handbag and dabbed a little colour on Susanne's cheeks, after which a bottle of perfume was deployed. Then Nadia took the two rings off her finger, slipped them on Susanne's and stuck her handbag under her arm. Finally her nimble fingers tweaked Susanne's hair into something one, with a bit of effort, might call a style, before she asked, "You can manage on your own, can't you? It won't work if I go with you."

It was unreal. In Nadia's clothes, with Nadia's rings on her finger and the bag under her arm containing everything that proved Nadia's identity. A little more lipstick, eye shadow and mascara, her hair freshly dyed and cut by an expert, Nadia's stud earrings in her ears – and the illusion would have been perfect. But her straggly hair did serve a purpose: a few strands concealed her un-pierced ears.

And on the photo in Nadia's passport her hair wasn't so brown. Despite her temperature, that made her feel as if lava were swirling round inside her skull, she still had the presence of mind to check the contents of the wallet. Hidden from Nadia in the Porsche by some tall bushes beside the door, she examined her ID card, passport, driving licence and credit cards. A packet of photos, mostly Polaroids, she ignored.

She did it for no other reason than to be prepared for all eventualities. She was convinced there would be doubts about her identity, which she'd have to counter with the ID card or passport. A woman who has to search though her handbag for her identity papers is not very convincing. Anyway, everyone should know their own address and date of birth. Private patients were bound to be asked where the bill should be sent. It was a slight shock to discover that Nadia was three years older than her. At the moment it looked the other way round.

After she had replaced everything in the wallet and stowed that in the bag, she rang the bell. A middle-aged woman opened the door, her questioning look immediately changing to one of pure concern. "Frau Trenkler? Good heavens! Peter, come quickly," she called back into the house.

Peter came. He didn't look offended. On the contrary, he seemed delighted to see a patient he thought he had lost. Frau Reusch led her to the surgery, where he washed his hands and quickly set about making his diagnosis. Her temperature was over a hundred and four, which gave rise to much shaking of the head and tut-tutting. He filled a syringe, found a suitable vein, then sounded her back, listened, got her to cough and immediately told her to stop – "My God!" While he was doing this, his wife got her file.

All the time alarm bells were ringing inside her head. He's a doctor, she told herself, he'll see the fraud as soon as he takes a closer look. But the risk of being unmasked by a doctor who hadn't seen Nadia Trenkler for a whole year was low. And she didn't have to talk very much. It was the doctor himself who expressed the thought that she hadn't come sooner because she hadn't had the time and wouldn't now have the time for a stay in hospital. Moreover he was sure, he said, that her smoking hadn't done her lungs any good. "How many a day is it now? Thirty? Forty?"

He didn't bother to wait for an answer. With a note of gentle admonition in his voice, he decreed, "For the next few days we're going to keep off the coffin nails entirely. We're very close to pneumonia."

Croaking, she swore she wouldn't touch a cigarette for the next few days, even weeks. He'd believe that when he saw it, he said, but for the next few days he was trusting her to use her common sense. Asking how her husband was, he wrote a prescription: antibiotics, something to bring her temperature down and something to stabilize her heartbeat. Finally he told her to make sure she spent the whole of the weekend in bed and let her husband pamper her good and proper. Here he wagged his finger and grinned: "But only as far as food and drink are concerned, of course."

Telling her to come back in a week's time for a check-up, he accompanied her to the door and peered out into the street. He couldn't see much, because of the bushes outside, and certainly not the Porsche. Only at that point did it occur to him to wonder how she'd got there. All she could think of was to murmur, "Michael's waiting."

"Then why didn't he come in?" Peter Reusch asked. She shrugged her shoulders and Reusch told her to give her husband his best wishes.

The door closed and she walked slowly down the path to the street. Her knees were wobbling by the time she reached the car. Nadia leaned across the passenger seat and opened the door, quivering with suspense. "Well?" She dropped into the seat and held out the prescription. "Great," said Nadia, taking back the rings and handbag. Then she insisted on a detailed report.

They drove back – at roughly the same speed. On the way Nadia stopped at an all-night chemist's and got Susanne's prescription. She wanted to know why she had no health insurance and reacted angrily when she heard the reason. "Why didn't you tell me? Did you think I wouldn't understand? What does it matter if you take a bit of money from your mother? You're going to inherit it eventually anyway."

Shortly after nine the Porsche turned into Kettlerstrasse. Despite her annoyance at Susanne's lie, Nadia had remained calm and proud of the success of the impersonation. Now she grew nervous. "Can you manage it up the stairs by yourself?"

"Of course." She felt better already, presumably because of the injection. Even in the car her head had gradually cleared. Nadia's reproaches hadn't stopped that, perhaps even helped to stimulate it. But they had reignited the fear that she wouldn't repeat the offer she'd made in her letter.

"Fine," said Nadia as she stopped the Porsche in the middle of the street. "Out you get. Make sure the main door doesn't shut and leave the door to your flat open. Then you can go straight to bed and won't need to get up again."

She got out. Hardly had she closed the car door than the Porsche shot off. There was no need to prop the main door open, it hadn't shut properly for ages anyway. It was fairly quiet in the building and she got to the third floor without encountering anyone. She left the door to her flat ajar and took the first dose of antibiotics. Only then did it occur to her that she hadn't told Nadia which floor her flat was on.

The tenement had five floors. There was no lift. Despite that, she thought she should go down again, to save Nadia having to check every floor, but now that her vision had cleared, the mess in the flat was all too evident. She quickly tidied up so Nadia wouldn't think she'd given her clothes to a slattern.

Finally she pushed the little table back into place, straightened the leg that had given way and picked up what she had assumed was a screw. Looking at it more closely, she saw that it wasn't a screw at all. There was no thread and it was rectangular in section, both the thin, elongated part and the thicker end, which in her feverish state she had taken for the screw head. But it had to be part of the table, there was no other explanation. She tipped the table on its side, knelt down and examined the place where the loose leg was attached.

She was still doing that when Nadia came in. She closed the door behind her and immediately started telling her off: "Are you out of your mind? Why aren't you in bed? What are you doing down there on the floor?"

Quickly Nadia came over and knelt down beside her. Susanne explained the problem and she took the mystery object from her. She also examined all four table legs and declared, "Whatever it is, it's broken off. It's no use any more, I'll throw it away, OK?"

Saying that, Nadia slipped the object in her pocket and helped her up. Outside an Intercity express hurtled past, closely followed by a local train on the neighbouring track. The windowpanes shook. Nadia started and said, "You get to bed. I have to go, but it won't be for long and then I've got plenty of time. I'll bring something to eat."

To make sure she did go to bed, Nadia took her into the bedroom, helped her undress, tucked her in, then picked up the worn imitation-leather holder with the house keys. "You don't mind? Then you won't have to get up when I come back."

The last time Susanne had enjoyed such cosseting had been when she'd developed a temperature and a rash after some vaccination or other. Her mother had petted and pampered her with everything she thought would do her good – chocolate and cocoa, crisps and Coca-Cola, custard creams and apple juice. Agnes Runge had had to change the bedclothes five times because Susanne's weakened constitution couldn't cope with her idea of an invalid diet.

Nadia was more sensible. She came back after an hour and a half with three tinfoil containers giving off a delicious aroma. Chicken with mushrooms, fried noodles with pork and prawns, and, in the third container, rice. She'd also bought several bottles of mineral water. "I hope you like Chinese."

"Sure, it's just that I've no appetite."

"You're going to get some food inside you," Nadia declared, and decided she should have her meal in bed. Without asking, she dragged over the two kitchen chairs, took a clean sheet out of the cupboard, spread it over one of the chairs, placed the containers on it and helped her to sit up. "Take whatever you like, I'll fetch some plates and cutlery."

The cutlery was in the kitchen dresser. She heard Nadia looking in the sitting room first. She couldn't really say whether she was happy with the way Nadia took it for granted she could rummage round among her pitiful belongings; all she felt at the moment was immense gratitude for Nadia's determination, for the money in the blazer pocket, for her understanding attitude when she told her about stealing from her mother's nest egg and her willingness to let her assume her identity so she could see a doctor and get the medicine she needed.

Nadia took some of the noodles, sat by the door on the other chair with her plate in her lap and ate with obvious relish. Susanne forced a piece of chicken and half a mushroom down, waiting, as she had at their first meeting, for Nadia's offer. But all Nadia said was, "If you don't like the chicken, try the noodles."

Noodles were the last thing she wanted if there was anything else on offer. "It's fine," she said, "it's just that I don't feel hungry. I am thirsty, though."

Nadia brought two glasses from the kitchen, filled them with mineral water and handed her one. "Have a drink then get some food inside you. You must, Susanne, you've lost a lot of weight. I don't think you were that thin before."

Nadia had observed her very closely when she'd helped her get undressed and into bed. She'd noticed that and found it a bit embarrassing because Nadia had insisted she take off her panties and bra. She'd never been subjected to such intense scrutiny by a woman before.

Nadia paused for a couple of seconds, then said, "I'll make sure I can get away tomorrow and I'll bring you some soup. That's probably best for you at the moment. I'm sure I'll have some chicken soup in the cupboard."

Nadia smiled. It was a strange smile, presumably meant to emphasize the jokey conspiratorial tone. "We'll have to see how many tins I can smuggle out of the house without anyone noticing."

But her humour seemed like a thin blanket concealing something utterly serious, something written all over her face saying that it could be extremely awkward if she was found smuggling out chicken soup. But it was presumably only meant as a joke. If necessary she could buy the soup, lots of shops stayed open till four on a Saturday afternoon.

"You've already done enough," said Susanne. "I don't want you to get into trouble because of me."

Nadia gave a quiet laugh. "It's too late for that. Michael didn't believe for one second that I've been stuck in a traffic jam for the last five hours."

She couldn't understand why she'd lied to her husband. "Why didn't you tell him where you are?"

With a sarcastic smile Nadia said, "Oh yes, I'm sure he'd have believed that. I'd have had to tell him to come and see with his own eyes that I'm with a sick friend – a woman friend."

It was nice to be called a friend. It put Nadia's help and generosity in a light that didn't make her look quite so poor. "Well," she said, "surely you could have told him that?"

Nadia's smile turned into a laugh. "Not likely! I'm not going to spoil the best chance I ever had of a weekend to remember."

Susanne had no idea what she meant by that remark. She stared at Nadia, uncomprehending, until she hung her head in embarrassment and said, "Now it's out. Pity. I'd have liked to spend a few more days feeling I was being altruistic. I hinted at it in my last letter, but when I saw you I thought I should let you get better before asking you to do me a favour."

She was quite clear that in her last letter Nadia had talked about a job as a stand-in, not a favour. But after everything Nadia had done for her, she was keen to do something in return. "I'm not at death's door," she said. "Come on, out with it."

Nadia looked at her thoughtfully and said hesitantly. "No, really. It can wait. I don't want to exploit your illness. I'd feel ashamed of myself."

She really did feel much better. Whatever it was Dr Reusch had pumped into her veins, it had completely cleared her head during the hour-and-a-half rest she'd had. And the way Nadia was stalling made her suspicious. It could hardly be a little favour or Nadia wouldn't be making such a fuss about it. One of her ex-husband's comments came to mind: "Development aid isn't pure charity. They're just investing their money in poor countries so their own industries can cream it off again."

Her ex-husband and his views meant nothing to her any more, but the thought still left a nasty taste in her mouth. Her tone was sharper than intended and the formulation somewhat unfortunate: "We can talk now. What do I have to do for a suitcase full of hand-me-downs, two hundred euros in a jacket pocket and a free visit to the doctor?"

"Don't forget the medicine," Nadia reminded her, clearly irritated by so much ingratitude. She stood up and put her plate down on the chair. One step took her to the doorway separating the bedroom from the rest of the shabby flat. There she turned round and breathed in and out audibly several times before going on. "I'm sorry Susanne. I can imagine that in your situation you can't be bothered with little games, but —"

"But what?" she asked when Nadia broke off abruptly. "Come on, tell me. What do you want from me?"

Nadia shrugged her shoulders and gave an innocent smile. "Nothing world-shaking. I've already told you that I... To cut a long story short, not long ago I met a man. We've had the odd hour together and I was wondering if I might manage to spend a weekend with him once or twice a month. If you can play the sulking wife for me meanwhile."

"You're mad." That was all she could think of to say.

Nadia laughed. "Of course. Mad enough to think it'll work. Reusch didn't notice who he was treating. With the right preparation I don't see any risk with Michael. There's plenty of time and if you're happy with it..."

She wasn't happy with it. It was absurd, unworkable. However Nadia imagined it could be done, sending a stand-in to share the house – and the bed – with her husband, was impracticable. Any of a thousand details could scupper it. Starting with the sound of their voices which, to her ears, were not identical, however hard she might try to imitate Nadia's tone. A person wasn't simply a face and a figure. Even if Dr Reusch hadn't suspected anything, he'd only glanced at her briefly, placed a thermometer against her forehead, measured her blood pressure and listened to her lungs. Nadia's husband, on the other hand...

Nadia interrupted the cascade of thoughts. "Naturally I don't expect you to do it for nothing. I'm quite prepared to pay for my weekends away." With an look of appraisal at the worn floorboards she was standing on, Nadia said brusquely, "Five hundred?"

Susanne gulped. Her mouth was dry, she couldn't answer. Five hundred! And Nadia was talking of once or twice a month. Twice would make it a thousand. If it did work, she wouldn't have to go to the bank to steal her mother's money ever again. But her own scepticism – which was maybe nothing other than cowardice, fear of something nameless, perhaps of something that might impel her to resort to a heavy stick or stone – was making her confused.

"You wouldn't be running any risk," Nadia insisted.

She couldn't see any risk in it for herself, either. If it all went pear-shaped, that would be Nadia's problem. The worst that could happen to her was being chucked out by Nadia's husband. And, according to Nadia, it wouldn't come to that if she made an effort – and only once a few little changes had been made to her appearance, of course. She still looked too pale and drawn, she needed a bit more padding round the ribs. And the hours on her kitchen balcony and her long walks had given her a somewhat irregular tan. It was, as Nadia insisted, only a matter of her external appearance. And to polish that up could only help improve her personal situation.

Nadia stayed until half-past eleven. How important the matter was to her could be gauged from the cigarettes. She only smoked four, and those standing at the open window. The ash and butts she threw out onto the railway track. More than ten times she automatically flipped open her cigarette case before closing it again, with a look of resignation, in order to spare Susanne's bronchial tubes and not retard her rapid recovery.

By the second cigarette it was clear that Nadia hadn't just thought this plan up on the spur of the moment. She'd gone through everything a thousand times. She listed what they needed for her external appearance: a good hairdresser to give Susanne's mop a professionally casual look and a dye that wouldn't wash out; a top-class beautician to teach her the tricks Nadia could do in her sleep; Nadia's perfume, plus deodorant and body lotion; a jeweller to pierce her ears; then a few sessions in a solarium to give her a seamless tan. Naturally Nadia would bear all the costs.

It went without saying that they'd have to spend a few hours together to enable her to copy Nadia's gestures and vocabulary, to learn a few standard phrases, with which to counter Michael's remarks, and to absorb a few patterns of behaviour. Two or three weeks of intensive training ought to be sufficient to enable her to pull the wool over the eyes of a man who had known Nadia for ten years and been married to her for seven, as long as she didn't let him get too close.

"But I'll see to that," Nadia promised. "I'll see to it that the atmosphere is decidedly cool before you go on stage. Then Michael'll make sure he keeps out of your way. Nothing can go wrong. Come on, say yes."

Something inside her had switched off minutes ago. Nadia's explanations washed over her like long-awaited rainfall in the desert. At least five hundred euros a month! It wasn't a dream come true and it certainly wasn't what she really needed, but as long as Nadia's affair lasted she wouldn't have to dip into her mother's account. With a thousand she'd even be able to start paying back, if she continued to keep her expenses to a minimum. And perhaps Nadia would be able to help her find a job. Once she looked the part. She nodded hesitantly.

Nadia registered her agreement with an exhalation of relief and went on with her explanations. The way it would go would be that they'd meet in the city on a Friday afternoon, she would take Nadia's car and – Susanne had another fit of coughing, after which she wheezed, "I'll probably need a few driving lessons before I can handle a Porsche…"

Nadia broke in with an amused laugh. The Porsche wasn't hers, she only used it for business. That was why she'd had to go, to take it back and get her own car which, at the moment, was parked a couple of streets away. Its engine couldn't quite match the Porsche's, it was only an Alfa Spider. It sounded as if she felt she had to apologize for it. "But of course you can have a few driving lessons," Nadia said, "that's no problem."

Nadia spent the last thirty minutes showing her the photos she'd seen outside the door to the surgery but not paid any attention to. The Polaroids had presumably only been taken to show to her once she'd accepted. To help her they had descriptions written on the back. Nadia had put a note on the back of the other photos as well.

The revelation of Nadia's home surroundings reminded Susanne of a school excursion to a castle where they'd slid round the parquet floor in felt slippers, admiring carpets, the names of which no one could pronounce. Nadia explained various details, regretting that she couldn't show her round the house personally. "Too much of a risk, because of the neighbours."

She also showed her photos of the neighbours, taken at some social gathering. Joachim, Jo for short, and Lilo Kogler, both in their fifties, pleasant and easy-going, but with an unfortunate tendency to organize parties at short notice.

"The idea usually occurs to Lilo in the morning," Nadia said. "Then she orders a buffet and rings round for a few people. Mostly it's impossible to get out of going. And Jo's a genius, there's nothing he doesn't know about. He has two or three patents currently under consideration, technology and electronics. The things he's done with my house, fantastic, I tell you, it's absolutely secure. You'll see. Lilo works in a gallery, which has its advantages. She's got me a few pieces at special prices, even a Beckmann."

"Really?" said Susanne, who had no idea what a Beckmann was. She looked at the second couple, who lived next door to Nadia, on the other side. Wolfgang and Ilona Blasting, both in their late thirties and not quite so nice. He was a policeman, she worked in Berlin as a member of parliament for the Green Party.

"She can be unbearable, she keeps lecturing you," said Nadia. "But she's mostly in Berlin. Unfortunately that gives him too much time to devote to his neighbours. If you know what I mean."

She understood only too well, she just had to think of Heller.

Then Nadia came to her husband. After the detailed descriptions of her immediate neighbours, Susanne assumed she would be given comprehensive information about Michael Trenkler. But Nadia just said vaguely that he worked at some laboratory and came home at irregular hours, often very late. Whether he was actually working or was having fun with his little laboratory mouse, she had no idea. She was no longer interested in his extramural activities.

Finally Nadia left. The door clicked shut behind her. Outside, a late Intercity express thundered past. It was stuffy in the room and, although she was tired, Susanne couldn't get to sleep. It wasn't the fever going round and round in her head any more, it was Nadia's voice, like a wind you can hear and feel, but can't grasp. And images of a life of luxury kept floating up before her inner eye.

On Saturday Nadia came back about midday. She had a scarf wrapped round her head, sunglasses covering half her face and was loaded down with two huge carrier bags. Two bottles of orange juice were sticking out of one of them.

"You can take those straight back with you," said Susanne. "I'm allergic to citrus fruits, strawberries, boiled carrots, lentils, celery, apples —"

Nadia interrupted her list: "Only to food, then?"

"No, I can't tolerate deodorants, I come out in a rash."

Nadia then checked for any other disparities she hadn't taken into account. They discovered their blood groups were different, but Nadia didn't think that was a problem. Susanne also had a slightly raised birthmark below her navel. Nadia had noticed it the previous evening. Her own skin was without any such irregularities. She didn't see that as a problem either. Susanne wasn't to let Michael get close enough to inspect her navel. A touch of foundation cream would be sufficient for a casual glance. Other darker patches of skin that might give her away would be scarcely noticeable after a few visits to the solarium, Nadia said.

The fracture to Susanne's skull could only be seen on an X-ray, the scar on her scalp was completely covered by hair. She had no other scars. Both had regular teeth, with none missing and no fillings that might betray Susanne when she laughed. Nadia checked everything thoroughly. The only difference to their finger and toe nails was in the length – Nadia kept hers a little shorter. A nail file would soon solve that problem.

Then Nadia unpacked the bulging carrier bags. As well as the orange juice, she'd brought mineral water, then salads from the delicatessen, sliced bread, ham, eggs and cheese, grapes and bananas, various kinds of biscuits and other confectionery that would help her put on weight. Susanne had no need to worry about where her food for the next few days was going to come from. And that wasn't all.

Three times Nadia went back to the car. From her final trip she brought a cardboard box full of clothes, and not just ones she'd discarded this time. On the top was a bag with the name of a classy boutique. Her shopping spree there provided her with an alibi for the hours she was spending with her stand-in; also she'd bought two of everything. Two sand-coloured suits with matching blouses, two pairs of identical court shoes and four sets of lingerie. Susanne couldn't believe it. Nadia was already completely taken up with her preparations and, like a little child whose dearest wish was about to be fulfilled, she was on a high. "Have you had breakfast?"

She hadn't. Nadia immediately set about making some. While she was brewing up coffee, making toast and boiling eggs, she asked about the man she'd met on the stairs who'd stared at her as if she came from another planet. From her description it had to be Heller. Naturally he'd treated Nadia to some choice obscenities. From the way he spoke she deduced Susanne was having an affair with him.

"Do I look as if I need it that badly?" she protested.

Nadia gave a brief smile. "You've been divorced three years. He's probably not that bad after a shower."

"I'm quite happy with Richard Gere," she said, thanking her once more for everything.

Nadia waved her thanks away. "No, no. You just can't imagine what this means for me."

No, she couldn't. When she'd been married to Dieter she'd been well aware that when he was abroad he didn't live like a monk, but she'd never really thought about it. The idea of looking for someone herself for a bit of fun on the side had never occurred to her. She'd had neither the time, the opportunity nor the desire. An invalid mother-in-law reduced your libido to zero. – Water under the bridge. Forget it. She'd become used to doing without a man.

Nadia put her new outfit in the wardrobe. Then they discussed who would see to what once Susanne was better. Nadia didn't have time to do everything. Susanne was to organize driving lessons and a visit to the beautician herself. Only the hairdresser Nadia insisted on arranging herself. She suspected Susanne's haircut was the work of some bungler from the tenement district where she lived. That kind of economizing could ruin everything. Nadia was going to make an appointment with her own hairdresser for the following week. That was to be her dress rehearsal.

At four Nadia put on her sunglasses again, wrapped the scarf round her head and took the boutique bag, the orange juice and the suitcase in which she'd brought the used clothes. She promised to come back on Monday afternoon and left reminding Susanne to eat her fill, get a lot of sleep and take her medicine.

Susanne spent the afternoon eating fruit until she felt one more grape and she'd burst. On Sunday she paid the price for her unaccustomed indulgence with vomiting and diarrhoea after a second helping of chicken salad. Dry toast for supper cured her overtaxed stomach. On Monday she felt fine. She was hardly coughing any more and when she did, though it sounded deafening, it was a relief.

It was pleasant outside: not too hot, not too cold, not too humid, not too dry, in fact ideal conditions for building up her strength with a long walk in the mild sunshine. But she made do with the kitchen balcony. She spent hours looking at the photos and wallowing in visions of a future in the lap of luxury, disregarding the fact that at most this "future" would amount to no more than one or two weekends a month.

By now the turmoil of pros and cons going round and round in her head had subsided. She made an effort to look at the whole thing rationally. She desperately needed the money. She would still look for a job and would ask Nadia at the first opportunity if she could do anything for her. Just at the moment, though, the opportunity wasn't there.

Nadia was completely taken up with the preparations for her first stint as stand-in, setting about them with such intensity that everything else went by the board. On the Monday she turned up shortly after five, once more in headscarf and sunglasses, with more provisions and with equipment to deal with the small discrepancies: a nail file that was worthy of the name, a concealer stick for her birthmark, an epilator for her legs, a ladies' razor for underarm hair, tweezers for her eyebrows and depilatory cream which was gentle enough to be used in the genital area.

Before Susanne knew what was happening, Nadia had taken off all her clothes and demonstrated what was needed. "I hope," she said as she did this, "you haven't got any hang-ups about getting undressed in front of a stranger. If you find it embarrassing, just tell yourself it isn't you Michael's seeing, but me. We sleep in the same room – naked. If you keep your underwear on, he'll think I'm hiding something."

Nadia gave her an apologetic smile and described Michael as a typical representative of his species. To be unfaithful was perfectly acceptable – for him but not for his wife. "A little affair's nice," Nadia said, "and to enjoy it for a whole weekend without wondering all the time what I'm going to tell my husband will be lovely. But it's not worth jeopardizing my marriage for. And then you and me, it's a fantastic opportunity. Who would have imagined it?!"

Nadia couldn't entirely rule out the possibility that Michael might feel there was something odd. But what could he do? Given their amazing similarity, he was hardly going to ask Susanne who she was. He'd assume Nadia was in one of her moods. And Susanne could make sure he didn't feel there was something odd. She just had to behave the way Nadia did, and going to bed naked was part of it.

Although Susanne hadn't said a word, and certainly not expressed any fears or doubts, Nadia repeated her reassurances: "You really don't need to worry. Normally he keeps well away from me when we've had an argument. If the worst comes to the worst you can always make a point of taking the tampons out of the cupboard."

Then Nadia put her clothes back on and laid several banknotes on the table. "That should be enough. It depends how many driving lessons you need. Can you see to that tomorrow and also make an appointment with a beautician?"

Susanne nodded, unable to take her eyes of the money. It was almost as if Nadia had placed a contract before her – stretching out her hand for the money would be like signing it.

"Good," said Nadia. "And make sure they let you drive straight away. You just want to refresh your driving skills, you don't need the theory. See the beautician on Wednesday. Buy your make-up there, also the perfume. And buy some body cream, its fragrance is more intense than a lotion and you're going to need that if you can't use deodorant. Then you can go straight on to the solarium and the jeweller. That all has to be done by Thursday. You're going to the hairdresser on Thursday, four o'clock. We meet on Friday, at five, in the multi-storey."

"Why?" She asked, just to get a word in. "You could come here."

"Better not," said Nadia. "When you come out of the flat yourself someone might notice there's two of you."

She thought this precaution rather excessive but said nothing. It was Nadia's game. That she wasn't going to stick too precisely to her rules was merely a matter of economy. A woman who'd been living on noodles for the past few months and came out in a cold sweat at the thought of her next fuel bill couldn't just throw away several hundred euros. Should Michael Trenkler realize in the first fifteen minutes that she was trying to put one over on him, there would be no second performance and no more money. If she was careful with what she'd been given for expenses and the five hundred for the first weekend she could save herself two raids on her mother's account.

The next morning she went, as instructed, to a driving school and enquired about the price for a single lesson. But it was much too high, and since it wasn't the Porsche she was going to be driving, she decided she'd manage. At the beauty parlour she just bought the required perfume and body cream. Together they cost over a hundred euros, even though she only took the smallest bottle. Everything else she bought cheaply in the supermarket.

Then she spent two hours in front of the mirror trying things out. She was a bit out of practice. At her first attempt the rouge was too dark, at the second she jabbed her eye with the mascara brush, but at the third the overall result was reasonably acceptable. She gradually started to enjoy it; it took her back to the time before Dieter and the first months after her divorce. Then it would have been unthinkable to turn up at the bank without make-up. After she'd washed it all off and redone it twenty times, it was almost perfect.

She spent the evening removing the unwanted hair. Her armpits and pubic area were unproblematic. Her eyebrows caused her to shed a few tears and the epilator proved to be a real instrument of torture. One hour later her legs looked as if they'd got the measles. By Wednesday morning, however, all the lumps and red blotches had disappeared.

She went to the jeweller. She was amazed how quickly and painlessly holes could be pierced in one's body and admired the medical studs, which she had to wear for a while. After that she stretched out on a sunbed. She had a slight attack of claustrophobia but the radiation was no problem.

And on Thursday she was a great hit at Nadia's hairdresser's with the amusing story of a man who managed to evade paying most of his taxes and made provision for his old age by sending it abroad by courier. Nadia had advised her to tell them about Herr Schrag and Röhrler so as not to let the hairdresser ask too many questions; she might arouse suspicion if her answers were wrong.

Nadia hadn't seemed concerned about the – to her ears – different sound of their voices. The bronchitis she was just getting over explained that. It also explained why she didn't use the ashtray they provided. No one seemed to harbour any doubts about her identity – and she'd only spent ten minutes on make-up beforehand. She was treated deferentially, pampered with coffee and biscuits, and addressed as Frau Trenkler every two minutes.

True, the hairdresser was a little annoyed at the awful state of her hair, but she just told him what Nadia had drummed into her: on holiday, forgetting to protect it from the blazing sun, then making the mistake of entrusting it to a foreign hairdresser. This mollified the hairdresser, at the same time providing an explanation for her efforts with the scissors.

While she was being manicured – which Nadia also considered essential, at least for the beginning – she discovered when Nadia had last been to the salon. It was in July, just one day before their encounter by the lift in Gerler House. Nadia had cancelled her appointment for the following week because of the holiday that she had used to explain the state of her hair.

In her mind's eye she could see the line in Nadia's first letter: "Perhaps I can do something to change that." And in the mirror she saw the woman who had come out of the lift towards her. A slightly suntanned face with the touch of make-up, which hadn't suffered under the hands of the hairdresser. The silvery studs glittered, her hair was the right shade and not one strand out of place. All at once her heart missed a beat, as if it had just dropped into a hole. The unpleasant sensation made her aware that it might work. The outward transformation at least was complete.

Nadia was waiting in her own car, a burgundy convertible, when her double entered the multi-storey car park shortly after five on Friday. Susanne got in and immediately noticed the holiday snap of the blond man on the dashboard. It gave her a sudden feeling of unease. Nadia must love her husband very much, otherwise she would hardly have transferred his picture from one car to the other. But to her way of thinking loving a man very much was incompatible with this kind of deception. Even if he was cheating on her.

Nadia surveyed Susanne's hairdo and face with a look of approval, checked the shape of her eyebrows and fingernails, and even went so far as to inspect her shins to make sure all growth really had been removed. Then she took the headscarf and large sunglasses out of the glove compartment and told her to put them on. Finally she drove the Alfa Spider out into the street, asking, "Did you manage to get some driving in?"

"Just one session," Susanne lied. "It went OK. I surprised myself. But the instructor said it's like swimming or riding a bike – you never forget how to do it."

"Great," said Nadia. "Then that shouldn't be a problem. There won't be any others, either, you look perfect. How was it at the hairdresser's?" She listened to Susanne's account and headed for the autobahn, telling her, "Remember this route."

There wasn't much to remember. They went past three exits – and that pretty quickly although the traffic was fairly heavy. Even if the Alfa Spider was less powerful than the Porsche, it was hardly noticeable. Nor was it inferior to the white sports car as far as manoeuvrability was concerned. When the fourth exit approached, Nadia finally cut down her speed. Then there came a country road lined with young trees. Nadia pulled in on the verge between two very thin trunks and pointed ahead. There was virtually nothing to be seen, just a hint of roof tiles in the green shade of countless leafy treetops.

"From here it's easy to find," Nadia said. "Stay on this road. After you get to the village you have to turn left twice, then right. You can't miss it. There are only five houses on Marienweg, two on one side, three on the other. My house is the middle one of the three."

Then came a long explanation of the alarm system. It sounded extremely complicated, as if she'd need an instruction manual just to open the front door. When she'd finished, Nadia did a three-point turn, which Susanne would have thought impossible on the narrow country road and drove back, explaining that in the coming week she had no time for further meetings and that her first appearance would be – next Sunday!

No more talk of weeks of intensive training. Nadia maintained that it was a good opportunity, not a full weekend and no risk of a short-notice party at Jo and Lilo Kogler's with Wolfgang and Ilona Blasting. Just a few hours. And Michael would have to go to the lab in the late afternoon.

"There's a new series of tests running," said Nadia indignantly. "That's always a good pretext for a rendezvous with a laboratory mouse."

But given the situation, Nadia said, it would be child's play. Michael would scarcely be in the mood for a close encounter of any kind before he left. At lunch she would express her resentment at having to spend the evening alone and then say she had to go out too. All Susanne would have to do would be to show Michael the cold shoulder and meet any excuses or attempts to make up with a scornful laugh before flouncing out of the room where he was or to which he had followed her.

"You won't have to put up with him for long, anyway," Nadia said. "He has to leave at five. We'll meet at three in the multi-storey, that'll give you time for the drive there."

She managed a nod. She hadn't expected things to move forward so quickly. Her heart was pounding, she could feel the throb right to the tips of her fingers and was relieved that it didn't occur to Nadia to get her to drive. There was no question but she would have seen through her lie about the driving lesson and realized that her money had been misappropriated.

Next Sunday! Time was getting short. She couldn't do anything about her driving on Saturday. On Sunday she was standing by the street outside her flat with her new hairdo and perfect make-up, wearing the clothes Nadia had bought in the boutique. Johannes Herzog gulped when she got into the BMW. "You look great," he said.

A compliment like that to a woman of her age from a man in his twenties was not to be sniffed at. It was just that inside she didn't feel anything like so radiant as she looked outside. After four or five months – she couldn't remember exactly how long it was – she'd woken at six on a damp sheet stained red. And with the period came that general out-of-sorts feeling and massive self-doubt. She couldn't possibly drive the Alfa down the autobahn and out into the country next Sunday.

Johannes raced round the bends in his usual style, surreptitiously giving her sidelong glances. Eventually he asked, "Don't you feel well?"

No. She felt anything but well. She was afraid she was going to fail miserably next Sunday right from the start, on the journey out. Johannes flung the car round the next bend. "All this hurtling round corners is making me feel sick," she said in answer to his question.

It was the first time she'd criticized his driving. He was genuinely puzzled. "Am I driving too fast?"

"I never do more than fifty on a road like this," she said. That was the speed limit indicated on the signs they'd hurtled past only a few minutes ago.

"I'd no idea you could drive," he said.

"I don't have much opportunity," she explained. "I haven't got a car of my own at the moment, of course. But I've just been offered a company car; they want me to take over the courier work. I'd love to do it, only I'm afraid my lack of driving practice would mean I couldn't."

Taking the broad hint, Johannes nobly pulled up at the side of the road. This time next week, she thought as he got out. In her mind's eye she saw the little photo of a blond man. Michael Trenkler, who else? As it was only for a few minutes, and as he wouldn't have time to devote himself to her to any extent, there really was no risk – provided she got there safely.

She slid over into the driving seat. The engine was still running, Johannes had put it in neutral and applied the handbrake. Left foot on the clutch, right foot on the accelerator, engage first, take off the handbrake. And slowly – the BMW shot out into the middle of the road.

"Easy does it," said Johannes, leaning back and coolly crossing his legs. "You should have said something and I could have let you try sooner, I'm not fussy about letting other people drive my car. But what's this about courier trips? I thought you worked in an office?"

"Yes. But these courier firms aren't a hundred percent reliable," she explained. "If something's urgent, you have to see it gets there yourself."

It all sounded somewhat laboured, but at least she was driving at almost twenty miles per hour on the right side of the road. The engine protested. She changed up into second, crept up to thirty in third and managed to reach fifty without having the feeling she was at the wheel of an uncontrollable rocket. Johannes just sat there and let her get on with it, listening to her telling him how much she was looking forward to the courier trips because, of course, they were paid extra.

A little later than usual they reached the car park at the old folks' home. Johannes looked for a space and pointed. "There," he said, indicating an empty place. The only one left. It was much too narrow for her.

"It'd be better if you parked it yourself." she said.

"No. Any idiot can drive. You have to be able to park the thing as well. As a courier you'll have to squeeze into much narrower spaces. Try reversing in, it's easier."

Some ten minutes later the BMW was parked between two other vehicles. Susanne got out, trembling at the knees.

"You see," said Johannes as they went over to the building, "you can do it, no problem. See you at seven. Or let's say half past, the car park'll be fairly empty by then and you can practice a bit and drive back."

This time next week, she thought, as she thanked him for his offer.

It was a terrible week, starting with her mother going on at her because she wasn't her usual chatty self. "Susanne, there's something wrong with you. Won't you tell me what it is?"

"It's just my time of the month."

Agnes Runge was happy with that and prattled on about the little events in her life. Finally she asked Susanne how work was going and how her friend Jasmin Toppler and that nice Herr Heller were.

All at once she felt like bursting into tears. All the lies and the two thousand euros missing from her mother's account. It would have been so simple to say in January, "I've lost my job, Mother." Her mother would have certainly supported her. And now she could have said, "Something funny happened, Mum. I've met a woman who looks exactly like me. Or, rather, now I look exactly like her. She was keen to splash out on it and now she'll pay me five hundred if I…"

This time next week! She was itching to talk to someone about Nadia Trenkler, but it was an itch she didn't dare scratch. She could still hear her mother going on about fidelity in marriage. Her father had often said, "Why don't you go dancing, Susanne. You'll see there are more men around than your roving reporter. He's never there for you. And don't imagine he sticks to his marriage vows the way you do."

Every time her mother had jumped on him. "How can you say something like that? What Dieter does is neither here nor there. I don't think it's right for him to leave her alone all the time either. But at the altar she vowed…"

To tell her mother she was acting as stand-in for a woman who was going to cheat on her husband was out of the question.

At half-past seven she got behind the wheel of the BMW for the second time. Johannes was a mine of useful tips and she spent more than an hour, under his patient guidance, practising in the almost empty car park, going backwards, forwards, sideways into a parking space, doing three-point turns, reversing round corners and all the other driving-school manoeuvres. Then she drove out onto the country road and later – in first gear – along the acceleration lane and onto the autobahn.

Johannes kept her amused with a stream of advanced driving theory: how to get a car that's in a skid back under control, finishing off with a handbrake turn; how to travel for a short stretch on two wheels; how much you had to accelerate to jump like a horse over ditches or other obstacles, all tricks he needed for his part-time job as a stuntman. Then he even offered to come round during the week so she could practise on a piece of waste ground where he'd been working recently.

It would probably have been more sensible to take a couple of ordinary driving lessons, to familiarize herself with city traffic and learn to drive up an autobahn approach road in third gear at least. But Johannes's course in skid control was free, so she said yes.

On Monday she spent half the day with the photos: interior and exterior views of Nadia's house, parties in the neighbourhood, Nadia with Joachim Kogler, Nadia with Lilo Kogler, Nadia with Wolfgang Blasting, Nadia with Ilona Blasting, Nadia with a dozen unknown friends. For the first time it struck her that the blond man did not appear in any of the photos. Perhaps he was the one pressing the button. It was still odd.

Although she and Dieter had only lived together properly as husband and wife for a year, there were several dozen snapshots from that time and the lovely photos that had been taken on their wedding day, both outside the church and in the photographer's studio. Where they were now, she had no idea. She hadn't wanted to take them when she moved out. Ramie, her successor, had presumably thrown them away by now. But she could still see them clearly in her mind's eye: the promising young reporter in dark suit, silver-grey tie and white shirt, and herself all in white, as was right and proper, with her sumptuous bridal bouquet.

Among Nadia's photos was one with "wedding" written on the back, though without that she certainly wouldn't have recognized it as a wedding photo. It hadn't been taken outside a church or in a photographer's studio. Whether the building, the steps of which Nadia was hurrying down, was a registry office, was impossible to say. No flowers, no white dress, not to mention a bridal veil and wreath. In her elegant suit, her handbag under her left arm, it looked as if Nadia were just coming out of a business meeting. There was another figure a few steps above her, rather blurred, but apparently wearing jeans and a leather jacket. Perhaps the bridegroom, perhaps just some passer-by.

In the evening she spent two hours driving on the bumpy but completely empty waste ground where there was no danger of her colliding with trees or other road users. Johannes did not teach her how to drive according to the Highway Code. Instead he got her to try several tricks that were as useful for driving in normal traffic as a freezer in Greenland.

At first he found her much too timorous. After he had repeatedly assured her his BMW was used to much rougher treatment, she became a little more daring. And he praised the speed with which she picked things up and her quick reactions.

On Tuesday she went for a long walk to calm her nerves. When she got back, she found Heller lurking on the stairs like an evil omen. Hands in his pockets and a broad grin on his face, he told her, "That guy came to see me recently, your opinion pollster."

"How nice for you," she said, trying to get past.

He took a step forwards and blocked the way. His grin became suggestive. "He was trying to tell me he only screws students. He said he was a student himself, doing the survey was going to pay for his next semester."

"I'm not interested," she said.

Heller's grin broadened. "Well you should be. He was a snooper, you can take it from me. Look what I found after he'd gone." He took one hand out of his trouser pocket and held it out. In the palm was a something like a small battery, those tiny round ones you put in your watch. "That's a bug," Heller insisted.

"You ought to watch a nature film or a variety show now and then, instead of all those horror videos," she said, squeezing past him and hurrying up the stairs.

On Wednesday she flogged Johannes's BMW round the bumpy waste ground again. On Thursday he let her practise in heavy traffic. On Friday evening he got her to scare the pants off HGV drivers on the autobahn with her overtaking. On Saturday she practised Nadia's walk, Nadia's smile, Nadia's way of speaking, her mocking pout, her sparing but deft gestures and her defiant toss of the head until she was getting dizzy. She felt she had mastered them really well. The only thing that was still beyond her was the – to her ears – slightly deeper tone of Nadia's voice.

On Saturday night she dreamed of Michael Trenkler. It started off as a romantic dream of an excursion to the Eifel hills, but the outing ended in the empty disused factory, where he hit her again and again with the butt of a pistol and threatened, "If you move, you're dead."

The worst thing was that it was Heller who found her. He played the heroic rescuer and demanded his due reward.

On Sunday morning she found that her period had finished. About time too. After lunch she had a good shower, applied her make-up, did her hair and put on the clothes Nadia had bought for them in the boutique and which had so impressed Johannes Herzog the previous week.

The weather was pleasant and she took her time going to the multi-storey, but she was still there before three. Nadia had suggested they meet on level two, but the red Alfa Spider wasn't there, nor on levels one and three, which she checked, just to be sure. She went back out again and strolled up and down outside the entrance.

When it was getting to four o'clock, she began to wonder whether Nadia was going to come. All sorts of things could have happened during the week. Perhaps Nadia had had a heart-to-heart with her husband, or he didn't have to go into the lab that day. She wondered whether she should ring up, she remembered Nadia's number from the visiting cards. She'd always had a good memory for numbers. She decided to wait until half past. A few minutes before her self-imposed deadline, the Alfa appeared.

She ran back and up to level two, somewhat out of breath. Nadia had got out and gave a sigh of relief when she saw her coming. "I'm sorry," she said, flustered, "I thought I wasn't going to be able to make it."

"I won't be able to get there by five," Susanne said.

"There's no need," Nadia said. "We had one hell of a row. I wouldn't want you to have to go through a sequel."

Nadia took the remote control for the garage out of the car. It was new and very complicated, one of Joachim Kogler's inventions, the prototype. Whether it would find a market was doubtful, but Nadia was fascinated by the technological toy and spent five minutes explaining how it worked, emphasizing that she always drove into the garage because of the important data on the laptop she kept in the car.

There followed a further lecture, this time on the house alarm system. It was permanently switched on and had to be deactivated pretty quickly since it went off if the code wasn't keyed in twenty seconds after entering the house. Since Susanne would be coming in through the garage, she had no time to lose. The keypad was in the hall closet where they kept their coats. It was on a black box that was hidden behind a leather jacket. She was to push the jacket to one side – on no account was she to take the hanger off the hook – and key in the combination.

Then Nadia took off her two rings and Susanne slipped them onto her finger. Nadia took out her ear studs and Susanne put them through the holes she'd had pierced. Nadia took off her watch and put on Susanne's. Nadia opened her handbag, took out her mobile, a packet of cigarettes and a disposable lighter then picked up Susanne's bag. The cigarette case and the gold lighter stayed in Nadia's bag.

"You don't have to smoke today," Nadia said. "Not later on either, if you don't want to. It's enough if you light one and put it down in the ashtray. I do that quite often."

"When should I be back here?" Susanne asked.

"Not here," said Nadia. "I'm going to call a taxi and go to your flat. You've no objection, I hope?"

She shook her head. Nadia took a laptop bag and the document case from the back seat of the Alfa. "I've brought something to stop me getting bored. Take as much time as you need. It doesn't matter when I get home. Michael will probably spend the night in the lab. How many driving lessons have you had?"

"Almost every day," she said – truthfully this time.

Nadia nodded. "Great."

Thanks to Johannes Herzog's thorough training, she got there sooner than expected. It was only a few minutes past five when she reached the narrow country lane with the young trees. Far ahead of her the luxuriant greenery appeared through the summer haze, rapidly growing larger. She found Marienweg immediately and drove past the Kogler's house with its open, well-tended garden. Joachim Kogler was in the front garden, doing something with a reel of cable. She recognized him from the photos, his wife too. She was standing in the doorway and waved to her.

She ignored her, concentrating on the middle house. It wasn't as grand as the photos suggested, but it was a snow-white villa. Beside the wide drive leading to the double garage was a narrower one which must belong to the Blastings' property. A low fence separated the two.

She stopped in front of the garage door. She didn't even attempt to open it with the complicated remote control. For such a short stay it wasn't worth rushing round to reach the alarm in the hall in time. And neither Nadia's important papers nor her laptop were in the car at the moment. She got out, locked the car by pressing the key, put the key in her handbag, took out the house keys and went round the front.

Lilo Kogler was about twenty yards away and giving her a suspicious look. She must have been feeling offended because she hadn't responded to her friendly wave. Joachim Kogler had straightened up and was also looking across at her. She raised her arm and sketched a wave, smiled and nodded casually then hurried on to the front door. She was getting palpitations from the fear that they might speak to her and she would have to answer, the higher tone of her voice revealing her as a cheap imitation.

Strange that Nadia hadn't been concerned about that at all. She must have noticed the difference in their voices as well. On the other hand, since she was to respond to everything Michael Trenkler said to her with icy silence or a scornful laugh, the risk was slight.

There were seven keys on the ring, each with a different colour marking. Since Nadia had told her to go in via the garage, she'd forgotten to explain which key fitted the front door. She tried the red one. It wouldn't go in. And now Lilo Kogler was on the lawn, with her husband. They were whispering to each other and staring in her direction. They had probably realized something wasn't quite right.

She tried the green key. It went in, but she had no opportunity to find out whether it would have turned in the lock. The door was opened from inside, a hand grabbed her arm and jerked her into the hall.

Her response to the initial shock was to close her eyes. When nothing else happened and she opened her eyes again, she found she was looking at the face of the blond man. Michael Trenkler, who else? He was wearing jeans with a sloppy polo shirt and looked so ordinary that the sight of him offset the grandeur of the imposing residence. The only thing she found disturbing about him was the fact that he should have long since set off for the lab.

He closed the front door and, with an exaggerated gesture of invitation, said, "Do come in." She didn't move, she could feel the pulse of her heartbeat in her throat, her fingertips and toes. With a swift movement, she threw her head back and tucked her hair in behind her left ear. It was a gesture she'd often observed in Nadia. It showed off the studs. Fortunately it didn't show their effect on her. She'd had her ears pierced too recently and her lobes were already starting throb.

The blond man leaned back against the door and fixed her with a stare she couldn't quite interpret. It could have been mocking; it could have been absolutely furious. "That was quick. Did Mr Moneybags stand you up?"

He obviously took her for Nadia. She sketched a nod and looked round. The walls were white, the floor was white, all the doors were white and the lattice windows beside the front door had white frames. It was so bright it hurt her eyes.

"Great," he said. "And why didn't you put the car in the garage? Have you got to go out again?"

She shook her head and rubbed her aching wrist. He gave a mocking grin. "Do forgive me, I didn't mean to grab you like that. But I didn't want to run the risk of you stopping for a lengthy chat with the neighbours. As you can well imagine, I haven't got that much time at my disposal."

His voice was oozing sarcasm. She turned away and ran over the ground-floor plan of the house in her mind: hall, lavatory, closet, living room, dining room, drawing room, kitchen. It had sounded large and spacious. It was.

The kitchen was on the right. On the left was a gently curving staircase going both up and down to the basement. Before it was an open space with a six-foot-tall palm standing sentry outside the coat closet. In the closet was the aforementioned leather jacket on a coat-hanger. She heard Nadia's voice telling her the alarm was always on. Not a word about what happened when the door was opened from the inside. By now at least eighteen seconds must have passed. Even though it meant she had to pass close to Michael Trenkler, she set off, keeping her eyes fixed on the green palm leaves.

He made no move to stop her – or do something worse – he just gave a puzzled frown when she carefully moved the jacket to one side. On the wall underneath it was the box Nadia had told her about. But she didn't get the chance to have a closer look and certainly not to key in the combination since he pushed himself off the wall and was beside her with a couple of steps. "Did you take a vow of silence while you were out?" he asked.

Quickly she put her handbag and key ring down on the chest underneath the coat-rack and slipped past him back into the hall. Let him deal with the black box, if it was necessary. With one more step he was beside her again. "You don't have to speak, it's enough if you nod or shake your head."

His head on one side, he looked her in the eye. Just ignore him, she told herself, and headed quickly for the living room.

"Stop playing the drama queen," he said. "I don't need money to burn. I thought the matter was closed."

The furnishings of the room, into which her flat would have fitted four times over, were vaguely familiar from the photos. An elegant three-piece suite in a contemporary style, with a low table on a large rug by the open French windows. Outside them a few well-cushioned chairs gleamed in the afternoon sun.

"Christ, Nadia," he said, "be reasonable. We're doing fine and I just want to stop anything changing that."

Her heartbeat had gradually returned to its normal rhythm. What he was saying seemed to be nothing more than the usual kind of stuff after an argument between husband and wife. The "Nadia" from his lips sent waves of relief though her brain and sharpened her eye for detail. On the wall over the three-piece suite was something that might be the Beckmann. It looked like a sheet of paper painted black in which a child had made holes. The holes had been sprayed with gold paint. This work of art had a thin metal frame, which must have cost a fortune itself.

Behind her she heard his hesitant footsteps and equally hesitant voice trying to formulate an apology, which he obviously didn't think he owed Nadia. "Sorry I got so worked up. We'll discuss this calmly when I've more time. I have to go now. You know how much depends on this new series. If I leave Kemmerling to play around with Olaf by himself we'll have all sorts of results in the morning, but nothing that's any use."

Just ignore him, she thought. Go into another room. Easier said than done. He was standing in the doorway out into the hall. To his left, also on a rug, was a grand piano. There were some sheets of music on the rest. Behind the glass front of the rustic-style dresser she saw some glasses – and bottles! A little tot of schnapps to calm her down! Her father had sworn by it. It had helped before her second interview with the bank and she certainly hadn't been more nervous then than she was now.

She went over to the dresser, opened one of the doors, took out a glass and examined the bottles. They contained a wide range of expensive brands of alcohol. She looked in vain for the simple schnapps her father had recommended for medicinal purposes. But vodka would do in an emergency. As she picked up the bottle, she heard Michael Trenkler say, "What are you playing at?"

It was a sharp reprimand and she presumed it referred to her silence until she felt him grasp her wrist again. It was impossible to ignore him any more. His grip was extremely painful and the sharp tone contained an unmistakable threat. "If you're really serious, then I might as well just pack my bags and leave."

He took the bottle from her, squeezing her wrist as he did so, as if he were trying to break it. He put the bottle back, closed the cupboard and dragged her out into the hall.

"You're hurting me, Michael!" Her wrist felt as if it were stuck in a vice. The words were out before she could stop them. She was just glad that his name came out naturally with them.

He dragged her into the kitchen, pushed her to the fridge, pulled open the door and pointed to a veritable battery of bottles of fruit juice, mineral water, lemonade and ketchup. "If you need a drink, help yourself."

At last he let go. She took a bottle of Diet Coke out of the fridge. Leaning back against the worktop, his arms crossed, impassive, he watched her pour the drink. As she took her first sip, he asked, "Do I have to take the bottles with me, or are you going to be sensible?"

It gradually dawned on her. Nadia must have a little problem with spirits. And her husband didn't like it. She just had to think of Heller to remember how much she hated drunks herself.

"I wasn't going to get drunk," she said softly, assuming a muted voice was less likely to give her away. "I just wanted a little pick-me-up because…"

For twenty seconds or so she rattled off something about the Mr Moneybags he'd mentioned who'd stood her up and really pissed her off. She hadn't intended to say so much, but it appeared to be exactly what Michael Trenkler expected. He certainly didn't look surprised. When she finally stopped, he just gave a snort of contempt. Then he turned back into the hall, leaving her standing by the open fridge with her Diet Coke.

Hearing him go upstairs, she examined her surroundings: luxury wherever she looked. Even a TV in the kitchen. There was a small set fixed to the wall above the fridge. Not very practical, she thought, you'd have to stand on a chair to switch it on. Presumably there was a remote control.

After a few seconds she heard steps on the stairs again and Michael Trenkler reappeared in the doorway, a light jacket over his arm. "If you feel the need to get drunk, then don't let me stop you. But I tell you, I'm not going through all that again."

"Don't worry," she murmured, took a deep breath and held up her glass of Diet Coke, "I'll stick to this."

Again he frowned. For a moment she wondered if he'd seen through her. Then she realized she'd picked the wrong bottle again. That should never have happened! Nadia had lugged gallons of mineral water up to her flat and just once the orange juice. She could have bet her bottom dollar Nadia never drank cola.

Without replying, Michael Trenkler turned round and went out. At first she was relieved, but then she started to wonder whether it was right just to let him go like that. Could her mistake with the vodka bottle have triggered off the very thing Nadia was trying to avoid at all costs? Pack his bags! That sounded like a separation. The front door was opened.

She put the glass down and hurried out into the hall. "Michael," she cried, "I'm sorry."

The door swung to. Once more he was leaning with his back against it, a car key in his hand, giving her a suspicious look. As well as the suspicion, she could see fear in his eyes, but didn't know how to interpret it. What lovely eyes he's got, she thought. She felt at a loss, she had no idea what to say now. She could have kicked herself for having started to talk at all. Every further word increased the risk of discovery. Quietly, tremulously, she repeated, "I'm really sorry."

Nothing changed in his strange look and tense posture. She desperately tried to think what was the best thing she could say to put his mind at rest before he went out. "I didn't want to make a scene," she said. "I wasn't going to have a drink, either. I just thought…"

She tried to act casual, giving him the shrug of the shoulders and the mocking smile with the little pout. "I thought you might stay if I pretended I was going to. But off you go, I know how important the new series is and that you can't leave Kemmerling alone with Olaf. I won't touch the bottles, any of them." To emphasize her promise, she said, "Cross my heart and hope to die." It made her sound like a little girl and would presumably never have crossed Nadia's lips.

Michael Trenkler's only response was a rapid exhalation of breath, but it sounded disbelieving, derisive and very hurt. He gave a mechanical nod, turned round and opened the door. As he left, he said, "You've changed your tune! We'll talk tomorrow, OK?"

"OK," she said, rubbing her wrist, which was still hurting. His grip had left red marks. When the door finally closed behind him, she took a deep breath and let the air out slowly in relief. Outside a car engine roared into noisy life. In all the excitement, she forgot that there hadn't been a car parked anywhere in the street when she arrived.

She went back into the kitchen, tipped the Coke down the sink and set out on her first expedition into Nadia's life. In the living room she picked out a few notes on the piano and looked at the music on the rest: Chopin, *Nocturne in G Minor*. It sounded very complicated and that was what it looked like, too. Under that were pieces by Wilhelm Friedemann, Bach, Tchaikovsky, Rubinstein, Saint-Saëns and Telemann. The last two names meant nothing to her. She wandered over to the couch and asked the black-and-gold wrapping paper if it was the Beckmann. No answer.

The kitchen cupboards were meticulously neat and tidy. She couldn't find a remote control of the TV above the fridge but she didn't waste time looking for it. In the drawing room with the open fire she found more framed works of art and a second television. It was fitted into the natural stone wall above the mantelpiece and was hardly bigger than the palm of her hand. The miniature format made her realize it must be part of the alarm system. Nadia had told her so much about sensors that registered movement or heat and surveillance units that she'd imagined something futuristic.

She went back into the living room and discovered a similar mini-screen there, which she'd missed on her first inspection. Now that she knew what she was looking for, she found the surveillance unit in the dining room straight away. Somehow it seemed ridiculous, grossly excessive. At the same time there was something unpleasant about it, she felt she was being observed wherever she went, even though all the monitor screens were dark. It was only the lavatory and the hall that seemed to lack the spying eyes.

She had another look at the box hidden behind the leather jacket in the hall closet. Nadia's handbag was still on the chest. The ring with the marked keys was beside it; she assumed the car key was still in the bag.

Then she turned her attention to the curved staircase, first of all going down to examine the basement area. There was a utility room and a larder with crates of drinks and shelves, which were mostly empty, just a few tins of chicken soup and ravioli on them. She'd expected more. But the two freezers were well filled, mainly with ready meals.

Then she suddenly found herself immersed in lime-green reflections. The swimming pool! It was roughly as big as the living room and presumably deep enough for a non-swimmer to drown in. Half of the outside wall consisted of sliding glass doors. Beyond them a lawn sloped up to the garden. A door in one wall led to a tiny chamber full of machinery, presumably belonging to the pool. She didn't examine it too closely, the place was too cramped and too dark. And Nadia wasn't paying her to find out about circulating pumps, water filters and the like. In an adjoining room she found fitness equipment, a sunbed and the sauna.

This was the life! It was an alien world, but familiar from her dreams. She'd read about it a thousand times, suffering with the maids or the daughters of destitute counts, hoping they'd be rescued from their poverty, yet not believing such things actually existed – at least not for an ordinary bank clerk.

After a few minutes she went back up the stairs and on to the first floor. Six closed doors gave the impression of forbidden entry. But behind the very first she opened was a room where she immediately felt at home. It had everything she'd looked for and not found in the living room. There was an archetypal comfortable couch with three dozen cushions scattered about. It looked infinitely more used and nothing like as sterile as the suite downstairs. Beside the couch was a cupboard with two drawers and two doors which concealed a stack of towels and two bottles. "Massage oil", she read. What that brought to mind was the tensed-up neck muscles, she'd been living alone too long for any other thoughts. On the wall opposite the couch was a proper television, a video recorder, a satellite box and a stereo system.

Behind the second door was a bathroom. On the edge of the bath was a jar full of pink balls. For a second she thought they were sweets – but only for a second. One sniff told her they must be bath salts. She used the lavatory and for a while couldn't see the how to flush it until she found the plate in the wall behind the loo, which looked almost the same as the tiles around it. She couldn't suppress a brief grin.

Behind the third door was the bedroom. At least she assumed it was the bedroom. She only realized it must be a guest room when she saw exactly the same furnishings behind the next door. Their bedroom was behind the fifth door. Top quality, expensive, tasteful, pure white relieved by glass here and there and a touch of brass. The royal suite, there was no other name for it. There was no wardrobe but a dressing room with large mirrors, drawers and rails full of clothes. And not only city clothes, there were several evening dresses on the hangers.

A further door led from the bedroom to a huge bathroom. In fact a double bathroom. The shower cubicle was a separate room and considerably bigger than the recess which figured in her lease as a bathroom-cum-shower. A few steps led up to the circular bathtub. There was a smell of Nadia's perfume and fragrant bath oil. Open-mouthed, she admired the two washstands with bathroom cabinets either side and a white set of basketwork shelves with a collection of men's toiletries. The inescapable surveillance monitor was beside the door and clearly visible from the bath. Having discovered the tiny screen, she decided she had sufficiently familiarized herself with everything. She would just have a quick look in the sixth room and then leave. But things turned out differently.

Behind the sixth door was Michael Trenkler's study. At least that was what she assumed. There was no security screen there. A monitor, keyboard, mouse, telephone, answerphone, a small photocopier and a flatbed scanner all fought for space on the desk. There were no papers lying around, but then there wasn't room for any. Beside the desk was a metal cabinet with an ultramodern laser printer on it. The computer was underneath the table. A green light glowed. Michael must have been working at it and forgotten to switch off.

All round the walls were shelves overflowing with books. It was mainly specialist literature: biology, chemistry, biochemistry, pharmacy, medicine; some in German, most in English. Among them she discovered handbooks for a variety of computer programs. One of them was about the word-processing package that had sealed her fate when she'd worked for the insurance company. She leafed through it until there was a clattering sound from somewhere.

She quickly replaced the book and listened intently. It had been a quiet, metallic noise followed by an equally quiet but perfectly comprehensible swear word. A man's voice. Michael must have come back, perhaps he'd remembered his computer was still on. She tiptoed to the door and listened for noises in the hall. Only when she heard a woman's voice behind her calling for Terry and a kind of whining did she turn round and see the change on the computer monitor.

There was a small image in the top right-hand corner. She recognized the front garden and a section of the road, even part of the properties on the other side. The garden on the right, as she was looking at it, had a high wall separating it from the road. A wrought-iron gate was open. On the ground at the edge of the road was a man's bicycle, one of those racing bikes on which young people terrorized the pedestrian precinct in the city centre. Next to the bike was a very large shaggy dog that was sniffing at a man in lurid shorts lying on the ground, only his back visible. A flustered-looking woman, who looked vaguely familiar though she couldn't quite identify her, came hurrying out to the road, shouted "Terry!" again and went over to the man on the ground. "Have you hurt yourself?"

She watched, fascinated, as the man stood up, felt his left knee, bent down to pick up his bike and started to swear again. "Dammit, Eleanor, can't you tie the bloody beast up?"

It was all spoken quietly, but perfectly comprehensible. She'd discovered the surveillance unit in the study; strangely enough, she didn't find it disturbing there. She picked up the handbook again and calmly turned a few more pages.

Next she turned to the metal cabinet. It contained several thin files and three fat ones. One had "House" written on it, another "Insurance policies".

The third, which only had an M on the cover to indicate what it contained, was the one that aroused her curiosity the most. The latest item to have been filed was a contract between Michael Trenkler and a pharmaceuticals company. The annual salary was astronomical and dissuaded her from examining the other documents. The only other detail she noticed was Michael's age. He was thirty-five. She would have made him younger.

In the file marked "House" the purchase of everything from the house to the last movement sensor could be followed. Everything was in Nadia's name and it didn't look as if there were any unpaid bills or a mortgage to pay off. In "Insurances" were documents recording everything an insurance agent could desire, among other things a life-insurance policy for Nadia.

And although she had only worked in insurance for three months, she saw at a glance that it was a term insurance, not one that built up capital. Only payable on death. With Nadia dead Michael Trenkler would be richer by a million euros!

Part Two

Susanne Lasko read the sum in words and in figures. In both cases the effect was equally disturbing. The policy had been taken out seven years ago and revised after the changeover to euros. Perhaps Nadia had just wanted to provide security for her husband, since during the first years of their marriage he'd had no income of his own.

By that time it was past seven and she felt she'd sufficiently familiarized herself with everything. She went down to the kitchen and drank a mouthful of mineral water to wash out her mouth, which had gone dry at the sight of the figures. Then she closed the French windows, went out of the house, locking the front door behind her – the blue key was the one that fitted – and walked round to the drive. She looked around, to make sure the shaggy dog wasn't still there, and felt in the handbag for the car key, but before she could establish that it wasn't there, she saw that the drive outside the garage was empty.

Beside the low fence in the neighbouring garden the man who'd fallen off his bicycle earlier was vigorously polishing up his machine with a soft cloth. Wolfgang Blasting, the policeman with too much time to devote to his neighbours. He stood up and asked, "Doc off milking his mice again, then?" There was something common about his broad grin. It reminded her of Heller and didn't seem to fit in with this neighbourhood. Nor did his next question. "Did he bring that switch for me?"

She just shrugged her shoulders.

"He said he would," said Wolfgang Blasting. "Go and have a look." It sounded like an order and made her furious – with him and with Nadia, who would have had no problem looking for a switch and wouldn't have been desperately wondering how to get away. On the other hand, Blasting's request made it easy for her to go back into the house without arousing suspicion.

She closed the front door and leaned back against it for a moment, as Michael Trenkler had done. That explained why he'd asked her why she hadn't put the car away. She'd parked the Alfa right in front of the double garage and blocked the way out. And since he urgently needed to go to the lab, he'd taken Nadia's car – without bothering to ask.

At that point she remembered the alarm, went to the coat rack, pushed the leather jacket to one side and keyed in the code. A metallic click went round the whole house. She registered it but assumed it represented no danger as nothing else happened.

Quickly she went over to the door from the hall into the garage. It was locked. The black key opened it. At once several neon tubes flared up, bathing the large space in harsh light. She saw a cream Jaguar – unlocked, as she found when she tried the door. The key was in the ignition, the remote control for the garage door was on the passenger seat.

She was sure Nadia wouldn't mind if she came back in this car. She dumped the handbag on the seat, picked up the remote control and pointed it at the closed door, which didn't seem to have anything so ordinary as a handle or a latch. At least she couldn't see anything like that, only the inconspicuous black box on the wall and the cable running to a motor on the top edge of the door.

She quickly keyed in the combination but, although she was sure she'd followed Nadia's instructions exactly, the double door didn't move an inch. For some reason, which presumably only Joachim Kogler would understand, the technology refused to function. That seemed to explain why Michael Trenkler had still been there. He'd obviously been waiting for Nadia to return because he couldn't get his car out. So there was no question of asking the genius who'd invented it to help. That would have been the first thing Michael would have thought of. Perhaps that was why Joachim and Lilo Kogler had been watching her so intently – to see whether it worked from outside, or to explain to her if it didn't.

There was only one solution. A taxi. There was enough money in Nadia's purse. She went up to the study and looked for the telephone book, but couldn't find it, so she lifted the receiver to ring directory enquiries. But there was no sound from the receiver. Again and again she jiggled the rest, but with no result.

Panic set in and for a few seconds she was back in the disused factory. But this situation was nothing like as desperate. She was neither seriously injured nor disoriented. In the drive next door was a policeman waiting for a switch. Even if she hadn't particularly liked Wolfgang Blasting, with his vulgar grin and his ordering her about, there could hardly be a better person to guarantee her safety. Suddenly the risk of being recognized as a fraud if she spoke to him seemed so small as to be virtually non-existent.

And she had a ready-made excuse to use his telephone. "I can't find the switch anywhere, so I'll have to phone Michael. Unfortunately there's something wrong with our phone, could I use yours?"

What if he accompanied her to the telephone? As she went to the door, she couldn't think of a lie to get Wolfgang Blasting to leave her by herself for a moment. But that was not something that occupied her for long.

The front door wouldn't open.

The second panic attack was considerably more severe than the first. She was absolutely sure she hadn't locked the door when she'd escaped back into the house, so it never occurred to her to try the key. She ran back into the living room, pulling this way and that at the French windows. No joy. The glass doors by the swimming pool wouldn't open either, nor any of the windows.

In her mind's eye she saw the insurance policy. Inside her head Michael Trenkler's voice was whispering something about a Mr Moneybags and not needing money to burn. She'd seen enough crime films to wonder what Nadia was really looking for: a stand-in sulky wife or a suitable corpse? Was that why it didn't matter at all that her voice sounded different?

It was some minutes before she remembered the metallic clicking noise. Now she thought she knew what the mistake was she'd made. The alarm system mustn't have been on. She must have switched it on instead of off. She tried keying in the combination again, but Nadia had only given her the one and nothing moved.

Now panic really was threatening to take over. She had to force herself to stay calm. There must be a way of getting out of the place. She went back into the garage and examined the box on the wall beside the door. It was perfectly smooth, apart from a few countersunk screws. She hadn't come across a workroom where she could expect to find a screwdriver, but in an emergency a kitchen knife should do the job.

The screws were pretty tight, but eventually gave way. She took off the cover and found herself confronted with a tangle of circuit boards and wires, which all ended up in the thick cable going to the motor. Ignoring the danger of an electric shock, she fetched a knife with a sharp point from the kitchen and set about taking out the tiny screws holding the cable connectors.

Twice the knife slipped and cut her finger, smearing blood over the box, the wires and the handle of the knife. After ten minutes the thick cable was disconnected. She went to the side and grasped the bottom of the door, smearing blood over that too — and saw the keyhole just above the floor with a recessed grip on either side.

It was the red key that fitted. Feeling both immeasurably relieved and horribly ashamed of her stupidity, she turned it and heard something click in the floor. The door swung up a little. The front door could probably have been opened in the same way. As she pulled the door up, she peered though the widening gap at the neighbouring garden. The bicycle was still there, but not Wolfgang Blasting.

Seconds later the door was fully open and she was sitting in the Jaguar convincing herself she could manage the automatic drive. Another person would have found the sheer number of switches on the console between the two seats daunting. She didn't find how to adjust the driver's seat, but she could just reach the pedals with the tips of her toes. In her haste, she forgot to adjust the rear-view mirror.

As soon as she touched the accelerator, the Jaguar shot forward. She stamped on the brakes, let the car roll slowly out of the garage, then stopped, got out, pulled the heavy door down and locked it. As she was about to get back into the car, Wolfgang Blasting appeared from his house and asked, "What about the switch?"

"No time," she said curtly and got back into the car.

Ilona Blasting appeared in the open doorway, adding her strident voice to her husband's: "Oh, come on. It's not a catastrophe if you miss a few minutes of the first act. I don't want to spend the whole evening sitting in the dark."

Susanne deduced from this that it was a light switch they needed. Remembering what Nadia had told her about Frau Blasting's political affiliations, she suggested, "Light a candle. It's romantic and environ-mentally friendly."

Taking advantage of Ilona Blasting's flabbergasted silence, she released the handbrake, fastened the safety belt and drove off. Her fingers were still bleeding, both cuts were deep, leaving blood on the steering wheel, the handbrake and the door handle. There were smears on the sand-coloured dress too. She stopped on the country lane with the young trees to look for the first-aid box, which she found under the driver's seat. After wrapping some gauze round her fingers, she drove on, slowly and carefully, well aware that the Jaguar was jam-packed with as much technology as the bloody house.

The traffic on the autobahn was heavy. She stuck to the inside lane, trying to work out how to tell Nadia about the mess she'd made of things. It was all over before it had really begun, that was for sure. She needn't worry about the insurance policy, after such a debacle Nadia couldn't afford to install her in her home for any length of time. She'd end up demolishing the place. She'd failed, it was as much of a disaster as her miscalculation regarding the pistol during the second bank robbery. It was more than just embarrassing – suddenly the engine cut out.

It was a reflex action to pull the car over to the right and she managed to get the Jaguar onto the hard shoulder. After that it didn't respond at all, neither when she turned the steering wheel, nor when she trod on the brake.

As the car rolled onto the hard shoulder, she burst into tears. For the first time since her father had died. It was all too much for her: the shame, the tension, the loss of the prospect of five hundred or even a thousand euros a month, her whole miserable situation. The traffic roared past, no one bothered with her. She sat there for more than fifteen minutes, leaning on the steering wheel, her face buried in the crook of her arm. With her bloodstained dress she looked like something out of a horror film. Eventually someone tapped on the window of the passenger door. She looked up to see a bearded face. "Do you need help?"

She nodded and furiously set about wiping her eyes and cheeks, smearing the cheap mascara all over her face. The bearded man glanced round the interior and, seeing the traces of blood, said, "You're injured."

She waved his concern away. "It's just a cut on my finger. The problem's the car, it won't go."

The man's smile was reassuring and at the same time severe. "It's not the end of the world. But you should have switched the hazard warning lights on. Do it now."

She looked at the multiplicity of switches on the console. "Which one's the hazard lights?"

At the his look of surprise, she quickly added, "It's my husband's car. I don't normally drive it, I've no idea which switch is which."

"Aha," said the bearded man drawing out the word a little. "You'd better show me your papers."

He opened the passenger door, as far as the crash barrier allowed, felt in his shirt pocket and showed her his warrant card. The police! That was all she needed. She looked round. Behind the Jaguar was an ordinary white car. It didn't look like a police car.

"Papers, please," he asked again.

She held out Nadia's handbag, but he didn't take it. "Driving licence and registration document are all I need to see."

"I've only got my driving licence," she said. "And my identity card, of course." As she pulled both out of the case, two credit cards and Nadia's passport fell out as well. Among them was the registration document for the Alfa. Placing it on the outstretched male hand, together with the driving licence and Nadia's ID, she explained, "That's my car. My husband simply took it and locked me in because I wanted to go and see a friend and he can't stand her."

He didn't respond, but studied the driving licence and registration document. Then he went round the to front of the car, looked at something, came back, stuck his head in the car again and demanded. "The registration number."

She had no idea what he was talking about.

"The registration number of this car, Frau Trenkler," he said, emphasizing each word. "If it's your husband's car, you ought to know it."

It was all over. Ridiculous, really, when she had such a good memory for figures. But she'd not even glanced at it in the garage, nor out in the driveway. She shook her head. "I'm sorry, I'm not..." Not Nadia Trenkler, she was going to say and explain everything. Then he would be welcome to come to Kettlerstrasse with her and see with his own eyes that she'd only been doing Nadia a favour. But it didn't come to a full confession.

He interrupted her explanation in the same tone as Wolfgang Blasting had ordered her to look for the switch. "Get out of the car." She started to open the driver's door. "No." He waved her towards him. "This side."

80

Silently cursing, she slid across and followed him to his car. Without taking his eyes off her, he pulled a mobile phone out of a holder on his belt, thumbed in a number and said, "Dettmer here, will you check a car owner for me?" Then he gave the Jaguar's registration. After a while, which seemed like an eternity to Susanne, he got a reply and smiled at her. "If you can just tell me your husband's date of birth, I'll be convinced."

That was no problem, she'd seen it in the contract with the pharmaceuticals firm. Dettmer returned her papers and went back to the Jaguar. "Memory loss under stress. It can happen. Did the car do anything before it gave up the ghost?"

"No."

He tried to start the Jaguar. The starter motor turned, a few lights appeared, but that was all. Dettmer gave her a reproachful look. "It must be completely empty. Check the fuel gauge before you set off next time. Running out on the autobahn can be an expensive pastime."

She felt she wanted the ground to swallow her up. The helpful policeman looked in the boot, but there wasn't a spare can, so he got out his phone again and called the recovery service. Then he went, though not before telling her to wait on the other side of the crash barrier for her own safety.

The recovery vehicle appeared not long after. The Jaguar was attached to a hook and lifted up. She sat in the front, with the driver. It was ten miles to the nearest petrol station. She used Nadia's money to pay for the recovery and the petrol, did basic repairs to her make-up and drove to her flat.

Surprisingly she found a space right outside the flat. It wasn't a particularly large one but, bearing Johannes Herzog's instructions in mind, she managed to manoeuvre the Jaguar into it. She got out and hurried into the old, ugly tenement. Just for once Heller wasn't leaning out of the window. As usual, though, the door wasn't locked. She ran up the three flights of stairs.

It was a strange sensation, having to knock at her own door. Nadia opened at once and had a quick look up and down the stairs, to make sure there was no one else around, trying with difficulty to conceal the strain she was under. But when, after a few seconds, she saw the state of Susanne's face and dress, her eyes widened. "Just look at you! Have you been in a crash?"

She shook her head and mumbled something about a sharp kitchen knife. Nadia gave a sigh of relief. "Thank God. I thought something had happened."

Then she went back into the kitchen and lighted a cigarette, the last in the packet. On the table was a saucer overflowing with ash and cigarette ends. Beside it was an open laptop, the screen swarming with letters and numbers. It looked confusing and to gain time Susanne pretended to be interested. "Can you really do proper work with a little thing like that?"

"Little?" Nadia's snort sounded more than mildly amused. "That's a P4 with three gigahertz."

"Aha," she murmured, watching as Nadia's fingers flew across the keys and the jumble of figures vanished from the screen in next to no time.

After another drag on her cigarette, Nadia pointed to the rough-and-ready bandage on her hand. "What were you doing with a kitchen knife?"

"Michael was still there when I arrived."

Nadia looked up in surprise and laughed uncertainly. "I hope you didn't slaughter him."

She just shook her head. Nadia was insistent. "And? How was it? You look as if you've had an encounter with the Devil. Were there problems? Did he notice something or did he fall for it?"

She wasn't convinced he'd seen her for long enough to say that, but she nodded.

"What then?" Nadia demanded. "A problem with Michael?"

"No," she said, "I got on OK with him. I don't think he noticed anything."

Nadia breathed a sigh of relief. "So it works. It'll work for several days, you'll see."

"I don't think so," she said and started her report. When she came to her need for a sip of vodka to calm her down, Nadia's face turned grey. Her voice sounded as if she had sandpaper in her throat. "You did what?"

She hastened to add that she hadn't actually touched a drop and that she was convinced she'd managed to calm Michael down. She repeated word for word what she'd said and what he'd replied. "I'm sorry," she said, "but I didn't know…"

Irritatedly Nadia waved her apology aside. "OK, OK. My mistake. I hadn't thought you'd have a drink if you were going to drive, otherwise I'd have told you. But I can sort that out, no problem," Nadia said, without seeming entirely convinced. She stubbed out her cigarette, jabbing it viciously on the saucer, and, though it obviously cost her an effort, gave an explanation. "I went through a terrible time when I found out he was being unfaithful. It took a while before I could get it under control. Since then he really loses his cool if it even looks as if I…" Nadia shrugged her shoulders and went on, "But if you didn't touch a drop then I'm sure I can sort it out with him."

She swore she hadn't taken even a little sip. Nadia relaxed a little. "And then? Was there anything else?"

She nodded. Now the words came easily. She told the rest of her story in reverse, starting with a friendly man who'd helped her on the autobahn – keeping quiet about the fact that he was a policeman – then the Jaguar running out of petrol and back to taking the box apart in the garage. Along the way she mentioned the telephone not working.

Several times Nadia breathed in sharply, as if about to vent her fury, but she bit her tongue and even managed a "Nothing too serious then" at the end. "I'm sure Jo can mend the door." From what she said, she'd tried to simplify matters and had reprogrammed the alarm to stop herself being locked out if Susanne should happen to make a mistake. The telephone in the study was her business line, which was always switched off at the weekend; the private phone was in the bedroom.

Susanne hadn't seen a telephone there, but Nadia insisted there was one, by the bed, all she had to do was look, though actually she'd had no business to be in the bedroom. Nadia couldn't entirely conceal her anger, but apart from that comment, it was mainly directed at Michael.

"He seems to think the car runs on air. You can't imagine how often we've had arguments about it. Only four weeks ago I had an important engagement and was just leaving when he rang. He'd run out of petrol halfway to the lab and expected me to go and drive him there."

Nadia got worked up then calmed down. She was partly to blame herself, she said. Four weeks ago she'd told Michael to be so good as to check the fuel gauge next time before he set off. And if he'd forgotten to fill up he should find some other means of transport. Of course, by that she'd meant a taxi, not the Alfa. Her final assessment of the debriefing was, "Well, it seems to me it hasn't gone badly at all. Not as planned, but the things that went wrong weren't your fault. And I can guarantee that the next time Michael won't touch the Alfa and the door'll be working."

She couldn't believe what she was hearing. An outburst of rage and vituperation for her stupidity she could have understood. But for someone to accept that kind of damage with a shrug of the shoulders – just to be able to spend an undisturbed weekend with her lover? It was inconceivable. And experience had taught her that others had considerably fewer inhibitions than she had. A million on death.

"No," she said. "There won't be a next time. I've seen the insurance policy. My voice sounds different from yours, but when you're dead you can't speak. Find someone else for your little game."

Nadia gave her a blank stare. Then, after a few seconds she started to laugh out loud. "You think I was going to kill you just to collect a million?" It sounded as if a million was little more than petty cash.

Nadia shook her head, still laughing. "There's just one reason I need you, Susanne, and one reason alone: the one I told you. Our voices are as identical as all the rest. The only difference is in your own ears, it's the body's resonance that causes it."

At this Nadia took a small Dictaphone out of her computer bag, switched it on and said, "Say something."

"What should I say?"

Nadia shrugged her shoulders and picked up her handbag. "Did you take your money?"

"No. It was only for a few hours."

Nadia counted out five hundred euros and placed them on the table. "But they count as triple time with all the trouble you had."

The Dictaphone was still running. Nadia switched it off, rewound it and let her hear that there was no difference between their voices. "Does that reassure you? Now show me your fingers."

Hesitantly she stretched out her hand. Nadia took off the makeshift bandage, looked at the cuts and said they didn't need sewing. "They'll leave some scars," she said. "Have you got a sharp knife?"

Without waiting for an answer, Nadia went into the kitchen and fetched a small knife from the drawer. After examining Susanne's cuts carefully, she drew the knife twice over her own fingers. It made a soft hissing noise.

Susanne felt sick when she saw the blood trickling down Nadia's hand. It spilled onto the floor and soaked into the old carpet. "Are you out of your mind?" she stammered.

"Only at the full moon," said Nadia. When she went on it was in an insistent tone. "We've got this far, Susanne, you can't let me down now. In fortnight's time I'm going for a weekend away with my friend. It's already agreed. I know it's not easy, the alarm system's a bit awkward. But it's not the alarm you have to cope with, it's Michael. That worked. And the next time there won't be any other difficulties, I swear. I'll change the codes so there's no problem."

She couldn't take her eyes of Nadia's bleeding fingers. And every drop soaking into the carpet was another reason to say no. She really could have done with the money, but the idea that Nadia might cut herself and she would have to take a knife to herself to restore the likeness… Shaking her head firmly, she took off the rings and pulled the studs out of her ears, which by now were throbbing fiercely. She put the jewellery on the table beside the money and took off the watch. "No," she said.

Nadia must have realized she was deadly serious. With a look of frustration on her face, she wrapped a handkerchief round her bleeding fingers, gathered up the jewellery, put the laptop and Dictaphone in the computer bag, tucked the document case under her arm and went to the door. There she stopped.

"I'll pay you a thousand for each weekend. You won't have to take any more of your mother's money, you'll even be able to pay back everything you stole from her."

It was moral blackmail. When she showed no reaction, Nadia said, "Think about it, Susanne. A thousand for each weekend, that's two thousand a month. When did you last earn that much? We'll meet on Thursday. In the multi-storey again." After that command, Nadia closed the door behind her.

Susanne stared at the patches of blood on the old carpet, while in her mind's eye she saw herself strolling round the white mansion. She heard the asthmatic wheezing of her second-hand fridge, saw her threadbare couch, her whole shabby flat and the money on the table. A thousand, after the mess she'd made of it! A lie about her mother falling ill would have been decidedly cheaper. But perhaps Nadia's mother was dead, or Michael got on very well with her. Whatever, the business must be damned important to Nadia.

Immersed in thought, she went into the bedroom, took off the bloodstained clothes and put on some of her old things. Then she scrubbed at the expensive dress for a while. The blood would wash out of the clothes. She didn't bother with the carpet, it merged in with the lurid pattern and the grime of years.

About a quarter of an hour later there was a knock at the door. She assumed it would be Nadia, coming back to try and persuade her again. But on the landing were Jasmin Toppler and Heller. Jasmin, in her leathers and with her helmet under her arm, was at the door, Heller a little further back. As she opened the door, she heard him say, "...left half an hour ago, in a new Jaguar." Jasmin tapped her forehead and said, "He's been seeing things."

Heller flushed with rage. "But I did see her," he objected. "She was wearin' diff'rent things, that expensive clobber again. I hate to think what she's been up to of late. I think I saw her before, in a white Porsche. 'S a while ago now. It wasn't parked outside. I was —"

Jasmin cut him short. "Pissed as a newt as usual. You don't need to tell us that." Then Jasmin turned to Susanne and asked if she had a minute. She asked Jasmin in, so as not to have to argue with Heller.

He was drunk, but not so drunk that he could be persuaded he'd been seeing things. His window looked out on the street. If he'd seen Nadia come out of the building and drive off, even his addled brain would tell him that there must be two women. Which was the case, of course. As she closed the door, she heard him mutter, "So that's it. There's two of 'em. Very handy. You could get up to all sorts of tricks and always have an alibi." He giggled and went down to his flat, still muttering to himself.

Jasmin was standing in the living room. The money was still on the table next to the blood-smeared knife and the saucer full of cigarette ends. She was looking at them with a thoughtful expression on her face. Susanne quickly went past her, picked up the money and put it in the cupboard.

As she closed the cupboard door, Jasmin said, "Er, tomorrow I'm flying off on holiday for four weeks," and told Susanne that the friend who'd promised to water her plants had broken her leg and was in hospital. "So I thought you might be good enough to do it, if it's no trouble and I gave you the key?"

She hadn't been listening properly, she still felt dazed by Nadia's increased offer and just nodded. Jasmin gave a grateful smile, went up to her flat and came back with some Elastoplast, with which she bandaged her cuts. Again her eyes were drawn to the knife and the saucer. But she asked no questions and, to judge by her leather suit, she hadn't been at home during the last few hours.

When she was alone once more, Susanne took the things into the kitchen, washed the knife and tipped the cigarette ends into the rubbish bin. Only then did she see the tiny scraps of paper in the bin. She fished them all out, blew off the cigarette ash and took them into the living room.

There was no particular reason why she did it, not even curiosity. At first it was just something to occupy her. With a great deal of patience, she managed to put the sheet of paper together like a jigsaw puzzle. At the top was an imposing letterhead: "Alfo Investment". She'd seen that somewhere before, but couldn't remember where. At the very bottom was a row of figures in small writing: telephone number, fax, bank account details. The tears in the paper meant she couldn't decipher them all, but they stuck in her mind. In the middle of the sheet were more numbers, written by hand in relatively large letters.

There were nine in total, all of them seven-figure numbers, each preceded by a name. The figures were listed in descending order. The smallest, the one at the bottom, was 1,300,000. At the top, alongside the name Zurkeulen, was 5,730,000. The total came to a little over twenty million, a sum of money that was beyond her imagining, if it was euros. "A million on death" briefly came to mind. After that she had no idea what to think.

For a while she just sat there, staring at the scraps of paper. Her cuts were throbbing unpleasantly. Everything went through her mind again, like a film being played backwards. Until it came to Michael Trenkler. He was leaning back against the front door, looking at her with that expression of fear and suspicion in his eyes. "I'm not going through all that again," he said, expressing exactly what was going through her mind. On the other hand, could she afford to pass up the chance of two thousand euros a month simply because she had some – possibly completely absurd – misgivings? And she could do something to counter those misgivings.

She took the pad she used for her applications and started: "On 25/7 I met Nadia Trenkler in Gerler House." Then she wrote down everything that had happened since then, even Heller's crazy claim that the opinion pollster had been a snooper. She concluded with the disparities: blood group, birthmark and fractured skull, and put the sheets in a large envelope, adding the scraps of paper with the names and figures.

Then she wondered where she could deposit it. To hand it to her mother saying, "If I stop coming to visit, get someone to read this to you and take it over to the police," would give Agnes Runge a heart attack. She didn't know a lawyer she could ask to look after this "life-insurance policy". Her divorce lawyer had been a scrawny little bastard, always in a hurry and only interested in his fee. Basically there was only one person who would make proper use of her notes, if the worst should come to the worst, despite the way she still felt about him: Dieter Lasko. But it would be a mistake to send him the envelope. He'd just tap his forehead and tell Ramie, "I suppose Susanne's spending all her spare time reading crime novels now." She had to think of another way. And another way did occur to her.

On Monday Jasmin Toppler gave her the key to her flat then got into a taxi, together with a large suitcase. Five minutes later she was hiding her envelope underneath Jasmin's bedlinen. She'd stuck it down and written her husband's name and address on it, as well as a message to Jasmin, asking her to hand it over to Dieter if she should suddenly give up her flat and forget to ask for it back. It might sound ridiculous and Jasmin's reaction might be the same as Dieter's. But it reassured her.

After she'd done that, she turned her attention to another aspect. If she was going to stand in for Nadia for any length of time, she simply had to be better prepared. In the days that followed she wrote down everything that occurred to her that seemed important: what she absolutely had to know, what she ought to know on top of that and what it would do no harm to know.

As requested, she met Nadia in the multi-storey on Thursday. When, to be on the safe side, she mentioned her notes, Nadia simply gave an amused smile. Her questionnaire, on the other hand, she found a prudent precaution. With relief she said, "So you're going to do it," confessing that she'd felt she couldn't ask her to learn masses of dates and events off by heart on top of everything else. Since she was only going to show Michael the cold shoulder, it had seemed superfluous. But, of course, it would do no harm if she was prepared for possible emergencies.

They took a drive in the country in the Porsche. Nadia told her a few anecdotes that occasionally cropped up in conversations with Jo and Lilo or Wolfgang and Ilona. If some topic cropped up where she had nothing to say, it should be enough to put them off with a "Don't remind me of that."

She wouldn't come into contact with other people, Nadia said, since she herself didn't have a lot to do with the people in the two houses opposite. One belonged to Niedenhoff, a pianist who'd only moved in at the beginning of the year and who was mostly away on concert tours. An actress lived in the other. They hardly ever saw her, she was a bit eccentric, grotesquely attached to her dog; she lavished twice much attention on it as on her son. Her real name was Eleanor Ravatzky, though she had a different stage name.

Celebrities everywhere, Susanne thought, at least on the other side of the road. A pianist and an actress. That would explain why she'd felt she'd seen the flustered-looking woman somewhere before.

Nadia gave her a few details about herself. She'd been born and had her early schooling in Düsseldorf, where she'd also lived and worked for some time later on. Her parents had moved to Geneva years ago. That was where her mother came from. Her father was completely occupied with his work, he didn't even have time for a short telephone conversation. Her mother was very much involved in cultural life and she never got round to ringing up to ask how her daughter was either. There should be no surprises from that side.

Michael's parents lived in Munich, though they originally came from Cologne. Paul, Michael's brother, had gone to Bavaria ten years ago because of his work and their parents had joined him there. Paul was married to Sophie and they had one son, Ralph, who was now eighteen. Susanne would have nothing to do with them. There might be a telephone call, but the answerphone was always switched on to take incoming calls.

The last time Nadia had seen Michael's family had been shortly after their wedding. They hadn't invited their families to the marriage ceremony, but to please Michael they'd organized a celebration some time later, putting their relatives up in a hotel because at the time they didn't have a house with guest rooms. It had been an unmitigated disaster. Ralph had done nothing but get up to mischief and his grandmother had taken his side all the time. After that, Nadia had decided to keep the family ties as loose as possible and they didn't exchange visits. Michael had come to share her view that too much family was not good for their own peace and quiet.

"Does he never go to see his parents?" Susanne asked incredulously.

"Rarely," said Nadia and went on to several other points. The sailing holiday that had been mentioned had been quite nice. Contrary to Susanne's assumption, Nadia didn't have a yacht of her own. Kemmerling, whom Michael had spoken of, had let them borrow his. Nothing special had happened: a lot of water, a lot of boredom, but on the whole it had been relaxing.

The ring with the striking blue stone had been a present from Michael for their fifth wedding anniversary. She must never take it off; it sealed, so to speak, the renewal of their marriage vows. From that Susanne deduced that the big crisis in Nadia's marriage must have been two years ago. Nadia didn't say much about it and what she did sounded bitter.

"When I first met him all he had in the world was three pairs of socks and a grotty room he shared with a physics student. He was supporting himself with part-time jobs and would probably have taken several more years just to get his first degree. Now he has two doctorates and you've seen his lifestyle. It doesn't make it easy to take it when he suddenly starts thinking he might have missed out on something."

Nadia stared fixedly at the path through the trees in front of them, but after a few seconds her expression relaxed and she recounted a few more anecdotes which Michael was in the habit of recalling with a "Do you remember?" Apart from that there didn't seem to be a great deal of conversation *chez* Trenkler. They only rarely talked about Michael's research and almost never about Nadia's job, since, being one of the old-fashioned kind, he didn't like her going out to work at all.

Although Susanne would not have anything to do with her professional activities, Nadia explained that fortunately, after Michael's infidelity, her despair and a certain amount of excessive drinking, she'd come across an old acquaintance who had set up as a financial consultant. Insurance, financing construction projects, short-term loans for small businesses, that kind of thing. A little investment advice too. At the moment he couldn't afford to take anyone on full-time, so Nadia helped him out, as a favour, but also to take her mind off her domestic problems. Since then she'd been able to delude herself two or three times a week into thinking she was an independent woman. Given Michael's income, she wasn't financially dependent on what she earned.

These details built up into a consistent overall picture and provided a satisfactory answer to Susanne's questions. When they got back to the car, Nadia picked up a bundle of papers off the rear seat. She had made a list of her own. Every security lever, every movement sensor, every heat sensor, every monitor, every locking device, every "if-then" was on it. "Do you think you can manage all that?"

"I think so," she said, then told Nadia that she went to see her mother every two weeks and that she'd like Nadia to arrange her weekends away accordingly.

"No problem," said Nadia.

Shortly after nine they were back in the city. Nadia stopped two streets away from Susanne's flat and gave her a new mobile phone with a battery charger so that she could contact her by phone if necessary. "If everything goes as we arranged, we'll meet in the multi-storey on Friday week at four. I'll let you know if there's any change, so you won't be hanging around waiting to see if I'm going to come."

Hardly had she closed the door of her flat behind her than the mobile rang. Nadia had forgotten to give her the PIN she needed to enter after it had been switched off. She gave her the four digits and wished her a good night's sleep. It was a good night's sleep. With Nadia's explanations going round in her head, she dreamed her way through several episodes in her life.

On Friday she had another session on the sunbed. On Saturday it rained. She didn't buy a newspaper. Instead of the vacancies pages, she studied Nadia's notes and learned everything off by heart. With two thousand euros a month coming in, looking for work wasn't that urgent. But she didn't intend to give it up entirely. As soon as her weekends as Nadia's stand-in had become a matter of routine, she would put some intensive effort into finding work. She abandoned the idea of asking Nadia to help her. If Nadia was only working for an acquaintance as a favour, she was hardly in a position to use her influence to get someone else a job.

She spent the Sunday afternoon with her mother. She asked about her old school books. What she was really interested in, she said, were her music books. However, contrary to what she had expected, Agnes Runge had not kept them. "There's not much room here, I had to throw a lot of things away. Why do you need your music, Susanne?"

"Herr Heller's selling his piano," she said, "and I thought... But it's not important. It would be too cramped in my flat anyway if I had a piano as well."

"Do you think you'll soon be able to afford a bigger one?" her mother asked. "And what's all this about you doing courier trips?" Johannes Herzog had told his grandmother about it and obviously expressed some doubt about this source of extra income, which Frau Herzog had promptly passed on to Agnes Runge. Her mother was slightly concerned, but easily reassured.

Late on Monday afternoon Nadia rang on the mobile again. She told her to come and meet her two streets away, where she handed over two bags with new clothes for cooler days and a handbag – the twin of hers and with identical contents. She didn't have time for a walk, just enough to bring Susanne up to date on what had happened since they last met.

Naturally Jo had repaired the garage door mechanism. It hadn't been easy to convince him that the alarm system had gone haywire and the lock had only opened with the key once all the wires in the box had been disconnected. Poor old Jo had checked the whole installation over twice and was starting to doubt his own ability. Ilona was still in a huff; only the previous day she'd absolutely refused to say whether they still needed the switch or not, adding, tartly, that Wolfgang now spent the evenings in romantic candlelight, doing his bit for the environment. Nadia was much amused by this and said it solved any problems Wolfgang might cause. If Susanne annoyed his wife, he wouldn't be allowed to talk to her. As an enforcer of the law he might be hard as nails, but at home it was his wife who wore the trousers.

Susanne wasn't worried about Wolfgang Blasting. It was Michael she felt she really needed to know more about, but Nadia finished her report by simply telling her there'd been no problems with Michael. With that she was gone. It was only then that Susanne remembered she'd forgotten to tell her what Heller had said. But it was hardly likely that Heller might meet Michael Trenkler and tell him his wife existed in duplicate. And what other use could an alcoholic with a criminal record make of his knowledge?

On Wednesday her mobile rang for the third time. Nadia sounded slightly agitated. Something had cropped up. Her lover wasn't free that weekend, his mother-in-law had decided to come. "However, he's going away on business beforehand," Nadia said. "I could go with him if you could manage it."

Of course Susanne could manage it. Nadia was delighted. "Fantastic. We're going tomorrow and coming back on Friday. You can go home on Friday morning, if you prefer. I'll ring you there and you can come and pick me up. I'll make sure you have two quiet days."

"You don't need to pick a quarrel," said Susanne. "I'll take the tampons out of the cupboard. It's only for the one night."

"As you wish," said Nadia. "If he says or does anything you can't cope with, just give him the cold-shoulder treatment or remind him who financed his studies. That'll soon shut him up."

Susanne thought that was mean but naturally didn't say so. Nadia went on, without even pausing for breath, saying they were to meet in the large car park at the airport then adding, "You'll need to pluck your eyebrows again. The rest as well. I'm relying on you. Wear the grey suit and be there on time."

All she said was, "Yes." She spent the next hour with the instruments of torture. She pulled and plucked, shaved, clipped, cropped and creamed until there was nothing growing that wouldn't stand up to close inspection. Her stomach was tensed and she didn't bother with dinner. She didn't sleep well, either. Her mind was already on the next night and she knew that, stretched out beside Michael Trenkler, she wouldn't sleep a wink for fear of giving herself away with a false movement, breath or something.

Some years previously Dieter had said that she talked in her sleep. Quite clearly too, apparently. At breakfast he'd repeated her negotiations with an insurance agent. According to him she'd asked about life insurance for a journalist working in international trouble spots. She'd no idea whether it was true or not, but it seemed reasonable to suppose she'd thought Dieter could easily drive over a mine in his jeep, or be caught up in an ambush. She found it disturbing to think that in the night that was to come she might talk quite distinctly about things she had on her mind:

"Tell me all about your life, Nadia. And when I know all about it, when I can act like you in my sleep, you can swan off and make your lover happy for the rest of his life. We can swap. As Susanne Lasko you don't have to justify yourself or be faithful to anyone. And I'm looking for a permanent position anyway."

On the morning of 12 September she awoke even before the early train from a nightmare in which Heller had played a leading role. She came back from standing in for Nadia to find her lying on the bed in her flat, covered in blood with her fingers cut and her head smashed in. Heller was in the kitchen, washing his hands and the knife. He grinned and said, "Get out! It's a once-in-a-lifetime opportunity. No one'll think it's not you lying on your mattress."

His voice was still going round in her head as she took a shower and it made the coffee leave a bitter taste in her mouth. She did without her usual slice of toast, dressed carefully according to Nadia's instructions, took great pains over her make-up and hair. She left shortly after seven and set off briskly in the direction of the station.

She took the bus to the airport. She was much too early and had plenty of time to find the large car park. Nadia wasn't there. After she'd waited for a quarter of an hour at the entrance, the coffee and her nervousness began to press on her bladder. There was nothing for it but to go to the terminal. To her surprise, the red Alfa was in the short-stay car park. Nadia was nowhere to be seen.

She hurried to find the toilets. When she went back out, she used a different exit. There she noticed a large, black limousine with tinted windows beside which a stocky man was standing, keeping a sharp eye on the surroundings. As she approached the car, the man opened one of the rear doors. Quickly she took cover. Nadia got out of the limousine, a black briefcase in one hand. On the other side of the car a tall, slim, fortyish man with dark hair appeared and spoke briefly to Nadia.

All the unease Susanne had felt because of the life-insurance policy immediately vanished into thin air. The lover, with chauffeur or bodyguard. The sort of man to whom a thousand euros for a night of love was nothing. It probably wasn't Nadia who was forking out, but the dark-haired man. He got back into the rear seat and the stocky man settled behind the wheel while Nadia went to the nearest entrance and vanished inside the terminal. The black limousine set off, coming towards her. She ducked down lower behind a car and waited until the limousine had gone before dashing back to the car park.

By this time Nadia was already waiting by the entrance and a few minutes later Susanne was on her way back to the terminal with the task of renting a car, with her first wages and a credit card made out in her name in her handbag. The clerk glanced at her driving licence, accepted the piece of plastic as security and offered her the choice of a range of luxury cars.

She chose a silver Mercedes, and it was only as she was driving back to the car park that she began to wonder why Nadia needed a hired car. As she got out and handed Nadia the key and the registration document, she asked, "Why don't you go in your friend's car?"

Nadia gave her a forbearing look. "And what do I do if his meeting goes on for a long time tomorrow? Ring up when you're in bed? Michael certainly wouldn't be happy if you said you had to go into the office at three in the morning." It seemed to make sense.

Nadia took the credit card back, promised to call as soon as she'd arrived and gave her a note of her mobile number, just in case. If Michael should be around, she was to tell him she had to make a quick call to the office. On the phone she was to say, "It's me, Helga. Can you check what time my appointment with Herr Müller is tomorrow please? But do it quickly, I'm just…" And so on. That would allow her to explain the situation to Nadia who could then steer her through the problem.

While she was talking, Nadia removed her jewellery and took four packets of cigarettes plus a disposable lighter and her purse out of her handbag. Then she transferred her luggage from the Alfa to the Mercedes: a suitcase, the briefcase – with combination locks, as she could see now – the document case and the laptop.

"Won't Michael notice I haven't got that?" Susanne asked.

"My laptop?" Nadia sounded surprised. "He's not interested in that. As I told you before, I always leave it in the car. This isn't just a pleasure trip, my friend's going on business and I'll be alone quite a bit during the day. I've no intention of sitting in a hotel room, bored out of my mind, or wandering round the city by myself. I prefer to use the time to do a couple of analyses."

That seemed to make sense too. "Apropos boredom," said Nadia. "Most evenings Michael usually watches a few music videos. He needs that to help him unwind, but you don't have to put up with them. Go to bed before him." With a meaningful smile, she added, "Then you can hide under the sheets and won't need to worry that he'll see any more of you than Dr Reusch did."

Until now she hadn't worried about that at all. "And in the morning?" she asked.

"You don't need to see to anything. Michael doesn't have breakfast and you're hardly going to help him shower."

They swapped cars and drove out of the car park. Once on the autobahn the silver Mercedes quickly disappeared from view. It was ten minutes before it occurred to her that she'd forgotten to take the key to her flat out of her handbag. It wasn't the end of the world, she was just slightly concerned that she couldn't go home in an emergency. But it was a challenge. It meant she had to cope, she couldn't afford to be chucked out.

As far as the traffic would allow, she drove rapidly and, at first, calmly, sure as she was of returning to an empty house, the technological mysteries of which she could recite off by heart. When she left the autobahn, however, she started to feel a slight queasiness in the pit of her stomach. She soothed her twitching nerves by reminding herself she had the whole day for her second confrontation with the technology and Nadia's mobile number for emergencies.

Once she was in the house and had ascertained she could get out at any time, she was going to spend the hours until Michael came home doing whatever she felt like. Take a bath in the round tub; perhaps carefully check whether the swimming pool had a place where she could stand on the bottom; devour computer handbooks until her head was throbbing and – very cautiously – do a little practice with the word-processing package.

At fifteen minutes past ten she turned into Marienweg. A middle-aged woman was sweeping the dust out of the Koglers' front door. On the other side, a Ford Fiesta was parked in the drive, which didn't look as if it was part of the Blastings' goods and chattels. Niedenhoff's and Eleanor Ravatzky's properties seemed deserted. She brought the Alfa to a stop outside the garage door, picked up the remote control and keyed in the code. As if by magic, the wide door swung up.

At once the fluorescent tubes in the garage blazed into light. She drove in on the left-hand side. Hardly had she switched off the engine than the door swung back down. Bolts engaged – in the silence it sounded like two gunshots, one immediately after the other. She flinched, even though she knew very well they were only set off by some sensors reacting to the engine noise, or perhaps to the silence after the engine was switched off. Just to make sure, she operated the remote control again. The door opened and stayed open. She started the car then switched off. As soon as it was quiet in the garage, the door came down.

It worked. Fantastic! It was even fun just pressing some buttons and turning the key in the ignition. She did it four more times before it occurred to her that the neighbours might hear the noise and wonder what was going on. Nadia certainly wouldn't spend hours playing with the garage door.

She made it from the garage to the keypad in the hall closet in just five seconds. Three seconds later she'd deactivated the alarm. The front door opened and closed perfectly normally. She switched the alarm back on and tried the key. The door opened that way too, as Nadia had said it would. She briefly leaned back against the door then switched the alarm off again, breathing a sigh of relief.

She'd made it. Her nerves calmed down. The nightmare with Heller was fading fast and the queasiness in her stomach had gone, leaving a hole which reminded her that she'd given both dinner and breakfast a miss. She decided to make up for it and read a little while she ate.

The fridge was well filled and half an hour later she was sitting with some expensive china in the dining room. There was a door out onto the terrace, which she opened as it was mild outside. The mobile at hand beside her plate, she devoured two slices of toast with ham and one with cheese while reading a chapter about setting up, processing and saving a document. She wondered briefly where Nadia was. In all the excitement she'd forgotten to ask where they were going. But she wasn't particularly interested anyway.

Shortly after eleven the dining room and kitchen were clean and tidy again. She'd also emptied an ashtray containing five cigarette ends. Carrying the book and mobile, she went upstairs and examined the huge box underneath the desk with a quiver of nerves in the pit of her stomach. The green light was glowing; obviously the current was permanently switched on, even if that didn't mean the computer was ready to use.

Beside the green light were two depressions – further lights, she suspected – and underneath it a raised disc, probably the on-off switch. Just a try! Just to see if she'd understood the section in the book. For a few seconds she was undecided. She felt a bit uncomfortable, Nadia had made it all too clear that the study was out of bounds.

But Nadia didn't need to know and it was important for her future. You had no chance as a secretary if you weren't computer-literate. Nadia's affair wasn't going to last for ever. A married man! When Nadia gave him his marching orders, or he her, she wouldn't need a stand-in any more. At most there'd be the approach Nadia had suggested with Herr Schrag. "OK Nadia, I'm not going to insist on continuing to play the sulky wife for you. From now on I'll get…" But she wasn't like that.

Her eye was drawn to the box under the desk. As she pressed the switch she felt like a little child disregarding a strict prohibition. A red and yellow glow appeared in the two depressions and a chittering could be heard inside the box. A few messages flashed up on the screen, then an instruction appeared in the middle: Enter password.

For a while she sat there staring at the request like someone caught red-handed, wondering what it meant. Was Michael worried his wife might nose around in his lab results? Or was he afraid she might find the telephone number of his little laboratory mouse on the computer? Disappointed, she pressed the button again to switch the computer off. Nothing happened. She crept underneath the desk, where she discovered the telephone plug, which had been disconnected. Examining the box, she found a switch on the back. She had to press it twice and everything was as it had been at first.

Phew, she'd got away with that. But no more experiments. The shot of the front garden and the street that she'd seen on her first visit had shown her that the computer was more than just a glorified typewriter. And it reappeared now, hardly had the green light gone on again. A mail van stopped outside, the postman got out and came up to the house. As far as she could see he fiddled with something at the wall beside the front door and then disappeared. Not long afterwards the picture disappeared as well.

She went downstairs, leaving the mobile on the desk. First of all she checked whether there was a letter box attached to wall outside that she'd overlooked in her agitation. There wasn't, just a slit in the wall. At about the same height in the inside was a flap with a little hole, which she hadn't noticed before. The letter box must have been built into the masonry. She couldn't open it, there wasn't a key on the ring that fitted the hole.

She went down to the basement, to work up an appetite for lunch. The decision was incredibly difficult given the choice in the two deep freezes. This time there was considerably more in them than a few ready meals. It was a culinary paradise that made her mouth water, despite her substantial late breakfast. She chose a pork escalope with mushrooms, green beans and asparagus, carried it all up to the kitchen and decided to have a relaxing bath while the food was thawing out.

Once more she was spoiled for choice. Should she have a bubble bath, pour in some bath oil or use one of the pink balls? The pink balls were the most tempting. She fetched the jar from the guest bathroom, dropped two in the water as it filled the bath and enjoyed the way they dissolved, spread an oily film over the surface and filled the room with a subtle fragrance. It was an experience in itself and went some way towards compensating her for the frustration with the computer.

When the tub was a quarter full, the mobile rang in the study. It could only be Nadia, since no one else knew she had the phone. She hadn't even told her mother because she didn't know whether she was going to be able to keep it. From a glance at Nadia's watch, she saw that it was half-past twelve. It must have been a long journey. She went out, dumping her underwear and the towel on the bed, rushed into the study, picked up the phone and said, "Arrived safely?"

"Frau Trenkler?" It was a harsh-sounding man's voice.

"No," she said and switched off. Seconds later the phone rang again. She ran into the bedroom and dialled the number of Nadia's mobile on the bedside phone. A female voice announced that the person she was ringing was unavailable at the moment and invited her to leave a message.

What was that all about? Why had Nadia switched off her mobile? And why hadn't she rung yet? She'd promised to do so as soon as she arrived and she'd been gone for three hours now. An accident? Given the way Nadia drove it wouldn't be surprising. She would be sure to have put her foot down to catch up with her lover. A terrible picture appeared in her mind's eye: the silver Mercedes a tangle of metal somewhere on the side of the autobahn; the police, fire brigade and a doctor freeing the woman stuck in the car, only to establish that she was dead. One picking up the handbag, taking out the papers and saying, "She's called Susanne Lasko."

She straightened up, her back stiffening. Her scalp tightened until it was painful and her old wound started to throb. She began to work her way through the consequences of her nightmare vision: a patrol car going to the old folks' home, a uniform policeman giving her mother the sad news, tears welling up in blind eyes.

Finally she remembered the taps were still running. She rushed to the bathroom and was just in time to prevent a flood. The bath had lost its attraction, as had the escalope, mushrooms, beans and asparagus. She looked for an explanation – any explanation – to reassure herself. A very long journey during which Nadia had her mobile switched off for reasons of safety? Using a phone while driving was forbidden. But hadn't the Mercedes had a hands-free kit? A short journey and straight into bed on arrival where they wouldn't want to be disturbed? Followed by a substantial meal, during which they left their mobiles switched off out of consideration for other customers in the restaurant? Who would remember the stand-in at home when they were finally free to do all the things they'd so far been prevented from doing?

She kept trying to get through to Nadia every ten or fifteen minutes, but by half past two she still hadn't got a reply. Anyway, no policeman would think of informing Nadia Trenkler of the death of Susanne Lasko. What now? Ring up her mother to ask whether the police had been to see her? It was too early for that, the police would have to go to Kettlerstrasse first before they could find out whom they needed to inform of her death.

* * *

Towards half-past three, by which time she had tried so often she'd lost count, the continuing uncertainty was making her feel sick. She went into the living room and opened the upper doors of the rustic-style dresser. Just a tiny drop to calm her down! She examined the level of each bottle and, after some hesitation, mixed herself a drink with a few drops from eight different ones. The fist sip burned her throat. The second she retained in her mouth for a few seconds so she could feel the effect. Minutes later she imagined the alcohol had already gone to her head. She felt slightly dizzy and finally did something about getting lunch. It took her mind off things. The mobile was at hand beside the sink.

As the water was just beginning to simmer in the pans, she noticed movement on the little monitor over the fridge. The next moment a large dog started to bark in the hall. It sounded dangerous and the growls which followed sent shivers down her spine. These turned into a hot flush as she remembered she hadn't closed the door from the dining room onto the terrace. Eleanor Ravetzky's hound must have got into the house through it. Fortunately she'd closed the kitchen door.

Instead of looking at the monitor, she went to the window to see if there was anyone across the road looking for the dog. There wasn't. But there was a man at the front door. He saw her and waved a large bouquet. She recognized Joachim Kogler and finally looked at the monitor. Not surprisingly, it was filled with Joachim Kogler's face. More barking and growls came from the hall. She opened the kitchen door a crack. No sign of a dog. Nadia had instructed her not to go to the door, but since Joachim Kogler had seen her, she picked up the useless mobile and opened the door, saying, "Just a moment, Helga."

Joachim Kogler was beaming all over his face. He pressed the bouquet into her free hand and took a piece of paper out of his pocket, at the same time pulling her to him, patting her on the back, despite the telephone clamped to her ear, and giving whoops of delight. "I couldn't believe it when you told us yesterday. But now I've got it in writing; it came this morning. I still haven't taken it in."

Clasped to his chest like a dressmaker's dummy, she let her hand with the mobile drop to her side and prayed he would say something, anything, that would give a hint as to the reason for his euphoria. Finally

101

he stopped pawing her, placed his hands on her shoulders, pushed her back a little and stuck the piece of paper under her nose. Alfo Investment, she read, but before she could see any more, he said, unable to contain his joy, "Thirty points! Now, of course, I'm annoyed I didn't borrow more. Should I wait a bit? Do you think they'll go even higher?"

It could only be shares he was talking about. Nadia must have given him a tip. And he'd taken out a loan on the strength of it? How reckless of him. She puffed up her cheeks then let the air out slowly, shaking her head thoughtfully. "Hard to say. I wouldn't take the risk."

Joachim Kogler sniffed, frowned and immediately came back to earth. "Have you been drinking?"

She imitated Nadia's casual shrug of the shoulders. She was about to say, "Just a drop," but he immediately went on, "Don't be stupid, Nadia. What's up? Has Michael been moaning again?" He waved the Alfo Investment letter at her. "I'll talk to him," he promised. "After all, this is a good argument."

"There's no need," she hurried to assure him. "Everything's OK. Really. I was just making myself something to eat."

"Then use plenty of onions and garlic," he advised her, still deadly serious. "And come over if there's a problem."

"Yes," she said. "But there's no problem, really there isn't." She held up the bouquet. "Thanks for the flowers, they're lovely."

Joachim Kogler laughed, a brief laugh, but a laugh nevertheless. "If anyone has to say thank you, then it's me. It saves me having to go on my bended knees to Brenner. He's going to be sorry he cut the subvention for my new programme. Now I can develop it from my own resources. If you ever have another tip like that —"

"I'll think of you," she broke in to get rid of him.

He laughed again. "I should hope so too. But remember the onions – and put the flowers in some water." Giving her one last pat on the shoulder, he left.

She closed the door and looked at the flowers. A magnificent bouquet and, to be honest, the first she'd ever had. Her bridal bouquet didn't count, that was part of the outfit. And if she remembered rightly, Dieter had neither ordered it nor paid for it, her father had seen to that. She already knew her way around so well that she found the right vase straight away, put the flowers in the water and saw to her meal. There were onions in the larder in the basement but she couldn't find any garlic.

Twenty minutes later she was sitting at the kitchen table. She couldn't stand the thought of the elegant dining room and she'd just gone in briefly to shut the door onto the terrace. On the worktop behind her was the mobile surrounded by a pile of pots and pans. The glass was still there too. The room was filled with an aromatic fragrance and the arrangement on her plate looked delicious. It would probably have tasted like that, too, if she'd been in the mood to enjoy it. As it was, she just picked at it. She couldn't get the bloodstained image of the crash out of her mind, she dreaded the next futile telephone call and she didn't know what to do. She recalled the nightmare about Heller, how he'd grinned and said, "It's a once-in-a-lifetime opportunity."

It wasn't an opportunity, that was ridiculous. She laughed, though it was only a short laugh and slightly hysterical: Susanne Lasko in the snow-white villa, with a husband who earned a huge amount, but she didn't know exactly how, with unknown parents in Geneva, Chopin in G minor in the living room, a swimming pool in the basement and a Beckmann somewhere or other. And the only thing she did know about, more or less, was the blasted alarm system.

She remembered the hired car and was temporarily reassured at the thought of the helpful assistant who'd arranged for her to have the Mercedes and who would certainly be informed of any accident. But only for a few moments. Even while she was wondering whether to ring the car-hire firm, or even go to the airport, she realized that Susanne Lasko having an accident in a luxury car was bound to lead to countless questions.

Where had a woman who lived a wretched life in a grotty flat suddenly found the money to afford a car like that? What did she need it for? Where was she going in it? And if she explained everything? The car-hire firm certainly wouldn't be happy that she'd passed the car on to someone else. They'd probably demand compensation. How much did a silver Mercedes cost? The conclusion of all this was the dismal realization that if Nadia actually did have an accident in the hired car it would leave her facing a mountain of problems.

One of the sensors registered a car door being closed outside. The monitor over the fridge lighted up and showed movement. She didn't even notice. The escalope lay there between the asparagus and green beans, almost untouched. As she speared a couple of slices of fried mushroom and some onion rings with her fork, she wondered whether she could risk driving to Kettlerstrasse and asking Heller if the police had been there.

Voices could be heard above the fridge. Now she did look. Her hands started to tremble when she recognized Michael Trenkler. He must be standing right outside the front door. And he wasn't alone. Whoever was with him was hidden from the camera by his body, but he asked them, "Why don't you come in for a moment?"

The next minute she heard steps in the hall and then he was in the kitchen, smiling at her. "Hi, darling."

She quickly stuffed three runner beans in her mouth, mumbled, "Hi," and peered past him, expecting to see some stranger, whom she would have no idea whether Nadia would have been pleased or displeased to see.

His eye ran over the dirty dishes on the worktop and his smile vanished. He'd seen the glass. He took a couple of steps, picked it up and sniffed at it. His eyes narrowed. Joachim Kogler appeared in the doorway, a look of concern on his face. He seemed relieved at the sight of the onions on her plate. With a conspiratorial wink to her, he told Michael he'd already been there to thank her. And he'd had a celebratory tot of the hard stuff. Michael relaxed.

Joachim Kogler stayed long enough for the food on her plate to get cold. He went on at Michael almost without interruption, praised her nose for a good investment and said that Lilo intended to throw a party on Saturday to celebrate their victory over Brenner and his lack of vision.

Several times he tried to draw her into the conversation, throwing out half a dozen names. Lilo was certain to invite Henseler and young Maiwald, of course – provided she could lure him out of his retreat. He reminded her how amusing she'd found Barlinkow at the last private view and he was sure to come. Discouraged by her monosyllabic replies, he turned back to Michael. "You're free on Saturday?"

"Of course," said Michael, with a suspicious glance at her.

She could already see herself confronted with a faceless Henseler, a shadowy young Maiwald, a similar Barlinkow and a dozen other strangers.

Joachim Kogler gave her a somewhat perplexed smile. "Right then, I'll be off. Things to do."

He left. Michael surveyed the chaos on the worktop again. "Are you OK?"

"Yes," she mumbled.

"That's not what it looks like," he insisted. "Something troubling you?"

"No."

"So why the clenched teeth? Is there something wrong with the notification Jo's been sent?"

"No, it's all right."

"I'm not blind, Nadia. I can see something's not all right. Can Jo not cash those shares in?"

He kept on at her for minutes on end. Only when she assured him everything was fine, it was just that she had this terrible headache, did he grin and finally change the topic. He sniffed the aroma in the kitchen and said, "That smells delicious. What gave you the idea?"

What gave people the idea of cooking something for themselves?

"I was hungry," she said. "But now it's cold."

"Shall I warm it up for you?"

A friendly offer, under other circumstances she'd have deduced things from it about his character and the way he approached his marriage. As it was, she just said, "No. I don't feel like it any more."

"Any objections if I have it?"

She shook her head. She didn't know where to look, whether to get up and go out of the kitchen or to tidy up, using the opportunity to get the mobile out from among the pots and pans so she could try Nadia again.

Michael took her plate and put it in the microwave. Two minutes later he was sitting opposite her, tucking into the pork escalope. He even used her cutlery. Watching him eat made her go rigid. She couldn't stop following every movement of his hands. He noticed and came to the wrong conclusion. "But you were going to eat something."

"No," she quickly assured him.

He clearly wasn't convinced. He cut off a piece of meat, stuck it on his fork and held it out to her. "Open you mouth," he ordered, "we'll share."

She opened her mouth, though with some reluctance, and let him shove the fork in. With a satisfied nod, Nadia's husband took the next mouthful himself. She chewed at the meat, which tasted like cardboard, feeling she ought to say something harmless to stop him getting suspicious again. "You're back early today." she said. She had to force the words out.

He raised his shoulders with an audible sigh and let them drop again resignedly. "Olaf's got a virus. It sounds as if it may be terminal."

She looked up, shocked. The name echoed in her ear. Olaf and Kemmerling, his colleagues at the lab. "That's terrible," she said. "Is there nothing that can be done?"

Her concern clearly irritated him. He didn't seem particularly bothered about Olaf's approaching death. He held out another forkful and said, "Kemmerling says the virus is pretty bad. The technician's coming tomorrow morning."

She accepted the mouthful, relieved that chewing saved her from having to continue the conversation. For the moment the wrecked Mercedes by the side of the autobahn faded into the background. Her thoughts revolved round Olaf's imminent demise, a virus and what a technician had to do with it. As he was loading the fork for himself, Michael said, "I suspect Kemmerling's been tinkering again and hasn't got the guts to admit it. You can't leave him alone with a thing like that, even just for half an hour. If we've got a virus in the system…"

He went on. It just went in one ear and out the other, but it did start to make some kind of sense and she felt herself flush. Thing. System. He was talking about a computer! No wonder he'd seemed unfeeling. With any luck he'd have forgotten her shocked response.

It was strange but not unpleasant to be fed by him. After she'd overcome her inhibitions about sharing a spoon, it created a certain intimacy. Despite that, she felt wretched. Incapable of sticking to her role for much longer, incapable of avoiding the little snares of everyday life. How often would he have talked to Nadia about Olaf and Kemmerling? In precisely the same tone as he was using now. He was chatting away about things going wrong in the lab. She listened in silence and only with half an ear, pondering what she could do.

At some point he started talking about a set of data that had to be processed by the next evening. They couldn't rely on Olaf. There was no guarantee the technician would turn up, and even if he did, there was still no guarantee the fault would have been identified and eradicated by the evening. But the processed data had to be ready for Monday.

She registered a change in his tone of voice. He was probably going to have to work at the weekend and was trying to break it to her gently.

"Does that mean..." She cleared her throat to gain time and to assess whether it was advisable to say more. He was watching her with an expression of tense expectation. Hesitantly she went on, "So that's another Sunday..." That wasn't saying too much, nor too little, and it couldn't be completely wrong.

He gave an embarrassed, possibly apologetic grin. "Not necessarily. If it's all right with you, I could ring Kemmerling. He took the streamer from yesterday home with him. He thinks he can manage if he segments it. Which I very much doubt."

The technical terms buzzed in her ears like angry wasps. What, for Christ's sake, was a streamer? Michael lowered his head and said, in pleading tones, "Go on. You've got enough capacity. We can take down the Sec temporarily." She hadn't the faintest idea what he was talking about. Only when he said, "I'll be there keeping an eye on Kemmerling. He won't touch your files," did it dawn on her that he was still talking about a computer and that he wanted to borrow hers. Only she couldn't understand why. There was one in his study. If that wouldn't do, he must mean Nadia's P4 with three gigahertz. "He's not interested in my laptop." Oh, yes? That was what he wanted and it might well be lying, shattered, in a crashed car.

"Sorry," she said, "I left it in the office."

Michael didn't say, "Pity." He just frowned again and said, "What?"

"The P4," she said, indicating something the size of a portable computer with a sorry-I-can't-help-you gesture, "I mean the laptop, it isn't here."

Now he was more than just puzzled. "What's this laptop you're talking about?" When he went on he sounded angry. "Enough of this nonsense. I don't like having to remind you who's been bringing in the money these last two years, Nadia." He jerked his thumb at the ceiling. "Can we work up there, yes or no?"

After all the thoughts going round and round in her head, after all the lightning deductions, it took only a fraction of a second to take in what this implied. "Enter password," she thought. But she suspected he wouldn't know it. And for him to ask her for it was a risk she couldn't take. She was in Nadia's house, sitting at Nadia's table, facing Nadia's husband, right in the middle of Nadia's life. There was nothing for it but to behave like Nadia. "No," she said.

After this curt answer there seemed to be no need to worry any more about the coming night and a possible customary goodnight kiss Nadia might have forgotten to mention. Michael went out of the kitchen, visibly disgruntled. From the hall he shouted, "I might be late, don't bother to wait up for me." Then the front door slammed.

The monitor over the fridge lighted up again. She saw Michael dashing off and gave the mobile among the pots and pans a speculative look. Ring up the old folks' home? Use all her powers of persuasion to convince her mother there was no need for tears? "Whatever the police have said, or might say in the future, Mama, I'm fine. I'll explain everything later." She hadn't the energy to do it.

She took the dirty plate off the table. It was the work of a moment to scrape the pathetic remains of the meal into the waste bin and another to put the plate in the dishwasher. Then she was confronted with another problem. The pans, including the frying pan and the colander, fitted in the machine and were quickly loaded; the detergent was in the cupboard under the sink. But she couldn't find the switch. Her mother-in-law had had a dishwasher and that had had several knobs on the door. All this one had was a smooth surface.

Since she didn't know what to do with the rest of the day anyway, if she wasn't to go out of her mind, she emptied the dishwasher and washed everything by hand. Then she polished the cooker, the worktop, the wall tiles and the sink until they gleamed, fetched a bucket and the latest thing in mops from the utility room and did the floor.

Shortly after five a muffled ring roused her from her gloomy thoughts. It came from the kitchen while she was in the basement putting the cleaning stuff back in the cupboard. The mobile had rung seven times before she reached it, but at the eighth she'd picked it up and gasped a breathless "At last!"

In her relief she missed the first word, presumably the caller's name. Again it was the man with the harsh-sounding voice. The second word had been "here". Ignoring her reaction and his first call, he said, "Frau

Barthel was good enough to give me your new number. Unfortunately I can't make the appointment on Monday."

"Pity," she said.

"How does Wednesday look?" the man asked.

"Fine," she replied.

"The let's shift our meeting to Wednesday. Is one o'clock OK?"

"Yes," she said.

"I'm looking forward to it," the man said and put down the receiver.

She spent some minutes trying to work out how she could discover who'd been ringing. The name Helga came to mind. Nadia's advice for emergencies suggested that Helga worked in the same office and could give information about Nadia's appointments.

In her mind's eye she saw the row of numbers in small writing at the bottom of the torn sheet of paper from Alfo Investment that she'd fished out of her rubbish bin. She risked it. After she'd dialled the first number she heard the fax tone and after the second a polite, businesslike female voice: "Alfo Investment. Please leave your name and number and we'll call you back." Closed, she thought resignedly.

The next call came half an hour later. By that time she was watching the television, which she had managed to switch on after a number of experiments with a variety of remote controls. The mobile was on the couch beside her. As soon as it rang she had it at her ear. Rather hesitantly she said, "Trenkler."

"Are you not alone?" Nadia asked.

A dam broke inside her and relief came spilling out of the gap, but anger as well. "Oh, I'm alone all right," she hissed, "and I've been waiting for hours. I kept ringing but there was no answer. I thought something must have happened to you."

"'I'm not surprised," said Nadia and poured forth her own problems. "The battery gave up the ghost. You can't imagine the problems I've had. The car conked out halfway there and I couldn't even call the recovery service. It wasn't how I imagined my weekend. Anything on at your end?"

"Only Channel Four."

Nadia laughed at the joke, such as it was, complimented her on her new-found quick wit and explained the various remotes: one for the video, one for the stereo, another for the satellite dish and a fourth for the television.

"I worked out what the fourth one's for all on my own."

"You don't sound very happy," Nadia said.

"You've a nerve! I almost went mad here."

"Oh, come on now," said Nadia.

"It's all right for you to talk. Everything's been happening here."

She told her about the appointment with a man whose name she didn't know being shifted from Monday to Wednesday. Nadia said that was nothing to get excited about. She was touched by Joachim Kogler's bouquet but also a little annoyed because Susanne wasn't supposed to answer the door when it rang.

"It didn't ring," she said. "It barked and growled. It almost gave me a heart attack."

"Oh God," Nadia sighed. "I'd forgotten the bell. Anything else?"

She was surprised at Michael coming back so early. That really wasn't usual, she said. She laughed at Susanne's misunderstanding about Olaf's imminent demise and she found her problem with the dishwasher amusing too. "If you pull the door down there's a row of sensor buttons along the top. I'm sorry I didn't think of such minor details, I didn't imagine you'd be slaving away in my kitchen. You're supposed to be enjoying yourself. Did you have to wrestle with the vacuum cleaner as well?"

Nadia's mockery annoyed her immensely. She couldn't resist getting her own back a little. "No, but with Michael I did. It's possible he may have noticed something. He wanted to work here with Kemmerling."

"He must have been out of his tiny mind," was Nadia's comment. "I've told him a thousand times, but he keeps on trying. That nerd's quite capable of compressing the hard disk into a stock cube. I hope you gave him a very clear no."

"Not at first," she replied, explaining that she'd assumed the big computer was Michael's. "And the pair of them working here wouldn't have bothered me."

She could hear Nadia's sharp intake of breath, but she rattled on, enjoying the effect she was having. She told her how the penny had only dropped when Michael had promised not to let Kemmerling touch her files. Then, she went on, she'd said she had to work herself and had left her laptop in the office.

This produced another sharp intake of breath from the mobile and Nadia's outraged voice. "Are you crazy?"

She had no problem giving her voice a slightly guilty undertone and serving up such a convincing mixture of truth and invention that Nadia wasn't the least bit suspicious: that Michael had asked a few stupid questions about the laptop, that she hadn't answered but had gone upstairs and tried to start the big computer; that he'd followed her and seen she was getting nowhere.

At the other end of the line Nadia let out a long breath. "I told you at the airport that I always leave the laptop in the car. I should have thought it was obvious. A simple no would have been sufficient."

She grinned but said nothing. It was a small victory, but a victory all the same. For a few seconds the mobile was quiet. Nadia seemed to be considering. Then she asked, "Where is he now?"

"At Kemmerling's." That was probably the truth, but then she proceeded to mix it with invention. "He wants to fetch the streamer from yesterday. And then have a talk about who's been bringing in the money for the last two years." It was a bit risky, but the prospect of Nadia rumbling her after a couple of exchanges with Michael was nothing compared with what she'd been through that afternoon.

"Shit," said Nadia. "On no account must you let him use the computer. And if he asks about the laptop again, tell him Philip lent it to you."

Philip! The name set off a faint echo in her mind. She hadn't heard it from Nadia, of that she was sure. But she had heard it, only recently, and she didn't talk to that many people. "Is Philip this acquaintance you work for?"

"Who else? Now go next door and start the computer up. I'll explain what to do."

She followed Nadia's instructions. The password was Arosa. Nadia told her how to start a particular programme. Something appeared on the monitor that reminded her of the timetables from her schooldays, one empty box beside another. "You can type in figures for as long as you need to," Nadia said. "But don't touch the other programs, do you hear." Oh yes, she heard. She looked at the empty boxes feeling she was bring treated like a child who's been sent out in the garden to play – "But don't pull up any flowers."

111

Nadia then explained how to shut down the computer and said, "Make a note of the number of the hotel. If there's any problem you can leave a message at reception if I'm not in the room. I'll call back as soon as I can." She read out some numbers. The first were definitely the dialling code for a foreign country.

"Where are you, anyway?" Susanne asked.

"In Luxembourg. If Michael's still determined to use the computer tomorrow, you'll have to stay in the house."

"I can't go home. You've got my keys."

"Oh," said Nadia, "I didn't notice. OK then, see you tomorrow."

She put the mobile down. Following Nadia's instructions, she shut down the computer, then started it up again. Enter password: Arosa. Combinations of letters and numbers scurried in rapid succession across the screen. Watching this with a sense of satisfaction, she folded up the scrap of paper with the hotel number and stuck it under the mobile. Later she took it down into the hall and put it in her purse. Much later. After she'd written her first letter.

The knowledge that it was Nadia's computer she was sitting at reduced her inhibitions enormously and tempted her to experiment. And Nadia's explanations of how to start the program with the empty boxes worked just as well with word processing. She started to type:

Dear Frau Lasko,

On 25 August of this year you applied for a position as secretary in our office. Unfortunately an error was made when we returned your documents. We beg you to forgive us this slip, for which we apologize most profusely, and would ask you to come and see us in the course of the next few days. We will be interested to hear your salary expectations and look forward to working with you.

Yours sincerely,
Behringer and Partners

In her mind's eye she saw herself standing at the acrylic-glass desk holding out this invitation to a bemused Frau Luici. But she didn't like the letterhead. On the letter from Behringer's it had been more impressive. And, lo and behold, the word-processing package offered an infinite variety of possibilities. With the help of the handbook, she managed not only to get the characters in exactly the same form and size that Behringer's used, she also managed to place the firm's logo in the top left-hand corner.

With that the letter was finished and she couldn't bring herself to delete it. She gave the printer a speculative glance and tentatively pressed the key. It responded immediately. It didn't need a password, nor was it locked, and it took no more than a second to spit out her masterpiece. It looked so genuine, it could have been from Behringer and Partners.

By now it was past ten. Her neck and back felt tense and her stomach was trying to tell her that, after the gourmandizing of the past few weeks, it was feeling rather neglected. She got a ready-made meal out of the freezer, heated it through in the microwave and quickly ate it at the kitchen table. Then she was ready for her bath. This time the fragrance she chose also produced mountains of foam.

The towel and underwear were still on the bed. She took the towel, washed off her make-up and eyed the electric toothbrush sceptically. She hadn't thought of bringing her own toothbrush. With all the fuss about computers she'd forgotten to brush her teeth after breakfast and after the shared escalope too, because of her worry about where Nadia was. Unforgivable. After some hesitation she settled on the blue brush head and washed it out thoroughly in hot water. As she used it, she thought of the fork she'd shared with Nadia's husband.

Ten minutes later she was lying in the warm water, dreaming away, when suddenly something disturbed her. At once she was wide awake. She thought there'd been a sound and opened her eyes. The tiny monitor beside the door was blank. She strained to listen. There was a noise downstairs: a rattling, but very quiet. Then a metallic click went right round the house, accompanied by the whirring noise of the shutters going down over the windows.

After two, at most three seconds of absolute terror, she calmed down. The alarm had been switched on, activating the central locking and turning the house into an impregnable fortress. So much was obvious. But there must be several combinations. The one she knew wouldn't have closed the shutters. Steps could be heard coming up the stairs. It could only be Michael.

Her initial reflex was to jump out of the bath, give herself a quick dry, slip under the covers and pretend to be asleep. It was too late for that.

He appeared in the doorway, a piece of toast and ham with a bite out of it in one hand, a pickled gherkin in the other. A perfectly ordinary man with nice eyes who was hungry. She gave him a forced smile and whispered, "Hi."

He showed no reaction, just leaned against the doorframe, took a bite of toast and looked at her appraisingly. It's Nadia he's seeing, she told herself, to allay the embarrassment she felt rising inside her. Hesitantly she asked, "How did you get on with Kemmerling?"

He shook his head. "A wasted journey. He'd actually managed to fit everything in. I didn't believe he could do it. But the sick machine's going to take three weeks to sort out."

The feeling of embarrassment refused to go away. The mountains of foam had long since disappeared. She squinted down along the surface of the water, trying to assess how much of her he could see from where he was.

"I'm sorry," she said, "but there was something urgent I had to get done. Anyway, you can't expect me to let Kemmerling get his sticky fingers on my machine. That nerd's quite capable of compressing my hard disk into a stock cube."

He gave a brief grin, stuffed what was left of the toast in his mouth and followed it with the gherkin. Then he pushed off the door post and came closer. "You know, if you'd said something, I wouldn't have asked."

Remembering Nadia's words, she said firmly, "Excuse me, but I've told you that a thousand times."

"Seven times in the last five months. I've kept count."

She assumed they were still talking about Kemmerling. "Good. Then you should know I mean it seriously."

"Oh, I know that," he declared. "I just hope that this time you can stick to it for more than just one day."

She had no time to start racking her brains as to what he might mean. He went over to the lavatory, lifted up the lid and seat with one hand, opened his trousers with the other and inserted his hand. It took a great deal of self-control, but she managed to keep looking at his face and not to stare, as if hypnotized, at what was in his hand. His complete lack of inhibition spoke volumes about the intimacy they enjoyed in their marriage and was clear proof that so far he hadn't had the slightest suspicion that it wasn't his wife he was talking to.

114

He looked across at the bathtub, running his eye over the water and, therefore, over her body. She was completely exposed to his gaze. It's Nadia he's seeing, she kept repeating to herself, like a mantra. Then she remembered she hadn't taken the tampons out of the cupboard.

He flushed the lavatory, went to one of the basins and washed his hands. Even as he did this, his eyes were still wandering up and down her body in one of the mirrors and the strange smile stayed on his face. She felt as if she were being frisked. Next he cleaned his teeth, taking, as expected, the blue brush. He didn't seem to notice that it had been used only a short time previously.

Then he came over to her, sat down on the top step leading up to the bath, dipped one hand in the water and trailed it about a bit. "Shall I keep you company for a while?"

"No," she said quickly. "I was just going to get out. I still have a headache."

That didn't put him off at all. With a tender gesture he pushed a damp strand of hair back from her forehead. "That's what I was hoping. Get out."

She had no intention of getting out of the bath as long as he was there. "I'll stay in here for a few more minutes. It does my back good."

With an understanding grin, he said, "What, a sore back as well. Shall I give you a massage?"

A tempting offer. While her mother-in-law had still been alive she'd sometimes enjoyed a massage prescribed by the doctor. Despite that, she shook her head and said, "Thanks, but no. It's not necessary."

He put his hand on her shoulder and pressed his fingers into the tense muscles at the back of her neck. "Really? I'll make a special effort and I can guarantee you won't think of a cigarette for the next half hour."

It wasn't only the tampons she'd forgotten. During his short return home in the afternoon he didn't seem to have noticed her abstinence. Now he must have noticed the empty ashtrays and drawn his own conclusions.

Heavy smokers became a bundle of nerves when they were forced to give up. They became irascible, unjust and unpredictable. She'd been through all that with her father, when he'd had to curb his addiction on doctor's orders. Gentleness and patience had flown out of the window, his response to the most harmless request had been more than just a sharp "No". Michael must have been through that as well and seemed willing to view her odd behaviour and her refusal in that light and to forgive her.

The pressure of his fingers on the back of her neck was by no means unpleasant. If it hadn't been for her inhibitions, for the frustrating knowledge that she wasn't the person he thought he was seeing, she could have enjoyed it.

"You really are tensed up," he declared. "Come on, out you get before you get all wrinkled. I'll fetch you a towel." Before she could say no he had gone and came back immediately with a large bath towel. "On the couch with you."

"No, really. It's not necessary," she hastened to assure him. "You're tired too."

"Not that tired," he said, spreading out the towel in a way that brooked no argument. There was no doubt that he wanted to help and would keep on at her until she let him do what he had resolved to do. She recalled the bottles of massage oil in the next room. Presumably it was a matter of course for him: Nadia's back was all tensed up so he gave Nadia a massage. And inside her head she could hear Nadia saying, "You can stop him getting suspicious. You just have to behave as I normally do."

She could feel a flush start to creep over her face again as she sat up in the water. He held the outspread towel to her chest and wrapped it round her back. Then he finally went out. She quickly dried herself and wedged the towel under her armpits so that it covered her back, breasts, stomach and thighs. She tried to tuck the end in over her chest. It wouldn't stick. But if she clamped it tight under her armpit and didn't make any too hasty movements, it stayed in place. To be on the safe side, she quickly took the tampons out of the cupboard, placed them in a visible position on the edge of the wash basin and followed him into the adjoining room.

He had spread another towel over the couch and with a sweep of the hand invited her to lie on it. A bottle of massage oil was open ready on the cupboard. All the cushions were on the floor. Two seconds later the damp towel had joined them as he whipped it off and she hurriedly lay face down on the couch. Hardly had she stretched out than he was on top of her and sitting astride her thighs. She pressed her face into the towel and found breathing difficult. Not because of his weight. She could feel it on her thighs and the sensation was not unpleasant.

Out of the corner of her eye she saw his arm reach out over her head for the bottle. He poured some oil out into the palm of his hand. Then he started – with her shoulders. With practised hands he gave her tense muscles a thorough massage, then stroked the back of her neck up to her hair with the tips of his fingers and down the side of her spine to her hips. Twice he asked, "Is that good?"

"Mhm," she replied.

It really was very pleasant and for a while it was almost like being at the masseur's. True, he hadn't sat on her thighs and she'd worn panties, but otherwise the difference wasn't all that great. It was obvious it wasn't the first time Michael Trenkler had given a massage. Gradually she relaxed as she felt a pleasant warmth spread over her back. Eight fingertips pressed against her hairline while two thumbs firmly kneaded the back of her neck. She took a deep breath and felt four fingers and one thumb run down the right-hand side of her spine. She enjoyed it and didn't wonder for one second what the other hand was doing.

He shifted his weight and slid back to her lower legs. His hand worked its way up her spine and slowly back down again. Something briefly brushed against her thigh, too briefly for her to register that it was the end of an undone belt. She only realized that when she heard the noise of a zip being pulled down and immediately after felt his fingers touch a spot that Nadia had not subjected to comparison. Because he was not supposed to see it from close to and certainly not touch it.

She should have taken the tampons out of the cupboard in the afternoon or the evening. If he saw them now he would know they were only an excuse. "No," she protested, "don't."

He did in fact remove his fingers, but only to take off his shirt, as she saw to her horror when she twisted her head to one side. It fluttered down to join the cushions and towel on the floor.

"No," she repeated, more vigorously this time, and tried to shake him off her legs. "Stop it. I really do have a headache."

He leaned over her, kissed her on the neck and whispered, "Of course. So have I. Come on, don't be a prick tease." He put his hand under her chin, lifted up her head and turned it more to the side. His face came nearer.

"Leave me alone! I don't want to!" she said, before her mouth was firmly closed.

It was a long kiss – and her first for a long, long time. Initially it was new and strange, then tender, if not particularly comfortable with her head turned to the side. Later it became urgent, rousing and more comfortable. He slid off her and down from the couch, then took off his trousers, underpants and socks. She closed her eyes, like a child imagining it won't be seen if it can't see anything itself. Yet despite the darkness, her senses, sharpened by panic, perceived every movement. She had no idea how to stop what was coming, nor was she sure that she wanted to stop it. In time with her accelerating heartbeat, her mind was hammering against her skull: No! No! No! Her body, on the other hand, simply responded.

He turned her over, continuing to kiss and caress her. At one point something did seem to give him pause for thought. She peeked through her half-open lashes and saw him looking thoughtfully at her breasts. Immediately she felt a rush of fear. He had discovered the deception! He was bound to realize! No. He bent over her again and slid his lips over the very feature that had briefly disconcerted him.

With unremitting tenderness he continued to arouse her. And there came the point where she rolled over on top of him and returned everything in full. The cause wasn't simply her long period of abstinence and her craving for love, it was more his occasional puzzlement. Several times he paused as he was about to do something. When she opened her eyes she could see his half veiled, half questioning look. He must have sensed that something was different, completely different. But he didn't understand, couldn't understand what it was because ultimately it was just too monstrous. Her growing arousal was matched by a surge of fear that he would realize at the very last second that he was being palmed off with a copy. Eventually there was nothing for it but to accept what he was offering and to hope that Nadia responded in a similar way.

Afterwards, lying with his arms round her on the couch, he checked out the points that had made him wonder and looked for rational explanations. Placing his hand on her breast, he said "You've put on a few ounces, haven't you? Don't even think of going on a diet. It feels good like that." Then he ran the tip of his finger round her navel. The bath had washed off the concealer. "Since when have you had that?"

Still dazed by what should never have happened and by the response it had released inside her, she looked down at her stomach. "Since yesterday. It's just a spot."

"That's not what it looks like to me," he declared. "But we'll leave the diagnosis to a specialist. You'll go and see Reusch about it. And no more sunbed until that's been sorted out."

She just said, "Yes."

He stood up and pulled her up off the couch. "Let's get to bed. I really am tired now. How's the back?"

"Fine. My headache's gone too."

"I should hope so," he said with a smile. "I couldn't offer you a second course of treatment today."

She went to the bathroom, used the toilet and put the tampons back in the cupboard before Michael saw them. In the bedroom she started to shiver. It wasn't the temperature; it was warm in the room. He hadn't bothered to put his trousers on again and was standing by the double bed throwing back the covers. Then he went into the dressing room. She couldn't get into bed because she didn't know which side Nadia slept on, so she scurried back into the bathroom.

A couple of minutes later he followed her in with clean clothes over his arm and a little alarm clock in his hand, which he put on the basketwork shelf. She went back into the bedroom together with him. He lay down on the left-hand side and patted the sheet. "Get in, I'll hold you tight, at least until twelve. By then you'll have stuck it out for almost a whole day."

She cuddled up to him, he put his arm round her and almost immediately fell asleep. She lay there, awake, not daring to move. The bed was too different, the pillow too firm, the sheet too cool, his skin warm against her back. She could feel his breath on her ear and neck. And she couldn't understand how Nadia could be unfaithful to him. He was perfect! At least that's what he'd been for her in the last hour, and in comparison with Dieter Lasko.

The doors out onto the landing and to the bathroom were open. She listened to the silence in the house, thought she could hear a faint ticking somewhere. His alarm clock in the bathroom or just the pulse throbbing in her ears. The buzzing, thrumming noise rose and fell. What a day! And what a night! Panic, excitement, release, triumph and the certain knowledge that she could stand in for Nadia as a wife in absolutely every respect.

At some point or other she fell asleep, perhaps at three, perhaps not until four. Since there was no clock in the bedroom, she had no way of telling. Contrary to expectation, her sleep was calm and dreamless. When she woke up, she was alone in the bed. The room was flooded with daylight and she'd neither heard the shutters going back up nor noticed him getting out of bed.

It was depressing. Friday the thirteenth, she thought briefly. But that wasn't it. It was just the return to normality: waking up and being alone. No, it was worse than usual because she'd known what it was like to go to sleep with a satisfied husband. She'd thought she'd wake up beside him, have a few minutes with him, the time to make it clear to him that the previous night was nothing special, that it wasn't worth talking about.

What if he asked Nadia that evening, "Did you see the doctor?" What if he said, "You were so different yesterday." What if he made any comment that gave the game away? There were a thousand ways he could let out that she hadn't played the sulky wife, but simply his wife. There was no way of preventing it. And she had to, she really had to.

The memory of the night was still fresh in her mind. And the desire for a reprise correspondingly strong. But what if Nadia found out? She instinctively knew now why Nadia had given her advice on how to keep Michael at arm's length. After the previous night's experience, her tips no longer seemed designed not to make things easier for her stand-in. A fling with a little laboratory mouse might be forgivable, but a woman who was a mirror image of herself was much more of a danger.

In order to force herself to snap out of the wretched feeling that, while she'd supplied the clearest possible proof that the deception had been successful, she'd still failed, she got up quickly, smoothed out the sheets, put the bedspread over them and went to the bathroom. The alarm clock had gone from the shelf. A glance at Nadia's watch showed that it was a quarter past nine.

In the shower she tried to think up some arguments. If she went about it in the right way, she might even manage to make it seem an advantage. "I took the tampons out and kept saying no, but he just ignored it. When I realized I couldn't stop him without arousing his suspicions, I did what I could to make sure he didn't notice. And he didn't notice." Then she'd just have to wait and see how important her extramural pleasures were to Nadia if it meant supplying her husband with a replacement for bed and board.

She had a long shower, rubbed Nadia's cream over herself from head to toe, used Nadia's make-up and took a skirt and blouse of Nadia's from the dressing room to save the grey suit. Then she went to tidy up the television room but couldn't bring herself to go in. The towel was still on the couch, the cushions, his clothes and the other towel on the floor. It brought everything so vividly back to mind that she had to close the door quickly to stop herself bursting into tears.

At ten she was sitting in the kitchen having breakfast. When she came down there'd been two letters, the *Frankfurter Allgemeine Zeitung* and the local paper on the table. The letters were addressed to Nadia. One had the address of a hotel in Nassau on the envelope, the other came from a Swiss bank in Zurich. She put them on one side, the *Frankfurter Allgemeine Zeitung* as well, and leafed apathetically through the local paper.

At eleven she was sitting at Nadia's desk. With no great enthusiasm, she started up the word-processing package in order to delete her invitation from Behringer and Partners. With the night still coursing though her veins, it was the action of a woman who didn't know what to do, filling in time. She called up the menu. For simplicity's sake she'd named the file Lasko. It was at the top of a list of nine. The other eight all had the same name and were numbered consecutively: Alin 1, 2, 3 and so on.

Unintentionally she let the cursor slip onto the second line and clicked on it, bringing Alin 1 onto the screen. The imposing letterhead of Alfo Investment immediately caught her eye. She registered the name Markus Zurkeulen with an address in Frankfurt. She had already seen the name on the torn-up sheet of paper with the large numbers that she'd taken out of her waste bin and put together like a jigsaw puzzle.

The text of the letter didn't tell her very much: "We are sure we have a range of products that will meet your aspirations. My colleague will contact you in the next few days and she will give you any information you require." It closed with the usual best wishes and the name of the writer – Philip Hardenberg.

Now she remembered where she'd heard the name Philip before. She saw herself walking across the reception area at Behringer's, she saw Frau Luici cover the mouthpiece of the telephone with one hand, she heard her whisper, "Hardenberg". And the six-foot giant with the receding hair grabbed the receiver and said, "Hi, Philip."

A call from the man Nadia was working for as a favour at precisely the moment when she was coming out of nice Herr Reincke's office, filled with the justified hope that she had finally found the job she so desperately needed. But only two days later the letter of rejection arrived! And now she was stuck here because Nadia needed a stand-in sulky wife in order to enjoy a couple of carefree days with her lover.

Coincidence? She didn't think so. What if Nadia had already been wondering about being able to spend a worry-free night with her lover when she got into the lift on that Thursday at the end of July? What if the only reason Nadia couldn't seriously consider such a night was that it might endanger her marriage? What if Nadia had had a revelation when the lift stopped and she found herself face to face with herself? In that case – bloody hell, Nadia had certainly been quick out of the blocks to take advantage of the chance meeting! Without giving a thought to the needs of the woman in the green suit, she'd set Philip Hardenberg on Behringer to make sure someone else got the job.

That suddenly made everything seem so mean, so despicable. So far there wasn't a scrap of proof. But the way the six-foot giant had behaved supported her suspicion. She could still hear him saying, "May I know why you're so interested in this property?"

Property, she thought bitterly. And then he'd talked about water damage. Hardenberg had arranged some insurance for him and now Behringer wanted a juicy pay-out for the favour.

She called up the other files in the folder. They all had the same content and the same date: 02/08, the Friday when she'd met Nadia in the Opera Café for the first time. The addressees were different – the names she knew from the torn-up Alfo Investment sheet. One was missing. Presumably it had been replaced in the folder by her Lasko file.

She switched on the laser printer. It spewed out the letters one after the other. She had no idea what use she could make of them. She wasn't important enough for Philip Hardenberg or for Behringer to get them to admit to collusion. And a minor insurance fraud would be impossible to prove. There was no point in fantasizing about going to Behringer with the letters and getting confirmation of the truth. And if that was what had happened, if Nadia had done her out of the job, then she owed her more than the truth, much more than a thousand euros for standing in for her once a fortnight.

A woman who lacked for nothing, who had everything others could only dream about. A woman who hadn't the remotest idea what it was like to have to steal from your mother just to cover your supply of noodles for the next thirty days and the rent for a filthy hole beside the railway track, where she was constantly pestered by an alcoholic with a criminal record. This woman had had the cheek to exploit a little hole in her mother's nest egg in order to put moral pressure on her – and that after she was the one who'd made it impossible for her to fill the hole by honest means. If that was what had happened, then Nadia had robbed her of a future reasonably free from financial worries and the prospect of a secure old age.

For a few minutes she felt a mixture of impotence and raging fury, which swept away all thoughts of the night and the emotions Nadia's husband had aroused in her. After a while, fury came to dominate the mixture. Two alternatives. Either: "From now on you'll pay me…" Or? There was nothing in "or" for her personally, but she liked it better. If preserving her marriage and keeping her husband in the dark were really so important to Nadia: a phone call to the lab and a frank discussion with Michael.

His contract only had the address of the pharmaceutical firm, no telephone number. And she didn't think he would be back home before she had to leave. If the technician had turned up on time and repaired Olaf, there would surely be a lot to keep him occupied.

She started her search for an address book or list of telephone numbers in the desk drawers. There she came across the Dictaphone Nadia had used to allay her fear their voices might sound different. It didn't appear to have been used since then – when she switched it on, the first thing she heard was Nadia speaking the brief text of the letters and then herself asking, "What should I say?" After that Nadia spoke again. And even if there wasn't any difference in the voices, the question whether she'd taken the money and her answer must make it clear to anyone that there were two women speaking.

With the Dictaphone in her hand, she went to the next room. This time the towel on the couch and the bottle of massage oil caused her no inhibitions, she simply ignored the objects that bore witness to her night with Michael. She spent more than fifteen minutes looking for a way of making a copy of the tape. It couldn't be done on the stereo system. In one of the drawers of the cupboard where the massage oil was kept she did find several tiny cassettes, but they wouldn't fit into the Dictaphone, so that ruled out taking the original tape.

It was a while before she realized they were replacement tapes for the answerphone on the desk. Suddenly she knew what to do. She swapped the cassette in the answerphone for one of the replacement tapes and dialled the house number on her mobile. The telephone beside the bed rang just twice, then Nadia's voice on the answerphone could be heard in the study. After Nadia's message and the bleeps, she switched the Dictaphone on and held the mobile against it. The recording quality of her copy was poorer than the original, but that didn't bother her.

After that she had a look through the contents of the second drawer in the little cupboard. She didn't find a list of telephone numbers but, right at the back, underneath an accumulation of odds and ends, there was an envelope which had been soaked in some dark liquid. The address was unreadable, all that could be made out was the sender: Nadia; the postmark: posted in August two years ago in Cologne; and a stamped message: *Retour à l'expéditeur*.

The envelope had been opened. In it were two sheets, handwritten, unfortunately in French, and also stained with the same dark liquid. The beginning was legible: *Jacques mon chéri*. That suggested to her an intimate letter to a lover. What was there to say that the dark-haired man at the airport was the first with whom Nadia had been unfaithful to her husband? The fact that the letter had been returned to sender could only mean that *mon chéri* had refused to accept delivery. In other words had terminated his affair with Nadia.

She took the two sheets back into the study. The computer had long since switched to standby, but pressing the space bar immediately reactivated the word-processor. She typed out everything in the letter that was legible. It fitted on one page, which she printed out.

Before continuing her search for the telephone number of the laboratory, she made herself something to eat, just a ready meal. Taking the plate back up to the study, she went through countless folders, hoping to find a list of telephone numbers. Everything that looked as if it might be a written document she sent to the printer, including the ninth letter with Philip Hardenberg's best wishes. The addressee was called Maringer and was the one with the smallest sum on the Alfo Investment list. The rest consisted of reports on various, mostly foreign, companies with a positive assessment of their future prospects. She looked in vain for the three letters Nadia had sent her.

After about two hundred pages had piled up, the paper in the printer ran out. She took a large envelope from the desk drawer, addressed it to herself, put all the printed pages and the tiny cassette with her copy from the Dictaphone in it and, with a touch of irony, put Dieter Lasko as the sender. She couldn't find any stamps, so she treated herself to: "postage to be paid by addressee". There was too much paper to take in her handbag or any other way without Nadia noticing.

Next she used the mobile to dial the number of the hotel in Luxembourg to find out the name of the dark-haired man at the airport. A young woman answered and told her, in excellent German, that Frau Lasko had already checked out. She asked about the man accompanying Frau Lasko, claiming it was an extremely urgent business matter. The woman at reception knew nothing about a man. Frau Lasko had had a single room, she said. That wasn't surprising for a married man on a business trip. But however much she insisted, the otherwise friendly receptionist refused to reveal the names of male guests in the nearby single rooms.

When Michael came back shortly after three, she was still going through the folders, hoping to find personal letters or anything else she could use to open his eyes. The window was open because of the odd smell from the printer. When she heard the car in the street, the cursor was highlighting something of which only Nadia knew the contents. But it was her last chance. She clicked on the file, at the same time watching the monitor as the garage door rose.

The screen showed an index card with a name, an address and a telephone number. That it was only Dr Reusch didn't matter, for there were more cards behind it, with the top line visible. She clicked her way frantically through them and found Jacques. Down below, the door from the garage into the hall opened and shut. Even on the index card Jacques had no surname, but there was an address in Geneva and a mobile number, which she quickly noted down. A few more clicks. She found Philip, but she didn't care a damn about Nadia's employer. Michael's voice came echoing through the house: "You up there, love?"

Love! In the early days of their marriage, Dieter had called her darling a few times, but only when they were making love, otherwise it was always Susanne. But Michael's "love" wasn't aimed at her, even if it did set her pulse racing. He came up the stairs.

"Yes," she shouted, slipping the paper with Jacques's mobile number in the envelope, which she hadn't stuck down, and closing the card-index file. She changed the folder, trying to get back into word-processing, but she was in such a hurry her double click started up something else.

Michael appeared in the doorway. When she saw him her anger disappeared in a flash. At the same time she realized she would gain nothing by telling him who she was and what she was doing there. How could she expect him, after one single night, to accept a woman who had tried to make money out of deceiving him?

"We're really up shit creek," he said, coming over to her. "It is a virus. Kemmerling's devastated. He had a crash half an hour after I left yesterday. It totally wiped his hard disk." He gave a resigned smile.

She'd put the bulging envelope address-side-down on the desk. Michael merely glanced at it, bent down and gave her a quick kiss. "Am I glad you said no." He looked at the screen. "Have you still got some important stuff to do?"

She looked at it too. The screen had the boxes Nadia had given her to play with. Only in this file they were filled in. On the first line she read "Kogler', followed by dates, figures and abbreviations. At the top was the file name: NTA. She looked up at him and smiled. "No. That's it for today, otherwise my head's going to burst."

"Headache again?" he said with feigned sympathy.

"Splitting," she said. "Can you do anything to get rid of it?"

"I'm pretty sure I can."

His hand clasped her neck, squeezed it lightly, then proceeded down over her shoulder and rested for a few seconds on her left breast, which must have been slightly fuller than Nadia's. It wasn't apparent to the naked eye, only revealing its secret to the gentle pressure of a hand.

And Nadia's husband liked that. Nadia's husband also liked the fact that she hadn't been smoking. He gave the desk a long hard look. Obviously he saw that the ashtray was missing and asked, "Have you managed to stick it out all day?"

126

She knew at once what he was talking about and beamed at him. "Yes, no problem."

"Wow," he said. "A day and a half already, you're going to break your record. Anything special on the agenda?"

She shook her head. He drew her up from her chair. "So we can have a nice cosy evening together, just you and me."

This time the kiss seemed to last an eternity, during which her skirt dropped to the floor and her blouse slipped off her shoulders. When nothing but her underwear was left, he said, "Let's have a swim."

"No." He tried to pull her away but she resisted. The only arguments she could think of to explain her refusal were her make-up and hair.

He gave way. "OK, then I'll make us a coffee, we'll have a bite to eat and after that I'll deal with your headache on dry land." She nodded, relieved. He let go of her and went out. With practised fingers she got rid of NTA and shut down the computer. Then she quickly put her skirt and blouse back on and hurried downstairs.

The coffee machine was bubbling away in the kitchen. He'd taken the cups and saucers into the drawing room and was opening a packet of biscuits. "What do you think about going away for a few days?" he asked. "Kemmerling's boat's on Walcheren. If I ask him, I'm sure he won't refuse."

"I don't know." The idea of him spending a few a days away from it all with Nadia on Kemmerling's boat almost made her sick.

He noted her dull tone of voice and gave her an encouraging smile. "Be brave, love. I know how hard it is. The first days are terrible, you feel like biting your fingernails down to the quick. But then it's all right, believe me. I managed it and I'll help you. I've plenty of time now. I have ways of taking your mind off it."

He gave a quiet laugh. "The advantages of a virus. I don't have to go into the lab until next Wednesday. Kemmerling'll be there keeping an eye on the technician. He's hoping he can pick up enough to get his own machine up and running again."

She liked his casual tone. Dieter often used to go on in such a bombastic manner. For Dieter life in general and his profession in particular were deadly serious matters. Michael seemed to take things as they came. Of course, with a double doctorate and his income he could afford to do so.

He tipped some biscuits out of the packet onto a plate, poured the coffee into a pot and took both into the drawing room. "So what's it to be? A few days on the boat or something else?"

"I don't know," she repeated as she sat down in one of the comfortable chairs and watched him fill the cups. "Let's discuss it tomorrow."

"We'll be on our way tomorrow." He seemed to regard it as all settled.

"And what about Lilo's party? You promised we'd go."

He rolled his eyes. "Oh, come on, Nadia. You heard what Jo said. It's by no means certain that Maiwald'll come. Anyway, happy as I am to support young artists, one of his daubs is quite enough for me. As for Barlinkow, you can take the piss out of him another time. You're surely not going to pass up a chance of four days on the boat just for that."

Take the piss, she thought. Joachim Kogler had talked of her finding Barlinkow amusing. She sighed wearily. "Of course not. But I might have to go out for a short time. Helga said she'd ring and…" She picked up a chocolate biscuit, bit off a piece and felt she was going to choke on it.

He sat down opposite her in the other chair. There was a sharpness in his voice. "Then I'll talk to her. A few hours a week is OK. But if you think you have to let Hardenberg tie you up every day and even monopolize your weekends, then I object. You know my opinion. Jo's jackpot has done nothing to change that, on the contrary. If Hardenberg wants to extend his business, then let him see to it himself."

At this point Nadia would certainly have reminded him who had financed his studies. She just nodded. Half an hour later he led her upstairs. He stopped in surprise when he opened the door and saw that nothing had changed in the television room. Then he nodded and smiled, went over to the shelves and put on some music. She let her skirt fall to the floor again, took off her blouse, sat down on the couch and stretched out her hands to him.

She didn't entirely manage to switch off her thoughts and let herself be carried away. Despite that, it was good, and she was more aware than the previous night. She sensed that she confused him again. But she also sensed that he enjoyed it.

Shortly before five the mobile in the study put an end to the languorous mood. Their clothes were scattered round the room and they were

128

lying on the floor among the cushions. From the stereo loudspeakers a man's voice was crooning, "When a man loves a woman." His hand was behind her head, gently, lazily playing with her hair. At the first ring his hand twitched, then closed firmly round the back of her neck. He drew her head to him, kissed her and murmured, "Let it ring. Think of your resolution. Stress is the last thing we need just now."

In the study the mobile rang for the fourth and fifth time. "She'll soon give up," he whispered and kissed her again, holding the back of her neck in an iron grip. "Giving up really suits you. You taste much better and smell so good. I noticed that yesterday."

It rang for the seventh and eighth time. She put her hands round his face and pushed him back a little. "At least let me tell her I'm not going."

He let go of her. "But be quick about it."

She nodded, got up, closed the door behind her and went, naked as she was, to the study.

"Why did you take so long?" Nadia asked indignantly. To go by the background noise, she was already at the airport.

"Hi, Helga," she said.

"Is Michael there?"

"I'm sorry, Helga," she said. "I know I promised, but I can't make it today."

"Does that mean Kemmerling's there as well?" Nadia asked.

"No, I really can't. My husband's got a few days off. The lab computer's got a virus. He wanted to work at home yesterday, now he's glad I didn't let him."

"OK," said Nadia. "Now see that you get away. Tell him you have to collect some documents from the office."

The soft music suddenly grew louder as Michael appeared in the doorway.

"Is that music playing?" Nadia asked suspiciously.

"Well if I really have to," she sighed. "OK, I'll be there in an hour."

Michael shook his head emphatically and came over to her. "Out of the question." Before she could do anything about it, he'd grabbed the mobile. "Give my best wishes to Herr Hardenberg, Frau Barthel, and tell him my wife needs a few days' rest. She is unavailable until next Thursday." With a slight frown on his face he listened, then grinned.

"She hung up." He put the mobile back down on the desk and took her hand.

And for a moment she imagined what it would be like if she gave in. Nadia waiting at the airport, Nadia realizing she wasn't coming. Nadia's impotent fury. She'd have no choice but to go to Kettlerstrasse and spend until next Wednesday stuck in one-and-a-half rooms. She had the key and she could only come back home when she was certain Michael wasn't there. But Nadia wouldn't put up with that a second time.

With a long sigh she withdrew her hand. "I can't leave her in the lurch. I did promise." She switched her tone to enthusiastic and was amazed how well she did it. "You know what? I'll fetch the documents and borrow Philip's laptop again. I just have to do a few company analyses and I can just as easily do that on the boat."

He exhaled loudly. "A holiday like that's no holiday at all." He shook his head in frustration. "You really do have a talent for putting a damper on things, Nadia. And just now I had the feeling…" He broke off with a gesture of exasperation, managing to look both disapproving and hurt at the same time. What are you trying to prove? How good you are? Don't worry, I know. And if you insist – every day I'm well aware I'm only earning my pocket money in the lab. And that you're just holding back so as not to sap my male ego."

She could well understand him, his anger, his disappointment. But it was a unique opportunity, with the right answer, to put him in a thoroughly bad mood. If he was furious with Nadia, he was unlikely to think of mentioning the previous night and that afternoon. It was cruel, shabby, mean and nasty – it was Nadia's way, not hers. But she managed it. She tilted her head back a little, raised one eyebrow and asked, "Do I have to remind you who financed your studies?"

His reaction was as expected, a "No" through clenched teeth. Glancing past her at the darkened screen, he went on, "One day I'm going the throw that thing out of the window. I could kick myself for having agreed to that crap. I should have known what was going to happen. Just arrange a few insurance policies and mortgages my arse. It wasn't long before it was short-term loans for small companies, and now you're right back in the thick of it. Hardenberg knew exactly why he wanted you. Once you've tasted blood there's no holding you. But I've not stayed with you because I'm gambling on a fortune. I've stuck by you through everything because I love you, Nadia."

She felt awful. It hurt, deep inside her something stung an extremely sensitive spot. Nadia! Of course, it was Nadia he loved. The previous night and during the last couple of hours it was Nadia he had made love to. Every kiss, every caress, every melting glance had been for Nadia. As a woman, Susanne Lasko didn't exist for him, however good she tasted and smelled. She dug the nails of her left hand into her palm until it hurt. "I know," she said.

He nodded slowly. "Yes, you know, but it's not half as important to you as your juggling with figures."

"That's not true."

He waved her objection away. "Don't keep lying to yourself. I'll just tell you one thing: what we went through two years ago is enough for the rest of my life. If you screw up again or make a hash of things with Hardenberg, you're on your own." He turned round abruptly and left the room.

His words, echoing round inside her head, set her mind in a whirl. No reasonable man would call it screwing up if his wife took to the bottle because he'd been unfaithful. Stuck by you! That must have been about her drink problem, which Nadia had admitted to her. Gambling on a fortune! Juggling with figures! Short-term loans. She didn't know what to make of it all.

She went back into the room, picked up her blouse and skirt and put on her underwear. Michael's steps hurrying down the stairs had died away. From somewhere far off she heard violent splashing. Clearly he was working off his anger in the pool. She tidied up, put on the grey suit and checked to see if any telltale signs were left. Finally she filled the printer with paper, picked up the mobile, then the thick envelope, put in the invitation with Behringer's logo she'd written herself, stuck it down and went to the garage.

She took her time driving to the airport. There was heavy traffic on the autobahn, and the concentration that demanded took her mind off the questions Michael's last remarks had thrown up and off the things she'd learned in the course of the day. Despite that, as she turned off onto the airport slip road, she was afraid she'd do or say something very stupid when she met Nadia.

There were no spaces free in the short-term car park. She left the car double-parked, ran into the terminal and looked for a letter box for her thick envelope. When she came back an extremely angry driver was standing beside the Alfa. "What do you think you're doing, leaving…"

She gave him Nadia's captivatingly mocking smile. "No need to get your knickers in a twist. Look, I've gone already." A few minutes later she reached the agreed meeting place. And suddenly everything was easy.

She conjured up an embarrassed smile. "I came as quick as I could. Have you been waiting long?"

Nadia waved her excuses away. "Trouble with Michael?"

"You bet." She got out. "I thought I was going to have heart failure when he grabbed the mobile."

Nadia dropped her cigarette and crushed it with her toe. "No need to worry. I thought that might happen when I heard him."

Nadia had already returned the rented car and completed all the formalities, and she made it quite clear she was taking over as Nadia Trenkler with immediate effect. She took her handbag, demanded the mobile back as well and insisted on a comprehensive report, at the same time holding out her right hand as if to say "Gimme."

Slowly Susanne took off her jewellery, going on as she did so at great length about Michael's initial good humour, his plans for a few days away and abrupt change of mood. Nadia was very pleased to hear what she'd said about borrowing the laptop from Philip and asked if she had time during the coming week.

"Not on Sunday. I have to go and see my mother."

"It's not Sunday," Nadia said. "On Wednesday my friend's flying to Geneva for three days. And since I got there so late yesterday, we thought…" She sighed. "He asked if I could arrange it so I could go with him. We'd have more time together. It doesn't make any difference to you whether you do it at the weekend or in the middle of the week. As long as you haven't got a job and I have the opportunity…"

She left the rest unspoken. Again Susanne felt a rage of fury rising within her. As long as you haven't got a job! Presumably it had all been about business trips from the very first moment – given that it was a married man. If she'd had a job with Behringer's, she'd have only been available at weekends, and would have been earning enough to refuse supplementary income that came from deception on principle.

"Well, then?" said Nadia. "Can you?"

"I don't know." She hesitated, her mind in a whirl. A man who had given her a few unforgettable hours. But he loved his wife. He wouldn't accept another woman. She needed more information, she needed to know everything. So that eventually… She didn't get any further. "It can't work indefinitely," she said. "Take my boob about Olaf. You just laughed, but I didn't feel like laughing. Or Joachim Kogler with…" Suddenly half a dozen names were buzzing round in her head, making her feel totally inadequate. "I'd need to know more," she said.

"Jo," Nadia said emphatically. "Never even think of calling him Joachim, he hates that. He won't bother you. They're going to Canada for a fortnight at the beginning of the week."

"But you have an appointment on Wednesday."

"It's been shifted to Tuesday. I'll write down everything that occurs to me for you, OK?"

YES! lighted up in her mind like a flashing neon sign. Outwardly she remained hesitant, sketched a nod, at the same time shrugging her shoulders resignedly. "OK. If it all goes pear-shaped, that's your problem."

"Correct," said Nadia. "But it won't go pear-shaped. We'll meet in the multi-storey on Monday at four. We'll discuss the details then. Do you mind taking the bus back into town?"

"Not at all," she said, feeling immense relief at not having Nadia with her any more as she tried to deal with the thoughts going round and round in her head. Nadia got in the car and the Alfa roared off. She stood there for a moment, motionless, then went to the bus stop.

Wednesday! That she'd see him again so soon! As long as nothing happened. She refused to allow herself to think of Nadia and him together, that he might after all mention the night and the afternoon. She didn't know him well enough to judge that.

An hour later she was back in her flat. She took Jasmin Toppler's key and retrieved her envelope. Her initial thought was to tear up her notes, but then she didn't, she put the envelope in the cupboard with the three letters from Nadia and all the photos. She sat with the television on until three in the morning, but all she could see was Michael's eyes when he was standing, naked, beside the bed. They way he'd smiled at her. "I'll hold you tight." Head over heels in love, just like a teenager! She really hadn't expected it to happen to her again, when she'd managed without a man for so long.

Towards morning she dozed off on the couch, dreaming of the path through the woods. Nadia, all unsuspecting, was three paces in front of her and didn't see her raise the heavy stick in her hand. It was shortly after midday that the postman brought her furious digging to an end. The hole in the ground simply refused to get any deeper. Dazed and confused, she staggered to the door and paid the postage for the thick envelope.

The weekend edition of the newspaper with its pages of situations vacant meant as little to her on that Saturday as the torrential shower of rain that flooded her balcony and left the floor of the mini-kitchen under water. She had a bite to eat some time late in the evening, she didn't have much of an appetite. What little life there was in the room came from the TV. She had the choice between a variety show, a quiz show and a crime film. She chose the latter and went cold inside as on the screen a young woman was killed by her lover.

That night she dreamed about it. And the worst thing in the dream was that she learned that Nadia's lover had murdered her and Michael Trenkler was mourning his beloved wife from the newspaper. There was nothing at all she could do, she woke up, bathed in sweat, and needed a moment to work out where she was.

Monday morning. Half-past seven. A good eight hours until the meeting in the multi-storey. She had breakfast, just a piece of cheese on toast – and it tasted of blood. She didn't bother with lunch, she couldn't eat a thing. She was afraid of herself and of what she was going to think of next. Shortly after one she got herself ready and left. Heller was at his window as she came out of the building. He shouted an obscenity and spat, but missed her. She ignored him and set off briskly for the city centre, past the multi-storey and through two boutiques she wouldn't have dared enter just a couple of weeks ago. Then she went on to the Opera Café.

She remembered what Ilona Blasting had said. "A few minutes of the first act." There had been a number of CDs beside the stereo, which revealed Nadia's taste in music. She doubted whether Michael shared it. "When a man loves a woman." It was still going round in her head.

Punctually at four she was at the meeting place and went through one last quarter of an hour of torment that a casual remark of Michael's might have given away what had happened during the night and the afternoon, and Nadia wasn't coming. Then the white Porsche came up the ramp.

Nadia was as friendly as ever and suggested a drive out into the country. She didn't say much on the way there. Michael's photo was stuck to the dashboard and she couldn't stop herself looking at it. It was only when Nadia had parked in the little car park at the forest walk that she asked how the Saturday evening with Jo and Lilo had been.

"We didn't go," Nadia said, switched off the engine, picked up her handbag and got out, adding, as she slammed the car door, "I had a terrible headache."

She couldn't repress a guilty start. Nadia regarded her with a smile. Not a friendly or unsuspecting smile any more. "Unfortunately," she said, drawing out the word as she locked the Porsche, "I had to make do with aspirin. My husband was still in a pretty bad mood."

It was the first time Nadia had called him her husband. The subtext was clear. Nadia strolled off along the narrow path under the trees, not bothering whether she was following or not. After a few seconds she shook herself and set off, stumbling along the path behind Nadia.

"There's aspirin in the dressing room, by the way," Nadia said. "If you should happen to need one. You might do with the old injury to your skull. You often get a headache with that kind of thing, don't you?" Before she could reply, Nadia went on. "Unfortunately I haven't got round to writing anything down. We'll just have to do it orally. What do you need to know?"

"I don't know," she stammered. "I thought you would."

Nadia, already ten or twelve steps in front of her, turned round. By now her smile seemed frozen to her face. "How should I know what's of interest to you? As far as I'm concerned, I've told you everything you need to act out your role. You're not supposed to have needless arguments with Michael. The cold shoulder, d'you remember? And —" Nadia paused, her frozen smile giving a frosty glint to her eyes, "— the cold shoulder means doing nothing at all. Particularly not anything that demands specific, not to mention intimate knowledge. But for that you obviously don't need special instruction. I wouldn't have thought it of a woman who's been without a man for three years and even before that was kept on short commons. You seem to have a natural talent for it. He was quite taken with my unaccustomed abandon and was hoping for a further helping when I got home."

Her cheeks were burning. Nadia pursed her lips briefly and asked, "Don't you feel well?"

She shook her head slowly. A hint of sympathy crept into Nadia's smile, just the tiniest hint, the rest was still ice-bound. "What's the matter? Missing my husband already?"

"I'm sorry." It was an effort, but she got the words out. She realized that it had been a serious error not to bring up the matter immediately on Friday. It could perhaps have been sorted out then, with the explanation she'd originally thought of.

Nadia continued to smile. "Sorry?" she asked, drawing out the word. "If you're sorry, he can't have been in form. Did he not make sure you'd had an orgasm? I hope you'll forgive him, with all the problems in the lab and his frustration with Kemmerling. Normally he's not selfish like that."

"No, I'm really sorry. I didn't mean to sleep with him. And because I'd forgotten to put out the... I thought a headache would be a good excuse and..."

"OK, OK." Nadia interrupted her stammering apology with a gracious wave of the hands. "My mistake. I should have told you that we have an unusual code word. It never occurred to me. But I believe I remember having told you how much my marriage means to me."

Her cheeks were still burning, but her brain gradually cooled under Nadia's icy stare. "Yes, and I wondered why on earth you were cheating on him. There's no need to get worked up. Your husband didn't notice anything and that's what counts. If I'd known how he'd respond to a headache I'd have used diarrhoea as an excuse."

Nadia raised her eyes to the treetops. "But on Friday you should have known. You might have just as well said, 'Fuck me.' "

"I could never say a thing like that!"

"No," Nadia mocked, "not you. You're a little innocent and you don't use obscene expressions. And why should you, when there's another way? And now you know how it works. What did you have in mind for

Wednesday? In bed for a change? I'd advise against that. In bed you just get the standard deal. You'd do better to go for the pool, there he's in a class of his own."

"Pity I can't try it out," she said. "I can't swim."

"All the better," Nadia snarled. "I'm sure drowning while making love must be a wonderful death."

Slowly Nadia came over and stood right in front of her. For a few seconds it looked as if she was about to put her hands round her throat. "The night," she hissed, "I could have ignored that. You didn't know what was happening until it was too late, no one could blame you for that. But on Friday afternoon you went too far. Got a taste for it, have you? Well, not with my husband."

Now that hostilities had been declared and Nadia was showing her anger openly, she became completely calm. "If at all," she said, "then only with your husband. Your boyfriend's not my type. Anyone who goes round with a thug can't be much of a man."

Nadia drew back in surprise. "Thug?"

"The guy at the airport," she said. "I got there a bit early on Thursday and I saw you getting out of the black car. What was that bruiser supposed to be? A chauffeur? A watchdog? The latter, I presume, since he had to wait outside like a good boy. Did he keep watch during the night as well? Or did he climb into bed with you to take over while his master got his second wind? That's not my style – with a substitute ready to come on. I'm more for a cosy twosome and I reckon I had the more pleasant night."

Nadia had also calmed down. "Then I hope you made the most of it, 'cause there's not going to be an encore."

"I take a different view," she said. "We stick to our agreement: once a fortnight at a thousand euros a time. That's cheap when you take into account that you cost me the job at Behringer's. I know you did. I happened still to be there when Philip Hardenberg rang. I'm not going to do anything outrageous like demanding extra payment for special services. You won't have to pay for your husband's pleasure. After all, I'm not a whore. What Michael needs, he'll get free of charge. He wasn't selfish, he was fantastic. And he thought I smelled better, tasted better and felt better."

Perhaps she shouldn't have said that, but she just couldn't resist. Nadia stared, her eyes spitting fire. She'd really got into her stride by now and went on without stopping, "If you're not in agreement I'll have to ring Michael and ask for a meeting. I can play him the little tape you recorded in my flat. I can show him my ID card and your letters to me. And one or two more. I can do all sorts of things to convince him there's a faithful version of his wife. And that he won't have to worry every time that version takes a drink."

Her heart started to pound as she listed everything she could do, but overall she felt strong, just as strong as she'd felt when she'd placed herself in front of old Herr Schrag during the second bank robbery and pushed him towards the door. For a couple of seconds she thought she was in the stronger position, too. Then Nadia started to smile. It wasn't a nasty smile, not an icy smile any more, it was just bored. It reminded her of the red stain on the branch manager's shirt.

"Don't try to threaten me. Given your life story, you must realize you'll come off worse. It would break Mama's heart to stand at the grave of her only daughter and I just have to snap my fingers to make it happen. Rest in peace Susanne Lasko. You couldn't have made anything more of your life anyway. Is that what you want? Then ring Michael."

Nadia turned on her heel and went back to the car park. She followed slowly, all churned up inside. She could hardly believe it when she found herself her eyes actually scouring the ground for a piece of wood or a stone she could use as a weapon. She couldn't stop herself. A few steps in front of her, dangling from Nadia's shoulder, was the handbag that contained everything she needed. And a few miles further on was a man for whom she obviously had something to offer that he didn't get from his wife! The Porsche was only a hundred yards away. But she didn't know where she was to go with it to swap it for the Alfa Spider. And she wouldn't know how to take the piss out of Henseler, young Maiwald or Barlinkow at the next party Lilo Kogler organized. You couldn't just slip into a forty-year-old life like a blouse someone else had taken off. She heard a strange grinding noise and realized it was her teeth.

When she reached the car, Nadia opened the passenger door and, with a gesture, invited her to get in. When she hesitated, Nadia asked coolly, "Do you want to walk back? Or are you afraid? Don't worry, I'll return you to your dump safe and sound. And we'll forget the whole thing. If you're sensible, your mother can enjoy an untroubled old age."

She got in. And Nadia drove her home, stopping two streets away from her flat. She got out and leaned in the car. "So what about Wednesday?"

"Fuck off," Nadia snarled. "And close the door."

She didn't close it, she simply walked away. Behind her she heard Nadia swear. The door slammed, the engine roared, the white sports car flashed past and disappeared. Heller was still – or once more – leaning out of the window, and shouted something when she approached the tenement. He vanished as she opened the door and she assumed he'd be waiting to catch her on the stairs. Fortunately for him he wasn't. Otherwise he might have become acquainted with her knee for the first time.

She spent the whole evening and half the night pacing round the flat, from the kitchen to the tiny living room, from there to the half-bedroom and on into the bathroom-cum-shower. Almost blinded by tears, she wailed her frustration at not having picked up a heavy stick in the woods. At one point the walls came in, threatening to smother her, then receded into the distance and the squalor was transformed into a snow-white villa where a sweet-tempered and affectionate husband was waiting for her longingly.

With the first trains passing outside, calm returned, at least inside her. Under the shower she washed away all the tears with lots of cold water. At half-past six she was having breakfast with Nadia's letters on the table. For the hundredth time she read, "Perhaps I can do something to change that."

There was so much Nadia Trenkler could have done. That she could get rid of her just by snapping her fingers – the very expression took all the weight out of the threat. She didn't believe Nadia could be a danger to her. And she was absolutely determined not to let her get away with the way she'd treated her.

Part Three

The first thing Susanne Lasko did on Tuesday 17 September was to go to the place where it had all begun, the entrance hall of Gerler House. It was shortly after nine and fairly cool. The sky looked as grey and dreary as her future. Only where the sun must have been could a faint blush of pink be seen among the clouds.

She was wearing light-grey trousers, a pullover and a dark-blue wool blazer, her elegant attire complemented by a discreet amount of make-up. She approached the four lifts hesitantly, trembling a little at the idea that one of the doors might open and leave her facing her double. A lift arrived. There were only two men in the cabin and they hurried out past her.

Taking a deep breath, she got into the empty cabin. She was about to press the button for the fifth floor when she saw it. Alfo Investment. A tiny brass plate beside the button for the seventh floor. She should have realized that sooner, even though she hadn't had another chance actually to see the plate. Nadia's appointment that had been shifted to Tuesday came to mind. That meant it was pretty likely Nadia would come to swap her Alfa for the Porsche. It was a reflex action to press the button for the underground garage.

Not long afterwards she was walking briskly along the rows of parked cars. There was still the odd free space. Eventually she found the white sports car behind one of the massive concrete pillars, next to a green Golf, beside which was a blue Mercedes. One space was free, then came the next pillar. And over the four spaces was written on the white wall: "Alfo Investment".

She recognized the dark-blue Mercedes, she'd ridden in it once. It meant that the friendly fat man who'd driven her into town when she'd had the temperature must have been Philip Hardenberg. That Nadia's employer of all people should have happened to be driving past the telephone box and stopped to help out of pure kindness of heart, she found hard to believe. But she did recall Nadia saying something about an acquaintance. It wasn't important just at the moment.

Almost automatically a bloody scene unrolled inside her head. A woman going towards her car, her double appearing from behind the pillar, a cudgel or, even better, an iron rod in her hand. A well-aimed blow and the woman by the car collapses, her head streaming with blood. The murderer prises the car keys out of her hand, opens the boot and heaves the dead body into it.

She could have spent hours standing by the pillar developing the scenario, but at least the thought did help her deal with her impotent fury. After what seemed like an eternity she returned to the lift, went up to the fifth floor and entered the offices of Behringer and Partners. Frau Luici's initial smile turned into a wondering frown as she enquired, "And what can I do for you, Frau?…"

"Lasko," she said. "I'd like to speak to Herr Reincke."

"Have you an appointment?"

"No." She returned the smile in Nadia's manner and took the invitation she'd written herself out of her bag. "But I do have this."

Frau Luici took the letter and glanced through it, muttering, "I don't understand." She hadn't tried to forge Behringer's signature. Frau Luici noticed it was missing, looked up at her and said. "It's not signed."

"Precisely," she said. "I'd like to know whether it's just a mistake or someone's playing a joke on me. Can I speak to Herr Reincke?"

"Of course," said Frau Luici. She stood up, trotted over to Herr Reincke's office, knocked briefly, opened the door, cleared her throat and said, "Have you a moment, Herr Reincke? I have a lady here. There appears to have been another mess-up."

Two minutes later she was sitting across the desk from nice Herr Reincke. He looked somewhat unsure of himself. Whether the invitation to a further interview was the cause or the confrontation with someone he hadn't expected to see again, was hard to say. One thing was certain: he found her appearance in his office embarrassing. "Yes," he said eventually. "Unfortunately, Herr Behringer isn't in the office today. He hasn't mentioned it to me. Perhaps it would be best if you were to make an appointment…"

God, she hadn't considered the possibility of Behringer being there! She quickly plucked the letter out of Herr Reincke's hand and explained, "That will not be necessary. I haven't come to discuss my salary expectations with Herr Behringer. I would have been delighted to do so, but in the meantime I have obtained a well-paid position with Alfo Investment – or Philip Hardenberg, if that means more to you."

144

Reincke nodded. He ran his eyes over her clothes. She'd taken her blazer off and laid it across her lap, letting the lining show – and the label, which indicated it wasn't from some cheap high-street store. "I found the letter amusing," she went on, "but that's not what brings me to you. You perhaps remember that my knowledge of foreign languages is deficient?"

Reincke nodded again and waited.

"My mother has suddenly fallen ill," she said. "Among her things I found a letter, in French. I can hardly understand a word and I wondered if you would help me translate it." As she spoke, she slipped the Behringer invitation back in her bag and took out her copy of *Jacques mon chéri*. Glancing through the first lines, Reincke informed her that there were gaps in the text.

"I know," she said. "But I don't need a complete translation, I just need to know what it's about."

She followed her words with a deliberately artificial looking smile as she told him her father had died years ago but now she had the impression her mother had managed to find some consolation.

Reincke nodded again and returned to the letter. He furrowed his brow in concentration as he began to read, now and then murmuring a few words, which she could make nothing of. After a while he read on in silence, apparently gripped by what he was reading. "Yes," he said eventually, looking as embarrassed as he had at the beginning. "I don't think this letter was written after your father died. I think perhaps the best thing would be for you to discuss it with your mother."

Assuming an expression of deep mourning, she whispered, "I'm afraid that's no longer possible, Herr Reincke."

"Well, then," he began hesitantly. "My French isn't perfect and the letter's rather fragmentary, but if I understand it correctly, your mother's asking for a reconciliation. She deeply regrets what she's done and reminds him of the wonderful times they had together when they were young. She knows he's split up with Alina and thinks that is an opportunity for them to get back together again. She's says she's very unhappy in her marriage, her husband has absolutely no understanding of her needs. She would leave him if he – I assume that's Jacques – could forgive her. Is that enough?"

"Yes. Thank you very much." She took back the sheet of paper. "You've been very helpful."

He blushed like a schoolboy on his first date. "You're welcome," he said. "And you really don't want to talk to Herr Behringer? I could get you an —"

She broke in quickly. "No, it's really not necessary."

"Then I'll do it for you. We can't just ignore this. The only explanation I can think of is that the new typist forgot —"

She broke in again. "Good Lord, no! I don't want to get the poor thing into trouble. It will just have been a slip. That kind of thing can easily happen in the first few weeks."

"It should not happen," Reincke declared firmly. "And Herr Behringer could hardly have expressed himself more clearly. I'm glad he's changed his..." He broke off and started again. "I wasn't happy with his decision. Before the interview we were in agreement regarding your appointment. Then suddenly Herr Behringer decided to give an opportunity to a young woman with excellent foreign languages who was looking for her first job. But when it comes down to it, I'm the one who has to sort things out after her."

"Please," she said, trying to stop him seeing Behringer about it, "it's not that serious. As I said, in the meantime I've —"

Reincke raised his hand and shook his head firmly. "Your desire to protect the young woman does you credit, Frau Lasko. But something has to be done. The letter to you is not the only blunder we've had in the last few weeks."

"In that case," she said, holding out her hand. She preferred not to think of Behringer's reaction. Much more important than the six-foot giant's possible telephone call to Philip Hardenberg – "Just imagine, that Lasko woman turned up here" – was Michael's reaction to his wife's letter to *Jacques, mon chéri*.

Reincke took her hand and shook it. She went to the door and before he knew what was happening she'd left his office, nodded to Frau Luici and shot out of reception. In her mind she ticked off item number one. Item number two was the telephone in Jasmin Toppler's flat, item number three a meeting with Michael. She was sure she could persuade him to agree to that.

She took her time going home. Now neither the drizzle nor the unpleasant cold wind bothered her. Reincke's translation had improved her chances. "I can convince him there's a faithful version of his wife."

And Michael didn't have to go back to the lab until Wednesday. It was all falling out nicely. At the moment Nadia was probably on her way to the rearranged appointment. From what she remembered of the man's suggestion, Nadia was probably meeting him around midday.

Back in Kettlerstrasse she just went to her flat for long enough to get Jasmin Toppler's key. She made sure Heller wasn't around, then slipped across. "Good morning, Herr Trenkler. My name won't mean anything to you, but my face will. I know you have some free time today and I hope we can meet. Don't say no, it's very important. It concerns your wife." Either that, or: "Hi, darling. He didn't turn up. I'm in the Opera Café, do you fancy coming over? I've a surprise for you." She was only going to decide which version when she heard his voice. She was confident she would be able to tell what kind of a mood he was in from the sound of his voice.

The planned revenge was followed by a shock as, after the second ring, Nadia's "Trenkler" rattled her eardrum. Her finger shot out and broke the connection. Half-past twelve! She refused to believe Nadia had met the caller with the harsh-sounding voice in the morning. She waited half an hour. Then she tried a second time. Again it was Nadia who replied and again she hung up without a word. The sensible thing to do would have been to go back to her own flat and wait until three or four before trying once more. But she couldn't bring herself to do that. Instead she watered Jasmin's plants and did a little dusting. She stuck it out until two, then tried for the third time.

Again it was Nadia who replied. By this time she was sounding nervous. "Hello? Hello? Who is that calling? Say something."

She was about to hang up again, when she heard his voice in the background. "Is it that joker again, darling?"

"I don't know," Nadia said.

"Give it to me," he said. And then he was speaking to her. "You have exactly two seconds left to say what you want. Then I'm going to hang up and after that no one will lift the receiver again. A hundred and one, a hundred and two – that's it."

Before she could even clear her throat, the line went dead. "Darling" went round and round in her head, like a cruel echo. Well, there were other ways. She could write to him at the lab. She managed to get back to her flat unseen and spent the rest of the day drafting a letter. The writing pad she kept for job applications was getting thinner and thinner. No words were good enough for him. After all, there were things you could only say to someone face to face. Finally she thought of directory enquiries. It was dark on the stairs but she didn't switch on the light, just left her door open. When, a little later, she closed the door to Jasmin Toppler's flat again, she was reasonably content.

She didn't get much sleep that Tuesday night, she kept waking with a start from terrible dreams. Finally an early train brought her back to the dreariness of the real world. She looked at the alarm clock. Six o'clock. Michael would be getting up, going to the shower. He didn't bother with breakfast. She cuddled up under the blankets and followed him in her mind's eye through the splendour of white to the garage. After a good hour she decided he'd be in the lab, so she got up, had a shower, dressed and crept to her neighbour's door once more.

Like Heller's, Jasmin's flat looked out onto the street. The telephone was on a little table right next to the living-room window. From the third floor the street could only be seen by leaning out of the window, but the street corner, round which the telephone box was, could be seen from beside the table.

She dialled the number she'd obtained from directory enquiries the previous evening. A porter at the switchboard answered, listened to her request and said, "I'm putting you through." Music came from the receiver, interrupted now and then by a soft female voice: "Thank you for your patience. Please hold the line."

Her patience quickly grew thin. The muzak got on her nerves. Her eye wandered along the buildings across the road to the street corner. Once more the woman's voice thanked her for her patience, but before it could ask her to hold the line it was interrupted by the matter-of-fact voice of the porter asking her again what she wanted. Again she asked to be put through to Michael Trenkler, pointing out that she'd already been waiting on hold for some time.

The porter simply said, "I'm putting you through," and the little tune came back. A fat man of medium height appeared at the street corner and stood there. She paid no attention to him but drummed her fingers impatiently on the little table. She was starting to get worried about Jasmin Toppler's telephone bill. It might be a good idea to anticipate her surprise with a few euros and an explanation. "I needed to telephone urgently and the box had been vandalized again."

While she was thinking about that, her gaze automatically went back to the street corner. Now the fat man wasn't alone any more, he was talking to a woman in a sand-coloured trouser suit who was wearing a headscarf and large sunglasses. Before she could get a closer look, the woman went round the corner. The man started to walk, came closer, then crossed over the street and thus disappeared from view. And for the third time the porter asked her what she wanted. In an irritated tone she told him, "You've already tried to put me through twice. I've been waiting for ages."

"Not everyone's in their office yet," the porter said. "Perhaps you could try again later."

"No, now," she insisted. "I don't want to speak to someone in an office. I need to speak to Michael Trenkler. Please put me through to his lab."

The porter remained a model of porterly detachment. "Which department, please?"

"I don't know exactly, but he works with a Herr Kemmerling. Please, it really is very urgent."

She heard the porter asking, "Hey, Heinz, Trenkler and Kemmerling, have you any idea which lab they're in?"

"Thirty-eight," a voice replied. "If no one answers, try seventy-four. They had a computer crash last week, it could be that they've…"

She stopped listening to the discussion coming from the receiver. Something was happening down in the street. Now the woman was back at the corner and looking towards the building. The wind was tugging at her headscarf. And those large, dark glasses – on such a dull day.

"I'm putting you through," the porter said. And a door nearby was closed. Her door! Two seconds later the woman at the street corner took a mobile out of her jacket pocket.

There was no reply from extension thirty-eight. She wouldn't have dared to speak anyway. Someone was in her flat and talking to Nadia on the phone. The walls were thin. She'd heard Jasmin often enough. At first the voice from her flat just came as a murmur, but suddenly it grew louder. "I'm not blind and the place isn't that large. Why didn't you keep your big mouth shut, you stupid bitch? Couldn't you let her have her little moment of pleasure? After all, you're getting your money's worth too."

The man in her flat must be Philip Hardenberg. She might have recognized him sooner, but not at that distance, especially as she'd only seen him once before, and that when she'd been running a temperature. He was urging Nadia to leave. "Off you go. Get on with it!" The last thing she heard him say was, "Don't worry, I'll see to that. I think I can manage a convincing heart attack."

Without being aware it, she whispered "Shit" half a dozen times in Jasmin's living room. She only realized she'd spoken out loud when she heard steps going down the stairs. She didn't dare look out of the window, they might see her. Despite Hardenberg's command, Nadia was still at the corner. After a couple of minutes he reappeared down in the street. Then they both left.

Her brain was awhirl with questions and answers. What had Hardenberg been looking for in her flat? Immediately Nadia's threat came to mind: she'd snapped her fingers. How had he got in? With a duplicate of the key she'd forgotten to take out of her handbag last Thursday. And it wasn't only the man at the airport Nadia had an intimate relationship with. Nadia surely wouldn't have allowed Hardenberg to call her a stupid bitch if they were no more than just business partners.

She didn't bother with the call to extension seventy-four. Either Nadia had drawn the correct conclusion from her silent phone calls the previous day or – and she would have bet the whole of her mother's nest egg on it – she'd been informed about her visit to Behringer and Partners. Nadia probably even knew the favour nice Herr Reincke had done her. And to stop anything going any further, she'd snapped her fingers. A heart attack! The words sent a tingle of ice through her veins. If she'd been in her flat – or gone to the callbox: that was the direction the two of them had come from.

She stayed in Jasmin's flat for another hour, spending the first ten minutes looking through the classified directory then calling a locksmith. Only when she heard the bell ring next door and had checked that there was a van with the firm's name on it down in the street, did she go out. The door to her flat was open. It hadn't been forced open, as the locksmith quickly established.

It cost a small fortune to have a new lock installed and a chain fitted. Once the locksmith had left, she gave the new key a double turn and put the chain on, then checked every corner. There was no sign that Philip Hardenberg had been doing anything other than looking for her.

It was about midday before she noticed that the three letters from Nadia were no longer in the cupboard. The envelope with the Alfo Investment document she'd pieced together and the notes she'd made for her own safety had also disappeared, as had the pile of photos of Nadia's house and surroundings. But Nadia's faithful servant had ignored the fat envelope containing all the printouts with "Postage to be paid by addressee" on the front and "From: Dieter Lasko" on the back. He'd probably assumed it contained documents connected with her divorce. The fragmentary letter to *Jacques, mon chéri*, the note of his mobile number and the copy of the tape were still in it.

She spent the afternoon and the whole of Thursday, Friday and Saturday sitting in her room with the door locked and the chain on. On the Sunday she didn't go down until Johannes Herzog stopped in the middle of the street and started blasting his horn.

Her mind was elsewhere during the whole of her visit to her mother. She must have heard her ask, "Is something wrong, Susanne?" twenty times, and twenty times she replied, "Just a headache." And every time she said the word she felt a lump in her throat as she imagined she could feel Michael's hand clasping the back of her neck.

On the way back she asked Johannes if she could borrow his BMW on Monday, Tuesday, Wednesday, Thursday or Friday. She claimed she wanted to visit a friend. The concern in her mother's voice had made her see that she must do something. Take the bull by the horns and call on Michael in the lab then go with him to see Nadia. To have him at her side when she came face to face with Nadia would be the best proof of what she had to tell him. And Nadia could scarcely take steps against her once Michael knew. By that time there'd be no point, anyway.

Johannes did not greet her request with any great enthusiasm. "Which friend," he asked. "One like Heller?"

He had been treated to Heller's abuse often enough. "It's none of my business, what stories you tell your mother," he said. "But she tells my grandmother and she tells me. I thought there was something wrong with my ears when she said you were thinking of buying a piano from Heller. He doesn't even know how to spell piano."

"What do you want me to tell my mother? That the guy's a drunkard, is always hurling abuse at me, has a criminal record and hasn't got a job?"

"Nor have you," Johannes declared. "Or if you have, there's something funny about it. Firms just don't send their secretaries out as couriers. We've known each other for quite a while now, Frau Lasko, and suddenly you look like a different person. It makes you think."

"I really do just want to go and see a friend," she said.

Johannes nodded. "Then tell me when and I'll drive you there. But I'm not letting my car be used for something that might be a bit shady."

"Forget it," she said. She hoped Nadia would do the same.

Nothing special happened during the days that followed. Long periods of lethargy alternated with brief moments of undirected energy. Sometimes she read the reports in which Nadia went on at great length, and always in very positive terms, about the future prospects of foreign companies. Sometimes she wondered about getting a bus out to the pharmaceutical firm, but most of the time she just sat there, seeing herself in her mind's eye lying on the floor in the TV room next to Michael. She heard the mobile ring in the study and then herself, saying, "That's Nadia. She said she'd phone when she got back from the trip with her lover."

Jasmin Toppler returned late on Friday evening, collected her key and thanked her for looking after her plants. She confessed to having used the telephone. Jasmin waved the offered payment away and gave her a searching look. "Are you unwell?"

"Just tired," she said.

Jasmin invited her in for a coffee. There was a tot of genuine Jamaica rum to go with it and she heard how wonderful the holiday had been. She also heard someone knocking at her door, heard Nadia's urgent voice: "Open up, Susanne."

Jasmin heard it too. "You've got a visitor."

When she didn't move, Jasmin asked, "Aren't you going to go?"

She just shook her head so that Nadia wouldn't hear her voice. For three minutes Nadia went on begging her, then all was silent outside.

Strangely enough, this roused her from her lethargy. On Saturday she got up early and bought a newspaper with a vacancies section. When she got back, she also checked her letter box, which she hadn't done for some time. There was a letter in it. It had no sender's name on the back, but the familiar block capitals immediately caught her eye. To go by the postmark, it must have been delivered on Tuesday or Wednesday.

Nadia apologized for her outburst in the woods, swore it would never happen again, begged her to put her anger behind her, begged her even more to stand in for her during the coming week, for two days, and finally suggested they meet in the multi-storey. Friday, three o'clock. That explained why Nadia had turned up at her door.

She tore the letter up. Then she read the adverts and found two office jobs for which it was worth using up the last two pages of her pad. As she was writing her applications, Jasmin appeared with a box of chocolates as a thank-you present. Naturally Jasmin saw what she was writing and asked, "Would you do something other than office work?"

"Like what?" she asked.

Jasmin picked up the box of chocolates. On it was a sticker with the name of a high-class confectioner's. "One of their assistants has gone on maternity leave and they're desperate for someone. I know the manageress well, it was she who told me."

Twenty minutes later she was sitting behind Jasmin on her motorbike, wearing her spare crash helmet. Jasmin had rung up the manageress to tell her they were coming, making it clear she could start at once.

From outside the shop looked very imposing and it wasn't much different inside – lots of chrome, lots of glass, lots of light. Only the back rooms and the rear entrance looked a bit dingy. The manageress, Frau Schädlich, offered to take her on for a probationary period of three months.

"I'm sure you'll understand that I can't offer you a permanent job straight away," Frau Schädlich said. "You wouldn't believe the problems I've had with some people. Just now, for example, a young woman kept quiet about the fact that she was pregnant when we appointed her. Half the time she was off sick. The management's not very keen on that kind of thing."

"I've been by myself for the last three years," she said, "and it doesn't look as if that's likely to change."

Frau Schädlich smiled. "It might not be nice for you, but it's music to my ears. We'll see. In three months we'll be in the middle of the Christmas rush and even after that we can use good people." After the details had been sorted out, Frau Schädlich gave her a firm handshake as she said, "See you on Monday, then."

"Monday it is," she replied, going back into the splendid shop and taking in its hustle and bustle and the sweet smell of all the confectionery.

When things were quiet for a moment, she introduced herself to her new colleagues. One was called Meul, one Gathmann. Then she was out in the street again. There was drizzle and a horrible wind driving low-lying clouds over the rooftops. She treated herself to a bus back to Kettlerstrasse.

Back in the flat she found a handwritten note that had been pushed under the door. Nadia repeated her apologies and again asked to meet: Monday at five in the multi-storey. Two thousand for two days. She crumpled the note up and threw it in the waste bin.

On Monday she left shortly after seven, went to the station and bought a weekly season ticket. Punctually at eight she was in the shop, where she was welcomed by the three other women, who explained the range of confectionery to her. At half-past nine one of the senior managers appeared, but he just wanted to know why a fully qualified bank clerk was selling chocolates. The two bank robberies convinced him that Frau Schädlich had made a good choice. He just asked her to call in at Health and Social Security as soon as possible to get the paperwork sorted out.

When she got home in the evening, the red Alfa Spider was parked about two hundred yards from her flat. As she approached, Nadia leaped out, blocked the way and said, "Get in."

"No way!"

Nadia took her by the arm. "I need you tomorrow morning, Susanne. Please. Don't leave me in the lurch."

She shook her off. "Don't 'please' me. And no 'thank you' either. Did you ask yourself where it would leave me when you got Hardenberg to lean on Behringer to give someone else the job?"

"That wasn't me," Nadia said. "It was Philip's idea. And if he'd had his way, you'd have…"

"Clear off, or I'll go to the police tomorrow."

"The police!" Nadia snapped. "What nonsense. What are you going to tell them?"

"That you were going to have me killed and —"

Nadia interrupted her with a sigh. "I didn't mean it like that. You say a lot of things when you get angry. I can only apologize. I hadn't thought Michael would make love to you. And then he gave me a lecture about the hopes that I'd raised, how much he'd enjoyed it when for once I'd behaved like…" She broke off and let out a sigh. "It's not very nice to

154

have to listen to something like that. But it wasn't your fault. When I'd had time to think about it later —"

"The first thing you did was to send Philip to lean on me."

"Lean on you?" said Nadia. "Nonsense, Philip just —"

Again she interrupted her. "Entered my flat with a key. Stole my notes and picked up your letters and the photos. And I could hear every word when he rang you. He wanted to make me have a heart attack. How do you do that?"

Nadia ignored her final question, just shook her head vigorously. "Philip didn't have a key. Your door was open. He was surprised."

She couldn't have said whether Nadia was lying or not. She was convinced she'd shut the door behind her when she'd gone to Jasmin's, but she couldn't be a hundred percent sure. After all, she had left the door open the previous evening. "So what was he doing there?" she asked.

"What do you think?" Nadia said irritatedly. "He was going to apologize for my outburst and ask you to stand in for me again. As you know, we wanted to go to Geneva on Wednesday. He was so looking forward to it and was furious that the arrangement fell through because of me after he'd put so much into setting it up. He was paying for it, you see. The main reason why he was furious was because I'd got so worked up about Michael and you. He doesn't like to hear that kind of thing. At the same time he's scared stiff his wife might find out. He rang Michael and told him my mother had had a heart attack and I was already on my way to Geneva. Only unfortunately it didn't work. So…" Nadia had put on an expression that would have melted a heart of stone. "I really need you Susanne. Please, just for two days. I'm offering a thousand a day."

Recalling Hardenberg's words in her flat and the conclusion she'd drawn, it sounded plausible. That he'd looked in her cupboard and removed all the evidence could have simply been a matter of precaution. But: "If Hardenberg's your friend, who was the man you met at the airport?"

"Just a customer," Nadia said. "He knew Philip was flying to Luxembourg and had asked him to take some documents. As Philip had set off at six, I had to see to it." That sounded plausible too when she remembered the document case with the combination locks.

"Will you help me?" Nadia begged.

"No," she said and set off towards her flat.

Nadia trotted along nervously beside then behind her. "Can't you forgive and forget, Susanne?" she said and raised her offer to two thousand a day. She only dropped back when Heller leaned out of the window.

The scene was repeated the next morning. Nadia was there waiting when she came out and walked alongside her, pulling a thick envelope out of her handbag. "There's five thousand, Susanne. Please. My flight goes at eleven."

"*Bon voyage*," she said and continued on her way.

"How much do you want for the two days?"

"I just want to be left in peace."

Nadia only gave up when the bus arrived. During the journey she felt very strong and also relieved. She was sure it was all over and that from now on her life would resume its course: quiet, modest – and lonely, yes, but honest and without fear.

The work at the confectioner's was tiring but not difficult. The warmth with which she'd first been welcomed didn't change. She came through the required health check. For people working in the food industry an X-ray was a standard requirement. When the assistant placed a lead apron over her abdomen, saying it was compulsory for women of childbearing age, she could only laugh. "You don't have to worry with me. My periods have taken early retirement. Sometimes nothing happens for months."

Her daytime existence returned to normal. But often in the evening everything still came back to her. After she'd closed the door behind her, she had a kind of hollow feeling. She didn't regret having turned Nadia down. On the contrary. She knew she couldn't have gone through it again, letting Michael make love to her knowing it was Nadia he was thinking of.

The memory of the night and afternoon with him was still so vivid. The little treats she bought in the first two months to console herself for the dreary evenings were no real consolation. She chewed and sucked her way right through the shop's range, spending one evening with crystallized fruits, another the liqueur chocolates and a third with champagne truffles. Her teeth didn't suffer, she continued to brush them thoroughly, but her stomach often reacted to the sweets with a feeling of nausea in the early morning.

At first it didn't occur to her that there might be another cause. It was only at the beginning of November when, after eating nothing but tea and toast for days on end, she was still regularly being sick and in addition felt an uncomfortable tightness in her breasts, that an awful suspicion began to form in her mind. She bought a test at the chemist's. The result was unambiguous.

That night she cried herself to sleep. It was so cruel. Something was growing inside her that could have brought a little light into her life: a person who would have belonged to her to the end of her days, who would have given meaning to everything. And now, just as she was getting her life back on track, she couldn't afford to give that person a chance. Of course, there would have been the possibility of going to Michael and admitting everything, showing him proof that she had been in the house at that time and demanding maintenance for the child. But would he cough up enough for her to live on and pay the rent? Perhaps for a few years, if she was very lucky, but then she would definitely be too old to find any work at all.

She went round in a daze, incapable of thinking clearly or coming to any decision. Frau Schädlich observed her with increasing suspicion because she was often sick when she came to the shop in the morning. At ten o'clock on the last Wednesday in November Frau Schädlich told her to take her morning break.

"If you don't mind," she said, "I'll take a little walk instead. I must have eaten something that disagreed with me. The fresh air will do me good."

Frau Schädlich had no objections and said that since she was going out, she might as well get some change from the bank. She fetched her bag and just her blazer from the rest room. It was sunny outside, not as cold as it was early in the morning, so she didn't need to bother with her shabby trench coat. There was a branch of the Deutsche Bank nearby.

It was very busy. There were only two positions open and both had long queues. She went to the end of the shorter, left-hand queue and waited. After a few minutes the feeling of queasiness returned. She automatically looked round the hall for somewhere where she could make a quick exit. There was a double glass door and the right-hand queue was nearer. She moved over to it and continued to look around.

At the back there was a door to the offices. That was the door they came out of. The stocky man in a leather jacket, open so he could easily get his hand inside. He looked as if he was holding his chest. The dark-haired man she'd taken for Nadia's lover at the airport – he would have matched Nadia better than the fat Hardenberg – was wearing an expensive-looking coat over an elegant suit and carrying a briefcase with combination locks. They walked rapidly towards the exit, ignoring the queues at the desk. Automatically she watched them leave. They reached the glass door. The stocky man went out but his dark-haired companion paused, said something, handed the briefcase to the other and came back. Quickly she turned her head away, but it was too late.

She felt a hand on her shoulder and heard his voice. "What a nice surprise." She was forced to turn round and face him. He smiled and she responded with a stiff smile, wondering how she could get rid of him. Taking in the queue with a mocking glance, he said, "I wouldn't have expected to find you here, but it's very convenient. I was sorry to hear from Herr Hardenberg that you'd gone your separate ways. I hope you've time for a little chat."

She shook her head, but he continued to smile. "That's a pity. And I can't accept it. Unfortunately Herr Hardenberg was unable to explain to me how Joko Electronics had come to collapse."

She'd read something about Joko Electronics. On five or six of the two hundred pages she'd printed out. It sounded like a Japanese firm that developed new computer chips but clearly didn't sell them as well as Nadia had imagined. She hurriedly pulled a couple of strands of hair down over her forehead and mumbled, "You're confusing me with someone else."

The stocky man had disappeared. The dark-haired man gave a low laugh. "I don't think so," he said, grabbing her arm and pulling her towards the door. "We can talk in my car, we won't be disturbed here."

"Let go of me," she demanded forcefully. "You've got the wrong person." Some of the people in the queue turned round to look, but no one made a move to help her.

He continued to drag her away. Now he kept his voice down. "In your own interest I advise you not to make a fuss. I want my money back, all two hundred thousand of it. Or did you think I could lose such a ridiculously small sum without noticing?"

Shit, she thought and the word slipped out before she could stop it. The man reacted in mock horror. "What an ugly word from such beautiful lips! May I take that as an indication that you are unable to fulfil my request? That leaves me no alternative but to get someone to establish your pain threshold."

By this time they'd reached the double glass door. He held one part open with his elbow and tried to push her out past him into the street. Using all her strength, she managed to free her arm, took a step back into the bank and explained, her voice firm and unwavering, "You're taking me for someone else. Look at my ID. I'm not Nadia Trenkler."

For a moment he was confused. "Who's Nadia Trenkler?" Then he grasped her arm again, tighter this time, and pulled her out into the street. "Come along, Frau Lasko. If that's your attitude, I've no alternative but to let Ramon continue this conversation."

He dragged her along forcibly towards a parked car. It was the black limousine with the Frankfurt number plate and tinted windows she'd seen at the airport. The stocky man was already in the driver's seat, but he got out when he saw them coming, watching them with an expectant smile on his face. She tried desperately but vainly to pull her arm away. Panting, she said, "If you don't let go at once, I'll scream."

The man just laughed and said, with mock politeness, "If you'll just bear with us a few moments more, Frau Lasko, you'll have plenty of opportunity for that." Then he nodded at the stocky man, who opened the rear door of the car. She was pushed forwards, then the grip on her arm slackened and instead she felt a hand in her back. It was almost like the second bank robbery.

How often had she imagined to herself all the things she could have done to avoid ending up with a fractured skull. Hit, kick, bite – anything to stop herself being led away like a lamb to the slaughter. Space was too cramped for hitting or kicking but she managed a reverse jab with her elbow, which landed in the dark-haired man's stomach. He was more surprised than seriously hurt, but he did leave go of her. His companion didn't seem to have expected such a reaction either. His hand went inside his jacket, but she didn't wait to see what he was feeling for, she shot off and ran until her lungs were almost bursting.

Frau Schädlich accepted her explanation that she'd suddenly felt unwell in the bank, though with a thoughtful look, and sent Frau Meul to collect the change. Then she asked her to come to the office for a private word. "I suggest," she said, "that you see the doctor about your stomach. Do it on Monday when you have your day off. Then we'll know where we are on Tuesday."

She just nodded and went back into the shop. She didn't take her eye off the street outside. Through the large shop window she saw the car with the tinted windows drive past twice in the next hour. He'd called her Frau Lasko!

There was nothing for it, she had to ring Nadia, but she didn't dare do so from the manageress's office, Frau Schädlich was always close by. Just before closing time she twisted her left ankle so convincingly that Frau Meul offered to drive her to the station so she could get a taxi to the hospital and have her foot X-rayed. She accepted the offer gratefully. There was nothing wrong with her foot, but the route to the bus stop went past several dark corners where a woman could be dragged into a car unnoticed. What if they were still waiting outside? The risk of being seen and caught seemed to be less if she didn't leave the shop by the front door. Frau Meul's car was in the little car park behind the building.

She rang Nadia from a telephone at the station. She tried her mobile first but the number no longer existed. It didn't occur to her to try the mobile Nadia had given her for a few days, she rang her at home, unconcerned that Michael might take the call. After two rings the receiver was lifted. It was Nadia.

She simply said, "It's me. I have to see you immediately – in an hour's time at the station. Your client from the airport spoke to me today. Called me by my own name! He wants his money back, the whole two hundred thousand. If you don't come, I'm going to the police." She hung up before Nadia could say anything. Then she waited – until almost eleven, growing more nervous with every quarter of an hour that passed and travellers became more sparse, dubious characters more numerous. Nadia didn't come.

Finally she hobbled demonstratively to the taxi rank, got a taxi to Kettlerstrasse and asked the driver to help her up the stairs. Which he did – for a generous tip. After she'd locked the door and put the chain on, she made herself a belated supper. When she got to bed at half-past twelve she was still wide awake and kept hearing imaginary noises on the stairs. And when the alarm went at six, her head was ringing as well, with the devastating knowledge that Nadia had done some business deals in her name.

On Thursday she left the flat at half-past seven, firmly resolved to get Frau Meul to drive her to the police during the lunch hour. She had the envelope with her meagre proof in the large bag she always took to work. On the bus she kept a look-out for the black limousine. The thought of the five hundred yards from the bus stop to the shop filled her with panic, which she had great difficulty suppressing.

The red Alfa pulled up at precisely the moment the bus drove off. Nadia jumped out. She was wearing an elegant trouser suit and, over it, a padded windcheater with a fur-lined hood, which she'd pulled down over her face. For several seconds they stood staring at each other in the cold and damp. Nadia was beaming at her as if she were a long-lost friend. "Unfortunately I couldn't manage it yesterday evening. Now tell me, what's happened?"

Wavering between anger and relief, she told her about her encounter with the dark-haired man and his chauffeur, bodyguard or whatever. Nadia pooh-poohed her fear. "It's nothing to get excited about. Zurkeulen likes to play the hard man but he can't do anything, he'd have big problems with the tax people if he did and he knows that very well. Believe me, he's harmless."

Zurkeulen – that was the name opposite the largest sum on the torn-up Alfo Investment sheet. Markus Zurkeulen and well over five million. That he'd only talked of two hundred thousand the previous day did indeed suggest it was just a matter of a bad investment. Still! "For you perhaps," she said. "But you used my name to —"

She got no further as Nadia broke in, "Book a hotel room," Nadia said, and claimed that Philip Hardenberg was responsible for the rest. But, she assured her, it was not done with fraudulent intent. Since he knew they'd swapped their identity documents, he'd told his client he would be meeting a Frau Lasko. He'd assumed Zurkeulen would ask to see some ID before handing a large sum in cash over to an unknown woman.

Documents, she thought. Documents, my foot! Nadia had collected a briefcase full of money at the airport. With Schrag and Röhrler it would just have been an envelope. Nadia and Hardenberg were clearly playing the same game, but in a higher league. As for all the rest, she didn't believe a word Nadia said. The Alin letters one to nine had talked of a "colleague" who would contact the recipients and who was referred to as "she". She didn't say anything about those letters but described the encounter in such a way that suggested Zurkeulen had mentioned a previous meeting.

"Yes," Nadia admitted. "He saw me once in Helga's office when he'd come for an appointment with Philip. And then I ran into his bodyguard at the airport because I needed to go to the toilet before I went to meet you in the car park. What could I have done? I could see there might be problems, because I only had my own ID card with me. Fortunately Zurkeulen was happy with the authorization Philip had given me."

Philip had sorted the matter out later on, Nadia continued, and that was why he'd told Zurkeulen Susanne Lasko had left Alfo Investment. Unfortunately that little firm – Joko Electronics – had gone bust shortly afterwards because their computer chips hadn't sold as well as expected. It was possible Zurkeulen had got hold of the wrong end of the stick there.

She didn't believe the half of it, but there was only one thing that interested her. "Can you give him his money back?"

"No," Nadia said. "I could make good the loss, but it's Philip who looks after Zurkeulen's portfolio and he's far too cautious. If he'd taken any risks during the last few weeks —"

She cut her short. "Can you at least tell him I've nothing to do with it?"

Nadia nodded and held out her hand, as if to make things up between them. She smiled. "People like Zurkeulen are not exactly the kind of client you'd wish for. Everything has to be absolutely secure, but has to give a high yield and the two can't always be combined. But, to be honest, I'm grateful to him. If it hadn't been for him, you wouldn't have got in touch again. Are you still angry with me?"

She shrugged her shoulders. She couldn't say whether she was angry or not. She was depressed. Nadia was still living as she pleased, while once again she was faced with an uncertain future. She deliberately ignored the proffered hand. Nadia withdrew it. "I hardly dare ask, but do you think you might…"

Before Nadia could finish, she shook her head vehemently.

"Just for two days?" Nadia said enticingly. "It would be a nice little extra for you. I assume you won't exactly be earning a fortune as a shop assistant. And you could fall ill at some point."

She looked past Nadia, down the street. "Even if I wanted, I can't any longer. I'm pregnant."

Dumbfounded, Nadia stared at her belly, which as yet showed no signs, put her hand to her mouth and whispered, "Say that again."

"Why? You heard me the first time."

Nadia nodded deliberately and asked, "Michael?"

"Well it isn't Heller," she said.

"Do you want to keep it?" Nadia asked.

"I can't afford to." Although she fought against it as hard as she could, her eyes filled with tears. "But I can't get rid of it, either. I always wanted a child. And at my age – it could be my last chance."

Nadia gave her a few seconds to recover her composure. Then she asked, "What if I help you? I got you into this situation, so it's only fair if I help you to deal with the consequences. You'll hardly want to take Michael to court for maintenance. He'll blow his top if he learns he's fathered a little brat. And he'd have to be told how it came about. Then we'd both be in for it."

"What kind of help do you have in mind?"

"Two thousand a month," Nadia said. "And a decent flat. As a quid pro quo you'll be prepared to stand in when I need you. Not in the coming months of course, but after the birth, when you've got your figure back. Have we got a deal?"

It would be a heaven-sent opportunity – if Nadia meant it seriously. But could she trust Nadia? She looked at her double sceptically. She searched her face for signs she could take as a guarantee but saw only the usual smile. "I don't know," she said.

"Give it some serious thought," Nadia advised her. "I'll go to the office now and have a talk with Philip so we can get this Zurkeulen business sorted out."

Frau Schädlich, Frau Gathmann and Frau Meul were already in the shop, but none of them had observed the little scene out in the street. Frau Schädlich was completely unsuspecting when, shortly after nine, she called from the office, "Quick, Frau Lasko. There's a nurse from the old folks' home on the line. Your mother's had an accident."

The receiver was lying on the desk. Her hand was trembling as she picked it up. At first even she was convinced something had happened to her mother. But then Nadia said, "You mother fell down the stairs – at least that's what your boss thinks, so keep up the pretence. The offer I made you just now stands, we can discuss the details when we've more time. Philip's already talked to Zurkeulen, as I have too. I explained that he'd never met you before and also why I was travelling with your ID card."

She heard a quiet laugh from the other end. "He's always having little affairs himself, I think he was amused. Whether or not, he was certainly understanding. As for the loss, I can recover that in two or three months, if he lets me take over his portfolio. He was very interested, but insisted on seeing me personally. He's in Geneva at the moment. I have an appointment there today anyway, so it fits in very well. But there's a slight problem: I can't see both him and my other client and get back by this evening."

Frau Schädlich was standing in the doorway, all ears.

"I'm afraid I can't get away at the moment," she said.

Behind her Frau Schädlich said, "Of course you can, Frau Lasko. It's an emergency. Do you want to phone for a taxi?"

Nadia had heard this. "Say no," she said. "Tell her you'll take the bus. There's a taxi coming for you. It'll wait where I stopped earlier on."

The driver of the taxi Susanne Lasko got into on the Thursday – it was 28 November – had been given precise instructions as to where she was to be set down. It was beside the Swissair terminal. Nadia was waiting. Already without her rings, ear studs and watch, she had nothing but her handbag, flight bag and a flood of instructions. The Alfa was in the short-term car park. First of all she was to go to the hairdresser's to get her hair trimmed and dyed. The rest she could see to once she was in the house. Then Nadia opened her handbag and took out a wad of banknotes.

"There's five thousand, Susanne. That should help you get through the next three months, and take things easy. In your condition you shouldn't spend hours on your feet. And that ought to give us enough time to find a half-decent flat for you as well."

She stared at the wad of notes, unable to take it in. But that was not all Nadia had to say, not by a long chalk. "If you want, you could have a job with Alfo Investment, that would solve all our problems. You don't have to start straight away, you can use the time until the birth for training – computers and foreign languages. You'll need excellent English, but there are courses for that. Behringer's would have borne the cost, now Philip will take care of it. In the meantime he'll also pay for the flat and I'll see to everything else until you're earning enough yourself."

Later on she could bring the baby to the office, Nadia said, it wouldn't bother anyone, certainly not Philip, he adored children. Of course, she could always employ a nanny. Nadia had no doubt that her salary with Alfo Investment would allow her to do that.

Susanne had to clear her throat before she could reply. She couldn't give an immediate response to Nadia's proposals, so she just asked, "Is there anything particular I have to be aware of with Michael today and tomorrow?"

"No. Things are pretty tense between us at the moment. We got back from a short holiday at the beginning of the week." Nadia shrugged her shoulders. "I wanted to give him a surprise – a little holiday house. He completely misunderstood, thought I was going to go off with someone else. We spent most of the time arguing. It's a good situation for you, you don't even need to have a session on the sunbed. He'll ignore you. If he does speak to you, say nothing. Just like I've been doing for the last few days."

Then Nadia held out her handbag. "Come on, take it. I have to check in."

"Just a moment. I've only your word for it, nothing more."

"You have Philip's word," Nadia said. It sounded as if it was God who was endorsing the promise. "He's going to talk to Behringer about a flat today. Three rooms, kitchen, hall, bathroom, balcony or, better still, a roof garden, that's what I told him. On the outskirts of the town, if possible. If Philip sees to that, it'll be quicker than if I do it myself."

It sounded too fantastic to be true. Nadia smiled. "Don't look at me like that. Our affair has caused you some inconvenience, to put it mildly. And we're not doing it simply out of the goodness of our hearts. But I'll have to insist you take a contraceptive after the birth. We don't want to start a kindergarten."

Nadia took a deep breath and exhaled audibly. "We'll go into the details when I'm back. I should manage it by tomorrow afternoon. When I know which flight I'm on, I'll ring you at home. I need the mobile myself and, anyway, it's not working properly. The battery keeps giving up on me. Mine only seem to last a few months. Now give me your bag, everything's in mine."

"Did you book your flight in my name?"

"No," said Nadia. "But you need my papers. Do you intend to leave yours lying in my hall? For weeks now Michael's been sniffing around my things. I've been off with Philip several times and had to think up stupid excuses, so naturally he's been suspicious."

"And how are you going to prove to Zurkeulen who you really are?"

Nadia patted one of her jacket pockets. "Replacement documents. Recently I lost my wallet and didn't expect the finder to be honest enough to return it. Now I've got two of everything. Take your things out, if you don't trust me, but then please leave them in your flat."

Hesitantly Susanne opened her bag, took out her purse, her wallet and the worn imitation-leather holder with her keys and said firmly, "For the moment I'm not taking any risks, I'll go to the shop tomorrow. I can't be absent on a Friday. It shuts at seven so I'll be here at eight. We'll meet in the car park. If you're back earlier and don't want to wait, go home in a taxi. You can tell Michael the car wouldn't start and come and get the Alfa on Saturday afternoon. Or you can ring me at the shop in the morning to arrange a time and I'll drive here."

Nadia just nodded and said urgently, "Now give me your handbag, your ear studs and watch." Then she was gone.

Susanne was in a daze. She didn't know what to think, what to believe. Clasping Nadia's handbag to her chest, she slowly walked out of the building. She soon found the Alfa. The hooded jacket Nadia had worn that morning was in the boot. She got in, took Nadia's jewellery out of the bag, put on the two rings and the wristwatch then inserted Nadia's diamond ear studs. After that she sat there for several minutes, trying to persuade herself it was a purely rational decision. It was just about getting Zurkeulen off her back.

But as she stared out of the windscreen at the images slowly passing before her mind's eye, it wasn't the man in the bank she saw, nor the stocky chauffeur by the limousine. It was Michael. Michael sitting on the edge of the bath, trailing his hand in the water. "Shall I keep you company for a while?" The touch of his fingers on the back of her neck. "You really are all tensed up."

She wasn't tensed up now, just in a daze from Nadia's promise of a future free of care. A large, airy apartment and a good job with Philip Hardenberg. And if she was earning enough at Alfo Investment to pay for a nanny, she'd also be able to afford a car. And drive out to the old folks' home every Sunday in her own car with her own child. Suddenly Dieter's pompous announcement of the birth of his and Ramie's child didn't seem so over-the-top after all. "In a time when hope has all but vanished, we are delighted to have brought a ray of sunshine into the world." Again the tears welled up, she couldn't do anything about it. But she would do almost anything to bring her child into the world. And perhaps that was the only reason: to bring a spark of hope into her own life.

It would have been madness to reject Nadia's offer – and unforgivable stupidity to trust everything she'd said. There were some contradictions in what she'd told her. Right at the beginning she'd claimed she'd got to know her lover only recently, but when she'd talked about the crisis in her marriage and her excessive drinking, she'd spoken of an acquaintance who had fortunately appeared. That must have been two years ago. And Nadia had kept insisting her friend was married. Most married men wore a wedding ring. Philip Hardenberg had not had one when he'd helped her up from the floor in the telephone box. She could still see that in her mind's eye.

She drove to her flat, immersed in thought. She picked up her toothbrush – she could hide it in the guest bathroom so Michael didn't see it. Then she took a shower, brought her armpits, legs and all the rest into line with the original, made herself up and put on a trouser suit with the hooded jacket on top.

She put the wallet with her documents in the cupboard. The envelope with the computer printouts, the note of Jacques's telephone number and the copy of the tape, as well as her key holder, she put in the boot of the car. Even if Nadia or Hardenberg didn't have a key to her new lock, it was better to be safe than sorry.

Her first call was at the bank, where she plugged the hole in her mother's nest egg at one fell swoop. The rest of the five thousand she paid into her own account. She had enough in her purse for the hairdresser, where she also had her fingernails brought up to scratch and left a generous tip. When she'd finished there, she had ten euros left, but she assumed she wasn't going to need any cash during the next few days. She intended to stock up for the weekend from Nadia's larder.

Even after she'd been to the hairdresser's, she didn't head straight for the autobahn. She wanted to be as sure as possible. If Philip Hardenberg really was going to rent a flat on the outskirts of town from Behringer's, then nice Herr Reincke would surely be willing to tell her as soon as it happened.

A few minutes after two she drove into the underground garage at Gerler House. Only the Porsche and the green Golf were parked in the spaces reserved for Alfo Investment. The dark-blue Mercedes wasn't there. From that she deduced that Philip Hardenberg wouldn't be there. And if the green Golf belonged to Helga Barthel – it was a risk, but it was worth trying. Perhaps she could get some information about Markus Zurkeulen from Helga which would be a sight more credible than anything Nadia told her.

It was Nadia she saw looking out at her from the mirror in the lift. She took a deep breath and pressed the button for the seventh floor. The plate on the door of Alfo Investment was as discreet as the one in the lift. Below it was a bell-push.

She pressed it. When she heard the buzzer and the click of the door opening, she threw back her shoulders, tucked her hair in behind her ears and went in. The lobby was smaller than reception at Behringer's – and empty apart from the carpet and a large pot plant in a tub. There were four doors, of which one was open, leading into a brightly lighted office. A plump, red-haired woman was sitting at the desk. She was playing cards on a PC and had her back to the lobby. She turned round. She would have been in her late forties, wore glasses and produced a friendly smile, which was immediately replaced by a look of astonishment. Before she could say anything, the woman took off her glasses and said in puzzled tones, "I thought you were in Geneva."

Helga Barthel? She didn't dare risk addressing the woman by name and just said, "I'm on my way. I just popped in to…"

"Get the laptop," the red-haired woman said with a sigh as she stood up. "I wondered why it was in Philip's room. I assume things were pretty fraught this morning. What was it all about?"

She just said, "Zurkeulen," and waited to see how the woman reacted to the name.

The woman rolled her eyes and gave a sigh of exasperation. "That guy's beginning to get on my nerves. He shouldn't get so worked up about a mere two hundred thousand. Others lost everything when the new market collapsed in 2001. Philip explained all that to him again yesterday afternoon."

As she finished, the woman went out of her room and across the lobby to a padded door. She followed slowly and asked, in as casual voice as possible, "Where's Philip just now?"

"If you hurry, you might just catch him," the woman said, continuing to speak from the other office. "He's gone down to Behringer's about a flat. He said it wouldn't take a minute. I hope he's right, he has to be in Düsseldorf at five." The woman returned with Nadia's computer bag and a small leather holder. "You'd left your office key here too."

She took them both and left, throwing a "See you" over her shoulder.

"When?" the woman called out as she disappeared.

"Tomorrow," she said, closing the door behind her. She slipped the leather holder into Nadia's handbag, hurried to the lift and went down to the underground garage. There was no point any more in going to see Reincke, she thought. It looked as if this time her distrust of Nadia had been unfounded. Presumably even a woman like Nadia had some kind of conscience. Or Philip Hardenberg had one and had made Nadia see reason.

On the autobahn her heart and stomach were already quivering with anticipation. As she turned into Marienweg everything swam before her eyes for a moment. The Koglers' front garden was empty. The old Ford Fiesta was standing in the Blastings' drive again, it probably belonged to a cleaning woman. Behind Eleanor Ravatzky's wrought-iron gate a boy of about ten was romping around on the lawn with the shaggy dog. There was a van with the name of a garden centre parked in the road outside Niedenhoff's house. A man in blue overalls was raking the last of the leaves off the lawn. With him was a man with dark hair, presumably Niedenhoff. He waved as she drove past. She returned his wave and drove the Alfa into the garage. The laptop, the envelope and the imitation-leather holder with the keys to her flat she left in the boot.

From the moment she went into the hall and switched off the alarm, it was like coming home. She went up to the study. She did feel a little shabby when she opened the desk drawer where she'd found the

Dictaphone in September. It was still there. However, the revealing tape and been recorded over and the singed and smeared letter to *Jacques, mon chéri*, had disappeared from the cupboard in the television room. Well, if Michael had become suspicious Nadia would have had to clear some things away.

The handset on the table had been disconnected, the answerphone switched on. She rang the shop from the bedroom and told Frau Schädlich her mother hadn't come round from the anaesthetic yet. That meant she wouldn't be able to get back to the shop that day.

"That's what I thought would happen," said Frau Schädlich. "Do you think you'll be able to come in tomorrow? You know what it's like on Fridays."

"Of course," she said. "I'll definitely come in tomorrow."

Then she went down to the larder to get herself a late lunch. In a fit of nostalgia she decided on pork escalope with mushrooms, onions, asparagus and green beans. Standing in the kitchen, she almost expected Joachim Kogler to appear. He didn't, of course. The aromas rising from the frying pan made her realize how hungry she was and she wolfed the meal down, treating herself to a huge helping of chocolate-chip ice cream from the freezer for dessert and following it up with a strong coffee. Shortly before five the kitchen was clean and tidy again.

As she cleaned her teeth, she wondered whether to ring the lab and ask Michael when he was coming home. Just the thought of seeing him again gave her palpitations. If she had a rough idea of when to expect him, she could prepare herself better, she thought, so she went back upstairs and dialled through to extension thirty-eight.

The phone rang twice, then it was picked up and a fraught female voice immediately launched into a moan: "Where have you been? The shredder's running at two hundred and twenty. I need you here. At once."

"Good afternoon," she said in friendly tones. "Nadia Trenkler here. I'd like to speak to my husband."

"So would I," the woman replied. "But he's still in a meeting."

"Perhaps you could tell me whether he's likely to be back late this evening."

"Later than late. We've got huge problems with one of the subjects. He'll have to deal with it himself."

"Aha," she said, "thanks. At least I know what the situation is."

It sounded as if something technical had broken down or was about to give up the ghost again. She'd have expected to see a shredder on a trailer from a garden centre, like the one outside Niedenhoff's house, but then, who knew what they got up to in laboratories?

She replaced the receiver, went downstairs, tinkled away on the piano for a while and wandered round the works of art, trying to identify the Beckmann. The signatures on most of the pictures were illegible. Only on the black-and-gold monstrosity over the three-piece suite she thought she could decipher the name Georg Maiwald. She remembered Michael saying something about supporting young artists and he'd used the word "daubs". He seemed to have the same taste in art as she did – and not only in art.

It was already dark outside when she fetched a towel and went down into the basement. At the back of her mind was Nadia's comment that he was in a league of his own in the pool. Of course she didn't intend to find out for herself, certainly not that evening. Perhaps later on, after she'd had the child – and some swimming lessons. She got undressed and sat on the edge of the pool, dangling her legs in the water. After a while she let herself cautiously down into the water, holding on to the side with both hands until she felt her toes touch the bottom. The water came up to her throat and was unpleasantly cool. Shivering and summoning up all her courage, she let go and waved her arms around like a swimmer. She didn't move from the spot.

Around eight she tried ringing the lab again. No one answered. That suggested to her that Michael was on his way home, so she started preparing a further large meal and set the table in the dining room for two. Nadia had talked about things being tense between them, but on the Sunday in August, when she'd had her practice run as stand-in, he'd been perfectly agreeable after having had "one hell of a row" with Nadia.

By nine the food was getting burned. She ate alone and decided to have soused herrings in cream sauce for dessert. Then she treated herself to another helping of the ice cream followed by an espresso. She didn't want to be fast asleep and miss him when he came home. At ten she settled down in front of the TV, leaving the door out onto the landing open. She also had another espresso, but despite that she

171

gradually found herself slipping down on the couch. That Thursday had been – after an almost sleepless night – a long, hectic and stressful day. Eventually she stretched out and let herself slide gently into a restful slumber.

Eleven o'clock passed, twelve o'clock passed and the light slumber became a deep sleep. She hadn't put the light on. The room was filled with the grey-blue flicker of the rapidly changing scenes on the screen. By now it was a gory horror film, mostly set in a nocturnal graveyard. Other sounds mingled with the panting and slurping of the monsters and the screams of their tormented victims. She registered them unconsciously, but they fitted in so well with the general background noise that they didn't bring her back to the surface.

The metallic click of the central locking as the alarm was switched on could have been the breaking of bones, the whirring of the shutters sounded almost the same as the shuffling of the undead, the steps on the stairs echoed those coming from the television. A movement sensor activated the landing light. Through the open door it shone on her face, disturbing her even behind closed lids. At the same time a woman on the television shrieked, begging for her life. All at once she was wide awake again, blinked blearily and saw that the light was on.

"Michael?" she called. There was no answer. She sat up and listened. Nothing could be heard apart from the nerve-shattering noise from the TV. She switched it off. Everything was quiet. The light on the landing went off again and the room sank back into darkness. She had the sour taste of sleep in her mouth. "Michael?" she called out again.

Again no answer. Nor were any other sounds to be heard. With a deep sigh she pushed herself up and felt her way to the door. Immediately the landing light went on again. The bedroom door was open but it was dark inside. And quiet! Everywhere was quiet. And since she didn't know what had woken her, she came to the conclusion that she was alone in the house. There could be a thousand technical explanations for the light going on.

She went down the stairs, saying a few words to her baby on the way, and drank half a glass of mineral water in the kitchen, to wash the sour taste out of her mouth. And then back up. Now there was a faint light coming from the bedroom.

"Michael?" she called out again.

There was no answer this time either. Slowly she went to the door. The light in the bedroom wasn't on, it came from the bathroom. Damn, she thought, he's in a huff. In a real huff.

He was naked, cleaning his teeth at one of the washbasins. He didn't deign even to glance at her although she stood, motionless, in the doorway for at least a minute, looking at him and trying to control the turmoil inside her. Finally he switched off his toothbrush, walked up to her and past her as if she wasn't there, and got into bed, throwing back the cover from his half of the bed alone.

"Why won't you answer?" she asked.

No reaction. He went into the dressing room. She followed him and watched as he took his clothes and alarm clock out of the wardrobe drawers. Ignoring her completely, he went back into the bedroom and took the things into the bathroom. Again she followed him. He put the alarm clock on the shelf and went back into the bedroom. Only when he got to the bed did he turn round and ask, "Why did you ring?"

"I wanted to know when you were coming home. Didn't they tell you?"

He sat down on the bed. "Yes, they did. It's just that I couldn't believe you really meant it. I thought there must be some special reason. Perhaps the house had burned down or you'd run out of petrol."

It didn't sound as if he thought Nadia was being unfaithful, more as if he were afraid she'd started drinking again. "Didn't you manage to sort out the problem with the shredder?" she asked cautiously. "You sound as if you're in a bad mood."

He gave a hoarse laugh. "Oh, you noticed? Remind me to ring the date in the diary." Then he lay down, pulled up the blanket and said, "If you feel like a chat, call Philip, I'm too tired."

He quickly fell asleep. She was lying only a couple of inches away from him, but she might just as well have been on the moon. Twice she felt she couldn't stand being so close to him like that, crept downstairs, stood there in the kitchen for a while, drank some more mineral water, swallowed a few tears as well, promised her child everything would turn out fine, then climbed back into bed beside him.

It wasn't until about five that she fell into a light, restless sleep. And just one hour later it was all over again. The covers were thrown back beside her, waking her up. A soft, regular buzzing was coming through the open door to the bathroom. He went in, naked as he was. The buzzing stopped. She got up as well and followed him. He was already in the shower. Through the glass door he looked like a ghost.

Despite his frosty behaviour, she felt the need to touch him, if only just for a second, as a parting gesture.

It was to be a parting – for many months. However hard Philip Hardenberg might push for her to act as stand-in during the next few weeks, Nadia wouldn't allow it. When they had more time than yesterday, Nadia would check whether there were any give-away signs yet. And Nadia would realize that now there was a big difference, a whole cup size difference. At that moment she didn't care if he noticed.

Her feet took her automatically to the shower. Her hands slid the door open. He responded with an irritated look and a dismissive, "You needn't bother, I don't feel like morning exercises."

At that moment the sickness hit her, a hot wave surging up into her throat. She just managed to get to the lavatory in time. He watched, dumbfounded, through the open shower door as she went down on her knees, heaving and retching until her stomach had been emptied of the last bits of ice cream and soused herring.

"Too much to drink again?" he asked when she finally straightened up. It sounded cold, as if the question had been asked too many times.

She stood up, staggered over to one of the washbasins and rinsed her mouth out. Her stomach was still sending up little waves of nausea.

"It's no use denying it," he said as he rubbed himself dry. "You went down twice. I did notice."

"I only had some water to drink," she said.

"Of course," he said. "That's why you were puking your guts out. Take an aspirin, it's good for a hangover."

"I haven't got a hangover," she said.

"You haven't?" he asked in astonishment. "Then why have my soused herrings disappeared from the fridge?"

She preferred not to explain that. Instead she said, "I've got to go out soon and there's something I want to tell you first."

He went over to the other washbasin, took an electric shaver out of the cupboard and grimaced. In the mirror it looked almost like a smile. "Go ahead," he said magnanimously, "I'm all ears. I can spare you five minutes."

He switched the shaver on and ran it over his cheeks and chin. The buzzing grated on her nerves. And his attitude, his icy coldness! She shook her head. "I can't. Not when you're like that."

His eyes were on her in the mirror. Again he twisted his mouth in the grimace that was almost a smile and seemed to express hurt, carrying on shaving all the while. "But I can, you think, whatever you're like." At last he switched the shaver off and put it back in the cupboard, turned round and looked her straight in the eye. "I'm sorry if I can't fulfil your expectations. I know you imagine that with all the money you invested in me you'd got someone who'd be at your beck and call day and night. But, damn it all, I'm not a robot you can switch on or off whenever you happen to feel like it." As he finished he was already heading for the door.

"I love you," she mumbled.

He stopped and turned round. "What did you say? I didn't hear it properly."

"I love you," she repeated, louder this time. "I shouldn't say it, I'm only hurting myself. But I want you to know that, even if my feelings don't count for you."

He took a deep breath, keeping his eyes fixed on her. "So you have noticed. To be honest, it surprises me. But you're right, at the moment there are at least a dozen things I can think of that are considerably more important to me than your idea of love."

He shrugged his shoulders and grimaced, as if to excuse his lack of interest. Then he went on, speaking slowly and deliberately, "On the other hand, if making that admission hurts you, then perhaps a discussion to clear the air wouldn't be a complete waste of time. Only unfortunately we'll have to put it off to another day. '

His sarcastic tone helped her a little to deal with the turmoil inside. He wasn't seeing her, he was seeing Nadia, and what he said was directed at Nadia alone. In September it had been painful to realize that, now it was a comfort. She finally got into the shower. As she was about to close the glass door behind her, she saw him leaning against the doorframe, looking at her again with a long, searching look.

"Did you really mean it the way it sounded?" he asked, sounding himself almost the way he had the first time she'd acted as Nadia's stand-in. She just nodded. He sucked in his lower lip and waited a few seconds before saying, "I'll be pretty late today. As you heard, there was an emergency yesterday. We've got to start from scratch."

"What happened?" she asked.

He sighed. "One of our old friends. Comes straight from another series and gets the TA to give him a full dose, without saying a word. His blood pressure shot up, we thought he was going to die on us. If everything goes as planned today, I could get to Demetros's by nine. It could well be half-past, though."

"Doesn't matter," she said, already fighting back the tears and wishing he'd go. He seemed to be wondering whether to take her in his arms or not. But she was spared that. With a final nod he left the bathroom.

When she came down to the kitchen half an hour later, he'd already gone. On the table were the *Frankfurter Allgemeine Zeitung* and an unsealed, unaddressed envelope with two tickets for a concert by Niedenhoff. Attached by a paper clip was a note with greetings from Frederik covering the Christian name on the tickets. Assuming Niedenhoff was called Frederik, she took the envelope into the living room and put it on the piano. Then she made herself a coffee and some toast and ham. The only other thing in the fridge was a packet of cream cheese, in September it had been decidedly better filled. She didn't like cream cheese. She took two bites of the toast and drank half the cup of coffee. The knowledge that she had paved the way to a reconciliation with Michael for Nadia made it impossible for her to eat more. She didn't know if she'd be able to take it, if it was always going to be like this later on.

Before going out to the garage, she went to the larder and filled a plastic bag with two tins of chicken soup, two ready meals that didn't need to be kept refrigerated and the rest of the ham from the kitchen. Nadia could get herself some more if she felt like some for breakfast over the weekend. She put her envelope in the bag as well, so that Nadia wouldn't see it in the evening.

She couldn't stand it in the house any longer and got the Alfa out at half-past six. She was much too early for the shop and she would have had time to take the bag with the food and the envelope to her flat. But when that occurred to her she was already in a multi-storey car park close to the confectioner's and couldn't be bothered to go out again. She parked on the first floor – without a glance at the list of charges.

Frau Schädlich was surprised to see the elegant jacket and her new hairdo, but delighted to find her waiting at the door. "How's your mother?" she asked.

"Just a broken leg," she said. "But she was very confused from the anaesthetic and insisted I buy myself a new jacket and have my hair done."

"It's not something to be taken lightly," Frau Schädlich said earnestly. "If she needed anaesthetic it can't have been a simple fracture." She went on about osteoporosis and saw her fears confirmed when, shortly after twelve, she called from the office, "Quick, Frau Lasko. I think it's the nurse again. I couldn't understand properly, it's a bad line."

As Frau Schädlich had said, it was a terrible line. Nadia's words were distorted and truncated by crackling and hissing. She sounded tense and stressed out. First of all she asked if there had been any problems with Michael. With Frau Schädlich listening in the background, she decided it was best to stick to a simple no. The manageress, presumably thinking she was refusing to leave the shop again to go and be with her mother, said, "It would be very inconvenient today, but as I said before, it's not something to be taken lightly. With old people broken bones can be disastrous."

She could hardly understand anything at all of what Nadia was saying while Frau Schädlich was speaking. "…won't get back until…" The time was swallowed up in loud crackling. "…stay… your best… I'll make sure… punctual." Then the line went dead. She said, "Hello?" several times, then put the receiver down and waited to see if Nadia would try again, but the telephone didn't ring. Probably the battery in her mobile had run out.

Frau Schädlich asked if she wanted to ring back. She said, no, it was just a friend who was offering to lend her her car so she could pay her mother a quick visit in the evening.

As she had told Nadia she would, she left the shop a few minutes after seven. In the multi-storey she discovered that her ten euros were not enough to pay for the Alfa. She offered the young man at the exit one of Nadia's credit cards, but he wouldn't accept it, directing her instead to a nearby cash dispenser, which she could have used – if she'd known Nadia's PIN number.

There was nothing for it but to take the bus to her flat, praying the Jasmin Toppler would be at home. She was relieved to see her neighbour's motorbike parked outside. Jasmin accepted her story of a friend's car that had been left an hour too long in the car park and was ready to help her out with twenty euros. She even gave her a lift back to the multi-storey, but she'd still lost a lot of time and it was half past nine when she turned off on the airport approach road and headed for the agreed meeting place.

She'd counted on finding Nadia waiting by the entrance, but no one could be seen in the headlights. She drove round slowly once, twice, three times. Even after the fourth circuit no one appeared waving furiously. It wasn't surprising. It was terribly cold and drizzling, and Nadia had only been wearing her trouser suit. Her flight bag couldn't have held much more than a clean blouse, a pair of stockings, some underwear and make-up. Nadia was not the kind of woman to spend a long time standing outside in those conditions.

She headed for the airport buildings, mentally preparing herself for the reproaches that were bound to come. Though after such a mangled telephone message she didn't need an excuse. Moreover it had sounded as if Nadia was coming on a later flight. Before doing anything else, she checked one coffee bar after another and walked all round the extensive terminal before finally asking the woman at the information stand to put out a call for her friend.

Within seconds "Will Frau Nadia Trenkler please come to the Information Desk, where someone is waiting for her," echoed round the building. It was repeated two more times. She thanked the woman, wandered away a few steps and waited. Five minutes – ten minutes – a quarter of an hour. Nadia didn't come. She went over to the Swissair desk. There was no one there, but from the display with the arrival times of the remaining flights she could see that no more planes from Geneva were expected that evening.

By this time it was already past eleven o'clock. She tried to ring Nadia on her mobile, but all she got was a polite, "At the moment the person you are calling is not available." Had Nadia followed her suggestion and taken a taxi? Was she home by now? But what if she wasn't? What if she'd said she couldn't get back until the next day? That until then she'd have to stay in the house and make the best of it?

That meant she had to see if Nadia was at home. She dialled the number, unsure what to do if it was Michael who answered. The receiver was lifted immediately it rang. And before she could say anything, he bellowed, "If you say you're sorry, I'll change the code." He had clearly assumed it couldn't be anyone else ringing up apart from Nadia and without pausing he thundered on, "I've been waiting more than an hour."

"I am sorry," she whispered, "really sorry. I've been held up." That did nothing to calm him.

"You don't say. And I suppose you didn't have a couple of minutes to ring and tell me?"

"There wasn't a phone nearby," she explained, "and there's something wrong with the mobile. Didn't I tell you?"

"No." He sounded a little calmer but by no means placated. "If I remember rightly, your mobile telephone was not one of the things we discussed this morning. I've spent the whole day under the illusion we were going to meet at Demetros's at nine. I even managed to be on time. Then I just sat there, feeling like an idiot."

Demetros's! It sounded as if it was a restaurant. After the streamer and the shredder and the subject who'd got the TA to give him a full dose she'd assumed it was something to do with the lab.

"Oh, what's the point," Michael went on. "I've had plenty of practice. After all, it wasn't the first time. But it's definitely going to be the last." There was a brief pause, during which he let out a deep breath. Only then did he ask, "Where are you, anyway?"

"On my way home," she said and quickly hung up.

There was no cause for concern. Presumably Zurkeulen had taken up more time than Nadia had allowed for. It was obvious that after his loss with Joko Electronics he would want a detailed explanation of which firms Nadia was proposing to invest his money in so that he didn't get caught again. Her only fear as she drove back was that Michael would launch into a lengthy diatribe and that the only answer Nadia had supplied her with would make him see red.

He was waiting in the hall. He'd presumably heard the garage door and come to be there as soon as she appeared. Hardly had she opened the door than he grabbed her by the arm and pulled her to him. A fraction of a second later his mouth was pressed to hers. Taken completely by surprise, she opened her lips for him. It was an extremely violent, almost brutal kiss. He put his hands round her neck so she couldn't evade it. As abruptly as he'd pulled her to him, he pushed her back and said, "You're in luck! And now I'd like to know where you've been."

Her bottom lip was throbbing. She licked it with the tip of her tongue and felt a swelling. Being breathalysed by Wolfgang Blasting would surely have been less rough.

Michael went to the kitchen, stopped in the doorway and turned round. "I'm waiting, Nadia. Where have you been?"

"I had a late appointment."

He leaned against the door frame, a derisive grin on his face. "So why didn't you order your Frau Barthel to ring me up and tell me?"

"It didn't occur to me."

"Fortunately it did occur to me." By now his grin was turning nasty. "And I'll give you three guesses what dear Helga told me."

His anger was setting her nerves on edge. Hesitantly she walked past him to the fridge and took out the bottle of mineral water, not daring to look at him. He was standing there like a wild beast ready to pounce. Any moment, she felt, he might resort to violence.

"She told me you flew to Geneva yesterday," he said. "And intended coming back today."

The kitchen floor suddenly started to sway. The bottle of water fell out of her hands and smashed with a loud clatter. She held on to the worktop with both hands to stop herself falling into the puddle and the broken glass. "Helga misunderstood," she said. "Philip had to go to Geneva. He asked me if I could do it, but I refused."

"I don't think Helga misunderstood anything," he said. "It's about time you thought up a better excuse for her. I've had just about enough of Geneva. Let's review the facts: on 18 September your mother had a heart attack. Philip was good enough to inform me because of course you'd left immediately and didn't have time to tell me personally. As it turned out, your mother was fit as a fiddle. You should have known I'd ring her."

Despite the terrible situation, it was a relief to hear him confirm Nadia's explanation. Gradually the kitchen stopped swaying. When she remained silent, he listed further excuses Nadia must have made for her excursions with Philip Hardenberg. Repeated visits to her parents in Geneva, sometimes using her mother as a pretext, sometimes her father. It sounded as if Nadia's parents lived apart. "Does anything strike you?" Michael concluded. "It happens every two weeks. It's a well-known fact that alcoholics need regular binges. Helga probably assumed you'd be incapable of driving yesterday evening."

She felt able to let go of the worktop, though not to bend down and pick up the broken glass. She went to the door – it was like walking on cotton wool – and tried to get past him. He grasped her shoulder and held her there. Her fear that he might hit her had gone. "Let go of me," she demanded. "I'm going to bed."

"You can go to bed when I know what's going on. You're hitting the bottle again. Don't think I can't tell when you've been drinking elsewhere. You must imagine I really am stupid. Why d'you do it, for God's sake? Just because I won't dance to your tune?"

"Michael, please, I haven't been drinking. I've had an exhausting day. And I have to go out early tomorrow as well."

"Tomorrow's Saturday," he pointed out.

"I know, but Philip asked me —"

At the name it was as if he'd been struck by a whip. He let go, turned on his heel and went up the stairs. When she went up, a little later on, all the doors were closed. Not a sound was to be heard. He wasn't in the bedroom, nor in the bathroom. She spent minutes looking in vain for his alarm clock and checking the two guest rooms. Then she opened the door of the television room. He was stretched out on the couch, wearing a headset, his eyes closed. Apprehensively she touched his shoulder. He opened his eyes.

"I need the alarm clock," she said.

He pointed at his ears to indicate he hadn't understood a word.

"I need the alarm clock," she said, louder this time and slightly angry. It was a stupid situation. Nadia would be sure to know where the bloody alarm clock was kept. It would be silly if such a minor matter should arouse his suspicions. Finally he took the piece out of his left ear. Rock music blared. "Did you say something?" he shouted.

She shouted too. "I can't find the alarm clock!"

He grinned. "Set your internal clock. I'm free tomorrow and I don't want to be woken early."

One pitfall avoided! He must have hidden the alarm clock. It seemed a futile, almost childish response and immediately mollified her. It wasn't really him she was angry with anyway. "Please, Michael, I have to get up at six. It's important for me."

"Not for me," he said. "Call Philip, get him to wake you. I'm sure he'll be happy to." He popped the earpiece back in and closed his eyes again.

For a couple of seconds she stood there looking down at him with a mixture of understanding, love and frustration. In bed she pulled the covers right up and still shivered. At two she got up – the bed beside her was empty. She went to see what he was doing.

A broad strip of light from the hall fell on the couch revealing a picture of peace. The stereo was switched off, the headset was on the floor. He was lying on his side, face to the door and so fast asleep not even the light disturbed him. She closed the door quietly, tiptoed back to the bed and dialled Nadia's mobile. Again the female voice said, "The person you are calling is not available at the moment."

In the morning she stayed in bed until half-past five, then went to have a shower, tired, almost shattered. She took some clean clothes from Nadia's wardrobe, though she couldn't change the bra. While the coffee was percolating and she was clearing up the broken glass and the puddle, she heard his footsteps on the stairs. He appeared in the hall and approached slowly.

"So it was you I heard. Your internal clock did work after all." He pointed to the percolator. "Is there a drop for me in there?"

She just said, "Help yourself."

He strolled over to the cupboard, took out a cup and filled it. "When do you think you'll be back?"

She shrugged her shoulders.

"Come on," he coaxed, "surely you can give me a vague idea. About lunchtime, this evening, around midnight. I'm just asking so I'll know how to organize my day."

"I really can't say."

"Pity," he said. "But then I could go to Munich for the weekend, cheer up the plebs. What d'you think? Should I go, or is there a chance we might sort one or two things out between us in the next couple of days?"

"That's hardly likely," she said. "And I'm sure your parents will be delighted to see you. Give them my best wishes. Paul, Sophie and Ralph too."

"I will do so," he promised. "So we'll see each other on Monday or Tuesday or some time in the course of the next week. It isn't urgent."

Another parting. She found it easier than the one on Friday morning. Just before seven she went to the garage, still convinced Nadia would call her at the shop in the next few hours to arrange a rendezvous for the afternoon.

The telephone in the office rang five times in the course of the morning. Frau Schädlich answered and had a personal or business conversation, but towards midday she noticed her increasing nervousness and asked if she'd like to ring the old folks' home. Taking care to use her body to hide the phone from Frau Schädlich's sharp eye, she dialled Nadia's mobile, gave her name and asked how her mother was, covering the polite monotone of the female voice.

A violent dizzy spell forced her to sit down. Frau Schädlich watched, full of sympathy, as she haltingly thanked the recorded voice. "Don't let it worry you too much," she said, maintaining, contrary to what she'd said on Friday, that old people were tough. Then her expression became serious as she reminded her she was to see the doctor on Monday.

She left the shop with her colleagues shortly after closing time. The Alfa was parked some two hundred yards away among other cars at the side of the road. Frau Gathmann saw her get in, but she didn't let that bother her. She couldn't find anywhere to park in Kettlerstrasse, so she drove round the corner, parked by the telephone box and walked back.

Unusually, Heller wasn't leaning out of the window and didn't appear as she went up the stairs. He'd be in the pub. Some children seemed to have used his absence to play a trick on him, sticking transfers on his door and over the lock.

She noticed them as she went past, but didn't give them a closer look, her mind being occupied with Nadia. She waited until the early evening for the taxi that would bring her to collect the Alfa. She passed the time by giving the flat a thorough clean. By half-past six there wasn't a hair, a speck of dust or a piece of fluff anywhere. She couldn't think of anything else she could do and she couldn't stand the waiting any longer. Taking her jacket and handbag, she went out to phone Philip Hardenberg. He would surely know where Nadia was and when she would be back. She hoped she'd find his home number in the telephone directory, she even had enough change to ask directory enquiries. All that was left in the telephone box, however, was a dangling piece of cord.

It seemed pointless to go back to her flat. There was a telephone in the house and Hardenberg's home number on the computer. At least she hoped the index card she'd deleted so quickly in September would have that information. If Michael had actually gone to Munich, Nadia could come back any time during the weekend. Knowing the house would probably be empty calmed her nerves a little.

When the garage door slid up to reveal an empty space, she heaved a sigh of relief. She switched off the alarm in the hall and ran up the stairs two at a time. Hardly had she sat down at the desk than all the lights on the computer were glowing. A few words glided across the screen, then the picture came to a standstill with the instruction: Enter password.

Hurriedly she typed in "Arosa" and pressed Enter. Nothing happened. She tried twice more, after that every time she pressed a key there was an unpleasant bleep. Nadia must have changed her password. Without thinking, she picked up the telephone. The extension on the desk was connected, Michael must have plugged it in. She dialled directory enquiries and requested Philip Hardenberg's number. She was asked where he lived, she assumed it was in the city. After a few seconds the operator said that she was sorry but the number was ex-directory. Her request for Helga Barthel's number met with the same result.

She was hungry and exhausted. She'd hardly had anything to eat all day and felt she couldn't think straight on a rumbling stomach, so she made herself two pieces of toast. She had to go into the garage to get the ham from the boot – and there she saw the laptop. Two minutes later she had it in front of her on the kitchen table and switched it on. All she got on that one too was an unpleasant bleeping, the screen flickered and went dark again. She swore angrily. Out of the corner of her eye she saw the monitor above the refrigerator flicker on. The screen showed the usual section of road, the front garden and the paved path to the front door.

A woman was approaching – on extremely high-heeled shoes, which gave her a stork-like gait. To go with the uncomfortable shoes, she was wearing a ridiculously garish trouser suit made from some floppy material, which hung loose round her figure like a parachute. Her face grew larger and slightly distorted by the lens as she came to the door and set off a brief barking in the hall. Lilo had come to see her – straight from a surprise party, to judge by her dress.

The visit was really no laughing matter, but she couldn't repress a grin. She definitely wasn't going to go to the door. Lilo seemed to suspect that and went round to the kitchen window. When she saw her sitting at the table, she knocked on the window to announce her presence, then reappeared on the screen. After three or four seconds the slightly squashed face on the monitor made a grimace of frustration followed by continuous growling and barking from the hall. With a long sigh she got up and went to the door. She'd got on well with Joachim Kogler, if things didn't work out with his wife, that was Nadia's problem.

Lilo greeted her with a caustic, "I'll never get used to that nonsense." She presumably meant the dog.

She grinned wearily. "I'd have preferred a crocodile, but Michael wants to keep the pool for himself."

Ignoring her joke, Lilo said, "I was here earlier, around lunchtime. There appeared to be no one in." It sounded as if she was implying that there had been someone in the house only they'd not answered the door.

"I had some appointments. And Michael's gone to Munich."

For whatever reason, this remark had Lilo positively oozing pity. "Oh, you poor thing. Jo told me, but I couldn't believe it." Then she beamed. "But that fits in perfectly. We've got a few old friends round. They'll take your mind off things."

"Don't think I wouldn't love to come," she said, "but I've got a pile of stuff to do."

"I won't take no for an answer," said Lilo in severe tones before announcing, with a roguish smile, "Henseler's there, Barlinkow's there, Hannah's there and *Georges* is bound to arrive any minute." She put such a heavy stress on the last name, that it looked as if she was about to burst with enthusiasm.

She tried again. "I'm really sorry —"

"A change is as good as a rest," Lilo broke in determinedly, "and that's what you need." She looked her up and down. She was still wearing the trouser suit she'd taken out of Nadia's wardrobe in the morning. The blouse and trousers were crumpled. "Get changed and come over."

"I really can't," she said, emphasizing every word. "I've a problem with the computer and I have to —"

Once more Lilo didn't let her finish. "Nonsense. Jo'll see to that tomorrow. You're going to put all these problems out of your mind, have a nice hot shower, put on something pretty – and a bit of rouge, you really do look pale. Then we'll have a lovely evening. We've got a surprise for you." Before she could refuse again, Lilo had stalked off back to the neighbouring house on her high heels.

She closed the front door, took the useless laptop and its case upstairs and dumped it on the desk. If Joachim Kogler could see to the large computer in the morning... a man who could transform a house into an electronic mantrap would surely be able to get round a password and conjure up an index card with a telephone number on the screen. Barlinkow, she thought, Henseler, Hannah and *Georges*. In her mind she could hear Nadia saying, "Do your best." What else could she do?

The shower pepped her up a bit. Make-up concealed the tiredness in her face. Then she had a look at the party dresses in the dressing room. There were a few formal gowns – presumably for the opera – and a few striking ensembles. She decided on a lime-green outfit, loose-fitting like Lilo's trouser suit. Armed with half a dozen fictitious but amusing episodes from the life of an independent investment adviser, she went out, with only the keyring in her hand.

There were seven cars parked out in the road, so it didn't look as if there'd be too many people. Wolfgang Blasting opened the door and, instead of a greeting said, "I've already heard Doc's in Munich. Word's got round that he didn't like the beach hut either. He talks too much, if you ask me." When she didn't reply, he jerked his head towards the interior. "Come in and vent your spleen on the rest of the assembled company."

He stood aside to let her past into the brightly lighted hall with a wide-open double door opposite. One look through the door and she felt like turning on her heel and going straight back. A motley crowd filled the Koglers' living room. Lilo's "few old friends" came to at least three dozen, of whom she only recognized four.

A little white-haired man extricated himself from the crowd and came towards her with outstretched arms and a warm smile. With a "How delightful!" he raised her hands to his lips and placed a kiss on both. He had a Slavic accent. Barlinkow? Joachim Kogler released her before it could become embarrassing.

Lilo had already told him about her computer problem and he wanted to know all the details, especially whether the security system had been compromised or whether it might simply be a joke Michael was playing on her. Then he destroyed her hopes of seeing an index card with Hardenberg's number. "I'll be happy to have a look at it, but if there really is a problem with the password, you'll have to insert a jumper."

"I thought that might be the case," she said.

Whatever else she had thought might be the case vanished in the hubbub. Her fears regarding all the unknown people turned out to be unfounded, there would probably have been more complications had it been a small group. In larger numbers no one was interested in the anecdotes she'd prepared or anything else. There were a few little scattered clusters talking about Cubism or Dali's love life, but most had gathered round a young man who was enthusing about Julia's symphonies of colour.

She did a circuit of the room, returning a smile here and a "Hello" there, then withdrew to an unoccupied spot beside the doors onto the patio, where she almost fell asleep on her feet.

About ten minutes later a man in his mid-fifties and a grey-and-black-striped silk suit came over and started talking about the increased value of the Beckmann. Without having to contribute to the conversation, she learned that she wouldn't find the Beckmann in the house any more. It had been bought in the spring as a present for a dear friend. Now *mon chéri Jacques* was enjoying it. After that had been dealt with, he realized she hadn't got a drink. When he brought her a glass of orange juice, which gave her something to hold on to, she decided to think of him as Henseler. Lilo called him Edgar.

For a while she wondered about *mon chéri* Jacques. The recipient of an expensive present as recently as the spring. There must have been a reconciliation. How was it that Nadia was still with Michael? And why was she carrying on with fat Hardenberg?

Wolfgang Blasting also ventured to approach her. Twice. The first time he offered her an olive branch. When she rejected it, he raised a mocking eyebrow. "Withdrawal problems again, eh? That explains a lot." The second time he brought her a plate filled with food from the buffet, which had already been fairly thoroughly plundered. He praised the Waldorf salad. "Ilona brought some from Carlo's recently, but it wasn't half as good."

Somehow – via Carlo's, the Waldorf salad and Ilona's new preference for vegetarian food – he got onto his own profession. She didn't notice the change, her thoughts were still with Jacques and Philip, until Blasting mentioned a serious road accident in which "friend Arnim" had been killed.

"Terrible," she murmured.

Blasting grinned and asked whether she intended to continue warming up her vitamin ration much longer or whether he should get her a proper drink. She just nodded. He swapped the orange juice for a glass of champagne, telling her she'd earned it and Doc wasn't around anyway. Then he went on about "friend Arnim" again.

She was too exhausted to concentrate on his story. It wasn't anything to do with her anyway. Nadia would presumably know who the unfortunate Arnim was. It made her feel uncomfortable, as did the way Blasting spoke to her, much too close, his mouth right by her ear, as if he was going to nibble it. She wished his wife would glance their way and call him off.

Ilona was ten or twelve feet away, with the group gathered round the young man, listening to his effusions on Julia's colours, a malicious smile on her face. At some point the young man – it must have been *Georges* – had insisted Julia be invited over. Lilo told Jo to ring Julia. Jo asked whether Julia was on fifteen or seventeen and, once he had been told, hurried off to the telephone.

"Are you actually listening to me?" Wolfgang Blasting asked.

"Of course," she said, her eyes and ears on Joachim Kogler in the hall. The telephone there was the same model as the one in the study. She saw that Joachim Kogler pressed one of the buttons at the bottom then just two numbers. Speed dialling! At once she was wide awake and all attention. She heard Blasting say, "I didn't expect you to jump for joy. Respect for the dead and all that, but I did think it would cheer you up a bit."

"Oh, but it has," she assured him, "it really has. I think I'll go and get myself something to eat."

He shook his head. "You really are a one-off. Where are you with your thoughts? The Bahamas? Munich? Surely you can manage one weekend without your stud? Let him have his bit of fun. Two days fraternizing with the plebs and Doc'll soon remember what he has in you."

Your stud! Revolting. Wolfgang Blasting was no better than Heller and he just refused to be shaken off. He followed her to the remains of the buffet with his empty plate, noted with relief that all the Waldorf salad had gone, checked with a quick glance that his wife wasn't watching and grabbed a piece of pork fillet.

Then he came back to the terrible road accident. "It didn't have to end like that but, as I said, he'd seen the lads were after him and went into the lorry at a hundred and twenty. He was squashed flat. The only thing that survived was his briefcase. There were no revealing documents, of course, just envelopes with numbers."

"It never does to build up your hopes too much," she said, taking a sip of champagne and adding a piece of pork fillet, some cheese, bread and a few grapes to her plate.

Lighting a cigarette, Wolfgang Blasting explained, "He must have been to see five clients that evening, he had twenty thousand on him. The lads were quite surprised."

"I can imagine," she said.

He gave a mocking smile. "With the sums you're used to dealing with I'd expected more. Röhrler was just a little fish. But how did you know he'd changed sides? Have you seen him recently?"

She thought she was hearing things. Röhrler? He couldn't mean the young man who'd got her last employer to fire her in January. Blasting kept his eyes fixed on her face, waiting for an answer. But before he could pressurize her, Lilo appeared, asking in dulcet tones, "Did I promise too much, darling?"

"Looks like it," said Blasting. "Röhrler's horrible demise didn't even wring a tired grin from her."

Lilo gave her an expectant smile. "A hammer blow, isn't it?" She did, indeed, feel something like a little hammer inside her head, felt the blood draining from her brain. She needed a chair, she had to sit down! Of course it was the Röhrler who'd collected the envelopes with undeclared earnings from Herr Schrag. She'd told Nadia about him the first time they'd been for a walk in the woods. Nadia must have tipped off Blasting and now Röhrler had had a fatal accident!

"That miserable wretch," said Lilo, getting worked up. "Went round like justice personified and was the worst kind of lowlife himself."

"Well, not quite that bad," said Blasting, unmoved. "Röhrler was just a courier. He didn't try to rip off the bank, like you." He grinned at her. "There's one thing I never understood. Why didn't you do a bunk while the going was good? Hadn't you got enough? Or was it your love for Doc that kept you tied to home-sweet-home?"

She could hardly understand what he was saying. Inside her head was a confusion of whispering voices. Röhrler in Schrag's office asking, "What are you doing here? You've come down in the world and no mistake." Michael saying, "If you screw up again or make a hash of things with Hardenberg." Zurkeulen demanding his money back, the whole two hundred thousand. "Do a bunk" echoed round and round in her brain. Then everything suddenly went black. She wasn't even aware that she managed to produce a couple of reasonably comprehensible remarks.

When she woke from her faint, she was lying on a sofa in a strange room. On the wall immediately above her was a milling throng of grotesque faces, one above the other. In the first few seconds she had difficulty sorting out her senses. Her eyes ran over the colourful spectacle on the wall, but at the same time they were in the queue at the bank and on the black limousine parked in the street and at the airport with Nadia scurrying off. Her ears were trying to listen to Röhrler, Zurkeulen, Michael and Wolfgang Blasting all at the same time. And the little hammer had beaten her brain to a pulp. Do a bunk!

A woman was bending over her. She had seen her face earlier in the crowd. She was wearing an Indian sari and holding a phial under her nose which gave off a pungent stench. When she coughed and pushed the hand with the phial to one side, the woman turned to the door and announced, "She's still in the land of the living."

Lilo came hurrying in, bubbling over with concern and discreet reproaches because her blackout had brought her lovely evening to an abrupt end. It wasn't even twelve and most of the company had already left. Voices and noises from the hall signalled the departure of another group. Placing her hand on the back of her neck, the woman in the sari lifted up her head and poured some herbal infusion with a disgusting aftertaste down her throat. Ilona Blasting appeared in the doorway to tell everyone, "I got him at his brother's. He's on his way."

This was immediately followed by Joachim Kogler's voice. "What did you think you were doing, tanking her up like that."

"Now just a minute," Blasting replied. "I offered her a glass of champagne. She's grown-up enough to say no. Anyway she only took a sip."

"And you had to drag up the old stories to get her to take a proper swig," Kogler said.

Listening with interest, the woman in the sari drank the rest of the revolting infusion. Lilo took the cup from her and said, "Thanks, Hannah, you've been a great help. You'd better go and get your coat, your taxi should be arriving any minute." Hannah left the room, albeit reluctantly. Lilo sat down on the edge of the sofa and stroked her forehead. "How do you feel, darling?"

All that she could feel was a black hole in her brain with the voices echoing in the blackness. "The old stories are back on the agenda," Ilona Blasting asserted. You heard what she said."

"You keep out of this," said Joachim Kogler in a loud voice. "She was completely confused. And we all know who we have to thank for that. Your husband's methods are common knowledge round here."

"I'd keep quiet if I were you," Ilona Blasting countered. "Before you know it you could be suspected of conspiracy to —"

"What d'you mean?" Joachim Kogler broke in angrily. "Are you suggesting —"

Ilona Blasting interrupted in her turn. "I'm not suggesting anything, I'm stating facts. As long as you butter her up, you're allowed to have a finger in the pie. Wolfgang's made a few enquiries. The Deko Fund's all window dressing with nothing behind it, my dear. And two hundred are —"

Lilo shot up off the couch. "For your information, it was only fifty."

"That was Maiwald's share," Ilona countered. "Jo could very well imagine you'd be investing in art again and hang a few more symphonies on your walls. Michael said —"

"Say it's not true, Jo," Lilo demanded.

Joachim Kogler said nothing of the sort. Instead, he came into the room, asked if she felt better and helped her to sit up. She felt dreadful about being the cause of such a scene. In the hall Wolfgang Blasting said, "Come on, Ilona, we're leaving. Can't you keep your big mouth shut for once? Delightful evening as usual, Lilo."

Lilo accompanied the Blastings to the door, then came back, her eyes fixed on her husband. Her breast swelled as she took a deep breath, but before she could speak, Joachim said, "We'll talk later. Nadia needs rest."

"No!" Lilo folded her arms across her breast. "We'll sort this out while she's still here. Whether it was fifty or two hundred's a secondary matter.

What I want to know is where the money came from. I've heard what I've heard. And Michael said she was absolutely determined to buy the house over there. I don't want any nasty surprises."

"If you say one more word," Joachim Kogler replied, keeping his voice calm, "that's what you'll get on the spot. What's wrong with her wanting to buy a little house —"

"Little?" Lilo asked. "Michael was talking about several acres and their own beach, Have you any idea what something like that costs in the Bahamas? You can't pay for that out of petty cash."

"It was only a little beach," she murmured. "And the house wasn't very big. It was just a beach bungalow, very small and basic."

"That's OK, Nadia," Joachim Kogler said gently, helping her up off the sofa.

Jo, she thought. Not Joachim, he hates that. With one arm round her waist, he led her to the door, across the hall and out to Nadia's front door. The tingling of the cold night air was like a thousand needles on her face. She could still feel the weakness in her knees and the thump thump of the little hammer behind her forehead. Do a bunk! As Jo unlocked the door for her, she murmured, "What do I do now?"

"First of all have a good sleep," he advised her in fatherly tones. "Give me a quick ring when you wake and I'll come and we can talk. Don't do anything silly, promise me that."

She just nodded. He gave her an encouraging smile, put the bunch of keys in her hand and wished her good night.

It was like being in a trance, but she made it to the bathroom and was soon in bed. She heard Nadia make her generous offer, two thousand a month, a nice apartment, a great job with Hardenberg – and heard her own hysterical laughter. The next moment she was asleep.

It was daylight when she woke. Nadia's watch showed a few minutes to nine. She felt nauseous and dizzy. She staggered into the bathroom and then to the telephone in the study. Dialling 01 gave her the Alfo Investment answerphone together with a display of the complete number. 02 had two zeros in the prefix. A woman, oldish from her voice, answered, "We?" At least that's what it sounded like to her. Automatically she said, "Good morning. Excuse me for troubling you, but I urgently need to speak to Nadia —"

Hardly had she said the name than the woman launched into a long complaint – in French. She quickly rang off. 03 was the lab. 04 produced a number with the Munich prefix, as did 05. In both cases she replaced the receiver before anyone could answer.

At the sixth number the response was an answerphone with the same female voice as on the taped message for Alfo Investment. Helga Barthel. This time she just gave the number on the display and said, "We are unavailable at the moment, please —"

It was a quarter past nine, perhaps too early for a Sunday morning. She was about to ring off when the recorded message was interrupted with a distraught, "Philip?"

"Hi, Helga," she said, ready to hang up if anything awkward should crop up. "It's me, Nadia."

Immediately the words poured forth in relief. "Thank God for that! Why didn't you ring sooner? Why didn't you say anything on Thursday? Then it wouldn't have happened." Before she could ask what had happened, Helga Barthel apologized that through her ignorance Michael had been told about Geneva, going on to complain that no one ever told her what was really going on.

"That's OK," she said to stem the flow of words.

Helga Barthel calmed down a little. "Are you at home? Can you come over?"

"Unfortunately not," she said, "I'm still in Geneva. There's a small problem and I urgently need to ask Philip —"

"He said he had to go to Berlin," Helga Barthel broke in, before she could put her foot in it by saying something about the laptop malfunctioning and having forgotten Philip's home number which, as became clear from the further course of the conversation, would immediately have been recognized as wrong. When Helga went on, it became clear that it was Hardenberg's home number she'd called and that Helga and Philip, though not married, lived together. And Helga was terrified something might have happened to him.

From one moment to the next Helga sounded as if she was close to tears as she told her how Philip had taken her to her sister's on Friday because, he claimed, he had to fly to Berlin that evening. "I was supposed to spend the whole weekend there, but I'd forgotten my pills, so I took a taxi home, just before eleven. He was in the bath, white as a sheet. He'd been sick, had a cut on his face and bruised ribs. His story was that he'd had a fall at the airport and missed his flight."

"Which you didn't believe."

"No," Helga wailed. "There's trouble with Zurkeulen. Did the guy lose more than his investment in Joko Electronics? When he turned up here on Wednesday he said something about Lasko. That was all I heard. Is that the furniture company you checked before you went on holiday? They haven't gone bust, have they?"

"No," she said, shuddering at the memory of Zurkeulen's tight grip and his companion's lascivious grin. "I don't know what you heard on Wednesday, but Zurkeulen has nothing to do with Lasko. And anyway, I've sorted things out with him."

"I thought you were in Geneva," Helga said, uncomprehending.

"Yes. Zurkeulen's here too."

"Don't lie to me, Nadia," Helga wailed. "He was here, knocking at the door yesterday, together with the funny guy that always drives him. I didn't let them in, it was already past eleven and I was alone in the house. Philip left yesterday morning. He told me to go and stay with my sister but I refuse to be kept out of the way when there's something up."

"Yesterday was Saturday," she said. "It was Friday we were talking about. That was when I met Zurkeulen. He didn't say he was flying back."

"And why were you going on at each other like that on Thursday?" Helga wanted to know. "It was only that stupid laptop you were arguing about."

What Helga had said so far had done nothing to dispel her own fears. And the information she managed to elicit by means of carefully uncompleted sentences, soothing words and a stern "Now calm down and tell me things as they happened" made sense – highly alarming sense.

She learned that there must have been a violent argument between Nadia and Philip Hardenberg on Thursday afternoon. Helga hadn't really heard what it was about. Philip had clearly fobbed her off with prevarications and she would have liked her to tell her the real reason.

She also picked up that Philip had been doing anything but renting a spacious apartment for a mother-to-be at Behringer's on Thursday afternoon. Behringer had insured a few properties through Alfo Investment and had summoned Philip regarding a claim for damages.

She also learned that Philip had reacted in a very odd way when he'd returned from Düsseldorf on Thursday evening and Helga had told him Nadia had come back to the office to collect the laptop. When he heard that, Philip had rung Nadia. He'd sent Helga out of the room on some pretext but naturally she'd listened at the door and gathered that it was to do with Zurkeulen and that furniture firm – Lasko – which was clearly not in as good shape as Nadia had maintained.

Helga, suppressing the tears, begged her, "Nadia, tell me honestly, is there something fishy going on? Did you talk Zurkeulen into taking some dodgy shares? And it's Philip who has to face the music? I'm pretty sure it was Zurkeulen's thug who beat him up on Friday evening. And where is he now? I keep ringing him on his mobile but he doesn't answer."

"Don't let that worry you," she said, "those things are rubbish. Mine's given up the ghost too. He'll be in Berlin, like he said. Do you know when he's due back?"

"Tuesday morning," Helga sobbed. "He said. What if he doesn't come, Nadia? What do I do then? I'm not going to the office on Monday, I'm too scared."

The conversation was brought to an end by the dog in the hall when Jo appeared at half-past nine. She hadn't had breakfast, but she didn't feel like eating. The bruises on Philip Hardenberg's ribs and the cut across his face were a leaden weight on her stomach. Unlike Helga she wasn't just pretty sure but absolutely certain that Zurkeulen's thug had given Philip a going-over.

Jo insisted she get something inside her. He fetched a tin of tomato juice from the larder, seasoned it well with salt and pepper and whisked it up with a raw egg. She could have drunk it, if it hadn't been for the egg. Then he sat down opposite her at the kitchen table and waited for her to start. She desperately needed someone she could talk to and his fatherly concern made it extremely difficult to keep everything to herself. Even more so when she learned that she had already let out some things. Fortunately they were not too clear, but still clear enough to suggest to the whole neighbourhood, or at least that section of it gathered in the Koglers' living room, that fraud on the grand scale was being perpetrated at Alfo Investment. One of Hardenberg's clients, she'd said, had gone berserk and threatened her, even though she'd had nothing to do with the man personally. She'd only just managed to get away from him.

What she really wanted to do was to tell Jo the whole story then let him take her in his arms and reassure her. But he was the one who wanted reassurance. From her. He started talking about the Deko Fund. His hesitant, embarrassed tone made it clear he felt anything but comfortable.

"You don't need to worry," she said quietly. "It's not just window dressing with nothing behind it. Deko's our in-house abbreviation, that's why Wolfgang couldn't find out what there is to it. But it's OK."

Jo sketched a nod. "So what did I earn thirty points with? Even though I'm pretty ignorant about this business, you could at least try to explain it to me."

She stared at the glass with the cloudy red mixture and took a deep breath. At least she'd been trained in this field and even if she herself had never had much to do with investment advice, she did know how one could quickly lose or gain a lot of money. "Commodity futures. Mainly Indian cotton, tea and fuel oil."

"Fuel oil?" Jo asked, baffled.

"Yes. With commodity futures you have to have a mixture," she declared. "Cotton was a big risk, you never know what the weather's going to be like in India. But if that market had collapsed, I could have offset it with tea. You wouldn't have made much of a profit, but not much of a loss either. Oil was stable."

It might have been complete nonsense, but it sounded professional. Jo relaxed, even though he still looked slightly sceptical. "Have you the figures on the computer?"

"Yes," she said. "I can show you them all if we can get the thing going." It was obvious what she should show him, since his name was in the NTA file. Let him rack his brains over the rest himself.

He stood up. "Then let's get on with it."

There was nothing to show him. The computer didn't respond to Arosa and even Jo couldn't find a way of circumventing the password. Again he mentioned his suspicion that Michael might have been playing a trick on her and offered to have a serious talk with him. Given the way things were, it wasn't beyond the bounds of possibility that Michael had messed about with her computer, perhaps only the previous day, because he was angry she had to go to work.

She hung her head and mumbled, "Don't bother. I haven't been too well recently. I don't know if you've noticed, I've been doing the best

I can not to let it show." She heaved a long sigh as she stared at the darkened screen. "I suppose it's just possible I changed something myself and can't remember. I have had the odd drink now and then – but don't tell Michael."

Jo looked at her with an expression of pity and understanding and advised her again to insert a jumper. "Do it tomorrow. If you've inadvertently changed more than the password you could have problems with the system."

She hadn't the least idea what a jumper was. "I won't be able to manage it tomorrow," she said, hoping he might offer to do it.

But all he said was, "Then I'll check things up above." He headed for the door. She had no idea where he was going. Up above?

As far as she was concerned, she was already "up above". Of course, the house didn't have a flat roof, so it must have a loft. Only there was no staircase up to it and so far she hadn't noticed a hatch in the landing ceiling where there could be an extension ladder, as there had been in her parents' house and her mother-in-law's.

Jo was already on the landing. All she could think of was to call him back. "The figures are on the laptop as well." She switched it on. Nothing happened. "What's all this?" she cried. "Everything's conspiring against me today. Now this one's not working either!" He came back and stood in the doorway. She pointed at the dark screen. "Perhaps you can repair this one?"

"No, no," he said, waving the suggestion away. "I don't touch those midgets, I don't know anything about them. You'll have to take it in. Come on now."

"Just a sec," she said tapping a few keys at random, "perhaps it's just… You go on ahead."

He went off. When she peeked out a few seconds later, the door to one of the guest rooms was open. Hesitantly she went up to it. Jo had opened the wardrobe and was pressing the back. It swung aside, revealing some stairs. A light immediately went on.

The roof space was huge and it was brightly lighted by a good dozen fluorescent tubes. Every last corner was illuminated. The first thing she saw was a massive safe. Beside it was a metal cabinet about three feet high. Jo was already crouching down by it. He opened the front, took some little instruments out of his pocket and started to check the beating heart of his alarm system. He took quite a long time looking at wires and circuit boards, checking the resistance here, measuring something there. Finally he was satisfied. It didn't look as if the security system had been affected.

Whilst he was working, she looked round. Nadia certainly didn't use the loft for storing junk. There were just two tatty cardboard boxes stuck under the slope of the roof, but the rest of the things kept there showed that at least one of the occupants of the house was very keen on sport: skis, a snorkel, diving equipment, a surfboard, a saddle and other articles.

After Jo had left, she went back up and examined the contents of the cardboard boxes. The first contained a motley assortment of old household equipment, such as you'd expect a poor student to have, the second some man's clothes that must have been there for several years. Only three pairs of socks and some holey underwear among worn jeans and shirts. Underneath were two photo albums.

The first had pictures of an adolescent Michael with his mother, father and brother, taken on various occasions. She opened the second expecting to see a grinning boy, showing his missing front teeth, on his first day at school, or pictures of him as a baby. There was a baby, held by a pretty woman. Standing beside her was a man who looked almost like her own father in younger years. So nature had played the trick once before. The man was looking down at the baby, a proud smile on his face. Underneath the photo was a date. Michael had been born five years later.

The photos documented the very good start Nadia had had in life, richly blessed with worldly goods from the very beginning. Countless pictures of her as a child, taken in various surroundings, each grander than the last, were followed by photos showing her as she grew up: boarding school – dozens of girls in front of an ostentatious, castle-like building; holidays – alone in the stables and with Papa on board a motor boat; Nadia at eighteen in evening dress at some ball, on the arm of her proud father; Nadia at twenty, seated at a grand piano, beside her a blond Adonis, probably two or three years older, in white tie and tails – they were playing a duet. Without exception the date was given under every picture, sometimes the place, a note on the occasion or details of the people who had been photographed with her. Beneath the picture showing her at the piano with the Adonis was: "Jacques".

A series of photos with palm trees, white sand and turquoise water showed Nadia from twenty-four to twenty-eight in a jeep, in diving gear, on water skis, at the wheel of a motor boat, on the back of a horse, in and beside an open-air swimming pool, at a hotel bar. And always accompanied by Jacques. The relationship must have lasted quite a while.

Then came Nadia's career. At a Christmas party in stately surroundings and the company of distinguished-looking men, Nadia, in her early thirties, was standing in the foreground, radiant, a glass of champagne in her hand. The last page had a single large-format black-and-white picture. Nadia, at thirty-five, was with an older man who was handing her a certificate. They took up most of the picture, hardly leaving enough space for the third person, who was standing beside Nadia and looking at her, adoration written all over his face.

It was a young man. She recognized him at once, even though he must have been a good five years older when he'd crossed her path in Schrag's office. Röhrler! In January he'd obviously taken her for Nadia. In her mind's eye she saw herself walking in the woods with Nadia, heard herself telling her about Röhrler and Herr Schrag and assuring her she hadn't had her fingers in the till. The bitch! Nadia must have known she was the one Röhrler had been talking about. But why had she tipped Wolfgang Blasting off about him? Hadn't she been afraid that under interrogation he might have revealed there were two Nadias? Apparently not. But perhaps Röhrler hadn't known that. Presumably he hadn't mentioned the name Nadia Trenkler to Herr Schrag, otherwise Schrag would have had no reason to fire Susanne Lasko on the spot. Whatever, that was two jobs she'd lost because of Nadia.

She went downstairs and dialled the number with the double-nought prefix again. The woman moaning away in French had presumably been Nadia's mother. They spoke French in Geneva. And that, according to the postmark on the card, was where Jacques had been living in August two years ago. But if Nadia had been born in Düsseldorf, then it could be assumed that her mother spoke at least some German. And she might happen to know if her daughter was staying with her former lover. Seconds later the woman came on the line with a questioning "*Oui?*"

"Good morning," she said in German, enunciating very clearly. "*Parlez-vous allemand?*"

"Yes," the woman replied in German.

"Am I speaking with Nadia Trenkler's mother?"

"Yes," the woman repeated.

Giving a sigh of relief, she went on, retaining the slightly stilted tone, "This is Helga Barthel of Alfo Investment speaking. I urgently need to contact Nadia. She flew to Geneva on Thursday and —"

At that point she was interrupted. Nadia's mother knew nothing about her being in Geneva and, for her part, wanted to know what Alfo Investment was. When told, she didn't seem to be at all pleased. She hung up without a word. Redialling immediately produced no result, no one answered.

She got the note with Jacques's mobile number out of the car boot and tried it. She didn't have much hope she'd be able to communicate with him, but if the Beckmann had led to a reconciliation and Nadia was with him, presumably it would be enough to ask for her. But the number appeared not to exist any longer.

Strangely enough, that seemed to calm her down and she went over recent events and what she'd learned. That she appeared at Alfo Investment as a furniture company didn't necessarily mean anything. Hardenberg could scarcely have told his partner what or, to be more precise, who Lasko really was. He could still have rented a nice, bright apartment on the outskirts of the city from Behringer on Thursday, though that wasn't what he would have told Helga. Perhaps Philip really had fallen over at the airport and only wanted to send Helga to stay with her sister so that she wouldn't be alone all weekend. If she needed pills then that probably meant she was ill. And the fact that Nadia hadn't rung up again to make it clear when she was coming back – well, Nadia couldn't know that Michael was in Munich.

Perhaps Nadia, aware that her generous offer would have spurred her stand-in on to make a special effort, was treating herself to a long weekend with Hardenberg in Berlin – where there was no danger of them being pestered by Zurkeulen. Nadia's last instructions at the airport and the first, reasonably comprehensible, question in her distorted call on Friday had reflected her concern that Michael remain in ignorance. If Nadia had gone off with her lover and Zurkeulen's money, why should she be bothered whether Michael noticed it was only her double in bed with him? And Wolfgang Blasting's odious remark about her stud suggested her marriage was very important to Nadia. Apart from that, would she abandon a house which, according to the title deeds, had cost one-and-a-half million marks for a mere two hundred thousand euros? Hardly.

She decided she must stay calm. Wait and see. At least until Monday. Monday was no problem, it was her day off. And until then the fact that Michael wasn't there meant she could live two lives at once. And for Susanne Lasko Sunday meant going to see her mother.

She got herself ready, tipped the tomato juice and egg down the sink, refilled the glass and seasoned it with salt and pepper. It perked her up. Shortly before one, without having tidied up in the kitchen or set the alarm, she got in the Alfa, used the remote control to raise the garage door – and took her foot off the accelerator.

The Jaguar was parked across the drive. Michael must have deliberately left it so as to block both exits. He wasn't in the car. She kept sounding the horn until he finally appeared in the Kogler's doorway – together with Jo, who was giving her the thumbs-up behind his back, while Michael strolled towards her.

When he reached the Alfa and bent down, she lowered the window. "Hi, there," he said, "you seem to be bright-eyed and bushy-tailed again. It looks as if I arrived just in time. Off on a short excursion? Or is it to be a longer one?" He looked at her. She couldn't have said whether his expression was angry, bored, tired, mocking or something else entirely.

"Let me out," was her only answer.

He shook his head slowly. "Not today." With that he put his hand in through the open window and switched off the ignition. The engine died. He took the key out and went round to the back of the car. Before she could do anything, he'd opened the boot and taken something out.

Immediately she was beside him and she saw the expression on his face change. He was weighing the worn imitation-leather holder with the keys to her flat in his hand. The glance he gave her no longer seemed tired, mocking or bored, not even angry. It appeared to register the realization that his worst fears had come true. Without a word he put the holder in his trouser pocket.

Then he turned his attention to the plastic bag. At first he must have only noticed the ready-to-eat meals and the tins of chicken soup. He laughed, clearly not knowing what to make of it. "What does this mean? You're travelling light. Off for a picnic?"

Jo was still standing at his front door. He'd stopped signalling to her, his look now expressed incomprehension and pity. And then Michael discovered the envelope, glanced at the address and looked her in the eye. "Who's Susanne Lasko?"

She felt the blood drain from her face. She didn't reply.

"Postage to be paid by addressee?" Michael said in mocking surprise. "Dieter Lasko seems to be a thrifty man. Or is he just poor?" As he went on, his voice took on a touch of sharpness. "Will you please explain what this means?"

When she didn't respond, he pulled out the printouts. The little tape cassette slipped out too and fell on the ground. While he was still looking, she bent down, grabbed the cassette, slipped it in her jacket pocket and tore the empty envelope out of his hand. "Give me that. It belongs to me."

"No," he said, "it belongs to Susanne Lasko, it says so here. Who is she?"

She tried to take the papers and the car key off him. He pushed her hand away. "Take it easy, sweetheart. Surely I can have a look."

Then he took her by the arm and called across to Jo, "You can go in now. There's nothing more your helping hand can do. We'll have a bite to eat, then go to bed. After the long drive I feel I've earned a sleep in the arms of my loving wife. Who knows how long I'll be able to enjoy that pleasure."

With these last words he dragged her into the garage, then into the hall and, naturally, to the alarm. His voice lost its mocking undertone and became harsh. "Now we can have a chat about your plans without embarrassing poor old Jo."

She had no intention of discussing anything with him, left him in the hall closet and went to the kitchen. He followed her and, seeing the dirty glass and empty tin of juice, resorted to irony. "That was a hurried departure, I must say. You didn't even have time to clear away the remains of your frugal lunch or raise the drawbridge."

All that she could think of was that she wouldn't be able to see her mother, nor go back to her flat, if he stayed there and didn't give her the keys back. "But you said you wouldn't be back until tomorrow," she said, folding up the envelope and putting it in her jacket pocket with the tape.

He shrugged his shoulders. "Another speculation that didn't work out. But one more or less is neither here nor there. When Ilona rang I thought I'd better see what was going on here. She thought you were about to do a bunk."

"She got hold of the wrong end of the stick."

"Yes, I know," he said. "That's the end we all get when it's your business dealings we're involved in. May I know what tore you away from your pick-me-up?"

When she didn't reply, he turned to the printouts. Perhaps he hoped they'd contain an explanation. She picked up the glass, threw the empty tin in the rubbish bin and peeked at him furtively out of the corner of her eye. He leafed through the sheets, the car key clutched in his fist. Her transcript of the fragmentary letter to *mon chéri* was printed out on the last one, but he didn't get that far, he'd drawn his conclusions before reaching it. "Let me guess. Philip called."

"No, Helga. She hadn't managed to get out to the shops and asked me if I could bring her some things. Philip's not there, he had to go to Berlin yesterday."

His lips twisted in a joyless grin. "Berlin? Are you sure it isn't Nassau? You'd better check before you board the plane."

It sounded as if he knew about Nadia's affair. "Spare me your suspicions and just give me the keys," she demanded. That was probably the way Nadia would have put it.

His grin became a brief laugh. "Don't overdo it, sweetheart. Jo said I needed to treat you gently, you were a bit confused at the moment. He told me a client had threatened you. Perhaps you'd like to tell me what's going on so I'm prepared for the worst. Will it cover it if we dispose of the shack here?"

She threw her shoulders back and, although trembling a little at the thought that he might grab her again and take the tape and the envelope, which had both her and Dieter's full address, walked past him, keeping her head held as high as possible. He made no move to stop her.

A quick call to the old folks' home to tell her mother that she'd gone out with her friend Jasmin Toppler, that the motorbike had broken down and they were stuck somewhere, but were still having a great time – that was all she wanted to get done. She also managed to reach the study unhindered and closed the door behind her. But hardly had she dialled the area code than the door opened.

She replaced the receiver. He came over to the desk, slowly, and pointed at the laptop. "Nice little toy," he said, keeping a tight hold of the car key and the printouts.

"It's not working."

"Oh, really?" He put on an air of astonishment. "What's wrong with it?"

Before she could reply, he'd put the printouts and key down on the desk, opened the laptop and switched it on. Then he started to laugh. He didn't notice her hand creeping towards the key, which she slipped into her jacket pocket. "You're priceless," he said. "You might pull the wool over Jo's eyes with an empty battery, but not me. Where's the lead?"

"In the office. It's Philip's laptop."

"Oh, really?" he said again. "Then why's it here?"

"I'm taking it to be repaired tomorrow."

His tone was a mixture of disparagement and concern. "Nadia, please. You're talking to me, not the neighbours. Have you been at the office computer as well? You couldn't just stick that under your arm. Unfortunately it won't be much help if you've already got an irate client after your blood. When can I expect him to turn up here? Is there a chance you'll still be around then? Or will I have the pleasure of conducting the negotiations this time? You can't count on your father any more."

With an irritated wave of the hand, she went to the door. "I need to eat," she said. It wasn't particularly brilliant, but it helped.

He took a deep breath and exhaled slowly. "Me too. There's no point in reading you a lecture if the damage is already done. Let's go to Carlo's."

For a few seconds she thought she might still be able to see her mother if she let him go by himself. But then she realized what a risk she'd be running. He might well throw the keys to her flat out into the bushes somewhere. There was nothing for it but to follow him to the Jaguar, hoping she could fish the holder out of his pocket some time in the next few hours.

It took a good half hour to get there. He went on at her almost uninterruptedly, revealing some details of the holiday during which the quarrel had broken out. They'd been to the Bahamas, as Wolfgang Blasting had already mentioned. Michael had suspected there was something in the wind when he chanced to take a call for her from a solicitor's secretary in the hotel. Nadia had been negotiating with the solicitor behind his back and tried to explain it by saying she'd been arranging a surprise for him.

He now interpreted her declaration of love in the bathroom on Friday morning as a farewell on the theme of: Sorry, darling, but since you don't want what I want, I'll have to head off into the sun on my own. Perhaps some day you'll remember I wanted you to come with me. The fact that she'd welcomed his idea of going to visit his family in Munich had been the final proof for him. She'd wanted him out of the house so she could clear off undisturbed.

His tone wavered between bitterness and sarcasm. He suspected the worn imitation-leather holder contained the keys to her new home. It appeared that Nadia had been given a similarly grubby object by the solicitor in Nassau so she could view the holiday house. Michael assumed she'd spent the Saturday getting the basic tools and trappings of the elegant lady together and out of the house. Large items of luggage could be checked in well ahead of the flight. The only counter-argument she had was, "You're wrong."

Finally he drove into a car park on the edge of the pedestrian precinct. Carlo's turned out to be an Italian restaurant that was very busy. It was clear that both the staff and some of the customers knew Michael well. Whether that was also true of Nadia was impossible to gauge. A waiter greeted them with an obsequious, "Good evening Madam, good evening, Herr Doktor" and led them to a table where a middle-aged man was already sitting.

He'd have been in his late fifties, had thick white hair and a similar, neatly trimmed beard. Tall and powerfully built, he made an imposing impression even when sitting down. He looked up from his almost empty plate, surprised and, as it seemed, pleased.

"Is that all right?" the waiter asked.

Michael and the white-haired man nodded simultaneously, Michael appearing slightly embarrassed. "I didn't expect to see you here, Herr Professor."

The professor stood up and, the perfect gentleman, pulled out a chair for her. At the same time a loud "Hi there" echoed from a group of eight at a large round table in one corner. Two arms were waved.

"Excuse me," said Michael. "I'll just say a quick hello," and with that he left her alone with the unknown man.

The professor gave her a friendly smile. She returned it. The waiter had disappeared. Michael was chatting with the people at the round table – the hello was definitely not going to be a quick one. He was particularly directing his attention towards a young woman whose hair was dyed an unnatural red and who turned round to look at her several times with an expression that was initially sour, later exultant.

The professor suddenly spoke. "I heard Niedenhoff's going to give a concert in the Beethovenhalle soon."

"I heard that too," she replied, continuing to smile. She felt her cheeks had already gone to sleep.

"I wonder if it's still possible to get tickets."

How should she know? All she knew was that there were two tickets on the grand piano in the living room – with greetings from Frederik. She couldn't keep her eyes off Michael and the young woman. A colleague from the lab? Those adoring looks at Michael! And the glances she cast at her. The laboratory mouse, maybe?

The professor noticed she kept looking across at the round table. He cleared his throat quietly. "Frau Palewi will be leaving us shortly." If he thought his delicate hint was any help to her, he was wrong.

"Whether that will change anything, I very much doubt," she said. "My husband's heard a nasty rumour that's going round the neighbourhood." She told him a little about Jo's profit from the Deko Fund, Ilona's envy, Wolfgang's dubious research and her idea of buying a little holiday cottage as a nice surprise for Michael. Only now he saw that in a different light, she concluded, after he'd heard the neighbours' gossip.

The professor listened attentively. He quite agreed, he said, envy was an all-too-common disease and he would have had no objections to a little holiday cottage. Michael placed his hand pointedly on Frau Palewi's shoulder and bent so low he was almost touching her cheek. He was flirting unashamedly. For the moment she forgot her mother, who would doubtless be worried, she forgot her uncertainty about Nadia's whereabouts and the fact that she was sitting at a table with a man of whom all she knew was that he was a professor and wanted tickets for the Niedenhoff concert.

With her eye on Michael's bent back, she said, "The way things are, it seems I can pack my bags anyway. It looks as if my successor's already been chosen. But he doesn't have to make it so obvious."

The professor cleared his throat again. Regretting what she'd just said, she smiled at him. "You must excuse me, I don't want to bother you with my worries. How many tickets do you need?"

He was surprised. "Two, if possible."

"As it happens," she said, "I've got two. I'd be happy to let you have them."

"But I can't take them," the professor protested, in a tone that made it clear he'd be delighted to accept the tickets on the spot. "I'm sure you'll want to —"

"At the moment I don't know what I want," she broke in. "If that should change in the next few days, I can always get some more from Frederik."

"But that would be marvellous," he said, delighted. "My wife has a particular liking for Niedenhoff. It's almost enough to make me jealous." Hardly were the words out of his mouth than his eye was drawn to the round table and his face set in an expression of embarrassment.

She felt like grinding her teeth and going over to grab Michael by the scruff of the neck and drag him away from his laboratory mouse. Finally he extricated himself, came back and sat down on her left. Without deigning to look at her, he asked the professor, "Wasn't your wife coming back today?"

The professor sighed. "She said she'd earned a short holiday after the strenuous conference. And the weather's so nice in Malta."

Again he smiled at her. "It's not easy with successful women. Young men especially find it difficult to accept. At my age it's not such a problem, the only thing solitude is likely to ruin is my eyesight."

She could have kissed him for that. Giving her a furious look, Michael enquired, "So you actually managed to realize your dream, then?"

The professor nodded with a mischievous grin, like a schoolboy who's just played a trick on someone and got away with it. At last the waiter arrived with two menus. Michael waved them away. "A light white wine, one number sixty…" He broke off and looked at her. "What about you? The usual?"

Since she didn't know what the usual was, she shook her head, took one of the menus back from the waiter and immersed herself in it. The man waited patiently until Michael told him, "Bring a cognac for my wife, Guido, perhaps she'll find it easier to make her mind up after an aperitif."

If he insisted! She handed the menu back to the waiter and pointed at the professor's almost empty plate. "I'll have some of that. And I'd like a mineral water with it and a vodka instead of the cognac." A nip would surely not harm the baby and it would calm her down.

The professor gave Michael a questioning glance, but he didn't bat an eyelid. A minute later the drinks arrived. There was a thick slice of lemon floating in her mineral water. She hadn't realized how dry her mouth and throat were. The sight of the water, which she couldn't drink if she didn't want to come out in an almost immediate rash, gave her an unbearable thirst. She downed the vodka in one, unconcerned by the professor's embarrassed look. The strong drink burned her throat, but she felt better after it.

The food came and it was delicious. Michael and the professor kept up a lively conversation, peppered with expressions that meant nothing to her. Not once did Michael address the professor by name. The fact that she didn't join in didn't seem to bother either of them. The waiter appeared at the table again and asked if everything was satisfactory. She praised the food and pointed to the mineral water. "Take that away and bring me a glass of that wine."

The man did as instructed and brought a very good and very light white wine. As he went off and she took her first sip, Michael was saying, "I think I've managed to get Beatrice to change her mind. It would be a real pity if she left, she's the best TA we've ever had."

So it was Beatrice Palewi! She gave a little laugh. "Sweetheart, you don't have to pretend to anyone here. Half the restaurant must have seen you flirting with the best TA you've ever had."

Then she stood up and looked the professor in the eye. "Excuse me. I feel sick."

Fortunately there was a discreet sign to the toilets by the cloakroom, so she didn't have to submit to people's stares while she searched for them.

She spent almost a quarter of an hour leaning against the cool tiles of the wall, trying to control the turmoil inside her. She was pregnant by him, dammit, and even if he didn't know – and must never know – she wasn't going to put up with any more of this behaviour from him. Nadia certainly wouldn't have accepted it, and whatever Nadia could do, she could do.

She checked her make-up in the mirror, went over her lips with the lipstick and rehearsed Nadia's smile. When she returned to the table, the plates had been cleared away and the professor had left. Michael had already paid the bill and was standing by Beatrice Palewi at the round table once more. Throwing her shoulders back, she went over to the group. They watched her approach, some embarrassed, others hoping for a scandal. Doubtless everyone at the table knew Nadia. And doubtless everyone was expecting a scene. Well, they were going to get one.

She put one hand on Michael's arm, bestowed Nadia's haughtily disdainful smile on Beatrice Palewi and said, "Come along, darling. You've just spent two days among the plebs, surely you can wait until I'm on the Bahamas for another dose?"

He did indeed follow her out – without a word and stony-faced. But once they were in the street, he snarled, "How dare *you*!"

"Me?" she asked, drawing out the vowel. "How dare you! That really was going too far. You seem to have forgotten who financed —"

"You don't need to say it," he broke in, very calm and collected. "You'll get every penny of it back."

"Don't bother," she hissed. "Stick it down your TA's bra instead. At least then you'll have something worth groping. And you read me a lecture because you've got it into your head that I'm going to leave you! You're an idiot. You've no idea how blind you are."

He stomped along beside her, a grim look on his face. When they got to the Jaguar he thrust the car key in her hand, saying he was too tired to drive back. That she didn't know how to adjust the seat to her height did nothing to arouse his suspicions. He did it for her, reminded her to check the mirror and showed her which buttons to press. Once they were out of the built-up area, he asked her how high she thought her blood-alcohol level was.

Now she realized why he'd made her drive and laughed. "No idea, but if it's enough for me to lose my driving licence, you'll lose yours too. It's your car and you insisted I drive."

He didn't seem to have considered that angle in his fury. "Pull in here," he demanded.

"No. I'm carrying on driving. I still can. Watch." The country road was empty in front and she was in the mood to brush up some of the skills she'd learned from Johannes Herzog. To start with she slalomed along the centre markings for a couple of hundred yards.

"Stop this nonsense, Nadia," he said.

She pulled the car back into the right-hand lane and put her foot down. The Jaguar was considerably faster that Johannes Herzog's old BMW. She took the speedometer up to a hundred and forty then, to the sound of Michael's strained breathing, stamped on the brakes. She assumed the rear wheels would skid, as regularly happened with the BMW, but the Jaguar held its line. There was a terrible knocking under the sole of her shoe, but she ignored that. When the car stopped, Michael took the key out of the ignition. He was pale. "You're out of your mind," he gasped. "Do you want to kill us?"

"Why not? Rather that than hand you over to your flat-chested cow. It's a touching thought really, the Trenklers in a double grave."

He got out and said, "Shift over." Then he drove on.

When they got to the house, he went straight upstairs. She waited a good hour before she followed. The bedroom door was open, but it was impossible to tell whether he was asleep or not. Nor was she really interested. She closed the door, went into the study and closed that door too. The laptop on the desk was now plugged in. Where Michael had found the lead was a mystery, it hadn't been in the computer bag.

That was not her first concern, however, the printouts on the desk and the call to the old folks' home were more urgent. Her mother wasn't half as worried as she'd assumed she would be. It turned out that she hadn't expected her to come anyway, because Johannes Herzog had crashed his BMW so couldn't bring her. Her mother was just glad she hadn't stood waiting for him for ages, since she'd gone out with her friend.

"Where are you, Susanne?"

Agnes Runge accepted the story she'd made up earlier with all the enthusiasm of a mother who is happy when her only child is enjoying herself. Her sole concern was that she was facing a long journey home on a motorbike. "Give your friend my best wishes and tell her to drive carefully. It could freeze."

"Don't worry, Mum, we'll be careful," she said.

Then she sat there looking at the laptop and the lead. Nadia must have hidden it somewhere in the house, perhaps in the dressing room. And left the laptop with its empty battery in Hardenberg's office. In a matter of seconds the machine was up and running. It wasn't password protected, it loaded up automatically and very rapidly – unfortunately with a different operating system to the one on the big computer.

She couldn't find a file manager and didn't know how else to get at the files. Eventually she picked up the telephone and tried Nadia's mobile again, only to hear, "The person you are calling is not available at the moment."

At the moment! she thought. She'd just have to wait. One more night. It wasn't nine yet, but she was tired, so she went downstairs and locked up. The only thing she didn't know how to do was lower the shutters. Michael's trousers were on a clothes hanger in the dressing room. The imitation-leather holder with the keys to her flat was still in the pocket. She shoved it underneath a pile of pullovers. In the bathroom the little alarm clock was on the shelf. It was already part of a familiar scene.

Shortly afterwards she was in bed. Her last conscious thoughts moved seamlessly into a nightmare. She was sitting in Schrag's office eating a piece of fruit flan. Röhrler came in. Not looking the way she'd seen him in January. He was squashed flat, there was nothing human about him any more. He came right up to her desk and muttered, "That's what happens when you get caught with your fingers in the till." His blood dripped down on the flan and on a fat envelope. And she was so horribly ashamed of her voracious appetite. "They were accounting errors," she cried.

"You could call it that," Röhrler said with Michael's voice, placing a bloody hand on her shoulder.

"Let me go," she screamed. "I didn't want you to die. I'd no idea the lying bitch knew you."

Röhrler grasped her upper arms, shook her and said, "Wake up."

She couldn't wake up. She fought against his firm grip with all her might. Only when he slapped her did the horror end. She was blinking up at an alarmed face. Michael's face. "Are you awake?" he asked.

"Yes," she mumbled, sat up and got out of bed.

"Where are you going?"

"Out," she said and went to the bathroom. He followed her and watched, standing in the doorway, as she let the water trickle into the hollow of her hand and gulped down a few mouthfuls.

"Should I get you a drink?"

Still bending down, she shook her head. He waited a few seconds, then he asked, "Who is Susanne Lasko?"

She was close to telling him. But what if he threw her out and Nadia didn't come back? "I don't know," she murmured, her face still over the washbasin.

"Is Dieter Lasko the client who's been threatening you?"

"No."

He didn't believe her. "Perhaps you can settle with the man if you sell the house," he suggested.

She straightened up and laughed hysterically. "That would be one possibility. I could sell the house and find an elegant little apartment with charming neighbours. An alcoholic with a criminal record would be nice, I'd fit in there."

He regarded her thoughtfully. "Go back to bed and try to get some sleep."

She followed him back into the bedroom, lay there awake for a while, then fell into a light sleep, from which she was roused by the buzzing of the alarm clock. Michael got up and went into the bathroom. For several minutes she heard him washing and getting shaved. Then her exhaustion blanked out every sound. She went back to sleep and had no idea how much time had passed when she next heard a noise: the metallic click of the central locking. The door onto the landing was open.

Still half asleep, she waited for the clatter of the garage door and the noise of the Jaguar's engine. But either it wasn't audible on the first floor if the windows were closed or – it was a couple of minutes before she completed the thought – Michael hadn't left yet. She blinked in the hazy light and lifted up the arm with Nadia's watch. The tiny hands were blurred and she had to blink several times before she could see clearly. Ten-past nine. He must have been in the lab for ages.

At the next thought, she shot up. Nadia! From one moment to the next all the difficulties of the weekend, all her anger were forgotten. Her hands and knees started to tremble, such was the relief. She swung her legs out of bed and, fighting against the rising nausea and dizziness, fetched a dressing gown. Then she went to the stairs.

All was quiet in the house. There were just a few faint sounds. They came from the basement. She stopped halfway down the stairs. She thought she could hear a voice. Nadia was not the kind of person to talk to herself. There must be someone with her. Her heart started to pound.

Not daring to call out to Nadia, she tiptoed down to the hall. She did briefly think about arming herself with a kitchen knife, but that didn't seem to offer enough protection. For her, threat was synonymous with a gun and a knife was no use against that. All you could do was hope it would jam. A rapid withdrawal as soon as she saw anything suspicious. Dash up to the study, lock herself in and call the police. That seemed the most sensible option.

When she was about halfway down the basement steps, she heard a voice, the irritation half-suppressed, say, "Stop that."

Then she was at the bottom. The door to the utility room was open, but all she saw at first was the chunky black gun.

Part Four

It was a strange sight. Standing between the washing basket and ironing board, a twenty-something woman in a brightly coloured housecoat and jeans was trying to wrestle the gun off a two-year-old child. The boy was twisting and turning like an eel beside the full washing basket, giggling with delight as he sprayed the woman and the washing with his water pistol.

She stood there, rooted to the spot, as the woman finally gained the upper hand, gave the boy a slap on the fingers and started as she straightened up. "Ooh, you gave me a shock here. I didn't know you were in the house. You did say I could come today."

With a quick glance at the child, which had started to cry after the smack, the woman gave her a guilty look. "I'm sorry, but I had to bring him. His gran's coming down with something today."

The child turned to face her and stuck his thumb in his mouth. "Yes," the woman said, stretching out the word. She put the water pistol in one of her pockets and, with a glance at the iron, said, "Should I maybe call it a day?"

She shook her head. It wasn't intended as an answer to the question, it was simply a response to the whole situation. Naturally the woman interpreted it otherwise and to show her zeal she said, "In that case I'll do the upstairs windows as well today. I should have done them on Friday. I'll make sure he doesn't get up to mischief."

She just nodded and went back to the steps. A home help! She should have thought of that ages ago. Lilo had one, Ilona had one, Niedenhoff had a gardener to mow his lawn. Would Nadia, of all people, go round her mansion wielding a duster? What could the woman's name be? That wasn't the only question on her mind as she made her way back up to the hall. Why had Nadia not thought to mention that a woman came in to do the ironing and clean the windows?

"Stop that, Pascal!" the woman in the basement bawled. "You're messing up all the washing, dammit."

She felt no urge to have a lengthy chat with someone whose name she didn't know, nor how – or how much – she was paid, but she couldn't

217

stand the noise. She went back down and said, "Don't shout at the poor thing. Why did you buy him such an awful thing anyway? Give it to me."

She actually gave her the water pistol and asked, "Don't you have to go out today?"

"I'm not sure yet."

"And what about tomorrow?"

"I don't know about that either. Unfortunately today I'm…"

She broke off. Don't explain anything until it's absolutely necessary; if she asks about being paid, say, "We'll see to that later. I have to go to the bank first."

The woman waited a few seconds, to see if she was going to finish the sentence, then asked, "I just want to know if I should come tomorrow if you're going to be here. So far it hasn't been a problem, but if it doesn't suit you any more, I'd prefer it if you told me in advance instead of sending me home halfway through like last Thursday."

That sounded as if, before setting off, Nadia had made sure she didn't run into someone she didn't know. But if Nadia had made sure they wouldn't meet on Thursday, she'd have done that for other days as well. Nadia must have assumed she wouldn't need her stand-in on the Monday. The realization sent a shiver down her spine.

She went back upstairs, stuck the water pistol under the pullovers, together with the imitation-leather holder, took out some clean clothes, had a shower, put on make-up to conceal how pale she was and made a further futile attempt to ring Nadia on her mobile. After that she tried Alfo Investment. Helga Barthel wasn't in the office, but then she'd said she wasn't going to be. There was no reply from Hardenberg's home number either.

She tried all the numbers stored on the phone, apart from Geneva, Munich and the lab. Five times she said, "Sorry, wrong number." Four times she listened to a recorded message, hearing two names that meant nothing to her; the other two just gave the number that was on the display.

Sixteen was the Henseler Gallery. It was Lilo who answered. She listened to her apology for bringing the party on Saturday to an untimely end and reassured her, "Please, darling, don't worry, it wasn't as if it was a real disaster." Jo must have managed to convince his wife that the profit he'd made from his speculation was all above board.

Seventeen was a travel agency. Saying she was Helga Barthel from Alfo Investment, she claimed her colleague, Nadia Trenkler, had told her that if she didn't appear in the office on Monday, she might have gone off on impulse, perhaps to Berlin or Nassau, and the travel agency would be able to provide the necessary information. They were very helpful but unfortunately could tell her nothing about the movements of Nadia Trenkler. No one replied on eighteen, nineteen and twenty. And Jacques's mobile had probably long since ended up in the rubbish bin with a dud battery.

When she came back downstairs again, the home help was sitting at the kitchen table drinking coffee and reading the regional paper. Her son was squatting on the floor turning the contents of a packet of biscuits into crumbs. Showing no sign of a guilty conscience, the woman looked up and tapped an article in the paper. "Have you seen this? Now they're cutting each other's throats. Good riddance, I say." Then she stood up, saying now she'd get on with the upstairs windows.

The problem of what she was called solved itself when the woman told the child, as she swept up the crumbs, "Didn't Andrea tell you not to crush them up like that, you mucky pup."

Andrea went back to the basement with Pascal. She decided to have breakfast first of all. There was a slice of ham left and she didn't need to make coffee, the pot was still half-full. To keep up appearances, she took it into the dining room, together with the regional paper and the *Frankfurter Allgemeine*. Andrea was up and down the stairs between the basement and the first floor, Pascal in one arm, the ironing in the other. She nibbled at her toast, washing it down with plenty of coffee, leafing uninterestedly through the regional paper until her eye was caught by the article in the local section Andrea had mentioned.

A woman living in a tenement in Kettlerstrasse had called the police on Friday evening because she'd been disturbed by the sound of fighting and cries for help coming from the adjoining flat. She'd assumed her neighbour had turned up the sound of his television too loud, as he often did. The police found the man on his living-room floor, dead from stab wounds. It was assumed there'd been a fight between two drunks, since shortly beforehand the victim had started a brawl in a bar where he was a regular and the landlord had thrown the two of them out. She didn't learn Heller's first name from the article, it was just given as a full stop.

His violent death gave her a shock that left her shaking all over and made her forget her uncertainty for the moment. Not that she'd been in any way sorry that Heller had not made an appearance on the Saturday, but the idea that at that time he was already in some refrigerated compartment…

She went out without telling Andrea. Parked in the drive was a rusty old banger with biscuit crumbs, a thermos and a child seat in the back. But there was enough room to get the Alfa out. She went to a bank and presented Nadia's ID, claiming she'd forgotten both her cheques and her bank card. They gave her a cheque she could use to access Nadia's account. She made a credible attempt at Nadia's signature, without having practised it very much. That at least solved her cash-flow problem.

When she got back, Andrea was in the bedroom changing the bed linen, which she saw as she went past. She installed herself at the desk, tried to make the telephone ring by sheer will-power and made a pretence of frenzied activity on the laptop. No message had been left on the answerphone while she was out.

Andrea and her small son left shortly after two, after Andrea had ascertained that she didn't need to cook anything but that her presence on the following day was desired. She didn't ask for payment, nor for the return of the water pistol.

The silence was almost driving her crazy. Nadia must know when her cleaner left the house, but nothing happened. One more attempt to call Alfo Investment. Only the answerphone. One more attempt to call Hardenberg's home number. Helga Barthel answered, considerably calmer than on Sunday. "I'm glad you've rung."

Philip had also rung by then and reassured Helga. He was in Berlin, the Hotel Adlon, and everything was as it should be. Helga had been instructed to tell Nadia to transfer the money and call Philip if she had any problems with the laptop.

Claiming she was still in Geneva, she said she'd see to the money transfer immediately and that she'd had no problems with the laptop. That meant there was no need to call Philip and if he was asking Nadia to ring, that must mean she wasn't with him. But then who was she with?

And where? With Jacques in Geneva? Or with Jacques on the Bahamas? Perhaps *mon chéri* had fancied the idea of a holiday house with several acres of beach.

Once more she tried Nadia's mother, who didn't reply herself. She spent minutes arguing with a young man who could have been a private secretary or a gardener and didn't speak a word of German. He larded his French with a few English expressions to make it absolutely clear that Madame was not available for Jacques.

"Prat!" she muttered, explaining in a loud and angry voice, "Jacques does not want to speak to Madame, I want to speak to Jacques. I urgently need his telephone number." When that got her nowhere, she summoned up her school English and tried, "I am the *Sekretärin* of Nadia Trenkler. I must a call make with Jacques. I must please have the number of the telephone of Jacques. It is very *wichtig*."

She couldn't remember how to make it clear her call was urgent, but that didn't really bother her, his English wasn't any better. And apparently he had finally understood. At least he said something that sounded like a series of numbers, though in French, of course. She did have the presence of mind to write down what it sounded like, but when she puzzled over her notes, all she could make out was that the first two numbers were identical, probably zeros. She gave up and she didn't bother trying Nadia's mobile again either.

At a quarter past four she dialled number three on the stored list of numbers. She wasn't really in any state to deal with another stranger, also she had the feeling she'd forgotten something important. She trembled at the very thought that Michael or Beatrice Palewi might pick up the receiver. At least in that respect she was lucky. A young woman answered – not immediately and she didn't say her name, the first thing she did after lifting the receiver was to shout "Michael! Keep an eye on the centrifuge." This was followed by a brief, "Yes?"

Since Michael was nearby, she didn't announce herself as his wife, she just said, as casually as possible, "Hi. Can I speak to Kemmerling?"

And the woman shouted out again, "You're wanted on the phone, Danny."

Danny. Somehow it fitted in perfectly with her image of a computer nerd who could compress a hard disk into a stock cube. In her mind's eye she saw a gawky young man pick up the receiver. Danny Kemmerling's voice gave no indication of his age or anything else, because he had to shout to be heard over a rising torrent of noise.

She had to shout as well in order to be understood. Pretending to be Nadia, she asked the man to say nothing about the call to Michael. Michael, she explained, had played a trick on her and she had to insert a jumper but didn't know where it should go. Danny Kemmerling promised she could rely on him to keep quiet about it, saying he was delighted to be of assistance and he'd be there in an hour.

She thanked him, then wandered round the house again, upstairs, downstairs and in my lady's chamber, nervous, wondering if she'd done the right thing. Or was it a serious error to invite into the house a man about whom she knew nothing except that Nadia didn't want him anywhere near her computer? But what Nadia wanted was of secondary importance now. She simply had to get on the computer and she didn't believe Nadia was going to arrive home in the next few hours.

Presumably at that moment Nadia was lying in Jacques's arms somewhere, laughing at the silly cow who'd swallowed the fiction of a rosy future and was now flogging her guts out to keep her cuckolded husband unsuspecting for a while longer. She would have sworn that was the truth.

Despite that, her eye automatically looked for the security screen in every room she entered. In the dining room she saw Eleanor Ravetzky's shaggy dog bound furiously across the road and into the front garden. The actress's little son dashed after it, looking apprehensively at the surveillance camera, caught the beast by its collar and dragged it back to the wrought-iron gate, where they were met by a middle-aged woman.

Barely thirty minutes later the tiny screen set in the stone wall of the drawing room flickered into life. A sleek two-seater, such as one would only expect from a person in the upper echelons of the salary scale, was parked at the kerb. The driver got out. And her heart started to pound. It was the professor, to whom she'd poured out her troubles and promised tickets for the Niedenhoff concert. At Carlo's she'd found his sympathy and understanding very agreeable. But alone in the house with him?

There was barking and growling in the hall. She thought she could see something like alarm on the tiny monitor and, since he seemed frightened of the dog, she was fairly sure she could get rid of him before

Danny Kemmerling turned up. "Sit!" she shouted and went into the hall, noisily slamming the kitchen door as she passed and shouting, "And not a sound from you." Then she opened the front door.

The professor gave her a friendly smile. "Good afternoon, Frau Trenkler."

"Good afternoon," she said. "The tickets are on the piano, I'll just go and get them."

"That can wait," he said. Peering over her shoulder, he asked, "Is the cause of all the trouble upstairs?"

"No, I've shut him in the kitchen," she said, adding, "but that won't keep him out for long, he can open the door himself."

At this the professor didn't look at all concerned, rather puzzled. "May I come in?" he asked. He gestured with a sweep of the arm at the front garden, and what he then said made it clear whom she was talking to: "Or do you want me to take your computer apart on the lawn?"

The boat! Seeing the car parked outside, she made a connection she'd missed in all the confusion. A yacht and a young, gawky computer nerd didn't really go together. And it must be quite a big yacht if you could spend your holiday on it. It was so embarrassing, she didn't know where to look. She just pointed at the stairs and whispered, "Up there."

Professor Danny Kemmerling set off. How did a man in his fifties come to be called Danny? A trendy English name like that really went with a younger man. And how come a young thing in the lab could call him to the phone in such familiar fashion? A "Herr Professor" would surely have brought the boat to mind and she certainly wouldn't have asked a favour of him. She closed the front door, leaned back against it and fought down a rising but completely inappropriate fit of laughter. Then she went upstairs too.

Danny Kemmerling had already located the study. He knelt down at the desk and pulled the computer towards him. "I thought if I came a bit sooner, there'd be no danger of Michael surprising us," he said. "He'll be occupied for a while yet."

Inserting a jumper took no more than five minutes, most of that being taken up with removing all the leads and unscrewing the housing. Danny Kemmerling placed a tiny object somewhere between the clusters of wire and circuit boards, replaced the housing over the tangle, tightened up all the screws and put all the leads back in. When the machine had been pushed back into its place, it worked perfectly. Danny Kemmerling started it up and immediately the operating system was loaded up and the familiar file manager appeared.

"I don't know how to thank you," she said.

"Don't mention it."

"No, no," she said. "You've no idea what a help you've been."

She took the mouse and quickly skimmed through a few folders. She felt somewhat easier, even though reason told her that it didn't make her situation any better simply because Nadia's computer was working. It was highly unlikely she'd find the address of the holiday house on the Bahamas on it, never mind the telephone number. And if that's where Nadia was, a new mobile number for Jacques was hardly any help either.

Danny Kemmerling was looking at the laptop, which was still on the desk, plugged in. It sounded as if he intended to buy one for himself and he asked if she was happy with it.

"Yes, very," she said. "It's a P4 with three gigahertz." At the same moment she remembered that Hardenberg had asked Nadia to ring him if she had any problems with the laptop. What problems could she have had? If Philip had spoken to Nadia on the phone on Thursday evening, then he must have known that it was she who had the laptop and not Nadia. Was that a problem? Or had Hardenberg not got anywhere with it because of the empty battery and had assumed the thing had broken down? Why had Nadia left the laptop with its empty battery in Hardenberg's office and the lead at home? To stop Hardenberg looking at something?

She shut the computer down and went downstairs with Danny Kemmerling, wondering how to get a few hints about the laptop's operating system from him without arousing his suspicions. But that receded into the background when she picked up the open envelope from the piano. She took out the tickets and removed the greetings from Frederik attached with a paper clip. And saw that that wasn't Niedenhoff's first name. Jacques Niedenhoff it said on the tickets.

At first she thought it must be a coincidence. Two men with the same Christian name, there must be thousands of Jacques in France or Switzerland. At the same time the holiday photos in the attic appeared in her mind's eye – and on one of them Nadia had been sitting at a grand piano beside the blond Adonis. Her first love and a pianist living nearby.

224

She also recalled that Nadia had told her Niedenhoff had only moved in at the beginning of the year. At the same time as the Beckmann had been bought – as a housewarming present perhaps? How convenient! *Mon chéri* just across the road.

Professor Kemmerling was in the hall waiting for the tickets. "Would you like a coffee?" she asked. "I have some delicious chocolate-chip ice cream in the freezer."

He accepted the tickets with thanks and her invitation with pleasure. Then he was sitting at the table with her and, despite her nervousness, the serious gaps in her knowledge and the urgent need she felt to dash across the road and ring the bell of the house opposite, it turned out to be an informative afternoon.

Danny Kemmerling devoured two helpings of ice cream and did almost all the talking. First he told her he'd taken advantage of his wife's stay in Malta to buy himself a new computer. Now he too had a P4, a dream of a machine with not just three, but three point four gigahertz. Then he turned to the work in the lab and to Michael.

Their project was at a critical stage of development and certain allowances needed to be made, he said. He didn't say what it was that was being developed, he just emphasized that at the present time research work was impossible without men like Michael. Then he dropped his friendly, chatty tone and asked what the point was of financing such an expensive course of study if, after a few years, one was going to object to him carrying out his profession? Should a man of just thirty-five, hard-working, able and ambitious, spend the rest of his days lazing in the sun? No one could object to a little holiday house. A bit of relaxation on the beach or out sailing now and then was fine, but that was the limit for Michael, any more and he'd wither like a plant without water.

She understood very well what he was getting at. "I don't know what gave him that idea," she said. "I have no intention of trying to get him to resign, my own work's much too important to me for that. I haven't got two computers upstairs just for fun."

Then she tried to exploit Danny Kemmerling's enthusiasm for the laptop. She was just about to bring it down and let him play around with it while keeping a good eye on him to find out how to work the operating system, when Michael returned home unexpectedly.

* * *

He came into the dining room with a look on his face suggesting he was uncomfortable with the situation. "What are you doing here, Herr Professor?" Another bad habit, she thought. Addressing him with his title to his face, but otherwise referring to him simply as Kemmerling. How could a person see the connection?

"Drinking coffee," Danny Kemmerling said and asked if Jutta had also gone home. When Michael replied that she had, he stood up, thanked her again for the coffee, ice cream and an enjoyable afternoon. "I'm the one who should be thanking you," she said, as she accompanied him to the door. When she came back into the dining room Michael had just established that the coffee pot was empty.

"I'll make you some more," she offered.

"Don't bother. What was Kemmerling doing here?"

"Collecting tickets for the Niedenhoff concert."

"Goddammit, Nadia," he snapped, "do you think I'll fall for that? You've been moaning to him again, haven't you? If you imagine you can undermine my position in the lab…"

His vehement tone sent her tumbling back into her shattered marriage and into uncertainty. "You don't need me to do that for you. You should have seen yourself yesterday! Like a lovesick baboon!"

With that she turned on her heel and went up to the study. She was left to herself for fifteen minutes and by the time Michael came in she'd established that the whole of the card index as well as the Alin Letters had disappeared. It looked as if Nadia had deleted everything that was of any importance. The discovery made her heart sink.

Michael put his cup and the coffee pot down beside the laptop, sat on the edge of the desk and asked, "Can we talk sensibly?"

"I don't know if you can." She clicked on the next folder. "I can definitely talk sensibly."

"But not with me, apparently. Did you talk sensibly with Kemmerling?"

"I certainly did."

He breathed in deeply and exhaled slowly. When he went on, her heart sank even lower. "Given the circumstances, I think it would be best if I applied for a divorce. I'd be happy to avoid the year's obligatory judicial separation. I'd prefer it if we could get it over with as quickly and as painlessly as possible. How do they put it? Separation from bed and board. Well, who could prove that we've slept in the same bed during the last twelve months. We've both got enough alternatives."

She could hardly bring herself to listen and clicked at random all over the screen. He gave a brief laugh. "And as far as board is concerned, we wouldn't have to lie. You've never cooked for me. The financial side? Your accounts can't be in all that bad a state or you'd hardly be talking about moving away. But of course I'm prepared to support you if it should be, or ever become, necessary."

She gave a quiet, slightly hysterical laugh. "And how much did you have in mind? Two thousand a month and the rent for a three-room apartment with balcony?"

"Fifteen hundred," he said. "And the running costs for the house. I'll move out. There's just one condition, Nadia. You don't come to the lab again; you don't ring either, neither me nor Kemmerling. I know I owe you a lot, but you haven't purchased the right to ruin my life completely."

She managed to make eye contact and hold it. "I've no intention of doing that. I only called Kemmerling because..." She indicated the computer with a gesture of helplessness, ready to tell him what she'd told Jo, that she must have changed something while she was drunk. "He inserted a jumper for me."

"Haha," he said, unamused. "If I want the piss taken I can do it myself."

"Go ahead, then," she said. "Go ahead and leave me in peace." She was starting to stutter, she couldn't do anything to prevent it. "I've said nothing to your disadvantage and I've done nothing to damage your reputation. Yesterday – I was just furious because of the way... you and that Palewi... and I'm..." She broke off. She was about to say pregnant. But if she told him that and Nadia came back after all... Nadia had to come back. Nadia couldn't simply leave her in her life, like a primary-school kid in a university lecture theatre.

He picked up where she'd broken off. "You're what?"

She managed to relax her clenched fingers and let go of the mouse. "Tired," she said, "very tired. Would you leave me alone, please?"

"Do you agree to a divorce?"

"I can't say yet. It's too sudden. But I'll think about it."

He sat on the edge of the desk for a few more minutes, apparently wondering whether he should say anything else. Then he picked up his cup and the coffee pot and went out. She didn't know whether to laugh or cry and went on clicking the mouse without seeing anything. A divorce! It was a possibility. She'd need to consider it if Nadia didn't come back. He could have the house, but she'd have to accept his money if she wanted to keep the child and not have to live on benefits. With his income he'd hardly notice the fifteen hundred.

She heard him clattering about downstairs. It sounded as if he was in the kitchen. You've never cooked for me. What for Christ's sake had Nadia done for him? Financed his studies in the States, helped him get two doctorates. Used it to keep a hold over him, to tyrannize him. Been unfaithful to him. Left him?

Shortly after eight he came up with a full plate and went into the television room. For a moment her nostrils were filled with a spicy aroma. It faded almost immediately and, anyway, she wasn't hungry. Despite that, she finally switched the computer off, went downstairs and got something for herself. Just a ready-to-eat dish. She took her plate and followed him.

He was sitting on the couch. Leaning forwards, his eyes glued to the TV, he was cutting large chunks off an almost raw steak and putting them in his mouth. He ignored the blood on his plate, just as he ignored her. On the screen Carlos Santana was abusing his guitar. She couldn't stand the blood or the sound of the guitar. Even less his silence and rigid posture.

"I love you," she whispered, almost drowned out by the racket. "Things could be all right again if I could talk to you openly and you give me a chance."

She put her plate on her lap, leaned back, fixed her eyes on his back and went on whispering, the same thing, again and again. Eventually he noticed. "What did you say?"

"Nothing."

He picked up the remote control, switched off the sound and turned to face her, a furious look on his face. "What's the point, Nadia?" Obviously he had understood her. "Be all right!" He shook his head in frustration. "You never change, as I've just seen. What do you want to talk to me openly about? All I get from you is excuses and lies."

The he talked about his fear of a repeat of the catastrophe they'd been through two years previously. Ripped off the bank, that was the way

Wolfgang Blasting had put it. What Michael said made her a bit clearer about it. Nadia had arranged loans with a private bank in Düsseldorf for major clients until it was discovered that one of those clients didn't exist and the balance sheets presented had been created on Nadia's computer. She'd used the money to speculate on the stock market, and made a profit, which was used to pay back the bank. Of course, that didn't stop her being sacked on the spot when the matter came to light – because Röhrler had grassed on her. Her father's influence and the fact that the bank wanted to avoid a scandal had saved her from worse, that is, being taken to court and prosecuted.

Now Michael thought she was might be playing the same game again, only in reverse: talking clients, who came to Alfo looking for a profitable investment, into buying shares in non-existent companies. It was almost impossible for ordinary people to check out foreign firms. They were forced to take what they were told and the figures they were shown on trust.

He wasn't certain because he had no proof. But why had she been so nervous recently? Because things were slack at the stock exchange. Because she knew as well as he did that in the long run it was bound to go wrong. As it had two years ago. It only needed one investor to demand back the money she'd lost on her speculations.

He talked about the nights when he'd wandered round the house, worried stiff she might have caused an accident with her blood alcohol well over the limit. And about the scenes in the lab when she turned up there. So drunk she could hardly stand up. Seething with such rage she could hardly get a word out. She'd called him a rat because he'd cleared all the alcohol out of the house and taken away her car keys and credit cards; because he'd held her fast to stop her killing herself. Now he'd decided it was time for the rat to leave the sinking ship. There were priorities to consider and his own life had to come first, so he'd decided, despite all his love and gratitude, to make a clean break. He wanted to get off before he went down with her.

He still believed she was going to disappear. If one client was getting suspicious that could presumably be taken as a warning signal. But first of all he was sure she'd move heaven and earth to ruin him on the principle of: "What's mine, I can break, no one else is going to have it." Even though he had no intention of taking up with Beatrice Palewi again.

How he'd ended up in Beatrice Palewi's bed… he wasn't trying to say he wasn't to blame at all, but he was only human. He'd been afraid, simply afraid, of going home because he felt he couldn't stand what was awaiting him there any longer. And then he was the one who was at fault, as if his reaction had been what had set everything off. She'd always been good at twisting things so they came out in her favour.

That would perhaps have been the moment for a full confession. Did you know that your wife wanted to divorce you and go back to Jacques two years ago? He'd just broken up with Alina and she thought that was a good opportunity. You know a lot about Nadia, but not everything, not by a long chalk. Don't look at me like that, I'm not Nadia, I'm just her stand-in. You wanted to know who Susanne Lasko was. Well, she's sitting right here, next to you.

But she was too exhausted. "Why didn't you let me drive away yesterday?" she asked. "Surely you don't care if I clear off?"

He shook his head and tapped his chest. "I'm the one who's going to clear off. I owe it to myself." Then he switched the television sound back on.

She went to bed soon after and cried herself to sleep. It was just past three when she woke up again. The bed beside her was empty and at first she didn't know what had woken her. Then it came again. The phone ringing in the study. She leaped out of bed and staggered to the door, her head spinning. She got to the desk at the same moment as Michael emerged from one of the guest rooms, blinking irritatedly in the light. She ignored him, grabbed the phone and put it to her ear before the message on the answerphone had finished. "Nadia?" she gulped, but the reply was a laugh and a tipsy-sounding voice saying, "Hello, my dear."

It was a woman, there was no doubt about that, but she couldn't tell whether it was Nadia from the short greeting in a foreign language. And the woman didn't manage to say anything else. A man's voice broke in, sounding just as tipsy, drowning her in a flood of English. All she could understand was, "…big surprise" and "…is Phil."

"Philip?" she asked, confused.

By this time Michael was beside her. Seething with rage, he tore the receiver out of her hand and bellowed, "Are things OK, Hardenberg? They won't be for long, I'll make sure of that." All at once his expression changed and he gave an embarrassed laugh. "Sorry Phil. That wasn't for you. What a surprise – in the middle of the night. What's the time in Baltimore?" Then he asked in surprised tones, "You're where?"

For a while she stood beside him, listening to him happily chatting away and understanding just about half of what he was saying. When he told her, "It's Phil," which meant nothing to her, she went back to bed, pulled the clothes right up to her neck and still shivered as she thought about the future.

A divorce! And fifteen hundred a month. It was a temptation, of course, but she couldn't do it, couldn't let him pay the bill Nadia had run up. Not even for the child, that wasn't his fault, not even an accident, since he'd firmly believed he was sleeping with his wife, who knew very well that he didn't want children and presumably took appropriate precautions.

So it was back to the grotty flat. At least Heller wouldn't be there to pester her any more. Back to the sweet shop and a private conversation with Frau Schädlich. She'd have to take all her free days for the next few weeks at once in order to go to a clinic and have the new life sucked out of her. It still wasn't too late for that. There was no other solution.

Sleep was out of the question. He'd taken the alarm clock into the guest room with him and she was afraid that, if she closed her eyes, it would be nine before she woke up again. Until she heard the shower in the guest bathroom, she lay there, eyes open, staring at the ceiling and wiping away the occasional tear. Then she got up and had a shower herself. He took advantage of that to get some clothes. He was pointedly avoiding her. Perhaps it was best that way.

Not bothering with make-up, she put on the clothes she'd worn on Thursday. They were crumpled, but who cared? They were the kind of clothes that went with her. He had long since left by the time she came down to the kitchen. The two newspapers were on the table. She spent a few minutes looking through the local section to see if there was a further report on Heller. There wasn't.

The violent death of an alcoholic with a criminal record had been displaced by a report of a new horror. On Sunday afternoon a fourteen-year-old boy had discovered a female corpse in the rubbish bin of a hostel for asylum seekers. At first sight it looked like a road accident in which the driver had made every attempt to get rid of all traces of the victim. Terrible, but she wasn't really affected by it; it was far outweighed by the child she was going to have to kill.

Shortly afterwards she left the house. There was heavy traffic on the autobahn. Her plan was to park the Alfa at the airport in the evening and come back by bus. Since she'd set off far too early, she had time to make a detour to her flat. Just to get the wallet with her own papers, leave her toothbrush in the bathroom and put on some clean clothes, that was all.

As usual there wasn't a parking space free in Kettlerstrasse. She parked the car by the phone box and walked back. It was half-past seven. Heller had never been leaning out of the window that early in the morning but she still missed him somehow. Jasmin's motorbike wasn't outside the building either. She got in unobserved and hurried up the stairs. On the second floor she saw the stickers on Heller's door that on Saturday she'd assumed were a prank played by some children. They were police seals.

She felt cold. She continued up the stairs slowly, the key ready in her hand. When she reached her door she was about to insert it when she saw the seal on the lock. There was also yellow-and-black striped tape across the door and the frame, half-concealing the marks, just a few notches in the wood, as if someone had tried to jemmy the door open.

She stared at the door and the seal. Her mind was a blank and she couldn't stop her fingers taking over and automatically scratching the tapes, which came away. One hand placed itself on the door and pushed. There was a snap as the twisted bolt came out of the plate. The door swung inwards, revealing terrible chaos. The doors to all the rooms were open, the contents of all the cupboards had been scattered over the floor: broken plates, cups and glasses amid masses of feathers. The bed had been completely taken apart, the mattress, pillows and sofa cushions cut up.

For a few second she was aware of nothing but her beating heart. Not daring to step over the threshold, she turned round, went back down the stairs and returned to the Alfa the way she'd come. There were a few people out in the street, but no one took any notice of her. Her ribs and her throat felt as if they'd been laced up tight. Later on she had no idea how long she'd sat in the Alfa, incapable of thought, incapable even of starting the car.

Eventually she set off, not knowing where to go, just hoping to meet someone she could ask something. And eventually she ended up in the underground car park of Gerler House. Philip Hardenberg's Mercedes was next to where she'd parked the Alfa. It was shortly before eleven. She got out and walked to the lifts, as if in a trance. Staring at her from the mirror in the cabin was an ashen face with dark shadows under the eyes. She spent some time using the make-up in her handbag to powder over her pale cheeks and give some colour to her lips. As she put the lipstick back, she noticed the leather key case Helga had given her on Thursday. That would save her pressing the bell.

The lobby was empty, the door to Helga's office open. There was no one at the desk. The upholstered door to Hardenberg's office wasn't properly closed either. She couldn't see the man who was in the office, but she could hear him loud and clear. "I'll tell you what bothers me: Nadia Trenkler."

It sounded polite and thoughtful – it sounded like a gun pressed against her head. It was Markus Zurkeulen's voice coming from behind the upholstered door and this voice was wondering, or asking someone, what Frau Lasko meant by claiming she wasn't Nadia Trenkler last Wednesday and then insisting vehemently that she was on Saturday evening. There must be something special about Nadia Trenkler.

"I don't know." It was Hardenberg speaking. He didn't sound polite, just breathless. "I don't know anyone of that name. I told you that on Wednesday."

For a few seconds all was quiet behind the door. Then Zurkeulen, as polite and thoughtful as ever, spoke again. "Yes, yes, you've already said that. We also met the lady on the way to Frau Lasko's flat. However, she had no keys on her and claimed you had taken possession of the keys to the front door and to the flat."

"But that's nonsense," Hardenberg protested. "Why should I —"

Zurkeulen cut him short. "That's what I wondered too. Naturally I felt it was important to clear the matter up. Things often look different when you're face to face. The lady gave us your address. Unfortunately no one came to the door." The way he spoke, it sounded as if Nadia had been with them when he and his companion had turned up a Helga's door late on Saturday evening. Helga had said nothing about that.

"I was in Berlin." Hardenberg sounded as if he was having to make an effort to stop himself retching. "Where is Frau Lasko now?"

"That is beyond my knowledge," Zurkeulen declared. "Ramon spent quite some time talking to the lady. Ramon, do you remember where you set the lady down?"

It was silent behind the door. She was still standing in the middle of the lobby, incapable of moving. After a few seconds Zurkeulen asked, "What do we do now, Herr Hardenberg? I must confess I have certain concerns and am already wondering whether it might not make more sense to have Ramon continue this conversation instead of me. I'm sure he would enjoy it. Wouldn't you, Ramon?"

Someone laughed. It wasn't Zurkeulen and certainly not Hardenberg. "Please, Herr Zurkeulen. There are absolutely no grounds for your suspicions. At the moment the sum in your portfolio amounts to six million or thereabouts. Any loss has been recouped by now."

"And it is at my disposal?"

"Of course, at any time, in the next few days, if you should wish," Hardenberg hastened to assure him.

"Good," said Zurkeulen. "I do wish. We'll see each other again on Friday, Herr Hardenberg. And I very much hope that, for your sake, there are no problems with payment. Otherwise I would have to turn to different methods."

Steps could be heard and she just managed to slip into Helga's office and hide behind the open door. Peering through the gap between the door and the wall, she saw Zurkeulen and the stocky man cross the lobby, followed by Hardenberg. The stocky man was the first to vanish from her narrow field of vision, then Zurkeulen as well. He left without a further word.

Philip Hardenberg went back into his office. The upholstered door stayed wide open, making it impossible for her to cross the lobby without being seen. Through the narrow gap she could see part of the desk and the back of a large monitor. She could only hear what Hardenberg was doing. First he made a phone call, getting no answer and several times angrily cursing and calling someone – presumably Nadia – a damn bitch.

Then his voice switched to affectionate. She could hear his side of the conversation, clearly with Helga. "It's me, darling... Yes, of course I'm back, the plane was on time... No, I popped in briefly at home, but I didn't want to disturb you. Has Nadia rung?... I don't understand... No, better not, you'll just get Trenkler's back up. You know how —"

She must have interrupted him. He gave an affected laugh. "I don't understand that either. That's the way some men are: imagine the wife's just there to cook for them. But what can you do?" Helga's reply was fairly lengthy. He laughed again. "No, that's really not necessary, darling. There's nothing to do here at the moment. You take it easy… Yes, I'll be back early. See you." There was a smacking noise, as if he was sending a kiss by telephone.

She was trapped in Helga's office for more than an hour, almost fainting with worry that Hardenberg might come in. After he'd finished on the telephone, he worked on the computer. Then he went to the bathroom with some papers in his hand which he burned in the basin. Finally he closed the door of the lobby behind him, turning the key twice in the lock from outside. At that moment she remembered that the Alfa was parked beside the Mercedes.

She dashed out of the office in a panic. The lift seemed too risky. At the end of the corridor was a door with the escape-route symbol. It wasn't closed, it led into a dingy staircase. Her heart was almost bursting through her ribs when she got to the bottom. She had to force herself to open the door to the underground car park, but with the massive pillars and all the parked cars there was plenty of cover.

And a pleasant surprise. The Mercedes was still there, the Alfa next to it. No sign of Philip Hardenberg. When a group of three approached from the lift, she risked it, dashed over to the car, jumped in and roared off to the exit in a squeal of tyres.

Around three in the afternoon she was in an exclusive lingerie shop, certain that neither Hardenberg nor Zurkeulen and Ramon were in the vicinity. That was all that mattered. She had three brassieres in her hand and paid for them with Nadia's Visa card. After that she had lunch in a restaurant she would normally never have entered. She paid for that with Nadia's American Express card.

Then she went shopping without having to think before she bought anything. A piano tutor: *Easy Pieces For The Piano*, food: ham, cheese, a few speciality salads and some fruit which wouldn't produce an allergic reaction, as well as an outrageously expensive blouse and trousers to match. Both were too big for her at the moment, but that would change in the coming months. One of the bags she put on the rear seat of the Alfa had a stylized cradle printed on it. Inside were a tiny vest and a pretty little romper suit with a butterfly embroidered on it. She hadn't been able to find one with an embroidered ray of sunshine.

She'd spent almost eight hundred euros, but money wasn't the problem. In her handbag were two statements she'd printed out from a cash machine with Nadia's bank cards. One account had a round thirty thousand euros. Fifty thousand had been paid into the second only three days before, bringing the amount in credit up to €127,000.

It was past five when she got home. And "home" was what she actually thought to herself. What else could she think after what Zurkeulen had said in Hardenberg's office and what she'd seen in her flat? No one could live in such a scene of devastation.

Ramon's doing, of that she was sure. Things were still too close for her to think them over logically but, despite that, she had a general idea of what must have happened to Nadia on Saturday evening. Nadia must have arrived back from Geneva after she'd gone to the house to get Hardenberg's home number. Nadia had probably taken a taxi from the airport to Kettlerstrasse. Where she'd run straight into Zurkeulen and Ramon. Perhaps she'd been taken with them to Hardenberg's, where no one had come to the door. She might have been left in the black limousine, which would be why Helga hadn't seen her. And then Ramon would have "talked to her". She didn't want to think about that – either logically or in any other way. Above all, she didn't want to think of what would have happened if she'd gone back to the flat from the phone box to wait for Nadia.

There was a car she didn't recognize in the Koglers' drive. Lilo was at the door, talking to a man, and waved to her. She waved back. She recognized the man, he'd been at the party on Saturday evening. She didn't know his name, but that wasn't important. People could change their names.

She drove into the garage and took her shopping into the house. Andrea had been there, had made the beds and returned the bathroom to its pristine condition. She got changed and hid the baby clothes behind a pile of towels.

Not long afterwards Lilo came round for a little chat, telling her how interested Kestermann had been in the picture that was on the wall above her when she'd come round on Saturday evening. So it was Kestermann. Things worked out one way or the other. Let Michael get a divorce. Losing him might hurt a bit, but he'd never really belonged to her and she'd managed without a man for years. Given her bank balance, she wasn't dependent on his money and it brought the risk of exposure down to zero. In theory she could even stay in the house. She got on well with the neighbours.

Shortly after Lilo had left, a white Mercedes drew up outside Niedenhoff's. A dark-haired man, presumably Frederik, got out and a few seconds later was standing at her front door. She didn't intend to answer, but somehow she found herself facing him. "Hi," he said. "I just wanted to check that the concert tickets arrived."

Presumably she should have thanked him. She did it now. He smiled and said, "See you in Bonn, then."

"Unfortunately not," she replied. "I owed someone a favour and passed them on."

"Ow!" he said. "You should have said so sooner. I don't know whether we…" Instead of completing the sentence, he said, "Jacques's in Paris. Should I give him a ring or do you want to talk to him yourself?"

She found it impossible to reply immediately. Jacques! In Paris! "Where can I get him?" she asked after a few seconds' pause.

"The George V," Frederik said, slightly puzzled, as if she ought to have been well aware of that. "He won't be in his suite just at the moment. Try in half an hour. Or better still, leave it for an hour. The rehearsal will definitely have finished by then."

She thanked him with a smile, which she hoped didn't appear too forced, and spent the next ten minutes on the telephone, at the same time wondering how she was going to explain her liberal use of the credit cards to Nadia. What Zurkeulen had said in Hardenberg's office no longer seemed so serious and might even explain some things. Ramon's "talk" with Nadia had presumably left marks, which Michael mustn't see. It was quite within the bounds of possibility that she'd decided to get Jacques to tend to her wounds in Paris.

As it turned out, it wasn't half so difficult to get the number of the George V from the international call service as she'd imagined. They didn't even ask for the exact address. Paris was sufficient. Then she was speaking to someone at the reception desk. He responded to her "*Parlez-vous allemand?*" with excellent German and gave her the number of the suite without hesitation. Unfortunately Jacques Niedenhoff wasn't there and no one else answered the phone.

She decided to try again in half an hour, but twenty minutes later Michael came home. He gave her a curt hello and even for that had to clear his throat twice. Then he got himself a towel, went down to the basement and swam a few lengths in the pool. She listened to his initially furious, then smoother splashing and risked a second attempt. Again no one answered.

By this time she was wondering whether Frederik – as a friend, co-tenant, lodger or whatever – wouldn't have been informed if Nadia had sought refuge with Jacques. And why Nadia hadn't rung during Monday from Paris. Despite that, she decided to try again after another half hour. However, fifteen minutes later Michael appeared by the desk, naked and sopping wet, rubbing his hair with the towel.

He seemed unsure of himself, no longer the man who'd presented her with a catalogue of her misdeeds only the previous evening. "Phil's at the Sorbonne," he said hesitantly. "They'd been out for a drink yesterday. They weren't aware of the time. He's sorry he woke us up."

At the Sorbonne. It had a ring of seaside and holidays. So did what he went on to say. "He sends you his best wishes, Pamela's too." He had to clear his throat several times before he could get the rest out. "They wondered if we fancied going over for a few days."

"What you fancy, I can't say," she said, forcing herself to look him in the face as he stood there, the embodiment of all her longings. "But I don't."

He took deep breath. "I just thought —"

She broke in with sudden vehemence. "What you think was made perfectly clear yesterday evening. What's the point of you going to the Sorbonne with a woman who mostly treats you as a doormat? Get out, this is a study, not a strip joint. If you stand around much longer I'll have to kiss you dry, whether you like it or not."

"What?" He was visibly perplexed. And she was ashamed of herself. It wasn't like her to express her feelings so openly. Of course, she'd hardly ever had the opportunity – and with Dieter she'd never really had the urge.

"You heard," she said. "I'm not made of stone. You may see me as a money-grubbing bitch, but I still see you as the man I love and desire."

"Sorry," he mumbled, looking down and wrapping the towel round his waist. It wasn't much help. Jacques was in Paris, but she no longer felt like calling him and hearing that Nadia was there and was only going to come back when the bruising had faded. And she definitely didn't feel like going back to her devastated flat after Nadia's return, back to Kettlerstrasse.

"I'm sorry," said Michael. "I shouldn't have brought everything up again. I spoke to Kemmerling and..." He broke off. Obviously the professor had confirmed that she hadn't poured out her troubles to him. He excused himself again, adding, "I could take time off until Wednesday. I thought you might like to do a bit of shopping —"

"Done it already," she interrupted. "There's cheese and ham in the fridge. I got fruit as well, though I'm afraid I forgot the soused herrings. And if you don't get out this very minute, I'm going to start."

He shook his head in bewilderment and finally went, leaving her alone with the slashed mattresses, the broken crockery, the feathers everywhere, the police seals on the door, Zurkeulen's thoughtfully polite questions about Nadia Trenkler and Hardenberg's claim not to know a woman of that name.

She went to bed early. It wasn't even ten. Michael was still sitting watching the television, winding down with pop music and a frenetic kaleidoscope of pictures. This time it was Shakira wallowing in mud and waggling her hips. She couldn't have sat beside him for two seconds without flinging her arms round his neck, making a full confession and begging him, "Let me stay with you. I'm having your baby. But I won't love you any the less once it's here."

At some point she heard the central locking going on, the shutters going down and Michael going to one of the guest rooms. Shortly after that she fell asleep. She was wakened by someone shaking her shoulder violently. It was only a few minutes after six. The ceiling light was on. He was leaning over her holding part of the regional paper in one hand. The expression on his face was a mixture of consternation, bewilderment, disbelief, denial; it reflected such a wide range of reactions that it was impossible to take them all in at once. In a hoarse voice he just said, "There," and held the paper out for her to read.

The headline leaped out at her like a wild animal: "Body of woman identified." Beside it was a photo of her face, but it couldn't have been that which he'd found so devastating. With the coarse-grained reproduction you had to look closely to see the striking similarity. It was an old, unflattering photo from the days when she'd spent her time at her mother-in-law's bedside, reading to her about princes' castles and poor serving maids. It made her look like a careworn housewife, not at all like Nadia. It was presumably Dieter who'd provided it.

The article referred to the report in the previous day's paper about the dead body in the waste bin. The police were asking for anyone who had seen her or had any information about her to come forward. Her name was Susanne Lasko and she was the divorced wife of the well-known journalist and writer, Dieter Lasko. It was the two names that had caused Michael's reaction.

When he told her, at half-past seven, that he had to go to the lab, she was reading it for the sixth or seventh time and surprised she didn't feel sick. There seemed to be no room in her head for anything other than morning sickness. Before going to the garage he commanded her to stay put until he came home. He was going to see to it that he got back early. It sounded like a threat, but she had no idea where else she could go.

Punctually at eight Andrea appeared, again bringing her son. The little boy came towards her, his thumb in his mouth and carrying a grubby soft toy, while his mother, out in the hall, took a pair of orthopaedic flip-flops out of her bag and put on her brightly coloured housecoat.

"Come here, Pascal," Andrea called.

"Come here, Pascal," she whispered. And, hesitantly, he took the last few steps towards her. She lifted him onto her lap, showed him the photo in the paper and asked him what she should do. Going to the police and telling them it was a case of mistaken identity was out of the question. It would simply mean that Zurkeulen and Ramon would be able to read in the next edition that Susanne Lasko was in the best of health. And the logical conclusion of that was that from now on she was three years older and married to a man who wanted a divorce.

Andrea, alerted by Pascal's disappearance, came into the kitchen, leaned over the article and declared, "She looks like you, don't you think?"

"No, not at all," she replied and turned back to the child in her lap, telling Pascal she was going to have a baby. And this started off a train of thought. Her mother! At first she ignored the fact that Nadia Trenkler could not afford to make contact with Susanne Lasko's mother after her daughter's death. What counted were the tears, the mourning, the terrible news that must have torn a blind old woman's world apart. She had to do something at once, but she couldn't get up from the chair because of the child in her lap.

Andrea smiled in disbelief and asked, "Really? What are you going to do? Will you sue Wenning?"

"No. Why should I?" She didn't even know who Wenning was.

"What does your husband say about it?"

"I don't know," she said, feeling she knew nothing at all apart from that one fact: Susanne Lasko was dead, probably as a result of a "talk" with Ramon.

She spent the morning as if in a trance with a barrage of flashlights picking out individual parts of a complex whole for a fraction of a second. Nadia claiming to have replacement documents. Nadia assuring her Philip had no key to her flat. Zurkeulen in the bank and his thoughtful voice in Hardenberg's office. Andrea with a bottle of oven cleaner. The telephone in Frau Schädlich's office, Nadia's fragmentary message. Andrea holding a dress shirt with a spot that hadn't come out. Andrea asking, "And tomorrow?"

"Wednesday, I think," she said and came to with a start. It was almost two o'clock. She was sitting at the kitchen table in her dressing gown, in front of her a newspaper covered in biscuit crumbs and smeared with chocolate. On the floor Pascal was playing with the cut-up *Frankfurter Allgemeine* and a whisk. Susanne Lasko was dead, Jacques was in Paris, the Chopin on the piano was as complicated as ever. And she couldn't swim either.

"Should I come tomorrow or not?" Andrea asked.

She took a deep breath and came to a decision. "Of course. Come as usual. We're letting the water out of the pool, I think it needs a good scrub."

Andrea just shrugged her shoulders, took the whisk off Pascal, gathered up the pieces of the *Frankfurter Allgemeine*, stuffed them in the waste bin and left. She sat at the table a while longer, staring at the local section of the paper. Her former face could hardly be seen under the smears of chocolate.

One hour later she'd showered, given her complexion a healthy smoothness with the help of a lot of cosmetics and a lot of effort, and blow-dried Nadia's hair to the same perfection as the coiffeur himself.

Every gesture was right, her brain was razor-sharp, well aware that anything that went wrong from now on was her problem alone.

In the dressing room she decided on the trouser suit Nadia had worn when she'd rung Philip Hardenberg from the corner of Kettlerstrasse. To go with it she selected a light-brown pullover and matching slip-ons. For the first time she also took some of Nadia's jewellery from the leather-bound casket. She chose a double string of pearls, that went marvellously with the pullover, stuck a ring with a large pearl on her left hand and swapped her diamond ear studs for dangling pearls. Then she went to the study and made an appointment as Nadia Trenkler.

The inn she'd proposed for the rendezvous was an isolated building on her Sunday route. Every time she'd driven past with Johannes Herzog, she'd noticed the board by the door on which some dishes were written in chalk. From the car she'd never been able to read them. When she walked up to the board one hour later, she regretted her proposal.

On the deserted gravel parking lot beside the building the Alfa stuck out like a sore thumb. She was close to turning back. But then she went in, her handbag under her arm and carrying the computer case. Beside the laptop, the case also contained the lead, as well as the envelope with the printouts and the tape from the Dictaphone.

The bar had a cosy, country air and was empty. A bell rang as the door closed behind her. At the back was an open sliding door into a large, gleaming kitchen. A busty woman appeared and scrutinized her from head to toe, as if she were some exotic beast. Perhaps the pearls and the mink jacket were a bit over the top. But what the woman at the bar thought was neither here nor there and for Dieter Lasko nothing could be too over-the-top.

Turning to Dieter Lasko of all people was a huge risk, but by no means as great a risk as anything she could have done herself, that much was clear to her. She didn't want Dieter to help her, just her mother. In return for all the hours she'd spent with trashy novels beside his mother's bed. Who else could she send to the old folks' home to reassure her mother? "There's no reason to be downhearted. You mustn't tell anyone, but Susanne's all right."

Dieter arrived only eight minutes later. She was already drinking a coffee and had ordered cheese and mushrooms on toast. She should have been surprised she could even think of having a snack, but there

242

was no time and no room inside her head for surprise. That was entirely taken up with a mountain of hope that somehow she'd manage to bluff her way through someone else's life with the means at her disposal.

Sitting in the semi-darkness at one of the tables at the back, she wasn't immediately visible. She had specially asked the landlady to switch off the light over her table. With a shrug of the shoulders, the woman had complied. Clearly one was allowed pointless requests if one was wearing a mink jacket and a pearl necklace and was setting up a P4 with three gigahertz.

She almost didn't recognize Dieter. He was wearing grey trousers with a crease, jacket, shirt and tie to match, and had neat, blow-dried hair and bronzed skin, as if he'd come straight from the Caribbean. She'd only seen him in worn jeans and sack-like pullovers, with a pale complexion, close-cropped hair and a three-day beard.

As expected, he didn't see her at once and turned to the landlady, who reappeared through the sliding door when the little bell jangled. She couldn't make out what he said. The landlady pointed in her direction. He peered through the semi-darkness, split the bronzed skin with a polite smile and came towards her. After two or three steps, he halted.

During the drive she'd imagined his reaction to her face in a thousand different variations. Only she would never have dared to predict what it would be – not from the Dieter she knew: a man who went on fanatically about justice, law, order, dignity and God knows what, but had nothing other in mind than a good story or a new book. And he knew her from the time she'd worked in a bank. She'd always been smartly, if not so expensively, dressed and nicely turned out.

A few agonizingly long and anxious moments passed. He'd recognized her. Or had he? Three years after their divorce, preceded by six years, during which he'd seen her about as often as a child from the lowlands sees the snowman it's built, and after what he'd been put through the previous afternoon, he didn't seem sure whether to believe his eyes or not. The way his expression kept changing was spectacular. He stood there like a waxwork in the blazing sun. As he forced himself to take the last few steps, he looked as if he was about to melt away. His speech did. "Frau... err... Trenkler... err?"

She'd never heard him stutter before. The relief that it had worked with him too was like a warm wave flooding through her body. She just nodded. Shaking his head, he sat down opposite her. "You must excuse me if I stare at you like this. The similarity is really amazing."

"Yes," she said, "nature can play some odd tricks." She asked him to tell her something about her double and the circumstances that had led to her death; only then would she explain the connection between her and his ex-wife.

It was close to a miracle that Dieter accepted this. Previously one would have got nothing from him before the quid pro quo was on the table. But he was presumably still influenced by the shock and by the number of questions it left him with. Beyond that, he was convinced he was sitting facing the woman the police were already looking for, though she only realized that in the further course of the conversation.

The landlady brought him a coffee. He fixed his eyes on the window; his voice was still without its usual steadiness. He'd had to identify the corpse the previous afternoon. The fact that they'd traced him so quickly – and that so far no doubts as to the identity of the dead woman had been raised – was due to identity papers found in her handbag, which had also been in the waste bin: a passport, a replacement driving licence and an ID card, which, like the passport, had only been issued in the middle of September.

It appeared, Dieter said, that Susanne had lost her papers in the middle of August and applied for replacements. He couldn't say whether the police had found an older ID card or the original driving licence in the flat. Nor did he know anything about a flight bag in the waste bin, only that they'd searched in vain for the keys to the outside door and to her flat, and assumed the murderer must have taken them.

He couldn't tell her anything about the circumstances of her death, he went on. He'd seen the autopsy report, but that raised more questions than it answered. Susanne had not simply been run over. Both hands had had petrol poured over them and been set alight – not post mortem. And she'd been subjected to a few further acts of brutality before the car had finished off the job. She'd been run over twice. The time of death was late on Saturday evening or during that night; more precisely they couldn't say.

"The police hoped I could give them some useful information," he said, "but I was unable to help them. Since our divorce I'd had no

244

contact with Susanne and I don't know with whom or in what she'd become involved."

Finally he dragged his eyes away from the window. "The police are looking for an acquaintance of Susanne's who used a pretext to lure her away from her work on Thursday. On Friday a woman – presumably the same – rang the shop again and put a car at her disposal. That doesn't necessarily have to be connected with the murder. Perhaps the two women just went out shopping together on the Thursday. But the police would naturally like to talk to the acquaintance."

He stared at her, as if challenging her to admit it was her. When she said nothing, he went on with his account. He told her about Heller, who'd been stabbed to death on the Friday evening – by a fellow boozer with whom he'd had a fight in the bar earlier, the police believed. They were also assuming there was a connection between the two cases. Two tenants of the same building so soon one after the other, a connection was an obvious conclusion. The more so as, according to her mother, Susanne had been a close friend of Heller. She must have sunk pretty low after the divorce, Dieter said, to get involved with a violent alcoholic who had a criminal record.

Had she been killed because she'd seen Heller's murderer? In their statements her colleagues in the shop had said she'd seemed nervous on the Saturday. But if she seen something, why hadn't she gone straight to the police? And if it was the same murderer, who was just getting rid of a dangerous witness, why the tortures? Why had her flat been broken into and wrecked? Dieter had the impression the murderer was looking for something. Why had no one in the building heard anything? True, if a train was going past outside, it would cover a lot of noise, breaking crockery, perhaps even cries for help.

She'd been wounded in the flat, Dieter explained. There were splashes of fresh blood that corresponded to old patches on the carpet. That she'd let the murderer in herself could be ruled out. Had she been in when he came? She'd gone out early on Saturday evening. Someone in the neighbouring building had seen that, but no one knew when she'd come back.

One question after another. The big mystery for Dieter was his ex-mother-in-law's statement. Agnes Runge swore by all that was holy that she'd talked to her daughter on the phone on Saturday evening. By that time Susanne was long-since dead, so couldn't have been out on a motorbike trip with her "friend" Jasmin Toppler. Jasmin Toppler had spent the whole weekend with other motorbike fans at the Nurburgring, but hadn't seen Susanne since the Friday. She denied they were friends, they just did each other the occasional favour, that was all. Had Agnes Runge got the day wrong? That would have been understandable after the shock of such news. But why had Susanne lied to her mother left, right and centre? About her "friend", about an office job she didn't have; she'd even pretended the drunk, Heller, had a piano.

She kept the smile on her face, though it was an effort. That it looked very strained as she heard this information didn't give her away. Dieter finished by explaining, "Susanne always lived in a dream world and tended to overestimate her ability to deal with critical situations. Perhaps she'd been influenced by the countless trashy novels she'd read in which there's always a happy ending."

She decided to bring the farce to an end and to risk it. "Very informative, your assessment of me."

He was struck dumb. When he recovered, he wavered between anger and denial. "I'm sorry, Frau Trenkler, but this isn't the moment for silly jokes."

"I'm not in the mood for silly jokes, either," she said. "I may have become a bit of a cabbage during the six years I lived with your mother, but I'm not that stupid that I'd try to pass myself off as a dead woman voluntarily. I made up stories for my mother because I didn't want her to worry about my situation."

He gulped, screwed up his eyes and murmured, "I don't believe it. It really is you, isn't it?"

"Not any more," she said. "Now I'm Nadia Trenkler." She showed him her ID card and driving licence.

He examined them. "How did you get these documents? Do they belong to the dead woman?"

She nodded and started a detailed report – at the lift in Gerler House, as she had when she'd written it down. Now there was a lot to be added. Dieter listened, flabbergasted, several times he shook his head but he didn't interrupt. Only when she got to the end did he comment that that was exactly what he'd just been saying. It was typical of her – any reasonably sensible person would have been suspicious after the increased fee offered following the disaster with the garage door. And no woman with a modicum of sense would have agreed to do it a second time, especially after such a dramatic danger signal as the encounter with Zurkeulen in the bank.

"I didn't have much choice," she said. "I may be lacking up top, but something down here's more important." She pointed at her belly.

For a moment Dieter forgot who he was and cursed and swore like any builder's labourer, at the same time giving her unacceptable pieces of advice. Get an abortion, go straight to the police, that kind of thing.

"I've not come to hear a sermon from you," she broke in and went on to explain what she wanted him to do.

He shook his head vigorously. Telling her mother he considered the craziest idea she'd ever had. "She couldn't keep it up. Christ, just think what you're expecting from an old woman, Su—" He broke off in the middle of the word and quickly glanced at the sliding door, which was open. The landlady couldn't be seen, the clatter of pots and pans came from the kitchen.

Dieter categorically refused to go to the police and name Zurkeulen and Ramon as Susanne's murderers. The things she'd heard in Hardenberg's office might well suggest that, but Dieter absolutely declined to go along with her proposal that he change his statement and say that in the last few weeks his former wife had passed incriminating evidence as well as the keys to the Alfo Investment offices on to him.

"OK," she said, "forget it. I didn't imagine I could expect much from you. But at least you can tell me where I can brush up my English quickly. There must be special courses."

He tapped his forehead. "You can't stay with her husband. How do you think that's going to work out?"

She didn't think it was going to work out. Since Michael was talking about a divorce, it would be a waste of time. She just wanted to be equipped to survive a short get-together with Phil and Pamela at the Sorbonne. If Michael suggested it again, she was going to agree. It couldn't do any harm to get away to somewhere safe.

Dieter broke into laughter, loud enough to bring the landlady out of the kitchen for a moment. "You? At the Sorbonne? And what are you going to do there? Give a lecture on castles in the air?"

At least she learned where Phil and Pamela were staying and that French was indispensable there. Dieter's amusement quickly subsided. He sighed. "You haven't got a cat's chance in hell."

"I've managed so far."

"Yes." He nodded for a change. "And how long have you been managing? For one weekend?"

"I got by in September as well."

"Perhaps you could survive for two or three days, but that would be it. Knowledge can be withheld, lack of knowledge comes out automatically."

The landlady finally brought her toasted cheese and mushrooms, and asked if they'd like anything else to drink. Dieter ordered another coffee, plus a cognac to help him digest all the revelations. After the landlady had returned to the kitchen, she pushed the laptop and envelope across the table to him.

"What am I supposed to do with these?" he asked.

"Keep the envelope safe and show me how this thing works." She told him about the lead that had been kept in the house, which suggested that Nadia didn't want Hardenberg looking at the laptop. While she was explaining this, Dieter took the printouts out of the envelope, leafed through them and quickly read the fragmentary letter to Jacques. "What's this about?" he wanted to know. "It sounds like a highly personal matter."

"I know," she said, "but it's not important at the moment. Jacques's in Paris."

"Is that where he lives?"

She just said, "Yes," to stop him giving her another sermon. He switched on the laptop. Even while she was explaining that it didn't work without the lead, he'd loaded up the program, rolled his eyes pityingly and muttered, "Oh, Susanne." He offered no explanation.

She set about her cheese and mushroom toast. It was excellent. "Wouldn't you like to eat something?" she asked. "On me."

He took no notice of this, nor of her assertion that she'd only have to get through a few weeks as Nadia at most; that as soon as possible she intended to find a flat somewhere where no one knew Susanne Lasko or Nadia Trenkler. His fingers were scurrying round the mouse pad. He interrupted her explanations with a curt, "What was the name of the file with your neighbour's name you found on the computer?"

248

"NTA," she said.

"There's an SLA here." With that, he turned the machine round so she could see the screen. It showed a list with figures, dates, series of numbers and sets of letters. There were no names, but the figures spoke for themselves. The first was 5,530,000. Combined with the date given – 12 September – and the letters MZ, there was only one possible answer.

"But on the torn-up piece of paper it was five million seven hundred and thirty thousand," she said. "If she'd only paid in five hundred and thirty thousand, then Zurkeulen's not lost anything."

"But these guys are always creaming off a percentage for themselves," said Dieter. "The gals, too, apparently."

She couldn't believe Nadia had taken money for herself. On 12 September Jo had been celebrating a rise of thirty points. And at Lilo's party she'd picked up a number, two hundred, but not been able to make any connection because her head had been full of other things. The Deko Fund was just window dressing after all. And Joko Electronics. It sounded somehow Japanese, a bit like John Lennon's wife. Yoko Ono. Joko equals Joachim Kogler, she thought. If you're going to lie, keep it simple. How had Ilona Blasting put it? "As long as you butter her up, you're allowed to have a finger in the pie."

Dieter ran his finger down the columns on the screen. All the other deposits corresponded exactly to the amounts on the Alfo Investment sheet. NTA – SLA. It was simple really: Nadia Trenkler – Susanne Lasko, the A presumably standing for account. And worst of all were the dates of the initial investments. After the twelfth and eighteenth of September – that was the Wednesday when Nadia had been so angry she'd cancelled her stint as stand-in – they corresponded to her days off from the shop.

"It looks as if this is her personal account book," Dieter said. "No wonder Hardenberg wasn't to get a look at it. But there's one thing I don't understand. Why didn't she make up Zurkeulen's supposed loss? I wouldn't risk my life for two hundred thousand when I'd got twenty million to play with."

"Perhaps she couldn't get at it. Michael said that the previous time she'd used the money to speculate on the stock exchange. Perhaps it's all gone."

"No," Dieter said. "There are regular increases, that must be interest coming in. The money's been profitably invested somewhere."

The landlady brought him his coffee and the cognac. After she'd gone again, he came to a decision. "I'll take this thing, but I don't think it's going to help you."

He assumed one set of letter combinations referred to banks, he went on. The series of numbers must be reference and account numbers. There were no sort codes, which made him think it would be impossible to work out where the money was. "But even if I do find that out," he said, "you can't get at it as Nadia Trenkler. I suspect everything's under the name of Lasko and you won't be able to get your old ID cards back. The police have them."

"I can get replacements," she said.

"Are you crazy?" Dieter hissed. Then, speaking in an undertone, he said he wondered how Nadia had managed to get replacement documents in the name of Lasko without the police finding out. Applying for them was no problem, but the council registration office would have sent notification.

"Getting them out of my letter box wouldn't be a problem either," she said. "I was at the confectioner's all day."

The landlady was at the bar now, making a show of wiping up. With a quick glance in her direction, Dieter pointed at the screen again. He spoke so softly even she had difficulty hearing. "For the moment you do nothing." No question of going to the police now. His finger tapped a column of pairs of letters. AR, she read, PR, DL, RL, LL.

It was presumably these initials alone that had made him change his mind and dissuaded him from leaving her to deal with the situation by herself. Agnes Runge, Peter Runge, Dieter Lasko, Ramie Lasko, Letitia Lasko. He was very angry that his wife and daughter had been drawn into this. Not knowing Johannes Herzog and Herbert Schrag, he couldn't make anything of the other sets of initials. And Nadia was the only one she'd told about her crush on Richard Gere.

Pulling at his lower lip, lost in thought, a gesture she remembered from earlier times, Dieter asked if she had the office key on her. Then, quite happy to let her pay, he followed her out to the car park. Next to the Alfa was a dark-green estate with a child seat in the back. Dieter put the envelope and laptop on the rear seat and asked her to go on ahead; he would follow as he didn't know the way.

"And if there's someone in the office?" she asked.

"I hope very much there is," he said. "It would be useful to know if Hardenberg has access to the money. If he does, you've one worry the less. If he doesn't, you'd better find a good plastic surgeon."

It took them just under an hour to get to Gerler House. As ever, the dark-blue Mercedes was in its parking space; the other three spaces were empty. In the lift Dieter took the leather holder from her, also demanding the keys to her flat in Kettlerstrasse. If she was caught, he said, it would be better if they weren't found on her.

He went on ahead, opened the door and strode swiftly across the lobby to the upholstered door. It was locked. Nothing could be heard. Instinctively she held her breath when he went in. He called out, "Don't worry, the coast's clear."

By the time she'd entered Hardenberg's office, he was already sitting at the desk, had started up the computer and set a search in motion. After only a few seconds he exclaimed triumphantly, "There it is!"

SLA. The next moment a spreadsheet poured over the screen. It only had Zurkeulen's investment account, split up into several smaller amounts. "Where are the others?" Dieter asked, telling her to have a look to see if there were any CDs around. "I'll make a copy of this."

She couldn't find any disks, neither in Helga's office, nor in Hardenberg's filing cabinets. All she came across there was a spring file which a firm of private investigators had sent to Hardenberg. Heller had been right, the opinion pollster was a snooper. And the funny object that, when she'd been running a temperature, she'd assumed was part of the table, was a bugging device. Both she and Heller had been under surveillance for several weeks. Dieter had also had a visit.

"What's that you're messing about with?" he asked irritatedly. He took the file from here and muttered, "The bastards."

The idea there might be a bug in his house drove him wild. He started rummaging through the filing cabinet himself and established that none of the documents he leafed through quickly hinted at dishonest transactions. Given their haste it was, of course, impossible to check every sheet, but Dieter still calmed down. He was no longer bothered about a CD. He took the private investigator's file then had a quick look at Helga's hard disk, dismissing the correspondence of Hardenberg's partner as harmless letters. Apart from that, there was only a small kitchen and a washroom. Nadia hadn't had an office at Alfo Investment, but then freelancers didn't need one.

They got back to the lift and down to the underground car park unseen. Dieter intended to have a look at the computer in the study and – if necessary – free up some memory. Then he was going to go back to Hardenberg's office and send all the material that seemed important by email, to give him time to examine it undisturbed. The way he put it, it sounded like child's play.

But she didn't think he'd find anything of significance. Hardenberg had spent too much time and effort on his computer after Zurkeulen's visit. And the papers he'd burned suggested he'd destroyed anything that might give him away. Apart from that, she remembered that Michael was going to come home early. "Let's do it tomorrow," she suggested.

"I'm having lunch with my publisher tomorrow," Dieter said.

"Then the day after tomorrow."

"No," Dieter insisted. He'd drawn the same conclusion about Hardenberg's actions as she had. "We'll get it done today. Hardenberg was panicking when he cleared up, he might have missed something. Once he has time to think, it might occur to him that a specialist can retrieve deleted files. If he wipes the hard disk or removes it, we won't find anything. And if they get onto you in a couple of days, I want to have as much evidence as possible to hand. Are you clear about what you might be faced with? How do you think Trenkler's going to react when he realizes who it was they found in the waste bin? You had nothing to lose when his wife met you. That she engaged you as a stand-in is about the most stupid argument you could use when there's twenty million lying around. You worked in a bank, you know about finance, remember? Which of you was it who saw it as her big chance?"

She'd never thought about it like that, but she just couldn't see Michael as a threat. And she was intensely irritated by the way Dieter was slipping back into his old way of treating her. And he was forgetting one thing. If Michael was already at home and Susanne Lasko's ex-husband turned up, that would considerably increase the chances of her being unmasked.

It was dark outside as they emerged from the car park one after the other. She led the way again through the heavy evening traffic and Dieter followed. In the city there was no real chance of overtaking but on the autobahn things were different. The Alfa was much more manoeuvrable than the dark-green estate. There wasn't a lot of room, but enough for a bit of motorway slalom. For a couple of seconds she could still see him flashing his headlights in the rear-view mirror. Then they were submerged in the sea of light.

Twenty minutes later she stopped in the drive. The Jaguar was already in the garage. She braced herself for an angry outburst or a breath test and went into the hall expecting her wrist to be grabbed. But Michael was nowhere to be seen. There were dirty pots and pans in the kitchen. It looked as if he'd made himself a meal but hardly eaten any of it. She went upstairs, hung the mink jacket back in the dressing room and checked all the rooms. No trace of Michael. When she went back downstairs, she heard him calling from the basement.

He was sitting on the side of the pool, naked and wet. His eyes were reddened, probably from the chlorine. His voice was completely toneless as he said, "I thought you'd gone."

"I just had to take a few things back to the office. Been home long?"

"Since half three. Who was Susanne Lasko and what did she have to do with you?"

"With me, nothing," she declared. "Philip was involved with her, I'm sure of that. The man who threatened me must have confused me with her. That's the only explanation I can think of."

He nodded, sunk in thought. Without indicating whether he believed her or not, he looked up and smiled. "Do you feel like kissing me dry?"

"Not just now," she said.

"Have you been drinking?"

She shook her head. He stretched out his hand and, thinking he wanted to do a breath test again, she took a couple of steps towards the edge of the pool. Before she knew what was happening, he'd pulled her down. For a second she could feel his thighs under her back, his hand behind her head and his mouth on her lips. Then, despite the fact the she was fully clothed, he gave her a push. She slipped off his legs and the water closed over her head.

He stayed sitting on the side, watching her desperate struggle. If she'd let herself slide into the pool carefully, she could probably have kept her head above water. Being thrown in was quite a different matter. Her shoes came off. She couldn't touch the bottom and there was nothing for her to grab on to either. Flailing her arms and thrashing her legs only took her further from the side. She didn't dare breathe in, holding her breath until she thought her lungs and her head were going to burst.

Twice she saw him, refracted through the water, sitting motionless on the side. Since he did nothing, she was convinced he was trying to kill her – that is, Nadia. Then he finally pushed off and was beside her in a moment. He pulled her to him and lifted her head above water. Only to kiss her. She didn't even have time to take a deep breath.

"Why can't you understand what I really want," he murmured, then dived down with her. He seemed to take the way she clung to him in panic as passion. Even under the surface he continued to kiss her, at the same time fiddling with the zip of her trousers. Then back up to the surface. Time for a quick gasp for breath before he clamped his mouth over hers again.

Her pulse was a deafening throb in her ears. The necklace tore as he pawed her. A few pearls drifted through the water, the rest of the string swirling as it sank to the bottom. It was green down there and blue, with the first dark patches as she began to lose consciousness. The last thing she felt was his hands round her waist, under her pullover, his lips on her breast and water up her nose. She didn't even get round to cursing her driving skills. Nadia had been wrong about one thing – drowning while making love was definitely not a wonderful death. But Nadia's had been even less wonderful, had been horrible.

She felt terribly cold when she came to. There was an immense weight on her chest. Then it eased and light returned. Michael was kneeling beside her, pressing rhythmically under her ribs with both hands. She coughed, wheezed, spat out water and heard him begging her breathlessly, "Yes, come on, come on, come on. That's it. Keep breathing."

He kept kissing her again and again, not letting her get enough air. Cradling her face in his hands, he asked, "What was wrong? Did you bash your head against the side? You have been drinking, haven't you? Admit it, you've been drinking. Tell me again that you love me. I love you too. You, just you, not the money you can make." He was stammering, as if he were going out of his mind. He squeezed the water out of her hair, brushed it off her cheeks, pulled her dripping-wet pullover off over her head and tugged her trousers down.

Her teeth were chattering. "I feel so cold."

"You'll warm up pretty soon." He took her in his arms and carried her upstairs. In bed it was anything but the standard deal. It went on and on, he couldn't get enough – of Nadia. The cold gradually faded, apart from one spot deep within, like an icy thorn that every "Nadia!" from his lips drove deeper into her flesh. Although extremely reluctantly, she realized that Dieter was right. When it came to the crunch, this man, who couldn't stop kissing her, caressing her, loving her, could represent a much greater threat than Zurkeulen and his thug. She had to get out of his life as quickly as possible.

At some point the telephone in the study rang. The answerphone clicked in. Nadia's voice with the message could be heard through the open door, then Dieter saying, "Are you mad? Where did you learn to drive like that? Ring me. I told you I haven't time tomorrow."

The question suddenly brought Michael back down to earth. He stopped his lovemaking and pushed himself up. "Who's that?"

"I don't know. Must be a wrong number."

She pulled his head back down to her. In the study Dieter was begging her for Heaven's sake not to try anything herself or what little was left would go down the drain too. She put her hands over his ears and clamped her lips to his until all was quiet again. He pulled away from her and looked down. "Nadia, I want to know what's going on. I have to know."

So she told him – that behind her back Philip had been indulging in some nasty chicanery with a double, a woman who looked just like her. The words simply flowed, she was at least as good as Nadia at lying, after all, she'd had plenty of practice with her mother. "For weeks I didn't realize what was going on," she said. "A few times when I came into the office, Helga asked me if I'd forgotten something. It sounded as if I'd been in already that day. But who would imagine something like that? No one expects there to be another version of themselves."

The possibility only occurred to her, she claimed, the first time someone addressed her by the name of Lasko. No, not the angry man in the bank, Behringer's friendly office manager had greeted her in the lift and asked how she was getting on with her job at Alfo Investment. It was from nice Herr Reincke that she had learned that Susanne Lasko had applied for a job as secretary at Behringer's and that Philip Hardenberg had torpedoed her appointment. Naturally she'd wondered why Philip had taken on her double – and that without Helga's knowledge. That was why she'd been travelling round so much recently, had had to stay away overnight and think up stupid excuses.

"I got the idea that Philip must be meeting this woman somewhere else, perhaps because Helga had become suspicious. I followed him when he went on business trips, but I never saw the woman. And I didn't like to ask Herr Reincke for her address. After that angry client went on at me last week, I tried to see what I could find in the office. I thought there must be some documents somewhere. But the only things I could find were that envelope with papers and the old key-holder, the things that were in the boot of the Alfa. On Friday I went to the address, in Kettlerstrasse. The keys fitted, but the woman wasn't there. I waited for hours, I wanted to have it out with her. That's why I was so late coming home. And I went there again on Saturday morning, again with no success. I wanted to have one more try on Sunday, but you stopped me. Now the woman's dead and Philip has clearly gone into hiding. Hold me tight."

He did that, for most of the night, on the damp sheets. He only got out of bed once, to put his alarm in the bathroom. Then he clung tight to her again, murmuring his fears and feelings against the back of her neck. That he didn't know whether to believe her or not. That he was afraid he'd never be able to lead a normal life if he stayed with her, because she didn't understand what really counted in life. But he knew what he owed to her. And he was the one person she could count on, if she made a mess of things again. It flowed almost seamlessly into a whispered "You sleep on." She felt his lips across her temple, then he was gone. An unpredictable factor. An incalculable risk. Nadia's husband.

She spent most of the morning brooding over the pain his inability to give up Nadia was causing her. It was just before midday that the telephone took her mind off it. Dieter was on the line. Andrea was cleaning the big windows by the pool. It hadn't been emptied. Andrea didn't know how to let the water out, nor did she.

Dieter had switched his meeting with his publisher from lunch to dinner. He could understand why she hadn't rung him. He was ringing from Hardenberg's office. He thought it highly unlikely he would be interrupted in the next few hours. "The Mercedes has gone and I'm convinced that means Hardenberg has too," he said. "From what I've seen so far, there's no mention of the other eight men on the list, but I'm a long way from having checked everything yet."

He wanted to know how much free memory there was on the hard disk in the study. Following his instructions, it took her only a few seconds to find the information. As Dieter had assumed, there was nowhere near enough storage space.

She sent Andrea home. Just thirty minutes later Dieter was there. She guided him into the garage. He had no objection to being shown round, but made no comment, neither admitting he was impressed nor suggesting mockingly that she fitted into the house like a pig in the parlour. When she mentioned the pool, all he said was, "I had a small pool installed in the garden last spring too." The sight of the shimmering green did, however, elicit an awestruck, "My God, it's a proper indoor pool!"

"Do you know how to let the water out?" she asked hopefully.

"Why? There's nothing wrong with it. Have you any idea what it costs to fill a pool like that?"

"I don't want to fill it," she explained. "I fell in yesterday."

"Then just keep away," he advised.

In the hall he quickly demonstrated how to open the letter box. It didn't need a key, she just had to stick her finger in the opening she'd assumed was a keyhole, press a tiny bolt to one side and pull out the flap. There were two envelopes in it. One was the telephone bill, the other came from a music agent's and had two more tickets for the Niedenhoff concert in the Beethovenhalle.

As they went into the study, the telephone rang. The answerphone switched in. It was Phil telling them, in incredibly fast English, that there was a small guest room available, but that Pamela could book them into a hotel, if they preferred. Dieter translated it for her, adding, with ironic emphasis, "You'd better get a sore throat." Then, recalling her request, "I must have some language courses somewhere. English definitely. I did have a French course, too, but it's possible that Ramie…"

He broke off and promised, "If I find the things, I'll send you them. Then you can contribute the odd remark to the conversation without making a fool of yourself. But you mustn't overdo it. No one'll notice if a woman whose husband thinks she's fucked up again keeps her mouth shut."

Then he sat down at the computer and fiddled around for a while to familiarize himself with it. "What's Sec?" he asked. She didn't know. All she could remember was that in September Michael had said something about taking it down. From that Dieter concluded they could do without Sec for the time being. He also deleted a few operational programs, commenting, "Better safe than sorry."

When he thought they had enough storage space, he explained what she had to do in Hardenberg's office. He was uneasy about leaving the data transfer to her, but he couldn't see to it himself because of the dinner with his publisher.

Before he went, he had time to report what else he'd heard. That morning he'd been to the police again to find out if they had any clues about the acquaintance who'd phoned Susanne at the shop. They hadn't. On the Friday evening Jasmin Toppler had dropped her outside the multi-storey and driven straight back home. On Saturday Frau Gathmann had only seen the Alfa from a distance, hadn't noted the number and couldn't say what make of car it was. Nor could they establish where the two calls from Nadia had come from, since the confectioner's didn't have an ISDN line. It appeared the police hadn't stumbled across Alfo Investment yet. Naturally they didn't tell him everything but they'd hinted that their money was on an opportunist thief disturbed in the flat.

"By the way, she applied for the replacement documents at the beginning of August," Dieter said. "Two days after she'd received the first report from the private eye and knew for certain that you had no contacts apart from your mother. It usually takes four to six weeks before you get the new documents. In the meantime you get a paper from the vehicle-licensing people certifying that you're permitted to drive. The council registration office also issues you with something you can use as ID if necessary. I suspect she'd have still put one over on you, even if you hadn't gone along with it. She probably only really needed you so her husband wouldn't get suspicious while she was off on her travels."

Now Nadia's concern about her marriage was working to her advantage, Dieter said. For the moment she was safe, at least from the police. So far they'd seen no cause to do a DNA test to confirm the identity of the dead woman. "They don't do that as routine, it's expensive and they're looking to save money. Let's just hope it stays that way – after the confusion your mother caused. She insisted you rang her on Sunday evening. I advised her to change her statement and not make a fuss."

"Did you tell her I was OK?"

He grinned. "Not likely. Or do you think she could keep it to herself?"

"What do they need for one of these DNA tests?" she asked.

"In principle just your toothbrush."

"I've got that here."

He shrugged his shoulders. "A hair-brush does the job just as well, though I very much doubt whether they looked for one in the shambles that had been made of your flat. If necessary, they could take a sample from your mother to rule out a family connection. But if they do that, I'll hear about it. She rings me up three times a day."

Then he handed back the office keys, emphasizing how important it was not to let anyone near her computer until he'd made sure Hardenberg had been thorough in deleting files. "Heaven only knows where that leaves you if all he's done is to save his own skin. Anyone who really wants to can view the smaller files in the editor."

He'd made a list of the files he wanted to have a look at. He told her to buy some CDs the following day and copy what he wanted onto them. He was going to do that at home. On no account should he stay close to her unnecessarily, he'd realized that much at least. "That's the last thing you want at the moment. Is Trenkler likely to start doing some digging off his own bat?"

"Why should he?"

"Well I would if my wife was involved in something like that."

"He's a scientist," she said, "not a journalist."

Dieter nodded pensively. "What about the neighbours? Policeman can mean almost anything and it's a pretty expensive area round here. He won't be driving a patrol car, that's for sure."

She told him about Lilo's party and the news of Röhrler's death. Dieter was immediately concerned. "Sounds like the serious fraud squad. He was probably onto her and she gave him Röhrler to get him off her back. Want to bet?" No she didn't, he was probably right.

Shortly after Dieter had left, she decided to go and carry out the data transfer. There seemed to be plenty of time, even though it was just after three. However, as she was watching the green estate disappear – and trying to establish whether the neighbours had noticed her visitor – Michael rang.

After he'd started to leave a message on the answerphone, he was audibly relieved that she'd picked up the phone. "I thought we could go to Demetros's this evening," he said. "I am going to be a bit late, but I could manage it by nine. You could go on ahead and we'll meet there."

"I hope you don't mind," she said, "but I just don't feel like going out."

"You'll wait up for me?"

"Of course."

The last thing she heard was a quiet, "I love you."

No, she thought, not me. Then she switched the alarm system on and went to the garage. There was heavy traffic on the autobahn into town, but despite that it only took her three quarters of an hour. She parked in one of the reserved spaces and went up by lift. There was no one in the lift nor, as Dieter had predicted, in the Alfo Investment offices.

The transfer presented no difficulties, but it took time. When she left, the building was almost empty. There were only a few cars among the massive pillars in the underground car park. She didn't notice any that seemed familiar and might have warned her. She did hear an engine starting up somewhere in the background, but paid no attention to it.

Driving through the city she noticed the car that was tailing her several times, only she didn't realize it was tailing her. It was a grey car. It never overtook her, but in the heavy after-work traffic that was impossible anyway. She drifted along – with the traffic and with her thoughts. Demetros's! A delicious meal in a pleasant restaurant would have been nice. But she could cook herself. And set the table with candles and all the trimmings. What she couldn't do was to go for complete reconciliation, the previous night had made that clearer than any quarrel could have. Even if it broke her heart, she had to get Michael thinking about divorce again. Or, even better, take off herself. Not necessarily in the next couple of days, but as soon as possible.

When the grey car followed her up the autobahn slip road, her mind was still fixed on Paris. If Michael could get off until Wednesday and Phil and Pamela were looking forward to a visit… A foreign city, it should be possible to slip away… She needn't stay there – it would be difficult, anyway, if she couldn't speak the language.

The grey car was practically stuck to her rear bumper. Eventually she noticed. She saw too that there was just one man in it. In the headlights of the car behind, his head appeared as a silhouette in her rear-view mirror. A square, squat head! Her heart missed a beat.

She pulled out. There was a small gap between a refrigerated lorry and an articulated lorry. It was one hell of a squeeze, but she managed it. The driver of the refrigerated lorry responded to her risky manoeuvre with repeated blasts on his horn. The radiator of the massive vehicle rose up behind her like a mountain and for a moment she could see herself getting squashed under the artic. She risked a quick glance at the outside lane. The grey car had also slowed down and was now right beside her. The driver's face could be seen more clearly. Ramon! Jerking the wheel, she pulled onto the hard shoulder and put her foot down.

On her right the dark bushes beside the safety barrier flew past, on her left an endless stream of HGVs. It was so narrow, it was like speeding down a tube. After a mile or so there seemed to be a space in front. She shot up to the gap, swerved back into the inside lane and stamped on the brakes. In front an ancient van was labouring up the hill, behind were the headlights of an HGV and beside her cars driving nose to tail. Another gap in the outside lane. She squeezed in and accelerated. On the right a sign appeared. Not far to her exit. The grey car had disappeared. She breathed a deep sigh of relief, convinced she'd shaken it off.

But when she indicated and turned right into the exit, it appeared from nowhere. And again it was right behind her. Just missing the exit crash barrier by inches, she shot back along the inside lane, then pulled out. She couldn't shake it off. She sped along for another ten miles, not thinking of Johannes Herzog, though her head was full of his instructions, switching from one lane to the other, then onto the hard shoulder again. There Ramon drove up so close behind, she was afraid he was going to force her up against the crash barrier.

Fifteen miles, twenty miles, all on a zigzag course accompanied by furious hooting from other drivers. Then another sign appeared on the right. Delaying until the very last second, she skidded into the long exit curve, the grey car skidding after her. But Ramon had not been taught by Johannes Herzog. He lost control of the car. In the rear-view mirror she saw it spin and come to a halt in the middle of the road. With a quick prayer that an articulated lorry or some other monster HGV would come and remove that threat entirely, she raced along the country road to the next slip road and drove back.

Twice she was tempted to reduce her speed, to see if she really had got rid of him, but she wasn't that stupid. It was only on the last stretch that she drove a little more slowly. Along the avenue of bare trees two cars came in the opposite direction. But there were none behind her.

She'd calmed down somewhat by the time she turned into Marienweg. There was a light-coloured car parked by Niedenhoff's fence. She noticed it as she turned into the drive, but she didn't give it a closer look. The garage door rose, she drove in and switched off the engine, without seeing someone come in through the still open door. After a moment's silence the door came down. And someone tapped on the side window. Her head swung round. All she could see was a section of a dark pair of men's trousers.

It was a chilling moment. To think that she'd shaken off Ramon, only to find Zurkeulen waiting for her here, where she thought she was safe behind a security system with surveillance cameras and sensors that registered heat and every movement. How much had they learned from Nadia? Had they forced her to reveal what was going on? Both of her hands had been burned to the bone, so that it had been impossible to take fingerprints from the body for comparison; that had also removed the mark made by the ring she wore on her right hand. And she'd been run over twice, so that the new fractures meant no one would notice the absence of an old one. It was horrific, but it had reassured her. And now this!

"Frau Trenkler?" It was a polite voice. She was staring straight ahead, she simply refused to look at that face, only separated from her by a sheet of glass. A man's voice she thought she'd heard once before. But she'd heard so many men's voices recently.

"Frau Trenkler?" the man repeated in polite, slightly hesitant tones. She finally managed to turn her head. He opened the car door. Her hands and knees were trembling so much, he had to help her get out. "I'm sorry, I didn't mean to frighten you. You remember me?"

Yes, she did. She remembered his beard, his warrant card, even his name. Dettmer, the suspicious policeman who'd helped her when she'd run out of petrol during the dress rehearsal on that Sunday in August.

Her heart was thumping. "Do you make a habit of creeping into people's garages?"

He let go of her arm and examined the Alfa with interest. "I thought you'd seen me."

"No." Still weak at the knees, she opened the door to the hall. Dettmer followed close behind. He hadn't yet said what he wanted and she didn't feel like asking him. She went into the kitchen, put her handbag on the table, took off her jacket and hung it over the back of a chair.

"I don't know if you've seen the paper today," Dettmer said. But he didn't get any further. Suddenly the ear-piercingly shrill wail of an alarm rang out. The twenty-second delay on the security system had passed. Both she and Dettmer jumped out of their skin.

Outside the kitchen window a red glare was flickering over the darkened lawn and the road. She dashed to the hall closet, pushed the leather jacket aside, saw the rhythmical flashing of a red light and hastily entered the code. The wailing and flashing continued. "Come on, switch the bloody thing off," Dettmer demanded, "it goes right through you." He had to shout to make himself heard above the racket.

It wouldn't go off, not with any of the key combinations she knew. She tried several. Her nerves finally gave way. She hammered on the box with her fists, burst into tears and shouted, "Jo! This thing's gone mad again. Why's no one helping me?"

Two minutes later Jo was there. It wasn't her cry for help that had brought him but the alarm, as it had Wolfgang Blasting, Frederik from across the road and Eleanor Ravatzky's housekeeper and her son. The two of them just peered through the wrought-iron door and Frederik left as quickly as he'd come.

Jo didn't even bother with the box, he dashed up to the study. Blasting asked Dettmer what he was doing there and was told there was the body of a woman in Forensic who looked like his neighbour.

The wailing and flashing continued unabated. Wolfgang Blasting also went upstairs to see why Jo couldn't stop it and she followed to make sure he didn't see anything he shouldn't. Dettmer followed her. And Dieter had said she shouldn't let anyone near the computer! Jo was sitting staring at the monitor, drumming his fingers on the desk, impatiently waiting for the data transfer, which he'd obviously set in motion, to finish. Then he discovered that his whole security system had been compressed and the two gigabytes needed to give the system enough space and allow him to switch off the alarm weren't there.

"What's going on here, Nadia?" Jo asked, horrified. The dog in the hall relieved her of the necessity to answer and she went back down, followed by Wolfgang Blasting. Lilo was at the door, wondering what had happened. A patrol car pulled up outside.

Her voice had gone, she couldn't shout, only whisper. "He always thinks he can do everything, then he fouls things up like this."

She meant Dieter, but Lilo, assuming she was talking about her husband, took her into the living room, sat her down in a chair and tried to reassure her. "Calm down, darling. It's a prototype, that's the problem, but I'm sure Jo'll get it working again."

In the hall Dettmer and Wolfgang Blasting reassured their uniformed colleagues. Just a false alarm because Dettmer had distracted the lady of the house. The patrol car drove off. Wolfgang Blasting offered her a cigarette and, like Lilo, told her to calm down. When she waved him away agitatedly, Lilo said, "I'll go and get her a Valium."

Jo went up to the loft and finally silence was restored, the red flickering died away. Lilo came back with two tiny pills, pushed them in her mouth and made her drink half a glass of water. And Dettmer said what had brought him there. He wasn't part of the murder squad, narcotics were his field, but naturally he talked to his colleagues. And a former boozing companion of Heller's, who was suspected of having killed him, had claimed under interrogation that Heller had told him there was a woman in the tenement who had a double and who was involved in shady dealings.

It sounded ridiculous. At first she giggled too, but that was pure desperation. A drunk with a criminal record, who'd made her life a misery, was putting the finger on her from beyond the grave. It was all over. Presumably they'd do a DNA test now.

Dettmer went on for almost ten minutes without anyone trying to interrupt or respond. But he asked no questions, merely related the facts. Heller had regaled his regular bar with more than just a reference to a chameleon – that was the expression he had used to describe her, Johannes Herzog would have been amazed he was familiar with the word and knew its correct meaning, given he had doubted whether Heller could even spell piano correctly. In a fairly inebriated state, Heller had talked about the supposed opinion pollster in the MG. Then he'd gone on to the white Porsche and Michael's Jaguar, and described in detail the elegant outfit in which Nadia had left the flat after the dress rehearsal in August. Exactly the same as the clothes Dettmer had seen that Sunday – worn by the woman calling herself Nadia Trenkler.

Dettmer must have an excellent memory. He could remember the scene beside the autobahn almost down to the very last word. Also the state she'd been in, sobbing, covered in blood, a cut on her finger, in a Jaguar that had run out of petrol, not knowing the registration number or how to operate the hazard warning lights. And had she not said she was going to visit a woman friend? He'd be very interested to know the name of her friend.

The little pills Lilo had pushed in her mouth gradually began to take effect. She stopped giggling and mumbled, "Helga." That was all she could manage.

Jo stepped in, explaining the problems his security system had caused that Sunday. Lilo confirmed this and was neither over-effusive nor, as her comments on Röhrler's death might have suggested, unfeeling. She was just a good friend, who had put her arm round her and was holding her left hand. That of itself gave her the feeling everything was going to be all right. In addition, Lilo was whispering, "Take it easy, darling. It's absurd, but Wolfgang will sort it out."

Not the least trace of hostility, envy or other negative feelings. They were a band of brothers – and sisters – in which each one had their allotted role. Jo was the fatherly support and also responsible for security. And Wolfgang Blasting wasn't just any old policeman, he commanded a whole department dealing, as Dieter had suspected, with high-level fraud.

That was what he was telling Dettmer, in a few sentences laced with irony. "I don't have much to do with pubs, despite what some people might think. But let's make a brief résumé, before things start getting out of hand." Then he summarized the facts: under the influence of drink, a notorious habitué of bars had imagined he'd seen his neighbour's double, had imagined he'd seen a Jaguar parked outside his flat, a Porsche close to his regular bar, had seen his neighbour getting out of the Porsche and an identical-looking woman getting into the Jaguar. Had anyone else, perhaps a more reliable witness, made any similar observations? Dettmer had to pass on that.

"And how did the officers dealing with the investigation respond to your suggestion of a double?" Wolfgang Blasting asked.

That put Dettmer on the back foot. He hummed and hawed, clearly he hadn't been taken seriously.

"How annoying for you," Wolfgang Blasting said, "when the living proof's sitting right here in front of you."

Assuring Dettmer that he was taking him seriously, he got him to confirm that Heller had died late on the Friday evening and Susanne at some time during the Saturday night. Then he switched from the friendly colleague to the man who was in charge of a whole department and used to putting subordinates in their place.

If Dettmer wanted anything from Nadia Trenkler, then it was the answer to two questions: Did you know Susanne Lasko? Where were you on Sunday night? And as far as that night was concerned, Wolfgang Blasting could vouch for her personally, even though Lilo's party had ended before twelve and she could, of course, have gone out again after Jo had taken her home. Jo and Lilo immediately confirmed that and named other guests at the party as witnesses.

But Dettmer had one further trump up his sleeve: the red Alfa Spider. His colleagues were looking for a woman among Susanne Lasko's acquaintances who owned a red car and had lent it to her on the Friday evening. Whether it was a convertible or not Dettmer couldn't say. Wolfgang Blasting commented that there must be umpteen thousand red cars in the area, but if the officers investigating the case thought it necessary, they were welcome to ask Nadia Trenkler if she'd lent her car to anyone. If they felt it was worth taking the trouble to come out there themselves.

By this time she'd calmed down sufficiently to see his treatment of Dettmer as a mistake. And she felt that Michael, when he came home, made an even greater one. He asked what the gathering in the living room was all about, demanded an explanation and then claimed she'd driven him to the lab on Friday morning and picked him up in the evening because he'd forgotten to get petrol. They'd gone to Demetros's, he went on, and only come back after midnight. At last Dettmer left. Hardly had the front door closed behind him than Wolfgang Blasting

266

said, "That was unnecessary. I can guarantee he'll go straight round to Demetros's."

Michael shrugged his shoulders. "Let him. I'll ring and tell them we were there."

And no one batted an eyelid. No one even thought of asking her where she really had been that Friday evening. Lilo patted her hand again. Jo gave her an encouraging smile. Michael sent a quick smile in her direction too, though a very cool one, and went upstairs. Wolfgang Blasting followed him, accompanied by Jo who was asking where he could find the necessary space for the security system. If the Security folder remained compressed, the leads in the loft would have to be cut again the next time the alarm went off. Lilo broke in, saying that Kestermann was going to come round to pick up the picture, and asked, her voice full of concern, "How do you feel, darling? Can I leave you with them?"

She just nodded and saw Lilo to the door. Before she left, she whispered, "If Wolfgang goes too far, just throw him out." She realized what she meant when she went into the study. Jo was sitting at the computer again. Michael and Blasting were standing either side of him looking at the masses of new data. Wolfgang Blasting's help had come at a price.

In the few minutes before she arrived Michael had already told them everything he knew about Philip Hardenberg's machinations with her double. Jo had established that some of the files that had just arrived already existed in another location on the hard disk and were thus duplicated. Wolfgang Blasting's opening salvo was the question, "Are you a hundred percent sure that this Lasko worked for Hardenberg?"

No mistakes now! Keep this awful trembling locked up inside you. She just nodded.

But Wolfgang Blasting wasn't satisfied with that. "What gave you that idea?"

Michael saved her having to reply. "Have you got many more of these intelligent questions?" he asked irritatedly. "What would you have thought if someone you'd never seen before addressed you as Frau Lasko and talked about an investment?"

Wolfgang Blasting shrugged his shoulders while Jo tried to open Hardenberg's customer list. The computer informed him the default application couldn't open it. "Why did you take the program down?" Jo asked.

Wolfgang Blasting gave her a thoughtful look. And suddenly, despite Dieter's warning, she saw her way clear, though she was skating on very thin ice. "I needed the space. I downloaded all of Philip's files so I could examine them without fear of interruption to find out what was going on."

Wolfgang Blasting's delight expressed itself in two words: "What? All?"

Less than a minute later Jo was loading the considerably smaller SLA file into the editor. It took a few seconds before figures and letters cascaded over the screen. They weren't as neatly arranged as on the account sheet Dieter had shown her, but it still didn't take Wolfgang Blasting's expert eye long to realize what he was looking at. He even worked out that the money was in Nassau. "Was that why you went to the Bahamas? To make enquiries?"

"No," Michael said quickly. "When we were over there she had no idea about the double. She only discovered that recently." He spoke in a firm voice, only his eyes showed that he was lying.

"Can I have a copy?" Wolfgang Blasting asked.

"What's the point?" Michael retorted. "The woman's dead. You can't ask her who the money belongs to."

"But I suspect," Wolfgang Blasting said, "that sooner or later the owners are going to want to ask Hardenberg some questions. I could post a man near his office."

Jo butted in. "Couldn't we at least delete some of it? How else am I going to get Sec running?"

Wolfgang Blasting had no time for Jo's worries. "Forget your Sec. It works, doesn't it? That –" pointing at the monitor, he looked at her – "is a much better lever than Röhrler. Have you at least some idea who the investors might be?"

The way the amount invested had been split up clearly suggested to him that the six million had originally come from several people. She shook her head and described Zurkeulen's car together with his chauffeur and the registration number. He looked at her reflectively and said, in a voice that brooked no argument, "You'll send me a copy. And the rest of the stuff. Or do you intend to continue working for Hardenberg?"

She shook her head again. With a nod of satisfaction he went to the door, then turned round. "And you'll do nothing off your own bat. Can I rely on that?"

"What could I do?" she asked.

He gave a soft laugh. "As I know you, you won't simply accept the fact that Hardenberg's dumped you after you'd pepped up his firm. But I think it's better if someone else put a stop to his game." In earnest tones he went on, "For your own sake, Nadia, no more little trips to the office. Even if you don't know the investors, your face will be very familiar to them, as we've seen already."

"We're going to Paris tomorrow anyway," Michael said.

"Good," Wolfgang Blasting said with a grin. "Then I'll get onto my colleagues in the murder squad before Dettmer stirs things up too much. Don't worry, I'll make it clear to them that their case has repercussions which are a bit beyond them."

Finally he left. Jo went with him. Once they were alone, Michael stood there motionless for a few moments, fixing her with an icy stare. Then he asked, "Why did you kill this Heller? Just because he'd seen you? And who's got the woman on their conscience? Philip?"

It was a horrible night. A hundred times she insisted she'd had nothing to do with Heller's death and certainly not with Susanne Lasko's. A hundred times he demanded she stop her lying. Hadn't she'd told him she'd been to Kettlerstrasse that Friday evening and had waited for Susanne Lasko? And he knew why she'd gone to the Bahamas. When she'd said she had to go to get some cash for the next day, he hadn't gone back to the hotel, he'd followed her – to the bank where the millions were deposited. And he thanked the Lord that he'd had enough sense to reject her surprise present. At least the money was still there. If Wolfgang managed to identify the investors, he might be satisfied with that.

Until two o'clock in the morning he kept pressing her to tell the truth. She came close to telling him everything because it sounded as if he simply couldn't put the two murders behind him. But on Monday he'd also sounded adamant and then had done an about-turn. And if he learned what had been done to Nadia… Dieter's warning kept her lips sealed.

It was towards morning before she got to sleep. When she woke at half-past eight, Andrea was already there. The two newspapers were on the kitchen table, together with a note from Michael. He asked her to book a flight and pack their cases. He wanted to be in Paris by the evening.

Through the travel agents it was easy to get two seats on a flight to Paris, the tickets to be collected from the Lufthansa desk. They pointed out that this was a scheduled flight, they had a cheaper offer for the Saturday morning. She insisted on the scheduled flight, she wanted to get away as quickly as possible. She booked the return flight for the following Wednesday, two seats again, even though she had absolutely no intention of coming back.

Shortly after ten a courier delivered a package. Dieter had sent four tapes with a little recorder and headphones. She phoned to thank him, also to tell him about the previous evening and what she planned to do, but it was Ramie who answered and she put the phone down without saying anything. Then she sat down at the desk with the tape recorder. She was disturbed just once by Andrea asking whether she should get anything special from the shops.

"Ten CDs," she said, handing Andrea fifty euros before concentrating again on the voice that spoke a sentence in French, then repeated it in German. It wasn't an introductory course for tourists who wanted to be able to order a coffee or ask the way, it was an advanced course that demanded her full attention.

Andrea went out. And Dieter, as if he were clairvoyant, rang at that very moment. He cursed when he heard her report. "So that's it then," he said. "You're in for it one way or the other. Blasting'll go after Hardenberg, and if they get him, he'll drag Nadia Trenkler in. And if this Dettmer gets Forensic to do what they should have done in the first place, you're in for it as Susanne Lasko."

Given the situation, he felt there was no point in his examining Hardenberg's files himself. He had the names and addresses of the other eight men who had accounts with Alfo Investment. The financial transactions were stored on the laptop. The portable computer was even set up for online banking and allowed you to shift amounts to and fro between various accounts.

"This thing's priceless," Dieter said. "Truly. It's a computer worth twenty million. Only NASA has one like that, if at all." He was relieved to hear she was going to Paris that very day. "Make sure you get away as quickly as you can," he advised. "That's the first place they'll look for you."

"That's what I mean to do," she said. "I'll go on to England, I can manage better with the language there."

"Romania," Dieter insisted. "I know a few people over there, I might be able to arrange something. They make good documents. Once the dust's settled I could try to transfer the money to Luxembourg somehow or other. Then you'd have to collect it. But we'll discuss that later. The first thing to do in France is to find a little guest house somewhere out in the country. Not a big hotel and don't use your credit card. Take enough ready cash with you. Ring when you've found somewhere, then we'll see what to do next."

Shortly afterwards Andrea came back with ten CDs. She put the fifty euros back on the desk with them. "They weren't that expensive. I took it out of the housekeeping, I had to go to the bank anyway." That was how she learned that Andrea had an account into which a certain sum was paid every month for food and the like.

After Andrea had left the house at two – and the bank had opened again after lunch – she went there herself, presented Nadia's ID card, as she'd done before, and took out two thousand euros. Hardly enough to finance the great escape, but she didn't want to arouse suspicion.

After that she copied a number of harmless-looking files for Wolfgang Blasting and put the CDs in an envelope, which she dropped into next door's letter box. Then it was high time she packed the cases. The maternity trousers, the new blouse, the bras and the baby clothes went right at the bottom, covered by a few pairs of Nadia's trousers, a few blouses and a warm pullover. She couldn't take too much or Michael might get suspicious. Anyway, in two months' time none of the things would fit any more.

She was still packing the cases when Michael came home. He was very distant. He urged her to hurry, took clean underwear from his drawer and went to the bathroom for a quick shower. She put the recorder and language tapes under the pullover in her case and had a look at Nadia's evening wear.

Paris – for her that meant things like the Moulin Rouge and the Crazy Horse, beautiful women, slim and tall, with feathers on their heads and swirling legs. Once she'd watched one of those shows on late-night TV in her old flat. She was sure Nadia would have actually been there. And Michael was probably planning to go to an exclusive bar. She packed two evening dresses and didn't forget a corresponding outfit for him.

Then Jo was given a house key so he could cut off the leads of the alarm in an emergency. They went in Michael's car. On the way there he didn't say a word, for which she was grateful, in her mind's eye she could already see herself disappearing somewhere in Paris. The Seine, Notre Dame, the Arc de Triomphe, the Louvre and the Eiffel Tower, that was more or less all she knew about the city. And of the two people with whom she was going to spend the next few hours she knew nothing at all. But that was the least of her worries. After all, she wasn't going to be there long. A "Nice to see you, Phil" or "Pamela" ought to be sufficient.

In the airport car park she was still on familiar ground. For the last time, it all went to plan. The tickets were there for them at the Lufthansa desk. Michael wanted to check in right away and then have a coffee and a bite to eat. From that point on it was all new to her but it didn't show, since all she had to do was follow him. He led her to an area of self-service snack bars, fetched two coffees and a piece of fruit flan for himself.

She didn't feel hungry. The parting lay heavy on her stomach. It sounded so easy: to disappear. To translate it into action was harrowing. To leave all the familiar places and faces behind, first and foremost her mother, perhaps supported by Dieter or Johannes Herzog at Nadia's graveside, as she had once dreamed. But she intended to ring her mother as soon as was feasible and later on to have her come and live with her. The thought was a comfort, if a small one.

While Michael was eating his cake, it finally struck him that she hadn't smoked for days. He expressed his surprise that she'd managed to stay off nicotine, given the way things were at the moment.

"It's not easy," she said. "I just have to grin and bear it. Both the withdrawal symptoms and your suspicions. How else can I prove to you that I'm no longer the woman you take me to be?"

She had absolutely no idea why she'd said that. But it was out. Perhaps she wanted him to realize, at some point or other, that she'd really loved him in the few days she'd had with him. He didn't reply, just looked at her thoughtfully.

Then they went through security and boarded a Boeing 737. Everything seemed smaller and more cramped than on a bus, but that didn't bother her once she was in her window seat. Flying! To be up in the air for the first time, above the clouds! Tense expectation gradually blotted out all other feelings.

There was just one awkward moment when Michael pointed out that she hadn't fastened her safety belt and she didn't know how to adjust it to fit her. But he ascribed it, as he had all the other moments that threatened to give her away, to her nerves. It didn't arouse his suspicions.

The plane started to taxi, then accelerated. She felt herself being pressed back against her seat. Then the Boeing took of and it was as if her brain was being squashed down out of her skull. There was immense pressure in her ears and her stomach clenched. She'd never felt so sick before. Mouth wide open, she took deep breaths. Her hands, her forehead, her back, her whole body was damp with sweat.

Far down below the world slewed onto its side. She couldn't look, she felt as if she was falling and kept her eyes fixed on one of the lockers where hand luggage was stowed. Out of the corner of her eye she saw the grey veil outside the tiny window thicken then suddenly clear. The plane had reached cruising height. Outside it was ablaze with light, the sky a radiant blue. In the gangway the stewardess was explaining where the emergency exits were and how the oxygen masks worked. It felt as if there was something like a whisk going round in her head and stomach. She put her hand over her mouth, trying to suppress the retching.

"What's wrong, Nadia?" she heard Michael ask.

"I feel sick," she groaned. She meant to say she felt rather queasy. She was sure that's what Nadia would have said. "I think I'm going to be sick." she didn't just think so, it was already coming up into her throat.

Michael took her handbag, which she'd stuck down the seat beside her. Presumably he was looking for paper handkerchiefs, but what he came up with was a bundle of banknotes. In the bank she'd just stuck them in her bag. Naturally he was surprised to find Nadia setting off with a large supply of ready cash when she also had two credit cards. "What's all this?"

Answering was impossible. She just swallowed convulsively and pressed her hand to her mouth. The stewardess was close enough to see what was happening. She passed over several paper handkerchiefs and indicated a brown paper bag in the net on the back of the seat in front. She was so wretched that she didn't even feel embarrassed. Michael apologized with a baffled shrug of the shoulders. "My wife doesn't normally have any problems flying."

It didn't get better. She needed another paper bag. She couldn't understand that there were people who enjoyed flying. By this time drinks were being handed out. With the best of intentions, the stewardess offered them a cognac. Michael categorically refused and insisted on mineral water. She decided on a tomato juice with a lot of salt and pepper. That had perked her up on the morning after Lilo's party. It did so now. But before her head and her stomach could get completely back to normal, the plane began its descent and everything started up again.

There was no looking out of the window for a first sight of Paris from the air. The lockers were better. The Boeing lurched as it landed, her stomach lurched too. Then, at last, it was all over. Michael unfastened her safety belt, commenting, not without a certain satisfaction, "It must all have been a bit too much for you in the last few days."

He waited for the crush in the gangway to subside, then helped her up. The stewardess asked how she was and wished her a pleasant stay. Michael led her out of the confines of the plane and along endless corridors. At some point he took their suitcases off a conveyer belt and looked round for a trolley because he couldn't carry two suitcases and support her at the same time.

"If you tell me where to check yours in I won't have to lug it all the way to the taxi." Once again he seemed think – correctly this time – that she intended to take off.

"You don't have to lug me along," she said, though she wasn't all that steady on her feet. The ground seemed to sway at every step. The lights on the ceiling were flickering. The throng all around her left blurred impressions, as if in a photo taken by a camera with the wrong exposure.

"Sit down," he told her. "I'll go and see where Phil is." He set her down on a chair somewhere, put the two cases beside her and went off. Ten minutes later he came back, surprised that Phil was nowhere to be seen. "Didn't you tell him when we were arriving?"

"I forgot."

Irritated, he pulled out his mobile to remedy her forgetfulness. Unfortunately he couldn't get Phil and Pamela, so he said, "We'll go round to their place. Perhaps they're only out for a short while. If not, we'll leave a message and go to the hotel. She decided not to tell him she'd forgotten to book a room as well.

She staggered along behind him to the taxi rank. He asked her to tell the driver Phil's address, where it was, Montparnasse, and that it was best to go via rue de Vaugirard. Fortunately the driver had understood him, she wouldn't have dared open her mouth. She crawled into the rear seat, feeling like death warmed up.

Paris, the beginning of December. It was a grey dream and bitterly cold. All she saw of the city was drizzle, the reflections of streetlights on wet tarmac and the taxi's windscreen wipers. Her brain was still throbbing. The slightest movement of her head produced a horrible dizziness. The feeling of nausea stretched from her eyes all the way down to the backs of her knees. They were presumably driving past some of the sights, but she didn't dare turn her head to the side to look out of the window.

The driver tried to chat with Michael, asking what the purpose of their trip to Paris was. She did get a few phrases. Michael obviously couldn't understand what the man was going on about, at least he didn't reply. The handwritten lines to Jacques, *mon chéri* came briefly back to mind. It clearly wasn't a great risk to leave something like that lying around if her husband couldn't read French. By now she could perhaps translate one or two sentences, but she hadn't learned much from Dieter's language course yet. Nor was she likely to as long as Michael was close by. And it was so important.

The very idea of having to use any kind of transport in the next few days made her stomach heave. She couldn't even think of a hired car without retching. The taxi ride or, rather, the way the Frenchman weaved through the traffic, made her feel even worse.

Finally they were there – in a street that didn't look much different from the one where she'd spent the last few years. Cars tightly parked either side and, beyond them, the dreary façades of tenement blocks. That the university wouldn't provide luxury accommodation for a short stay by a visiting lecturer made sense. But she still had no idea why Phil and Pamela were here in Paris and just felt as if she was back in Kettlerstrasse.

The drizzle was getting heavier. Michael asked her to tell the driver to wait as they might have to go on. Then he got out and went to the entrance of one of the buildings. Only a few seconds later he came back, paid the driver – from her handbag – took the two cases out of the boot and told her to stay there until he came for her.

The driver turned round and asked something. Not wanting to start a conversation with him, she got out – with some difficulty. Michael was at the entrance. He hadn't noticed that she was following him, squeezing her way through between two parked cars. He pushed the door open and peered into the dark hall. Squeals of delight came from one of the upper floors. Michael dropped the cases and threw his arms round the man who had come rushing down to meet him. As they thumped each other on the shoulders and back, she leaned against the wall, feeling her knees about to give way as the first black spots signalling the arrival of a faint appeared before her eyes. Then the nausea and the terrible dizziness were no more.

Her awakening was almost the same as at Lilo's party: a gaudy picture on the wall and the face of an unknown woman. She was lying on a couch and the woman was holding a cup to her lips, giving her something to drink. It was just water. She took a few sips. "Are you feeling better?" Pamela – who else? – asked in English.

She sketched a nod and tried to sit up. Pamela pushed her back down onto the cushion. "No, stay in bed." Then she turned to the door and shouted, "Mike!"

The room was even smaller than her "half-room" in Kettlerstrasse. A naked bulb was dangling from the ceiling, the window had no curtains. Apart from the couch there was just a small cupboard and when Michael came in the room was more than full. He was furious. "I told you to stay in the car. Did you hurt yourself?"

Just a scratch on her forehead. Her clothes were wet and dirty because she'd fallen in a puddle.

"We ought to call a doctor," he said. He'd presumably never seen Nadia in such a state, apart from the time when she'd been on the bottle. But now, without a drop of alcohol in her blood, she was white as a sheet and her teeth were chattering so badly she could barely speak. "It's just a dizzy spell."

"Nonsense. You've never had that kind of problem before."

Phil appeared behind him. He was shorter than Michael and had to stand on tiptoe. He gave her a wink over Michael's shoulder and made signs – which Nadia might have understood. "Hi, there. What's the matter?"

Michael explained something to him. She couldn't understand a word. He was speaking too fast. Phil nodded and went out again. Pamela

276

looked down at her, full of sympathy, and also said something. For the sake of simplicity, she just nodded. Pamela then set about taking her wet clothes off, fetched an old bathrobe, helped her put it on, took her into the little bathroom and stayed there with her.

A few tears mingled with the hot water of the shower. Paris! And the first steps of her new life had ended in a puddle. It was a bad omen. Pamela said something. In the shower she could pretend she hadn't heard, but she couldn't stay in the shower for ever.

When, half an hour later, Pamela brought her out of the bathroom, Michael and Phil were sitting in a kitchen-cum-living room with another man. He stood up, then bent down to pick up his bag, clearly a doctor's bag. Saying a few words in French to the two others, he went with her and Pamela to the tiny bedroom. Pamela stayed discreetly outside the door.

She got through the first few minutes with half a dozen "*oui*"s, on the assumption the doctor was asking her about her symptoms. He measured her blood pressure, felt her stomach. Her blood pressure was extremely low. He didn't need to tell her that, she could see it on the gauge. He felt lower down, looked puzzled and asked something.

"*Oui*," she said.

His fingers continued to squeeze her lower abdomen. Behind him the door opened. Michael came in, with Phil peering over his shoulder, despite the fact that she was lying half-naked on the couch. The doctor covered her up with the bathrobe and said, "*Madame, vous êtes enceinte, vous comprenez?*"

He had long since realized she couldn't understand him.

"What did he say?" Michael asked.

Before she or the doctor could reply, Phil thumped him on the shoulder and let out a whoop of delight that filled the dreary little room. "Congratulations, Dad!"

She understood that, she could even make sense of Michael's "Impossible." Then he turned to her, to make it absolutely clear to the doctor that he must have made a mistake: "What's the French for 'sterilized'?"

But the doctor didn't need a translation. He took out his stethoscope, put the two plugs in his ears and pressed the cool disc against her lower abdomen underneath the bathrobe. It didn't take him long to find what he was listening for. He handed the earplugs to Michael. Michael listened intently.

Her heart was in her mouth. Now he must realize! Because an operation had made a distinction. He looked down at her, his face a battlefield of emotions. In her panic she could almost hear him saying: You aren't Nadia. Instead he asked, "Do you want to hear its heart beating?"

She shook her head. He handed the stethoscope back to the doctor and went out of the room. The doctor packed his bag and followed him. In the kitchen he wrote out a prescription and received his fee – again out of her handbag. Then she heard him leave the flat.

Paris! Alone in an old bathrobe on a worn couch under a naked bulb, its light reflected in an uncurtained window. Inside her head she kept hearing Andrea ask, "Are you going to sue Wenning?" Now she knew what she'd meant. The door from her room into the hall was open and from the kitchen she heard the sound of voices and the clatter of plates. She spent about half an hour alone with her panic. Then Pamela appeared in the doorway and asked icily, "Would you like some chicken?"

She just nodded. "Dinner is ready," Pamela said. It sounded as if she were being invited to a meal of deep-frozen chicken.

The mood in the kitchen was sombre. They all spoke a little more slowly with the result that she could understand some of what was said. There was no problem with names, anyway. They still thought she was Nadia. Michael told them about Hardenberg, Heller, Susanne Lasko, Wolfgang Blasting and Nassau. A house with its own beach, one size up from the villa her father had given her. She could only think on that scale. And it didn't matter how much she had, she always wanted more. Money, money, money, nothing else counted. And she thought a balm of luxury could soothe the pain she caused. A Jaguar for the terrible time after her first disaster. A nice car, true, but he didn't really need it.

Now and then he threw her a hostile glance. Phil and Pamela behaved as if she wasn't there. Perhaps she should have been grateful for that. Michael mentioned the bundle of banknotes in her handbag, commenting sarcastically that it was presumably enough to pay for an abortion in a clinic. When Pamela served the coffee, it occurred to him that it was high time they contacted the hotel. He'd just give them a quick call, he said.

"Sorry," she mumbled, "I didn't think of booking a room."

"That doesn't surprise me at all," he snarled. "Presumably you didn't think you were going to need one."

Paul asked what was the matter and offered them the guest room again. It was the room in which she'd come round. The couch could be pulled out, Phil explained, making a passable bed, not very wide but – very *gemütlich*. At the German word – and presumably the idea of them spending a cosy night together – he grinned.

"That's OK for me," Michael said, "but you don't have to put up with it if you don't feel like it. Ring your clinic, I'm sure they'll take you now, even at this hour."

"I don't think so," she said. "I booked in for Monday." His assumption suited her quite well. If she got into a taxi on Monday and he thought she was going to a clinic, it would be longer before he realized she'd gone.

Shortly after midnight he followed her into the little room, closed the door, leaned back against it and asked which clinic she'd booked into for Monday.

"What's it to do with you?" she asked. "You don't need to hold my hand, I can manage perfectly well on my own."

He nodded. "The police are sure to have a few questions about the Friday evening. I could tell them you'd gone to Kettlerstrasse and I had to wait until twelve for you. And that's what I will tell them, if you keep behaving as if it didn't concern anyone but you. I played a part as well, remember."

She had no idea where this was leading. It sounded almost as if he wanted to be there when his child was scraped out of her womb. At that moment she was no one but Susanne Lasko. "As far as I care, you can tell them what you like. I know only too well that you don't trust me an inch. And in this particular case you're even right for once. I didn't get pregnant deliberately, but now it's in my belly and it's staying there until I go into labour. Whether you like it or not."

"You want to keep it?" He was stunned. And she'd believed Nadia when she'd said, "He'll blow his top if he learns he's fathered a brat."

"Why did you book in for an abortion, then?"

"I didn't," she said. "It was you who said that, I just didn't contradict you. What would be the point? You don't believe anything I say. And

I don't need you to have my child. You want a divorce. Go ahead. I'll manage on my own."

With two steps he was there and she was in his arms. From that moment on everything was different, though it was hours later before she understood what she'd done for him. She! Not Nadia! And if one day he came to know who she really was, perhaps he would be able to love her for it. If, at some point or other, he became aware he was living with a copy, perhaps he would already have realized that her idea of love was closer to his than anything Nadia had ever done for him. She'd financed his studies in the USA and bought him a Jaguar, but she'd never been able to give him the kind of life he wanted. And two severed Fallopian tubes had denied his longing for a child.

Since a pregnancy had occurred despite that, they could sue Dr Wenning, who had performed the sterilization. On the other hand, they could simply rejoice at the bungled operation. Michael was overcome with joy, wanted to forget everything and start all over again with her. If only it was that simple.

On Saturday morning he wasted no time telling the others she wanted to keep the baby. There were a few language problems, which were interpreted as the natural agitation of a happy mother-to-be. And after breakfast they solved themselves. Pamela asked if she would speak German with her and correct her mistakes. In contrast to Phil, who assumed his language was universal and thought anything else was a waste of time, Pamela wanted to learn. So they all got on famously, Michael with Phil and she with Pamela.

Shortly before midday Michael finally got round to booking a hotel. Phil drove them there. They just deposited their cases. Saturday was a slight improvement, cold but dry. She still didn't get to see the sights, however. Nadia had been to Paris so often it never occurred to Michael to do a sightseeing tour with his wife. After booking in at the hotel, they went back to Phil and Pamela's.

On Sunday they went for a stroll along the banks of the Seine and had lunch in a little bistro. On Monday Phil was busy at the Sorbonne. Michael had something to he wanted do by himself in the hotel, so took her to Pamela's by taxi. He still didn't seem to trust her entirely.

That would have been the chance to do what she had planned to do in Paris. Instead she went out with Pamela, who took her to some little shops, not the big stores where Nadia would presumably have gone on a serious shopping spree. She bought some baby things, two more maternity bras, some underwear and a pretty dress she would presumably fit into nicely in three or four months' time. Pamela, like her, was used to comparing prices and had never met Nadia. After two miscarriages when she was younger, she'd had to have an operation. She felt her inability to have children deeply and envied her, but they laughed a lot too, and were laden with bags when they came back to the flat which reminded her so much of Kettlerstrasse.

Michael was astonished at the prices she'd paid. She could laugh and said, "I'm out of work, love, or had you forgotten? And we have to fend for three from now on."

He laughed too, though he had been anything but economical himself. He'd bought her a ring, the third seal of their union. He laughed at the evening dresses and the dinner jacket that she took, completely crumpled, out of the suitcases on Monday evening. He laughed on Tuesday when she had to borrow a warm pullover from Pamela since she'd spilled coffee over hers – because she'd laughed too much.

There was one more worrying moment in bed on Tuesday night. He looked at her birthmark again. Until then she'd always been careful to cover it up with concealer stick. "Why's that suddenly popped up again?" he wondered.

"It's not that sudden," she said. "It reappeared a while ago. I just didn't want you to get worked up about it and stop me going on the sunbed. I'm sure it's harmless. Your skin changes during pregnancy, that's all. Everything changes then."

"Yes, he said with a laugh, "even your immunity to airsickness."

On Wednesday morning, while Michael was in the bath, she thought about ringing Dieter and asking how things stood. But before she could bring herself to lift the receiver – perhaps to be told it was high time she disappeared – Michael came back into the bedroom.

They went to see Phil and Pamela one more time and had lunch with them. Phil gave her a farewell kiss on the cheek. Pamela hugged her and told her she must ring often and keep her informed about how the baby was doing.

Their plane went in the early afternoon. She might perhaps have had one last chance of disappearing in the airport throng, on the excuse of going to the toilet. But he would probably have accompanied her there and waited by the door. And she didn't really want to get away any more, not after the last few days.

Again it was a Boeing 737 and again it transformed her into a bundle of misery. With the stimulant the doctor had prescribed, it wasn't as bad as on the outward journey, but it was bad enough. Michael's concern was touching.

Only after they'd landed did he tell her that he'd phoned Wolfgang Blasting that morning, while she was in the shower. They were already in the car park and he was putting the suitcases in the boot as he told her, "Wolfgang wants to talk to you himself, right away. He thinks you were incredibly lucky to get away from those guys in the car with the Frankfurt number."

Through her information the police had quickly found the owner of the black limousine. In former times Markus Zurkeulen had been a big noise in the Frankfurt underworld. More recently his influence had been seriously reduced by East-European gangs. That was presumably why he'd decided to retire, selling a number of establishments in the red-light district to a Russian – officially for a derisory sum. The actual value, Wolfgang Blasting had told Michael, would be around five-and-a-half million. He now appeared to be assuming they were just dealing with an investor who'd been swindled.

Michael didn't say whether he took the same view, but during the journey home he made it clear that he still had doubts about her version, namely that Susanne Lasko was the culprit. How did she think she could convince him of that when he'd seen her in the bank in Nassau? And how could a sweet-shop assistant have managed to transfer five-and-a-half million to the Bahamas? Wolfgang Blasting had told him that morning that Susanne Lasko had originally worked in banks, but her contacts wouldn't have gone much beyond the next branch of the local savings bank, Michael said. If Susanne Lasko had ever had anything to do with investment advice, then at most she would have recommended a few government bonds. How could such a woman have persuaded a streetwise gangland boss to take up a particular investment and then cleaned him out?

He didn't even suspect how close he was to the actual facts. And he was sure Wolfgang Blasting saw things in the same way. "Wolfgang told me he'd gathered some interesting information on Susanne Lasko, though he preferred not to go into it over the telephone. Nor did he want me to tell you anything. It would spoil the element of surprise, he said, he can't wait to see your face. Tell him how it really was, Nadia. Give him what he wants. Do it for us and for the baby. All he wants is to put Hardenberg behind bars for investment fraud and Zurkeulen for tax evasion. I'm convinced he'll make sure you get away with a suspended sentence. There's always that arrangement whereby people who agree to give evidence get a reduced sentence or even get off scot-free."

Even when they'd reached the country road lined with young trees he was still begging her to be sensible. It was too late for that. It would have been sensible to have said to Pamela in one of the little shops on Monday, "I just have to go to the toilet." And then to slip out by the back door. Michael would probably have understood that.

He was still going on at her as he turned into Marienweg. If she really loved him, now was the time to prove it. But she couldn't. She couldn't even listen to him any more. The element of surprise, she thought. Interesting information. Yes, the most interesting information was probably the result of the DNA test. That Wolfgang Blasting didn't want to go into that on the telephone was understandable.

You didn't tell a man on the telephone that the woman he was travelling with wasn't his wife. You just made sure the man brought the wrong woman back with him. So that she could be handcuffed and taken to face the charges against her.

Part Five

She felt terribly sick as she went into the hall. She just managed to climb the stairs to freshen up a bit. Less than half an hour later Wolfgang Blasting was in the living room. He had been burrowing away while they'd been in Paris. It took a while before she realized what he was saying and that it wasn't all over. He still had no idea who he was talking to. All he'd done was to fill out the picture.

He didn't think it necessary to pass his information on to the murder squad, he said. He wouldn't put it past them to go rushing round like bulls in a china shop. It really wasn't a case for simple-minded detectives and, anyway, he wanted to keep her out of the firing line. And not just out of neighbourly feeling. He wanted something from her, first and foremost access to her computer. The CDs were quite nice, he said with a grin, but not what he needed to nail Hardenberg and Zurkeulen.

"I can understand that you had certain concerns and therefore only copied harmless files," he said. "But you scratch my back and I'll scratch yours, Nadia. I'll have a look at everything and immediately forget anything that in any way incriminates you. OK?"

She just nodded. The knot in her insides gradually loosened, allowing her to breathe more easily. Wolfgang Blasting went on. From what he had found out so far, there was nothing to suggest a sweet-shop assistant could not have transferred five-and-a-half million abroad on Hardenberg's behalf. The Lasko woman, as he commented disparagingly, but with a certain respect, had gone about it very cleverly.

She'd been leading some kind of double life. On the one hand there was the retiring, poorly-off Susanne Lasko known to her mother and her neighbours in Kettlerstrasse. "But," Blasting went on, "there were some clothes lying around which an out-of-work woman couldn't afford. She'd only had a proper job for a short time after her divorce. No one knows what she lived on after that, but it must have been regular work. At least she behaved as if it was, went out in the morning, came back in the late afternoon and paid the same measly little amount into her bank account every month. Until January. In August she opened a second account and immediately the money started rolling in. She opened it with twenty thousand in cash, applied for a credit card straight away, paid for her purchases with it, for hired cars. The last was a burgundy Rover 600. It was parked two streets away from her flat. The guys in the murder squad have taken it in. That knocks the story of a car borrowed from an acquaintance on its head."

He gave her a grin, a friendly one. "Heller didn't dream up those fancy cars. In October she twice hired a Jaguar and earlier, in September, she had a Mercedes for two days. From the mileage she did she must have used it to go to Luxembourg; Zurkeulen's money was paid in there on the twelfth. The usual trick: take a briefcase across a frontier where there are no checks any longer. You don't take five-and-a-half million on a plane. We don't yet know when she was in Nassau. She never left from a German airport, my guess is she drove to Amsterdam or somewhere when she had to fly. A really clever girl. But presumably she was following Hardenberg's instructions. And he'll have lent her his Porsche now and then."

And in Wolfgang Blasting's opinion Susanne Lasko knew perfectly well she was getting involved in something risky. "She took special driving lessons," he said. "From a stuntman. And oddly enough, the reason she gave for needing them corresponded precisely to her work: acting as a courier."

It was incredible how well her fabrications were working out in retrospect – for Nadia. Michael was listening, head bowed. Wolfgang Blasting went on: now the murder squad were assuming it was all to do with drug smuggling. Was it Dettmer who'd given them the idea – drug crime was his area after all? It was impossible to say, but as long as they believed that, they couldn't do any harm. The investigation into the Heller murder had come to an impasse.

"I believe it's possible," Blasting said, "that Heller had to be got rid of because he'd seen Hardenberg with the Lasko woman. Hardenberg must have gone to see her in her flat more than once. But we'll look into that when we've sorted the rest out. Can I come and work on your computer tomorrow?"

"No problem," she said, only with difficulty keeping her tone casual. The Lasko woman! Perhaps that was what really made it clear to her what it meant to live as Nadia Trenkler. Disowning her own self.

Wolfgang Blasting left. Michael saw him out, then came back and looked at her with a pained expression on his face. "I'm sorry. I really am terribly sorry, darling."

He didn't have to explain what he was being sorry about, after the sermon he'd given her on the way home. On 12 September Susanne Lasko had been on her travels and Nadia Trenkler at home. It all came back to him now. It had been a great evening and a fantastic afternoon on 13 September. He had wrongly suspected her. That the bank she'd gone to while they were on holiday on the Bahamas had been the very bank where Zurkeulen's money had been deposited – pure coincidence. "Can you forgive me?"

"Of course," she said. "You've forgiven me a thing or two in the past. Am I wrong, or would you even have been able to accept the fact that I'd killed someone?"

He shrugged his shoulders and gave an embarrassed smile. "I don't know. At first I thought I could never come to terms with that. Then I thought, every child needs its mother. And now I'm just glad I don't have to wrestle with that problem any longer... Will you make us something to eat? Escalope, but just with mushrooms. Then we'll have a swim. It'll do you good."

"No," she said. "Then we'll go to bed. That'll do me even more good."

It was almost midnight when Michael finally put out the light. He quickly fell asleep. She lay there a while. She could feel the ring he'd put on her finger in Paris. Somehow it seemed to mean he belonged to her now. Then she thought of her mother and briefly of Dieter, who was probably surprised or concerned that she hadn't rung him from Romania during the last few days. Telling herself she'd ring him in the morning, she fell into a troubled sleep shortly after one. At some point she was woken by a familiar sound. The metallic click of the central locking as the alarm system was switched off.

There was a slight difference in sound between switching on and switching off, and by now she'd heard it often enough. Once it had been Andrea, mostly it was Michael. At first she didn't wake fully but dozed on, assuming it was early morning and he was setting off for the lab. It was the muffled cry that didn't fit into that and suddenly she was completely awake. As she sat up, she felt Michael still beside her.

* * *

It was dark in the bedroom, the door out onto the landing closed. Clumping steps were coming up the stairs. Someone was making sure they were heard. She shook his shoulder and whispered, "Michael, wake up, there's someone in the house." A narrow strip of yellow appeared under the door. A movement sensor had activated the landing light. She shook his shoulder again, more vigorously this time, and whispered more urgently, "Michael."

He didn't move until the door opened. A bright beam of light swept round the room and settled on her face, dazzling her. From the landing came the sound of a stifled exclamation, followed by a hoarse voice saying, "Will you shut your trap." There was a sound like a groan and a dull thump. The bright light meant she couldn't make anything out, but it became clear what was happening when she heard Markus Zurkeulen's voice saying, in reproving tones, "Must you be so impetuous, Ramon?"

Finally Michael sat up beside her, blinking in the light. "What's going —"

The hoarse voice broke in. "Take it easy, mister. One false move and I'll blow your brains out."

The two of them were standing in the doorway. She only recognized them when the ceiling light went on. With a polite smile, Markus Zurkeulen came closer. Ramon stayed where he was. Michael made a sideways movement, as if to pick up the telephone beside the bed. Ramon told him not to do anything stupid. "Otherwise it's curtains for you."

Once more Zurkeulen reproved his companion and suggested he adopt a different tone, pointing out that a serious conversation was impossible in that kind of crude German. "I'm trying my hardest to teach him good manners. Unfortunately his poor upbringing keeps coming through." His polite tone was almost worse than the gun Ramon had in his right hand.

She was sitting there, upright and naked, and all she could do was stare at the gun. She felt as if she'd been transported back into the second bank robbery and the muck of the abandoned factory. Michael took the sheet, pulled it over her breasts and pressed her hands to it. "Get out," he ordered Zurkeulen.

"Certainly," Zurkeulen replied, as he got to the bed. His eyes were still fixed on Michael, not on her. "It is not in my own interest to take up too much of your time." He emphasized the "your". "If you would be so good as to leave me alone with the lady for a few minutes."

"Certainly not," Michael said, placing his arm protectively round her shoulders. "And you're running out of time. The police should be here any minute. The silent alarm goes direct to the station."

Without warning, Zurkeulen took a swing at him with the back of his hand, splitting open Michael's lower lip. "How unfortunate," said Zurkeulen, looking at his hand. "I'm afraid I don't always have my reflexes under control. It must be because I can't stand people trying to pull the wool over my eyes."

She saw and heard everything, but she was incapable of thought. Being constantly dragged backwards and forwards between apparent security and acute danger had so worn her down that she could have wished herself back in one-and-a-half rooms with no prospects. The encounters with Heller on the stairs had been easier to put up with and, above all, she'd known where she was with him.

Zurkeulen told his companion to take Herr Trenkler to the bathroom. The swelling on his lip, he said, would not be so bad if he bathed it in cold water. Given the gun that had long since been pointing at him, Michael realized he had no chance against the two men. He got out of bed but didn't go to the bathroom, he went to the dressing room instead. Before opening the door, he said to Zurkeulen, "Don't you dare touch my wife."

With a smile, Zurkeulen enquired, "Are you absolutely certain this lady is your wife?"

Michael spun round and stared, first at Zurkeulen, then at her. Ramon grinned and licked his lips with relish. She couldn't even breathe as she felt the blood seep out of her brain.

"I recently had the pleasure of meeting another lady who insisted she was Nadia Trenkler and was unable to help me for that very reason," Zurkeulen explained.

"You killed that woman!" Michael whispered, but in the tense atmosphere it echoed like thunder in her ears.

"No, no," said Zurkeulen, "I would never think of killing a woman. There are too many pleasant things one can do with a woman." He ran his eye over her face and her hands clutching the sheet to her breast. "Now may I ask you to grant me a few minutes with your wife?"

He pointed to the dressing room and jerked his head at his companion. Then he came round the bed and looked down at her, a smile on his face. "Nadia Trenkler," he said, following it with a sigh. "If your husband's convinced of that, then I suppose I'll have to accept it. Presumably a man will sense whom he's sharing his bed with."

He sat down beside her. Ramon was still standing in the doorway. He looked almost as if he was expecting a special performance he didn't want to miss.

"Ramon." Zurkeulen was insistent. "Will you please go and keep an eye on Herr Trenkler. I would like to ensure he doesn't do anything stupid." Then he grasped her wrists and pulled her hands and the sheet down. The smile stayed as his eye moved downwards from her face. "Pretty," he said. His eye was followed by a hand in a black leather glove. "And very sensitive, aren't they?"

She didn't feel it at all, her attention was entirely focused on Ramon as he crossed the room and went into the dressing room with the gun. And the red stain on the manager's shirt quickly spread. "No!" she cried. "Leave my husband alone. If you —"

Zurkeulen put his other hand over her mouth. "Shh," he said. All was quiet in the dressing room. Gradually she felt the leather on her left breast, the painful pressure of his hand. "You're hurting me."

He squeezed harder. "That's my intention. It could get even more painful. It's up to you whether it does or not."

Perhaps it was the pain that kept the panic at bay. Perhaps it was the certainty that Zurkeulen wouldn't hesitate for one moment to kill her – and Michael, and the person who'd helped him get into the house and must be lying on the landing. She was convinced it was Jo. He hadn't returned the house key and he knew how to operate the alarm system.

"What do you want from me?"

"Six million."

It would definitely have been more sensible to say, "OK, I'll give you the money." For Nadia it would have been more sensible, not for her. "We haven't got that much in the house," she said. "Have a look if you don't believe me. The safe's in the loft, I'm sure my husband will be glad to open it."

He looked at her thoughtfully. And as he'd done to Michael, he struck out unexpectedly with his left hand again, so hard that she flew back into the pillows. She could taste blood, her lip was swelling. At the same time his right hand squeezed her breast so hard she couldn't repress a cry.

"Nadia?" Michael shouted.

"Tell your husband to restrain himself," Zurkeulen said. "Otherwise I won't be able to guarantee that he'll survive the next few minutes. Nor the lady outside." As he said that, he also drew a gun out of his jacket and pointed to the door onto the landing with it.

Lilo, she thought, as she called out, "It's OK, love." Then she stammered, "What do you want. I haven't got six million, for goodness' sake."

"I know," said Zurkeulen. "But perhaps you can get hold of that amount if you're prepared to come with me. Ramon will keep your husband company until we're back. And if you're both sensible, no one will get hurt."

He was going to go with her to 83 Antoniterweg, he explained, keeping his eyes fixed on her face as he said the address. He appeared to be looking for some specific reaction. But whatever he was waiting for, she couldn't provide it. Eighty-three Antoniterweg, it meant nothing to her. She'd deleted the file card too quickly in September.

"And the name Philip Hardenberg?" Zurkeulen asked.

She shrugged her shoulders.

"That's a pity," said Zurkeulen. "Herr Hardenberg also claimed he didn't know anyone with your name."

By this time she was calmer, though not free from fear, quite the contrary. Inside her chest, everything seemed to have gone numb, just her brain was working, but that with a strange clarity. "Why's it a pity?" she asked. "I don't know the man."

Zurkeulen's smile broadened. "Herr Hardenberg or, rather, his partner had second thoughts." He finally took his hand off her breast. The pain remained. "Unfortunately I'm in no position to assess the accuracy of her change of mind. For that reason I suggest you get dressed and we'll go and pay her a visit together."

She hated the very thought of getting out of bed with his eyes on her and going to the dressing room, where Ramon was waiting. At the same time that was the one place she wanted to go. Ramon was standing close behind the door, his gun aimed at Michael. Michael was leaning with his back against one of the mirrors, wearing a bathrobe with large patch pockets. His cheek and lips showed the marks of Zurkeulen's hand. He'd wiped the blood off. He didn't take his eyes off her. He said nothing, just followed every one of her movements, making it easier for her.

She took some underwear out of one of the cupboard drawers and put it on, ignoring Ramon's nauseating grin, got a pair of trousers and said, "I'm going to put a pullover on, it's cold outside."

Michael nodded, following her hands with his eyes. It was only a water pistol, a useless toy. But that wasn't obvious at first sight. The chunky black gun was in the middle of a pile of pullovers. Michael closed his eyes in horror when she picked up the top three and took one out of the drawer. Then he had himself back under control again and managed to give his look of alarm a plausible explanation. "I'm not letting that guy take you with him."

He pulled her to him, positioning their bodies in such a way that Ramon couldn't see him slip his hand into the drawer. He gave a start of surprise. The weight must have told him what he was holding. And he hadn't seen Zurkeulen's gun. "Be sensible," she said. "They're both armed. We have to do what they ask."

He understood. The water pistol disappeared in the left-hand pocket of his bathrobe. "OK," he muttered, moving away from her and letting his arm hang down beside the pocket. He looked harmless, defeated.

Zurkeulen was already out on the landing when she came back into the bedroom. He waved her over. He'd put the gun back in his jacket pocket. She came out and almost stumbled over Andrea, who was lying on her stomach, her arm over her face. As she passed, it was impossible to say whether she'd been injured or in what way. But her shoulders were twitching so she wasn't dead, thank God. Zurkeulen made her lead the way down the stairs and followed close behind.

"Take the jacket, Nadia," Michael shouted from the dressing room. "It really is cold."

Zurkeulen gave a mocking smile. She saw it as she quickly looked back. "If anything happens to my husband…" she said.

"Nothing's going to happen to him," Zurkeulen promised. "As long as he does nothing to provoke Ramon."

Michael called out again, telling her to take the jacket. She felt there was something urgent about his tone. There was only the leather jacket in the closet. And underneath the jacket was the alarm with all the buttons. Zurkeulen kept his eyes on her hands as she went to get the jacket. She didn't go too close to the box, just took the jacket off the hanger and slipped it on. It must have belonged to Nadia, it fitted perfectly. Zurkeulen gestured towards the front door.

The street was empty, the nearby houses dark. The street lamps made pools of glittering light on the damp tarmac. No one noticed anything, not even Eleanor Ravatzky's dog. The black limousine was in the drive. Zurkeulen unlocked the doors, waited until she was settled in the front passenger seat, then got in himself. The engine made a soft hum as the car drove almost silently out into the street.

Something was digging into her hip. There must be some object in the right pocket of her jacket, the seat belt was pressing it against her hipbone. She passed her hand over it and felt a longish object under her fingers.

Zurkeulen noticed. "Lift your hands up," he demanded, as he pulled up at the side of the road. Then he felt in her jacket pocket and took the object out. It was a cigarette lighter, fairly large, with a firm's logo on the side. In the left pocket was a slim cigarette case. He put them in her hands. "I must ask you not to smoke in my car."

"I gave up some time ago," she said. "I'm pregnant." Why she said that, whether she hoped it might make him treat her more gently, she couldn't say. Men like Zurkeulen knew no mercy. He was sitting at the wheel like a stone statue, cold, stiff and silent. She almost wished he'd asked who she really was. And perhaps realized that they'd both been taken for a ride. But if not even Nadia had managed to stay alive…

On the other hand, she wasn't Nadia and she'd already managed to get out of one apparently hopeless situation. The two awful days in the abandoned factory after the second bank robbery suddenly took on meaning. Dieter's opinion that she occasionally tended to wildly overestimate her own abilities was neither here nor there. It might be crazy to imagine she could somehow outwit Zurkeulen, escape and rescue Michael and Andrea, but it was precisely that idea which kept her from slumping down listlessly in her seat.

She wondered whether it would help to start a conversation. He must know that she'd lied and Helga had told the truth. She herself had shown Ramon that she knew Alfo Investment. Even though she couldn't say for sure at what point the grey car had started to tail the Alfa, there was only one place he could have picked it up and that was the underground car park of Gerler House. Should she tell him her marriage had broken down and that she'd already discussed getting an apartment with an estate agent's, Behringer and Partners? What would be the point? After the way Michael had reacted, he would hardly believe her. And Hardenberg would presumably render anything she did in that direction futile.

He accelerated when they were on the autobahn. Her thoughts went back to the house. Would Michael have any chance? With a water pistol against Ramon's gun? Or would he rather not take any risks so as not to endanger her? And Andrea? She'd been crying, though silently, what in Heaven's name had they done to her? Or to little Pascal? Or to Andrea's husband, if she had one? She'd also mentioned a grandmother.

The suburbs were approaching far too quickly. If she'd been the only one involved, she'd have tried using her fists, her teeth, holding the cigarette lighter to his hair, even at the risk of it ending up with two dead bodies being recovered from a crashed car. But there were two other lives to consider. Even if it had just been Michael alone, she wouldn't have taken the slightest risk. She played with the useless lighter in her lap. It came apart and she thought she'd broken it. But it wasn't broken, it was a knife. A thin, narrow blade attached to a plastic ring that formed the bottom of an ordinary plastic disposable lighter. The urgency in Michael's voice suddenly made sense.

Zurkeulen was staring concentratedly into the darkness of the autobahn exit. She pushed the blade back in as the car swung into the long curve. He slowed down and turned off to the right. On the right-hand side were detached houses. Again he turned off. Antoniterweg she read, a blue sign on a white wall. They passed large houses with extensive gardens. Feeling with her fingers, she pulled the plastic ring out of the lighter in her lap. Zurkeulen was looking ahead, she out of the side window. Number fifty-three. There were several building sites on the other side of the road. The thin, narrow blade was almost completely hidden in her hand.

Number seventy-five. The car slowed down and stopped outside number seventy-nine. "You lead the way," he said, pointing to the car door, "I would like to stay in the background initially. And it would be sensible if you didn't indicate my presence to Herr Hardenberg. I would like you to allow me to see you greet each other in a relaxed manner. It could turn out to be highly beneficial for your future.

Whatever he was promising, he couldn't afford any witnesses, that much was clear. When she didn't move, he leaned over and stretched his arm out across her lap for the door handle. One second later the thin blade was at his throat.

"Don't move," she said. "If you move I'll cut your throat. And don't delude yourself that I'll have any inhibitions." She felt in his pocket, grasped the gun, pulled it out and placed the muzzle against the back of his neck.

He didn't move. Half lying across her lap, he said, "You're making a big mistake, Frau Trenkler. I'm afraid it's going to cost your husband his life. And that is quite unnecessary. I wasn't thinking of violence, more of cooperation."

"You don't believe that yourself," she said. "But you've no need to worry about my husband. He's got a gun, a much bigger one than the little thing your companion was waving around. And now turn the car round. We're going back."

She thought she could hear him grinding his teeth. "First take the knife away," he said.

She withdrew the hand holding the blade. Immediately he made a downwards and sideways thrust with his head. It was a violent butt to the solar plexus and stomach that winded her. She didn't deliberately squeeze the trigger, it was just a reflex action set off by the pain. But nothing happened.

Zurkeulen took the gun away from her and said, almost sympathetically, "The safety catch is on." Then he forced the little knife out of her clenched hand.

He gave her three minutes, just three minutes, to get over his head butt. Whilst she was doing so, he rang Ramon. It turned out to be unnecessary to warn him about the water pistol. He'd overpowered Michael long ago, Ramon said. Zurkeulen passed the information on to her. "Was there any difficulty?" he asked. "You sound rather strained."

Ramon said that had been caused by Michael's violent resistance, which had cost him one of his front teeth. "You didn't shoot, I hope?" Zurkeulen said, asking whether Herr Trenkler was still conscious and wanted to say farewell to his wife. Ramon informed him that he was no longer capable of that. "Then take him down to the cellar," Zurkeulen ordered. "The woman too. Throw the pair of them in the pool."

After he'd rung off, he looked at the knife in his hand. The thin blade was a beautiful little toy, he said, more delicate than the implements Ramon normally employed. He described in graphic terms how he intended to use it. Then he said, "Will you get out now, please. Can you manage or shall I help you?"

She would rather have let herself be cut to pieces than allow him to touch her, even in support. Somehow she managed to get out of the car, without seeing or hearing anything. A veil had come down over her eyes. All dead. Nadia tortured and run over, Andrea knocked unconscious and drowned. Michael as well. She could still feel his arm round her shoulders, his hand putting her fingers over the sheet and pressing it to her breast. She saw him spin round in the dressing-room doorway.

Dieter would probably say, "Now don't get all worked up, it wasn't your fault. And for you it couldn't have turned out better. Trenkler was a serious risk. Sell the house and you'll be set up for life." Dieter had always been an idiot, even if his opinions were mostly correct.

The veil over her eyes was water. And once again she felt it close over her head, felt Michael draw her to him and kiss her. And Paris! He'd been so happy, so full of plans, so looking forward to having a child.

Philip Hardenberg's house lay in darkness behind a six-foot hedge almost bare of leaves. Gravel crunched under her feet. She could hear it. Zurkeulen was five or six steps behind her and from him she heard nothing. He was walking on the grass. She could hardly see and all she felt was the icy wind on her tear-damp cheeks.

Zurkeulen had promised he would let her live, if she helped him get his money. And he was convinced she wanted to live. Even without a husband it was worth it for the child, he'd said. And he believed it would be worth it even more, once he'd shown her how he dealt with people who cheated him. He was only going to use the little knife on Philip Hardenberg. Helga Barthel would have a quick and painless death. He hated having to cause a woman needless pain. He left that sort of stuff to Ramon, he couldn't even watch such unpleasant things.

She was almost at the front door. Everything was dark. She stumbled on the first step, steadied herself against the wall and took the next two steps without being conscious of them. There must be a bell-push somewhere but she couldn't find it in the darkness. And Philip Hardenberg didn't seem to go in for movement sensors that switched a security light on. She knocked on the door and turned round for Zurkeulen. But all she could see were two tall pine trees on the lawn.

She heard the door being opened. No light went on. Instead, a hand shot out and dragged her into the hall – it was a repeat of the Sunday of the dress rehearsal. Before she realized what was happening, the door was closed. She felt an arm round her waist, a hand over her mouth, someone's breath on her ear. "Are you all right?" a man's voice she didn't recognize asked. Somehow she managed to nod.

Outside the house all was silent. There was silence everywhere apart from some dark corner where muted groans could be heard. The pressure from the hand over her mouth slackened a little as the man behind her changed his position.

"Michael." She felt the sob rising in her throat, she could do nothing to stop it. "Ramon's killed my husband." Under the man's hand her shoulders twitched, as she'd seen Andrea's shoulders twitch on the landing.

The hand closed over her mouth again. The voice behind her whispered. "Your husband's OK. Frau Gerling as well." That must be Andrea. In that moment all she felt was her knees giving way. But the man held her. They were still standing close to the front door in complete darkness.

There was a crackling sound quite near and a distorted voice saying, "He's leaving." A few minutes later the same voice said, "You can put the light on now."

The hand was taken off her mouth, the arm let go of her waist. The light went on in the hall. She turned round slowly and found herself facing a man in a grey suit. The light was switched on in the living room as well. For a brief moment she saw two legs in dark trousers sticking out from behind a table. There were two of them in the house, one man in the hall, the other seeing to Helga Barthel and Philip Hardenberg. The third was on the building site opposite. The man in the grey suit opened the door. His colleague was coming across the lawn. He grinned as he closed the door behind him. "I've never seen anything like it," he said. "Why didn't he go to the door with her?"

The other laughed softly and said, "He rang up. It must have been a nasty shock for him to get a dead man on the line instead of his thug."

During those first minutes no one felt the need to explain things to her. Perhaps she wouldn't have understood anyway. She hadn't come to terms with the previous hour yet and already new events were piling up on top: three unknown men, very young and so inappropriately dressed in their suits. They looked as if they should be in a bank, not on building sites or in other people's houses. And they were behaving as if the last half hour had taken them back to their childhood, pure adventure, a welcome change from the tedious hours in the office.

One sat her down on a chair in Hardenberg's living room and took a mobile out of his trouser pocket. Helga Barthel was lying on the sofa, within reach of her, without her glasses and without any visible injuries, completely motionless, her face a pale blue. Philip Hardenberg was kneeling on the gleaming parquet floor between the table and the sofa. His head was resting on Helga's breast. He didn't move. His breath came in short gasps, interrupted now and then by groans or sobs.

The man with the mobile was making his report. It had been quite simple, he said. They'd expected it would be much more difficult, that Zurkeulen would come with her to the door. That would have complicated things. On what plausible pretext could they have let him go after three night-time attacks with several injured? As it was, Zurkeulen must have assumed Philip Hardenberg had summoned up his last resources of strength and played the hero to rescue Nadia Trenkler.

At some point she started to cry out for Michael and couldn't stop until the man handed her the mobile. But instead of Michael she heard Wolfgang Blasting. "Calm down, Nadia. Doc's fine. He's not even seriously injured."

"I want to talk to him. I want to talk to him straight away."

"He's not here, Nadia, he's taking Frau Gerling home. Now put me back on to Schneider."

Schneider was the one who'd pulled her into the house. He took the mobile from her and continued his report to Wolfgang Blasting. Frau Barthel was in a bad way, a serious problem with her heart. She'd taken some medicine, he said, and now she was sleeping – or unconscious, she urgently needed a doctor.

He didn't like Blasting's answer. "Frau Trenkler can't do that," he protested, "she can hardly stand up herself. And Hardenberg needs help too. He's got a couple of broken ribs." Again he listened, looking at her with an embarrassed grin on his face. Finally he handed the mobile back to her. "He wants to talk to you again."

"Listen, Nadia," Blasting said. "The men will help you get Frau Barthel and Hardenberg in the car."

"Are they police?"

"They're from my department. You drive the other two to the nearest hospital."

"Why did they let Zurkeulen go?"

"Do I really have to explain that to you, Nadia? Now do as I say. Hardenberg's to tell the doctors they were attacked while they were out for an evening walk. That kind of thing. He'll think up something."

"I want to get out of here."

"Nadia!" Wolfgang Blasting's voice took on a sharp tone. "Pull yourself together. You've held your nerve so far. It was really something the way you let Michael get that toy. He almost had a stroke when he realized what he had in his hand. But you were fantastic, both of you. And you can manage the rest. Hand me back to Schneider."

Schneider said he could take Hardenberg and Frau Barthel to the hospital himself but Blasting wouldn't have it. Schneider gave in, rang off and told his colleagues the boss needed them to help clear up. Then he turned back to her and, with flattery and high praise for her iron nerve, repeated Wolfgang Blasting's order.

"I'll go with you as far as the hospital. You drive behind and if there's a problem, flash your headlights."

Helga didn't move, even when two of the men lifted her off the sofa and carried her down to the garage. Helped by Schneider, Hardenberg managed to get to his feet and, with a glance full of hatred at her, let himself be led outside. The two men carefully lay Helga down on the rear seat of the dark-blue Mercedes, then Schneider helped Hardenberg

301

into the passenger seat, handed her the keys and got into Helga's green Golf. His two colleagues went over to the building site opposite where they'd left their car.

As she sat down in the driver's seat, Philip Hardenberg said, in a strained voice, "If she dies, you're going to die too." What followed made it clear that he, like everyone else, assumed she was Nadia. He was beside himself with fury and went on at her uninterruptedly, as if he'd just been waiting for the opportunity, revealing things he wouldn't have wanted anyone else to know.

Somehow she managed to follow the Golf and listen as well. Several times she was tempted to flash her lights to get Schneider to stop because she felt she couldn't stand it any longer. At the same time she knew Hardenberg wouldn't repeat what he'd said if Schneider or anyone else was listening.

"You and your blasted fad for playing the good Samaritan," he said. "First of all a poor student, then this bimbo. Is that the lot? Oh no, there's the inventor genius, he enjoyed your largesse too. They go down on their knees before you if they get a few crumbs from your table. You need that, don't you? A good deed now and then and you feel like Lady Bountiful."

He could hardly speak for the pain and every sentence he managed to squeeze out made it clear she should have been dead long ago. He'd intended to get rid of her on the last Wednesday in November. That would have been the best opportunity – in his opinion. There would have been at least two dozen witnesses to her encounter with Zurkeulen in the bank, consequently the police would have concentrated their enquiries on Zurkeulen.

He'd intended to exploit the opportunity, without bothering to let Nadia in on his plan. After Zurkeulen had turned up with a few stupid questions in his office that Wednesday morning, Hardenberg had gone to Kettlerstrasse in the evening. Unfortunately he hadn't been able to get into her flat. His duplicate key didn't fit any more and she hadn't come to the door – of course, at that time she'd been waiting for Nadia at the station.

On the Thursday Nadia had got him to agree to two more pleasant days for her stand-in, he went on. She'd said it fitted in nicely because she had appointments for the Thursday afternoon and Friday anyway and had to be away overnight. But there had certainly been no mention of a large, airy apartment and a good job with Alfo Investment after the child was born.

Nadia appeared not to have mentioned the fact that her stand-in was pregnant. She'd just promised to get rid of the problem herself – after her return on the Friday evening. He could still kick himself, he said, for having agreed to that. Nadia, he claimed, hadn't dreamed of keeping her word. He hadn't seen hide nor hair of her at the airport on Friday evening, nor of the Lasko woman.

"Did you warn her?" he hissed. "Of course you did. I waited for more than an hour in the car park. Then I went to her flat, but she wasn't there either. Instead I got into a fight with that drunken sot." And Heller hadn't let himself be dispatched without resistance. Hardenberg had had to take some hefty blows from him, so that Zurkeulen's thug had only had to tap him to leave him with a few broken ribs.

It didn't sound as if Hardenberg had ever seen Nadia without her clothes on. It had been about money, that was all. From the moment Nadia had told him about the woman she'd encountered by the lift, he'd had only one thing on his mind: the millions he could get men like Zurkeulen, who weren't exactly on Christmas-card terms with the taxman, to entrust to the dependable hands of the woman they would know as Susanne Lasko.

It was clear that Nadia hadn't been immediately enthused by his plan. She'd already come unstuck once before and didn't want to put her marriage at risk. Hardenberg assumed "the Lasko woman" had never found out that her identity was being used to defraud investors. As Dieter had said, they only needed her ID cards, and they were easy to procure. You just went to the passport office etc. with new photos and claimed you'd lost your handbag.

But Nadia always knew better, he went on, and didn't want to arouse her husband's suspicions when she stayed away overnight. That Michael would make love to his stand-in wife was something she hadn't reckoned with. Nor was she happy with it.

"I told you straight away it wouldn't work. You can't let a woman you don't know stay in your house and not expect her to have a snoop around. She wasn't half as stupid as you thought. Or did you let her in on our scheme on that Thursday in order to dump me? Yes, you did, admit it. There's no other explanation. You got together with that woman because you're never satisfied. You wanted me out of the way. I should have known you weren't to be trusted. I should have suspected something like that was going on when I found your letters in that woman's cupboard.

"Perhaps I can do something to change that," he said, imitating Nadia's way of speaking. "How did you think it was going to work? She'd have been more than happy with half a million, wouldn't she? You wouldn't have had to split the proceeds with her. You sent her to the office to get the laptop. You gave her my address. You were counting on Zurkeulen getting rid of me. Where's his money? I was in Luxembourg and it wasn't there. But you can't do that and get away with it, not with me, you damn bitch."

"Yes I can, just with you," she said. "And for your information, I have all this on tape. If you open your trap once more, you'll end up inside for longer than you'd care to think. You see, I haven't killed anyone. I haven't even defrauded anyone."

When she looked back, she had only a vague recollection of the next two hours. She knew it had been a few minutes before five in the morning when she'd backed Philip Hardenberg's Mercedes out of the Antoniterweg garage. And when she came to a halt in the Marienweg drive, it was shortly after seven. She must have got something done in those two hours. She'd deposited Helga and Hardenberg in Emergency at a hospital, then driven on. At one point she'd stopped on the hard shoulder because what she had come to understand made it impossible for her to drive on.

Hardenberg's bitter whispering refused to fade, even though he was no longer sitting beside her. And Nadia kept smiling and repeating her generous offer of a future free from worry, even though she had long since been consigned to the mortuary freezer. And had she looked at the list of parking charges in the multi-storey on the Friday morning, instead of taking everything to the bank, had she been able to get the Alfa out immediately after work in the evening, she would have been on time in the car park, where Hardenberg had been waiting for her. She found it impossible to get over the fact that it was only through her muddle-headedness that she was still alive.

And what had been Nadia's intentions? After all, she had rung her again at the sweet shop on the Friday morning. To warn her? Perhaps. But perhaps Nadia had gone to Kettlerstrasse on the Saturday evening to get the laptop back and to do what Hardenberg had failed to do. To get rid of her. That was the last thing Hardenberg had heard from Nadia. Early on Saturday morning she'd rung him again and said that unfortunately she hadn't managed it the previous evening. But he shouldn't get worked up, she'd gone on, there was plenty more time over the weekend. She could even make the body disappear without trace. Everything would be all right.

All right! The expression was still going round and round in her head like a tape on a loop as she walked up to the front door. She hadn't given a thought to her handbag and her keys when she'd followed Zurkeulen to his car, so for the first time she had to set the dog barking in the hall. Wolfgang opened the door. No longer was he Blasting, the dangerous policeman, he was just another friend like Jo.

Michael was standing by the rustic-style dresser in the living room, twiddling a half-full glass. He wasn't all right. He was a little drunk, a little unsure of himself, a little despairing. A little of everything. He threw his arms round her, dribbling some whisky down her neck because he hadn't put his glass down first. "You smell good and you taste even better," he murmured. His kiss tasted of salt and whisky. "How can that be?" Her held her a little away from him and scrutinized her face.

"I've stopped smoking," she said. "But maybe it's the hormones too."

He nodded. "I hit him just once and he didn't get up."

More information. And no room left for it in her brain. Michael had broken Ramon's neck. It had been Wolfgang speaking when Zurkeulen thought he'd been talking to his thug. She didn't feel sorry for Ramon. She didn't feel sorry for anything. Apart from the drops running down her neck perhaps. She freed herself from his arms, took the glass out of his hand, emptied it and said, "I need to eat something."

Wolfgang went to the kitchen with them. Since he intended to spend the day at her desk anyway, he helped her prepare a lavish breakfast. That is, he did almost all the preparation himself because she kept stopping all the time to remember – to remember Nadia's mangled message on that Friday. She would have loved to know what Nadia had actually said. But however much she racked her brains, she could make nothing of her last call. On the other hand, a lot did occur to her about Nadia's last hours. Clearly, despite all the tortures, she hadn't told Zurkeulen and his thug where to find Susanne Lasko that Saturday evening. Otherwise the two brutes would have turned up at Marienweg much earlier. It seemed unlikely that Nadia would have refused to reveal her own address to protect her double. For Nadia, all that mattered was Michael, she would have bet the life of her unborn child on that. Nadia must have loved him very much, at least in her final hours.

A few minutes later Michael came into the kitchen as well. The three of them sat round the table. Wolfgang hungrily devoured an omelette, several slices of toast and a bunch of grapes. She chewed away mechanically on something, with no idea what it was or how it had come to be on her plate. Andrea must have done some shopping in the last few days. It could hardly have been difficult for Zurkeulen to find out how to get into the house.

Michael spent minutes stirring his coffee and murmuring, "I just hit him once."

Wolfgang put his hand on his shoulder. "Forget it. No one's assuming you hit him as hard as you could with that intention in mind. You were furious, you were…"

"No," Michael replied, "I wasn't furious." Suddenly he was strangely calm. He looked at her thoughtfully, sceptically. "The alarm. You didn't —"

"I couldn't," she broke in. "Zurkeulen was right next to me. I was afraid he'd notice something."

His speech was slightly slurred, he was more than a little drunk. But his mind was still functioning clearly. "What was there for him to notice? You want to put a jacket on, you take the hanger off the hook. There's nothing in that. Why didn't you?"

It was only then that she remembered Nadia's warning not to take the coat hanger down. The silent alarm, she thought. And she'd assumed he'd only said that in order to scare Zurkeulen into making a quick exit.

"Frau Gerling didn't feel able to do it either," Wolfgang said.

Michael ignored Blasting's comment. "That swine asked me whether I was absolutely sure," he said, running his eyes over her face, with that sceptical expression, as if he wanted to check every pore. She waited for her heart to start pounding or for the awareness that this was the end to express itself in some other way. But nothing happened.

"Tell me something," Michael said. "Anything. Tell me where I sprained my ankle."

"You poor darling," she said. "What has that guy done to you? It was in Arosa. I'd warned you. There was more ice than snow on the piste. But you insisted on showing me how good you were on skis."

He gave a sob and, ignoring both Wolfgang and his cup, leaned across, drew her up and kissed her. His coffee spilled over the table. There must have been a thousand other "do-you-remember?" anecdotes, she'd just been lucky that he'd chosen one of the half-dozen Nadia had provided for her. That was something of which she was all too well aware.

Wolfgang took him upstairs. Into bed with you, my lad, sleep it off and let us get some work done. He didn't actually say that, but it was clearly what he was thinking. As they went up the stairs, she heard Michael talking of the horrible thought he'd had that Zurkeulen was taking away everything that made his life worth living; that he had perhaps already taken it, since the silent alarm hadn't been set off. The thought had been driving him mad, so that it wasn't fury, it was a simple destructive urge that had made him lash out at Ramon. He knew very well that the back of the neck was a weak point and at that moment he hadn't cared whether he himself was hit by a bullet or not.

"Of course," was the last thing she heard Wolfgang say, "I can understand that. I'd probably have reacted in the same way myself."

Wolfgang didn't come back downstairs. She went up to join him in the study, though what followed was like dancing on a knife edge. First of all he remarked that Zurkeulen really had put an idea in Michael's head, but in his view any man would know whether it was his own wife in bed with him or whether he'd been sleeping with another woman for days. Because it must have been for several days, he said, and in such a case there was considerably more to consider than just a striking facial resemblance. Apart from that, what reason could the Lasko woman have to move in with Nadia's husband?

Wolfgang saw things rather as she had done at first. That there were a thousand things that differentiated one woman from another. Sterilization, for example. But he suspected that was a trick. "Are you really pregnant," he asked, "or are you just trying to keep Doc happy?"

"To the first question the answer's yes, to the second, no," she said. "And if you're going to ask me if I intend to sue Wenning, the answer's another no. It was funny when I first noticed it. It's easy to say you don't want something when that something isn't there to want. But then suddenly there is something there you didn't expect – and at my age it's my last chance to have a child."

He listened with an odd grin on his face, murmured, "Piece of luck, then," and demanded information about Hardenberg's business affairs. For a while she managed to get him off that subject and even learned a few more things herself. His men had taken Ramon's body out of the house and dumped it somewhere among the flora and fauna. However, they assumed Zurkeulen would lose no time finding a replacement.

He eventually accepted that she couldn't tell him all he wanted to know. Whether he believed her when she said she'd had nothing to do with Hardenberg's shady deals was quite another matter. He opened the SLA file and pointed to the initials AR. "Most people lack imagination and choose code words with personal associations," he said. "If you'd set up this account, I'd bet on Arnim Röhrler. But if you've got nothing to do with it…"

He broke off. Perhaps he'd noticed her hesitation. Of course she'd had something to do with Röhrler. It was quite possible that Nadia had chosen Röhrler's initials. When she remained silent, Wolfgang went on. "Her mother's called Agnes Runge. She had no other relatives. It could be an absolute disaster, but I think we should try it."

"What do you mean, 'we'? I don't want anything to do with it."

"You'll have to give us a hand, I'm afraid," he said. "None of my men would make a convincing Susanne Lasko."

He was about to go on, but he was interrupted by the telephone. The answerphone was still switched on. First of all Nadia's voice was heard, then Dieter's, saying, "I've got some interesting information for you, Susanne —"

As if it was his own phone, Wolfgang picked up the receiver and switched off the answerphone, so she could no longer hear what Dieter was saying. He kept his eyes fixed on her face. He didn't say who he was, he didn't say anything, he just kept listening attentively. He watched her, deep in thought, as she got up and left the room.

She went to the bedroom, got into bed with Michael and put his arm round her. He was so fast asleep he didn't notice. "Hold me tight," she murmured. She had no idea what story she should tell them when

Wolfgang came through the door, no longer a neighbour, friend and helper, just a policeman.

It was quite a long conversation. In the first three or four minutes she heard Wolfgang Blasting give several brief answers and couldn't understand why Dieter didn't hang up once he realized it wasn't her on the line. Finally Wolfgang Blasting expressed his thanks. After that all was quiet in the study for a while. It seemed he still had things to do on the computer. Perhaps he wanted to get the full picture before he arrested her.

But when he finally appeared in the doorway, he was still Wolfgang. Dieter hadn't called to talk to Susanne, but to talk about her. He had no idea she was back. Wolfgang had contacted him some days ago to find out more about Susanne Lasko. Very early that morning, when she was still parked on the autobahn hard shoulder trying to come to terms with how close her brush with death had been, Wolfgang had rung Dieter from the study, explained what had happened and told him he could be contacted at that number for the rest of the day.

"I'm going to see Lasko," he said. "He's willing to help us as far as he can. If we get nowhere with Agnes Runge, perhaps he can give us some other idea for AR. Apart from that, I need him to nail Hardenberg. I'm sure we can cook something up."

His intention was to get Dieter to make precisely the statement that she had been refused, namely that shortly before her death Susanne had passed incriminating evidence on to him, in a closed envelope, of course, which was only to be opened if she should die.

"It always works," Wolfgang said. "You wouldn't believe how many people fall for such a hackneyed ploy. But Lasko wants to meet you, he was very insistent. So, are you coming along?" he grinned. "There's nothing for you here at the moment. Doc's downed four double whiskies and he won't be able to get it up for the rest of the day, that's for sure."

No more than an hour later he was parking outside her ex-mother-in-law's house. It had changed a lot over the last few years. New façade, new windows, a new roof – and no more flowers in the front garden, where she'd spent hours on her knees pulling out the weeds. Dieter had gone for the low-maintenance option: a lawn.

He dutifully started in surprise when he opened the door, and gave her a textbook wide-eyed stare. "Frau Trenkler?" When she nodded, he said, "Herr Blasting did warn me, but it's still quite a shock." Then he stood aside and gestured them into the house.

It was small, it was cramped. It hadn't struck her like that before. She'd been sorry to leave it. Now it looked like a doll's house that had been relegated to the attic when you grew out of dolls. Everywhere Ramie had put signs of her sovereignty. It was also very clear that there was a young child in the house. Even in Dieter's study there were toys lying around. But he'd sent his wife and daughter out, to the supermarket or somewhere.

Dieter was magnificent. He managed to chat to Wolfgang in such a way as to pass on information to her, all the while staring at her as if she were some exotic animal. Perhaps that was what she'd become for him. He must have been amazed that she'd managed to maintain the persona of Nadia through five days in Paris, being abducted by Zurkeulen and the confrontation with Hardenberg.

Dieter absolutely refused to provide the favour by which Wolfgang wanted to prove Hardenberg had been involved in dishonest dealings. It was possible, he said, that Hardenberg had been used by Susanne, rather than vice versa. Would it not then perhaps be better to shift the whole of the blame onto her? The way he described it, the time she'd spent reading trashy novels to his mother had given her a taste for luxury. He claimed that even while they were still married she'd made inordinate demands. And as a qualified banker, she knew how to siphon off money into her own account.

His ex-mother-in-law – Dieter felt obliged to do something for the old lady, she had no one else. But something she'd said suggested Susanne had at least dropped hints to her mother about a carefree future together in the sun. It sounded as if she'd intended to flee the country and take her mother with her.

However, Dieter didn't think Agnes Runge would repeat what she'd told him in front of a policeman. But perhaps, he said, he might be able to squeeze a little more out of her that would throw a clearer light on Susanne's plans – provided the police left her in peace.

Wolfgang nodded. "No problem."

Two hours later they took their leave. Dieter saw them to the door and gave her a furtive tug on the sleeve. Wolfgang went out to the car, while she stayed with Dieter for a moment. "Your mother knows," he whispered. "I'm taking her out for a drive on Sunday. It would be nice if you could be with us. Otherwise I can't guarantee she'll go along with it much more. Three o'clock, the car park at the inn." In his normal voice, he added, "I hope you understand why I have to refuse, Frau Trenkler. I don't want to be dragged into this business. But, anyway, I don't believe proving Herr Hardenberg was involved in investment fraud would help you."

"Don't worry about me," she said. "So far I've managed quite well on my own in this affair."

Wolfgang was unhappy and he made it clear on the journey back. If she'd whined and moaned a bit, he said, perhaps Lasko would have helped them nail Hardenberg after all. He didn't like the idea of Hardenberg getting off scot-free. She liked the idea even less, but what Dieter had suggested couldn't be rejected out of hand. It was doubtful whether it could be proved that Hardenberg had murdered Heller. He would deny to the police what he'd admitted to her. Perhaps he might even try to shift the blame for everything onto Nadia.

Michael was still asleep when they got back to the house. Wolfgang immediately went back on the computer again and checked the smaller files. It was just stuff to do with insurance together with finance for a couple of properties. He couldn't open the larger files without the appropriate program.

He deleted masses of data he didn't need for his investigation. What he did need was storage space and he hoped he could gain enough kilobytes by the evening to be able to reinstall the operating program. It was probably in the safe. Fortunately he was still a few hundred kilobytes short when evening came, so it wasn't worth sending her up to the loft. He just instructed her to thin out her own files. By that time Michael had joined them again.

After Wolfgang had left, she sat down at the computer to make sure he didn't find out the truth about the two hundred thousand for Jo. The sensible thing would perhaps have been to go up to the loft with Michael and watch what he did, as she had done with Wolfgang. But there was sure to be an opportunity to do that some other time. At the moment NTA was more important. She didn't want Jo to get into difficulties too.

"Would you be an angel and get me the program?" Of course Michael would be an angel. When he returned, the NTA file had disappeared. She continued deleting – all the analyses, reports and notes of discussions. Finally there was enough space. It was a bit tight, but that only affected the speed at which the computer worked. Michael took over to reinstall the program because she'd suddenly developed a sore back and was hungry too.

They spent a peaceful night. On Wolfgang's instructions Andrea, her little boy, her husband and grandmother had been put up by relatives. Jo and Lilo were protected by their own alarm system. Moreover one of Wolfgang's men was in a car in the street outside, bored to tears.

On Friday morning Michael set off for the lab at the usual time. She got up with him and made breakfast. He just drank a cup of coffee, refusing the toast with ham and a gherkin she'd so lovingly prepared. "You know I can't eat a thing this early in the morning." One more thing she knew for certain.

When Wolfgang appeared, shortly before eight, she'd had time to ring Dieter. He read out an English text and she repeated it three times, until he was satisfied with her pronunciation. Then he reminded her of the outing with her mother on Sunday afternoon.

Schneider came with Wolfgang. He was to relieve the man outside in the street. Wolfgang wanted her protected during the day as well. He was nervous when she picked up the telephone, explaining that they only had one attempt. If the code word "Agnes Runge" didn't work, she'd have to fly out to Nassau to get Zurkeulen's money transferred back to Luxembourg. And if it turned out that AR wasn't Arnim Röhrler either, he could forget the whole plan. But it worked – with her mother's name.

"That's that, then," Wolfgang said in satisfied tones as she replaced the receiver. He made a brief call himself, sending one of his men to get Susanne Lasko's passport and ID card from his colleagues in the murder squad. Then he said, "We're going to Luxembourg on Monday," handing the receiver back to her.

Her call was transferred several times, finally to the office of a bank manager. As she started to speak, Wolfgang gave her the thumbs up, though all she had to do was to introduce herself with the name she'd used for years, make an appointment for Monday and ask for the money

312

that would arrive from Nassau in the next few hours to be ready for collection.

On Tuesday she was to hand the money back to Zurkeulen and perhaps somehow get him to confess to the murder of Susanne Lasko. Wolfgang doubted very much whether she'd manage that, but handing over the money would be enough to get Zurkeulen on a charge of tax evasion. Solving a murder case wasn't really his business and, anyway, he doubted whether Zurkeulen would have got his own hands dirty. And Ramon was beyond justice.

On Saturday she went shopping with Michael. There was always someone close to them, but he didn't let that bother him, he was full of plans again. The guest room that didn't have the access to the loft had to be cleared out, wallpapered and equipped with a cradle, a table for changing nappies and so on. And he'd already been thinking about a name. He was hoping for a daughter and would like to call her Laura – after his mother – but he wasn't sure how she would feel about it.

"Why not?" she said. "Laura's a lovely name."

Her reward was a long kiss. Then he started talking about Wolfgang's plans for the next few days. He wasn't at all happy with them, but he realized there was no alternative. His concern gave her the opportunity to make arrangements that would allow her to go and see her mother. Repressing a sigh, she said, "If only we could be sure that'll be the end of it. But I can't get those other letters out of my mind. You remember, the same letter nine times over?"

He nodded.

"Who's to say Zurkeulen's the only one who's been cheated?" she went on. "The fact that Wolfgang's not found any evidence of other investors means nothing. Philip must know if there are more of them. But I'm afraid that once Wolfgang starts working on him we won't get any more out of him. Philip will be happy to let me walk straight into any trap."

Michael saw it that way too. She didn't even have to hint that she needed to talk to Hardenberg alone, he suggested it himself. He even arranged it so that she could slip out of the house unnoticed shortly after midday on Sunday. It didn't prove difficult to persuade Schneider, who by now was staying in the house, not outside, to have a swim in the pool.

Before he went down with Schneider, he reminded her about the Niedenhoff concert. In all the excitement she'd completely forgotten it. That evening in the Beethovenhalle. "We'll go, yes? It'll do us good to switch off for a while. And Jacques would be disappointed if we didn't turn up."

She would have preferred imagining Jacques's disappointment to meeting him face to face. On the other hand, what could happen at a concert? She'd be sitting there among the audience, while a man played the piano up on the stage. She'd never been to a concert before.

She got to the inn punctually at three. Her mother was in Dieter's estate. Dieter demanded the keys to her car and pressed his into her hand, urging her to get off to avoid anyone happening to see her. There was scarcely time to greet her mother properly. Agnes Runge just said, "Off we go, then." Dieter followed in the Alfa for a while then turned off and disappeared.

"I didn't go to the funeral," her mother said. "Dieter said it would be better if I didn't. I knew very well nothing had happened to you. After all, we'd spoken on the telephone. It's just that they wouldn't believe me. But tell me all about it. Why does Dieter have to tell the police those horrible things about you? You didn't really steal those people's money, did you?"

Only yours, Mum, she thought. It wasn't easy to think up a harmless beginning for the gruesome end. She felt more churned up inside from seeing her mother again than she'd expected. For several minutes she was just Susanne Lasko, a woman who'd put her mother, the only person she really loved, through a lot of uncertainty and pain. It was difficult to hold back her tears and sound reasonably convincing while driving Dieter's estate, at the same time pushing away her mother's hands, which were either feeling her face or hampering her own hands on the steering wheel.

Agnes Runge listened attentively. Eventually she asked, "But why didn't you say anything, child? You could have told me the truth."

At that all her self-control went. "I'm really sorry, Mum. I didn't want to lie to you, but I didn't want you to worry, either. That's why I thought —"

"That's all right," Agnes Runge broke in. "The main thing is that everything's all right now. It is, isn't it?"

"Yes," she sobbed.

"Then stop crying, child."

Dieter had prepared the ground a little, hinted at the arrival of a grandchild and painted a rosy picture of her only daughter's new life: a splendid house, a nice, good-natured husband, a scientist with a decent income and regular hours – all the things she hadn't had with him.

That it could never be a "proper" marriage, with a marriage certificate and the priest's blessing did take a little of the gloss off it. But a priest would have refused to bless a second marriage anyway and a certificate was just a piece of paper. Agnes Runge was looking forward to meeting Michael Trenkler. She couldn't see why that should be impossible. "You can't spend the rest of your life behaving as if you were his real wife, child. You have to tell him the truth. He has a right to know."

So as not to cause her mother any more worry, she promised to have a full and frank discussion with Michael as soon as the matter of the stolen money was sorted out. Agnes Runge was already dreaming of her first visit to her daughter's new home. Even if she wouldn't be able to see the splendour Dieter had described, it would be enough for her to be able to run her hands over this or that.

When they got back to the little car park at the inn, her eyes were red-rimmed and her lids swollen. Dieter was already waiting.

"When will I see you again, Susanne?" Agnes Runge asked.

"Soon," she promised.

"And I really can't tell anyone, not even Frau Herzog? I'm sure Johannes would be happy if he knew. Frau Herzog said he took it badly. And if he's told he mustn't talk about it, I'm sure he'll keep his mouth shut."

Dieter had already opened the driver's door. He pulled her out of her mother's arms and took her aside. "I'll see to that," he said. "Have you a moment?"

"Actually, no," she said. "I've got to go now, or I'll be late for the concert."

"What concert?" Dieter asked. "You'd be better having a nice evening in. Given the circumstances, I'm sure your husband will understand that you'd rather not go where you have to meet a lot of people."

"But he wants to go," she said. "He's looking forward to it."

Dieter shook his head, muttered something about not being able to understand how people could be so stupid, then added, in a louder voice, "Don't overdo it." As she got into the Alfa, he said, "Look after yourself."

"I have so far," she replied and drove off.

Michael was waiting for her nervously in the hall. He started when he saw the lines of tears down her cheeks. "Problems?" he asked in a whisper. It wasn't possible to speak any louder. He was dressed for the concert and not alone in the house. But her shake of the head and whispered, "Everything's OK," weren't enough for him. "So why have you been crying?"

"I went to see Helga too," she whispered. "She's in a bad way." That he could understand.

Schneider was in the living room with Jo and Lilo, looking at the Maiwald and listening to an explanation of the significance of the holes with gold paint sprayed round them. It wasn't clear whether he really was interested or just passing time. He looked at her, an embarrassed grin on his face. "You weren't meant to be going out for a spin."

"Your boss doesn't need to know," she said. "And I had to get out, otherwise I'd have suffocated."

Michael pushed her towards the staircase. "Unfortunately his boss does know and has already given him a rocket. Get dressed so we can calm him down. He's gone on ahead with Ilona. Jo and Lilo are coming with us. Schneider will escort us as far as Bonn."

Lilo followed her into the dressing room. She too declared, "That wasn't very sensible of you, darling," but immediately went on to express her sympathy. She'd have gone crazy, too, she said, if they'd dumped a policeman on her. You couldn't give free rein to your feelings if there was a stranger watching. Lilo assumed it was the strain that had made her cry and assured her, "Wolfgang's already let off steam. I wouldn't like to be that young man. Let's see if we can find something to take his mind off it."

Lilo looked through the evening dresses and decided the red was the right one, she hadn't worn that for ages. Round the waist it still fitted perfectly but it was a bit tight round the bust. Lilo thought it chic. "It looks very sexy, darling." Lilo also got the accessories together and was very keen for her to wear the necklace with the sapphire, pointing out that it was probably in the safe. But she was allowed to make excuses. "I just don't feel up to going to the loft at the moment."

After the make-up on her tear-stained cheeks had been renewed, Lilo said, "You look perfect."

Michael, too, was happy with the way she looked. They went in his car. From the rear seat Lilo kept them amused with an account of Maiwald's latest affair. No one really knew why, but *Georges* had definitely split up with Julia. Yet she'd been such an inspiration to him. Edgar was terribly sad about the whole thing. He was afraid *Georges's* new pictures might be very different from his previous work, because his new lover was more of a severe type. Jo's contribution was a short tirade against Brenner, who was now positively forcing money on him, when recently he'd been refusing him any funding.

She listened with half an ear, associated Edgar with the Henseler Gallery, Brenner with Jo's inventions, and contemplated Michael's profile and his hands on the steering wheel, pondering her mother's opinion that he had a right to the truth. Of course he had. And the truth was that she was expecting his child and loved him. Nothing else counted, she decided.

Their seats were close to the platform. Along with many others, Wolfgang and Ilona had already taken theirs when they reached the row. Jo and Lilo went in first, followed by Michael, leaving her the aisle seat, thus making it impossible for Wolfgang to give her a telling-off.

The large hall was filled with the murmur of quiet conversation. Almost immediately after they'd sat down the platform also filled as well. Jacques Niedenhoff made his entrance once all the other musicians were settled. Like a young god in white tie and tails, he came to the microphone and said a few words. He had a pleasant voice with a strong French accent. Most of his welcome or explanation was drowned out in a torrent of applause. Jacques bowed and sat down at the piano.

It was exactly as she had imagined it, completely without risk. And it was a quite special kind of enjoyment. A large space filled with music, nothing but music. She had no idea what was being played, but the violins brought a lump to her throat. It was so beautiful she couldn't find words for it. She was glad she hadn't let Dieter persuade her not to go, she could have sat there listening and enjoying the music for ever.

Michael next to her was listening with his eyes closed. It was perfect, two hours of perfection.

Then Jacques got up and bowed. There was thunderous applause and voices calling for an encore. Nadia's *Jacques, mon chéri* ignored them, thanked the audience again and disappeared. The other musicians followed and the audience started to get up and leave.

Michael stayed in his seat until the worst of the crush was over. Leaning across Jo and Lilo, he was talking to Wolfgang. The only thing she heard was: "With a helmet or not at all."

He wasn't pleased with Wolfgang's reply. As they went out to the car park Michael was still going on at him vehemently. Ilona shook her head in frustration several times, while Lilo listened intently. Jo, who was walking beside her, was also getting worked up. "I don't know what Wolfgang's thinking. He can't ask you to —"

She didn't let him finish. "It'll be OK," she said. "Don't worry, so far luck's been on my side."

Jo gave her an odd glance, but said nothing. Michael was already in the car and drove off the moment they were in. "Wolfgang's going to get a motorbike for you." He said, satisfaction in his voice. "Then you won't just have a bulletproof vest, he'll get you a helmet from the special unit as well."

"Are you crazy?" she exclaimed. "I'm not going on a motorbike, I'm going in my car."

"Be reasonable, Nadia. If Zurkeulen shoots…"

"He won't do that," she said. "He just wants his money back."

Jo joined in. "Yes, you must be reasonable, Nadia. Zurkeulen can't afford to let you go."

They almost got into an argument. Of course Michael knew that she hadn't been on a motorbike for ages, though he didn't mention when the last time had been. She couldn't imagine Nadia on a motorbike, it wasn't marked in her driving licence. "But with a little practice…" Michael said. It was for her own safety. She could familiarize herself with the bike on Tuesday.

"Out of the question," she declared. "In any other way, yes, but not like that."

In the heat of the argument, she didn't notice that they weren't heading back to the autobahn. She only realized when Michael asked Jo

318

if he thought they'd be able to park at the hotel. "I don't know," Jo said, "but I assume we can."

She didn't dare ask for an explanation, but that quickly turned out to be unnecessary. Lilo wondered whether Eleanor Ravatzky would be bringing half a dozen uninvited colleagues to Jacques's reception again. The possibility of a reception hadn't occurred to her. The unavoidable meeting with Jacques made her very nervous.

But she relaxed when she saw the mass of people. Taking her arm, so as not to lose her in the crush, Michael led her into the crowded room. Unknown faces wherever she looked. The few she recognized were those of two politicians and other media celebrities. Wolfgang and Ilona were nowhere to be seen. Jo and Lilo plunged into the throng and disappeared as well.

A waiter, squeezing his way between the evening gowns with his fully laden tray, offered them champagne or orange juice. Michael took a glass of champagne for himself and put an orange juice in her hand. She placed it back on the tray.

"I can't drink that any more. Recently it's been giving me heartburn."

Michael told the waiter to bring her a glass of mineral water. "But no lemon, please," she said. "That doesn't agree with me any more either."

While they were waiting for her mineral water, he finally had the chance to ask her what had come out of her meeting with Hardenberg. "I don't think we're going to have any more problems," she told him. "Philip said the others had merely been credited with the sums."

With a snort of contempt, he said, "And you believe him?"

"Yes," she replied. "He was still in shock and almost out of his mind with worry about Helga. I don't think he was lying."

The waiter brought the mineral water. Michael took her arm again and led her through the crowd, slowly but inexorably towards a group on the edge of which were Wolfgang, Ilona, Jo, Lilo, Frederik and Eleanor Ravatzky. The actress was engaged in animated conversation with Frederik. At the centre of the group was Jacques Niedenhoff.

It was the same feeling as she'd had at the bank when Zurkeulen had turned back at the glass door and come straight towards her. Just as in the bank, turning her face to the side was no use here either. Jacques spotted her and fought his way through the crowd, saving them having to take the last few steps. When he got there, he grasped her hands and help both to his lips, as old Barlinkow had done at Lilo's party. He spoke with a strong accent, as he had on the platform. "I am glad that you have come, Nadia."

She thought his accent charming, his behaviour brazen. Her heart started pounding unpleasantly. He didn't just look at her, he devoured her with his eyes. Despite the presence of Michael, he caressed her with his looks – and not only her face. The red gown had a provocatively plunging neckline. But Michael didn't bat an eyelid.

Summoning up her courage – and grasping Michael's arm a little tighter – she put on an arrogant smile, gave her voice a mocking tone and said, "Oh, but I wouldn't have missed it for the world, *mon chéri*. That wasn't the worst I've heard you play tonight, not by any means."

Jacques sketched a bow and replied in similarly mocking tones, *"Merci bien."*

And that seemed to be it. Wolfgang took her aside and gave her a real tongue-lashing. What the fuck was the point, he said, of getting his men to sacrifice their free weekend to make sure she was safe, if she was going to go swanning around all over the place?

"Simmer down, Wolfgang," she said. "I came back in one piece, didn't I?"

"And where did you go?"

"To see Lasko. I thought he might tell me a bit more about his ex. I was wrong."

Michael and Jacques were engrossed in a conversation in which Michael demonstrated that he knew considerably more about music than she had supposed. He was familiar with Tchaikovsky's first piano concerto and he could tell that Jacques had modified de Falla's *Fire Dance* a little. She didn't even know when, during the two hours, she'd been listening to Tchaikovsky and when to a fire dance. She sipped her mineral water and looked at the unknown faces all around.

Professor Danny Kemmerling emerged from the throng. On his arm was a creature less than half his age wearing jeans embroidered with pearls and a tight velvet bodice. And he'd told her how much his wife was looking forward to the concert. For a couple of seconds she wondered whether it was his daughter. The young thing beamed at her, all the while peering past her at Jacques, and said, "I hope Danny thanked you properly. It was a fantastic experience."

The cheery voice sounded familiar. And with the laid-back Danny on her arm it wasn't difficult to make the connection. It was the woman who'd answered when she'd phoned the lab to ask to speak to Kemmerling. Clearly even professors weren't immune to the charms of a little laboratory mouse.

Michael exchanged a few words with the professor's girlfriend and a few with the professor. Jacques took the opportunity to turn to her again. Since he suddenly switched to French, and very fast French at that, she didn't understand a word.

She gave him one of Nadia's haughty smiles and said, "I hope you don't mind, *mon chéri*, but before we chat I must get something to eat." The trick with food clearly worked in all situations. Ignoring his look of pique, she turned round and left the group. Jacques spoke to Michael again and out of the corner of her eye she saw Michael introduce him to Kemmerling's girlfriend.

A sumptuous buffet was laid out at the side of the room. She found a plate and sauntered along the besieged tables. No one took any notice of her and she took no notice of anyone else. She lost sight of the group round Jacques and concentrated on selecting her food. The salads represented a certain risk, because she couldn't identify all the ingredients for certain. Meat and cheese were no problem but were blockaded at the moment.

As she was wondering whether to take some smoked salmon from the middle of the dish, where it was untouched by the slices of lemon, a hand was suddenly placed on her shoulder. Jacques was close behind her and said something. All she could understand was *"Ma chérie"*. But his look was clear.

With the hand on her shoulder, he turned her to face him. His eye wandered down, paused at her neckline then continued its descent, ending up either on her plate or her stomach, she couldn't precisely say which. According to Dieter's Advanced French Course he was asking her if she couldn't decide.

"I have decided," she said.

At that Jacques, with a mocking smile, subjected her to a longish lecture, which included Michael's name twice and once the word with which the doctor in Paris had caused such confusion and rejoicing. Could he be asking who the father was? Not knowing exactly what he had asked made her more than just nervous. But she had to make sure he understood her. "Speak German," she demanded. "You can, you know."

He frowned, irritated, but did as she asked. "Michael says that you've got problems."

"None I can't manage," she replied.

He looked round. He clearly felt uncomfortable with so many people in the immediate vicinity. Naturally everyone knew him, some were smiling at him and even appeared to be following their conversation. He switched back to French, took her arm and drew her away with him.

Thanks to Dieter's cassettes she was familiar with a few of the words. Sea, house and Nassau needed no translation. Presumably he was talking about the villa with its own beach that Michael had refused. Jacques seemed to regret that. Not wanting to ask him to speak German again, so as not to arouse his suspicions, she concentrated hard and picked up a word or two here, a syllable there. She began to form the distinct impression that not only did he know about Nadia's plans, but he was at the centre of them. That, at least, was her interpretation of his agitation.

He mentioned Wolfgang, Luxembourg and six million, then went back to Nassau and the bank there, immediately going on to talk about her baby. He seemed to imagine the child was his. And the villa with the beach on the Bahamas was still for sale. She was pretty sure she'd understood that correctly.

By now they'd reached the end of the buffet. Beyond it was a door, which led God knows where. He was drawing her gently but unerringly towards the door. She jerked her arm free of his grip. "*Non!*" she said firmly, throwing her head back and pushing a stray lock of hair behind her ear. "I'm sorry if I raised your hopes, but lots of things have changed in the last few weeks. The baby's Michael's and I'm not going to leave him. Nor am I going to move abroad. I like it here. I hope you can accept that."

With a look of incomprehension, Jacques muttered something that sounded like an oath and made a gesture to his forehead that was understandable in any language.

"I know I'm crazy," she said, "but you must understand that I'm not crazy about you any more."

322

He clearly understood but he was just as clearly unhappy about it. He engulfed her in a torrent of words and grasped her shoulder again. Shaking herself free, she snarled, "Don't cause a scene, dammit. And if Michael gets to hear anything of this, I'll wring your neck."

He looked as if he was going to respond, but then, with a gesture indicating it was futile, turned on his heel and left her standing, staring at a mountain of something or other at the end of the long table. Once he had vanished from view, she turned her attention back to the by now considerably depleted spread.

Shortly afterwards she set off, with a well-filled plate, to look for Michael. By this time the group where she'd left him had dispersed. Kemmerling and his girlfriend were nowhere to be seen. She spotted Eleanor Ravatzky and Ilona in the crowd but she didn't feel like asking them where Michael was. Wolfgang was talking to one of the two politicians and she didn't want to interrupt.

She ate her food first then took her plate back and continued looking for Michael. Lilo and Frederik told her he'd gone to the buffet with Jo a while ago. She was somewhat alarmed. The idea that he might have witnessed her scene with Jacques didn't bear thinking about. Saying a quick prayer, she looked for him with growing unease. But her fears were unfounded. He appeared from outside, alone and immensely relieved to see her. "Thank God. I've been looking for you everywhere."

Jo was still looking – in the car park. They went out together to relieve the poor guy. "All those people were making my head whirl," Michael said. "Anyone who's determined enough can get in without an invitation."

"Then let's go home," she suggested. He immediately went to fetch her coat. Jo and Lilo could get a lift from Wolfgang.

She had an excellent night's sleep on Sunday. When the buzzing started in the bathroom and Michael kissed her on the back of the neck, a few fleeting images from her dream came back to mind. It hadn't been a nightmare. He'd put the baby in her arms and watched her suckle it.

He went to the bathroom and, thirty minutes later, to the garage. But not before he'd begged her a hundred times to be careful. And she'd told him just as many times that nothing would happen that day because she was just collecting the money and Wolfgang wouldn't let her out of his sight. Then he reappeared, just as she was drying her hair. "Can I take your car?" he asked. "You don't need it if you're going with Wolfgang."

"Will you never learn?" she asked.

He gave an embarrassed laugh. "Sorry. Filling up was the last thing on my mind yesterday. Wouldn't you rather take a motorbike tomorrow?"

"Darling," she said, "I really don't think riding a motorbike's a good idea in my condition. Just imagine if I fell off." That made sense to him.

Shortly after seven Wolfgang was already there at the door with her old driving licence, her ID card and a passport she'd never applied for. "Nervous?" he asked.

"No," she said.

Wolfgang seemed tense. During the journey he explained again what was to happen once she'd received Zurkeulen's money. She really didn't need to worry, he assured her. He'd wire her up and have a dozen men covering her. She was hardly listening. What did she care about his dozen men? For her there was only one who mattered, the one who, before he'd gone down to the garage for the second time, had said, "It would be more than I could bear if anything happened to you tomorrow."

They reached the outskirts of Luxembourg shortly before eleven, which gave them time for a brief rest. Wolfgang suggested a leisurely breakfast and found a small café near the bank. They spent half an hour over croissants, milky coffee and a discussion of what was to happen the next day. Then he handed her a briefcase, told her the combination to the locks, showed her how to attach it securely to her wrist and sent her off. "Don't worry," he said, "I'll be right behind you."

For Nadia it would presumably all have been a matter of course: entering the bank, asking for the manager, reminding him of their telephone conversation and receiving six million euros. She felt as if she were in a film. But there were no problems. The money was ready, high-denomination notes in thin sealed bundles. It didn't even look that much.

They checked her identity documents, full of understanding for her client's difficulties, and helped her pack the bundles so that they all fitted in her briefcase. By the time she'd attached it to her wrist, she couldn't remember what she'd said about her client and his difficulties. Something or other. By now she was an expert at that.

Wolfgang was waiting for her at the entrance. His hand inside his jacket, he covered her as they went to his Rover. He demanded the identity documents back immediately but the briefcase stayed where it was, chained to her wrist. It lay on her lap during the whole of the drive home. Six million! And somewhere there were another fourteen.

They were back by the late afternoon. Michael wasn't home yet. Wolfgang had had to withdraw his men, at the start of the new week they had other obligations. He thought it wasn't worth asking for police protection for the last day and thus involving other departments. He went into the house with her, unlocked the handcuff from her wrist and told her to take the money up to the safe.

"I'd rather you looked after it."

"You've a cheek," he said. "I haven't got a safe. D'you expect me to stuff the briefcase under my mattress?"

For the moment she put the briefcase down in the kitchen. "I'll make us a coffee." They hadn't stopped on the way back and had missed out on lunch.

"Not for me," Wolfgang said. "I have to go to the office. Now get the money in the safe."

She had no choice but to go up to the loft. Fortunately he didn't go with her. She wedged the briefcase in between the housing of the alarm system and the safe and went back down. "Mission accomplished," she said.

He nodded. He looked tense as he glanced out of the window. "Doc won't be too late coming back this evening, will he?"

"Don't keep calling him Doc," she said. "I hate it."

With a brief grin he placed a sheet of paper with several telephone numbers on the table. "One of those should get Zurkeulen. If not, ask him to call back. It'd be best if you rang immediately. That way we eliminate any danger between now and tomorrow. With the prospect of getting out of the affair gracefully, he won't be tempted to try any tricks. You know what you have to say."

She didn't know exactly because she hadn't been listening to him properly. But the time and place were presumably sufficient.

Wolfgang left. Only ten minutes later Michael arrived home – and he wasn't alone. She was standing by the desk and after three tries she'd finally got Zurkeulen. That was enough to explain the way her hands were trembling. As the two men came up the stairs, Zurkeulen was saying, "I'm delighted you've been able to persuade Herr Hardenberg to return my money. Unfortunately, however, I can't manage tomorrow."

On the stairs she heard Michael say, "Let's ask her what she meant."

"And I can only manage tomorrow," she said to Zurkeulen. "I'll be at the airport car park at precisely four o'clock. If you're on time too, then we can get the matter over and done with in a few seconds. If not – my flight leaves at five. Don't expect me to tell you the destination. What I can tell you is that it's beyond your reach."

Without waiting for Zurkeulen to reply, she replaced the receiver and turned to the door. Her smile was more than forced. "Hi there," she mumbled.

Michael smiled at her. "What have you been doing to poor old Jacques? He doesn't know whether he's coming or going."

Her hands started to tremble even more and her knees decided to join in. She had to sit down. It had never occurred to her that this idiot would dare to ask her to explain herself in Michael's presence, possibly even insist on some putative prior claim on her.

Michael looked at her, somewhat puzzled. "Is everything OK?"

"No," she said. "I think Wolfgang should ask for police protection for us."

Jacques had stopped in the doorway. Ignoring her comment to Michael, he unleashed, as he had the previous evening, a torrent of words, of which she could only pick out a few meaningless syllables.

"Just a moment, Jacques," Michael said, his gaze still fixed on her. He looked worried as he asked, "Did you not get the money?"

"Yes we did, it's in the loft," she said. "But Zurkeulen…"

Ignoring Michael's request, Jacques continued to pour out further incomprehensible French. He sounded furious. Michael flapped his hand at him, said, "Hold on a sec," then asked her, "Is Zurkeulen refusing to meet you?"

"Yes," she said. "But he will come. I —" She broke off and let fly at Jacques. "Oh do shut up. What's all this hoo-ha about?"

Jacques did pause in the middle of a sentence, but then he started up again – a little more moderately so that she could catch some of it. The few words and expressions she could identify beyond doubt corresponded to what he'd been going on about the previous evening and added up to an explosive cocktail. He had no compunction about reminding her – in Michael's presence! – of the plans she'd made with him. A villa on the Bahamas. Michael listened, his brow furrowed in concentration, his eyes switching back and forward between them.

"Did I not make myself clear enough yesterday?" she said in an attempt to stem the flood of words.

"*Non,*" he said.

"Then I'm sorry," she said, adding, with a meaningful glance in Michael's direction, "but I can't make myself any clearer."

"Dammit, Nadia," Michael said, "what the hell's going on here?"

"I don't know," she said. "I really don't know what he wants from me." In fact, she thought she knew all too well, so she got up and headed for the door with her by now familiar ploy. "I need to eat something."

Michael held her back. "He thinks you can't understand him."

It was a decision that had to be taken in a few seconds. Admit that she couldn't understand Jacques, or hope that Michael would forgive her. He would probably even have forgiven Nadia a murder – for a baby. He couldn't give that much importance to a brief fling with a sweetheart from the days before she'd known him.

"I'm sorry," she whispered again and bowed her head. "I didn't want you to hear about it. I – it wasn't anything serious, really it wasn't. You must believe me, it was just…"

She started to stammer. She knew nothing at all of what had gone on between Nadia and Jacques in the last few months and she was trying to fob Michael off with a few hints. It had happened, in memory of old times, which were meaningless now because she loved him, him alone, the father of her child. Jacques had nothing at all to do with that, whatever he imagined.

Michael's grip on her arm tightened, it started to hurt. He listened with his jaws clamped together and looking daggers at Jacques. "You slept with him." It was a toneless whisper, half-question, half-statement.

She sketched a nod. Jacques shook his head vigorously, at the same time waving his hands in denial. "*Non!*" he declared emphatically. What he went on to say she couldn't understand. Dieter's language course contained no sentences that came anywhere near expressing the mood of a furious man. All she could grasp was the name Alina. Coward, she thought and demanded, "Speak German, so Michael can understand."

"I can understand enough," Michael said, letting go of her arm and stepping away from her. He kept his eyes fixed on her face, seemed to be waiting for something. "He says you're lying. He says you've no idea what he's talking about."

It was the critical moment. Of course she had no idea. All she knew was that, after he had separated from Alina, Nadia had written a heartrending letter to Jacques asking if they could make things up again. Was it perhaps Alina with whom he made things up? He'd presumably never read Nadia's letter. "*Retour à l'expéditeur.*"

"It was when I was going through a bad time," she said, keeping it deliberately vague – and accepting the risk that Michael might send her packing. "You know, when I was on the bottle. You'd taken up with that Palewi woman and that hit me hard. He'd just left Alina and I thought perhaps things might… with him rather than… I was completely drunk when I… I really wasn't in my right mind…"

Michael stared at her, stunned. After some seconds he passed his hand over his eyes and forehead in a weary gesture. Then he patted Jacques on the shoulder. "Don't worry," he said, "I won't say anything of this to Alina."

Jacques continued to swear and curse and to give further explanations. Michael pushed him out onto the landing. She sat down at the desk to get the trembling under control. She'd come through again, by the skin of her teeth, but at what cost? She heard the two of them go down the stairs, heard the front door close and Michael hurrying down the stairs to the basement. He must be beside himself. She knew him well enough by now to know that he worked off violent emotions in the water.

After a while she risked a call to Dieter. It was Ramie who answered, but that wasn't a problem any more. "This is Nadia Trenkler. I'd like to speak to Herr Lasko."

Dieter was delighted that everything had gone according to plan in Luxembourg. "So why do you sound so depressed?"

She told him and he tried to reassure her. He found Michael's reaction perfectly understandable. "He'll get over it," he said. "If not today, then tomorrow. And if he doesn't, a divorce would really be the best solution anyway."

Then he offered to contact all the other investors before any of them got as bolshie as Zurkeulen. He'd found out with which banks the money was deposited and was convinced he could persuade the eight men to bide their time until the dust had settled.

"But we can't get at the money," she said.

"No, but I imagine Hardenberg can. And after his experiences with Zurkeulen, I'm sure I can get him to see what's in his best interest."

She was grateful to him for taking her mind off the man down in the pool, if only for a few minutes. "Why didn't you give Wolfgang the letters or the laptop?"

Dieter interrupted her with a soft laugh. "The letters have long since been burned to ashes, the rest as well. As for the laptop – no one would have let that out of their hands, except to give it to an accomplice. I didn't want to come under suspicion of being involved in the fraud if you'd been found out."

He couldn't rule out that still being a possibility, he said, but he felt there was somewhat less risk now that she'd even dealt with Jacques.

But at what cost! The thought of what Michael must be going through at that moment hurt terribly. She waited half an hour before she ventured down and stood there, six feet from the edge. He was halfway down the pool, thrashing the water with long strokes. When he reached the end, he saw her and panted, "I don't believe it. I simply don't believe it."

She didn't know what to say. That she was sorry, that she loved him? Nadia would presumably have done that, but she wasn't Nadia. She knew from her own experience the agony of feeling betrayed – even if her marriage hadn't been perfect. Perhaps the hurt went even deeper then, because you were suddenly forced to face up to the fact that what you'd been holding on to was an illusion.

He levered himself out of the pool and said, "I need something to eat. Let's go to Demetros's."

"No, let's stay here," she begged. "I'll make us something."

"Don't bother. I have to get out of here before I go out of my mind."

Perhaps he was right. With other people around they'd be forced to keep themselves under control. And perhaps once he could stand back from it a little… After a brief hesitation, she nodded. On the stairs he asked, "Where's the money? Can I see it?"

There was no reason not to let him have a look at the contents of the briefcase. He made no comment on the fact that it was beside the safe instead of in it. After he'd stared at the neat bundles of banknotes for a few seconds, he wanted to know if she found it difficult to hand the briefcase over to Zurkeulen.

"No," she said.

With a scornful laugh he went into the dressing room and put on a shirt and trousers. He brought the mink jacket for her. He hadn't filled his car and since the Alfa was still parked in the street, they took that. He drove. Hardly had they got away from the houses than he asked, "Whose child is it?"

"Yours," she assured him. "Really. You must believe me."

Presumably Jacques had given him a different version. Michael just nodded, his jaw clenched, and asked, "Does Alina know you're pregnant?" When she shook her head, he went on, "Then you should tell her as soon as possible. Perhaps the prospect of becoming a grandmother will make her amenable to a reconciliation."

For a second her brain seemed to freeze. Ignorance comes out sooner or later. As Dieter had predicted. Michael was calm, much calmer than he ought to have been. All the feelings that must have followed his realization seemed to have been washed away in the water of the swimming pool. But now he knew she wasn't Nadia, there was no doubt about that. He spoke in a monotonous voice that made her quiver with fear.

He listed the differences, starting with minor ones. Everything could have been explained, had been in most cases. Her difficulties in the pool – she'd hit her head when he pushed her in. That she hardly spoke a word of English in Paris and no French at all – Pamela had been determined to improve her German. That she hadn't taken the clothes hanger off the hook with the jacket in the cloakroom – she'd been afraid Zurkeulen might kill him and Andrea; Ramon wouldn't have hesitated if a patrol car had driven up outside. That she hadn't put the briefcase with the money in the safe – it wasn't worth it because she had to hand it over to Zurkeulen the next day. And she had known about Arosa. But she didn't know her own mother's first name.

Jacques Niedenhoff had never split up with Alina, that was Nadia's father. And Nadia had always called her mother by her first name. Alina had been born with a silver spoon in her mouth and had never had much sympathy for people who endeavoured to make as much money as possible. It was just about acceptable for men, but when a daughter tried to tread in her father's footsteps, that was it for Alina.

It was Nadia's unbridled pursuit of money that had led to the break-up of her parents' marriage because Alina blamed it on her husband. Michael told her that because it was something she couldn't know. He assumed she'd got her information about his wife from Hardenberg or by snooping round the house. Nadia would certainly never have said a word about her parents, it was not for nothing that she'd burned almost everything that might remind her of them: her school reports, her certificates, her whole past. He had managed to salvage one single photograph album and hidden it among his old things in the loft.

Michael knew the touching letter to *Jacques, mon chéri* only too well. He'd been the one who'd been in the house when it had been returned from Geneva. Not because Jacques had refused to accept it, but simply because he was no longer staying in the hotel where Nadia had sent it. And Nadia hadn't been asking Jacques for a reconciliation but for mediation. She wanted him to put in a good word for her with her father, whom she loved dearly. Jacques had done so, though unfortunately in vain.

As he'd already told her, Nadia's catastrophe had ushered in a terrible time for him. Only it hadn't been just the alcohol and the scenes Nadia had made in the lab, it was the realization that he could only play second fiddle in Nadia's life. The first fiddle, however, was not Jacques Niedenhoff. It was Nadia's father. Michael had imagined he had been promoted to first fiddle when, after his father-in-law had broken off all contact, Nadia had marched into the lab and threatened to feed Beatrice Palewi to the mice if she so much as touched him ever again.

At that point, he gave a laugh, though it came out more as a sob. Nadia had definitely been in love with him, he said. In her own way she had even been deeply in love with him. And she'd been unfaithful, if at all, perhaps once, with Wolfgang. In the summer he'd come across the two of them in a slightly compromising situation. Nadia had presumably relished the idea of getting her hands on a man who could be dangerous to her or to Hardenberg and twisting him round her little finger. But an affair with Jacques Niedenhoff?

Nadia had given him several nasty surprises, which was why his suspicions hadn't been immediately aroused when she'd started to act out the farce with Jacques. An affair with Jacques would have been a bit much, but he couldn't entirely rule out the possibility. Even Jacques's vehement denials could be seen as fitting in. It would have been more than simple adultery. Jacques Niedenhoff was Nadia's cousin. That was why he'd got so worked up and made such a fuss: "If she should take it into her head to tell Aunt Alina this nonsense!"

She was trembling all over and couldn't reply when he asked, "Did you kill her?"

She couldn't even shake her head, only stare at him in horror. He gave a hollow laugh. "No. You left that to those swine and moved in with me. What did you think you'd achieve by that? Or was it Hardenberg's suggestion? Did he think there was incriminating evidence against him in the house? Nadia had frequently downloaded files from him, was he afraid she might have got hold of the wrong files?"

At least she'd got her voice back, if only a hoarse whisper. "No. That wasn't the way it was. I was here before that."

"What?" He cleared his throat. "Since when have I had the pleasure then?"

"Since the twenty-eighth of November," she whispered, "And twice before that, once in…" She couldn't finish the sentence.

"My God!" he exclaimed. Then, more vehemently, "Nonsense! The twenty-eighth was a Thursday. I know that because we had a lot of bother in the lab. She rang…" He broke off and bit his lip.

"I rang the lab," she whispered. She couldn't tell whether he'd heard and understood.

He shook his head, again and again, at the same time making short, harsh sounds. When, after a few seconds, he went on again, she realized that he couldn't believe her because he didn't want to believe her. For him Nadia had died because he'd upbraided her so scathingly that Thursday night and been so nasty to her early on the morning of the twenty-ninth. Because on the thirtieth, the Saturday, he'd driven off to Munich in the morning. He spent minutes wallowing in self-reproach. All the things he'd reproached her with in the bathroom that morning no longer seemed true, nothing more than a toy that could be taken out of the drawer when required. All that counted now was that he hadn't been there when Nadia had truly needed him.

He had his own idea of what had happened. Wolfgang had told him that the presumed Susanne Lasko had been killed at some time on the

Saturday night. And on that Saturday night Nadia had been at Lilo's party, where she'd collapsed and been seen safely home by Jo – only to then be lured into a trap by her or Hardenberg. After she'd been killed they'd planted the false papers on her. And she'd taken up residence in the house.

But then she'd found she couldn't get on the computer, so she'd decided to clear off again. If he hadn't returned unexpectedly from Munich on the Sunday she'd have been miles away with Nadia's papers and Zurkeulen's money. And he would never have found out the truth about what had happened to his wife.

She tried once more. "No. It was quite different."

And he laughed again, a contemptuous laugh, and insisted on details. She started with the first meeting by the lift in Gerler House. He brushed it aside. Wolfgang, he said, saw that quite differently, namely that she and Hardenberg had met. Otherwise Nadia would definitely have told him about an encounter with a double.

His image of Susanne Lasko was based entirely on what he'd heard from Wolfgang: a crafty little devil, an artful bitch who'd hoodwinked everyone and even stolen from her own mother. Wolfgang – with Dieter's all-too willing help – had unearthed some ugly facts about Susanne Lasko.

She was far too churned up inside to pay attention to where they were going. And every time she tried to clear something up or said Nadia's name, he interrupted her. She did manage to get as far as mentioning Nadia's request that she stand in for her as the sulky wife, but when she went on to the dress rehearsal on the Sunday afternoon in August, he didn't want to know. And he refused to hear anything about the twelfth of September. He apologized sarcastically if, given the situation, he felt he couldn't take any more lies. All he wanted to find out was who he'd been duped by for days on end, as if he was a complete idiot.

The Alfa bumped slowly along an unmade track, coming to a halt on a tiny patch of rough ground. He switched off the headlights. Immediately it was pitch dark. Nothing, absolutely nothing could be seen. Not even his face. Only after several seconds, which seemed endless, did her eyes adjust to the darkness. She could make out vague shapes outside the car. Tree trunks! Massive tree trunks. "Where are we?" she asked.

He'd put his face in his hands and didn't reply. She repeated her question, unable to keep a quiver of panic out of her voice. He lowered his hands and, staring fixedly out into the darkness ahead, said, "Demetros's."

"But there's no restaurant anywhere around here?"

He laughed. "Who said Demetros's was a restaurant? It's a club, a meeting-place for like-minded people or whatever you want to call it. We often came here, my wife and I." He made an odd sound that was almost a sob. Then he went on. "A relationship needs a breath of fresh air now and then. It was her idea. She was afraid I might get the feeling I was missing out on something. It's very relaxing – jacuzzis, saunas for two. There's things to eat, too."

He got out. She followed him, forgetting to take her jacket and handbag. She stood by the Alfa, trying to get her bearings. He locked the car and disappeared into the trees. "Wait," she called and stumbled after him along a narrow footpath. "Wait a minute Michael, I —"

She broke off as she ran into him. He'd stopped at the edge of a small clearing. Not even the outline of a building was to be seen. She was almost choking with panic, but there was something inside her that refused to believe he'd lured her out of the house and driven with her to this lonely spot with a specific purpose in mind. And not as a spontaneous decision, he must have made it while he was still in the pool.

"But there's no one here at all," she stammered. "And anyway, I don't believe you. Nadia was immensely jealous. She'd never have gone somewhere with you where there were women you…"

He had turned towards her as she started to speak. In the darkness she couldn't see his face. But she felt his hands round her throat. He didn't speak, he panted, "Correct. She was immensely jealous. And you're trying to tell me she put another woman in my bed. You're the one who set those swine on me. How did you think it was going to work out? I'm there with my water pistol, the other guy puts a bullet into me and the way's clear for you."

The first red spots appeared in the blackness before her eyes. She couldn't respond, she couldn't even breathe. She did grasp his hands and try to bend his fingers back, but her fingers just slid off. Her movements got weaker. He kept pressing until she couldn't feel it any more.

* * *

She had no idea how long she'd lain there unconscious under the trees at the edge of the clearing. She couldn't even say how long she stayed there on the ground after she'd regained consciousness. Breathing was incredibly difficult and painful, it felt as if her throat were still crushed. Eventually something tickled her cheek. An insect was crawling over her face. Finally she found she could lift one hand. And a few minutes later she managed to get up off the ground, though at first only onto her hands and knees.

She crawled back along the footpath to the patch of rough ground. There was no one there and she didn't know where she was. Her head hadn't fully cleared yet. The one thought going round and round inside it was that Michael had tried to kill her. The question was – did he think she was dead when he left her there?

She stayed on the patch of rough ground for a while. For the first time she noticed the cold. It was bitterly cold. All she had on was a skirt, a blouse and nylon stockings. The jacket she'd worn on the trip to Luxembourg was hanging over the back of the chair in the study. It was more instinct than anything else that made her continue crawling, then at some point pull herself up onto her feet and feel her way along from tree to tree. Just keep going! One more step, then another, keep moving so as not to freeze to death. Perhaps someone might turn up eventually, as they'd done in the disused factory.

There were no dossers in the woods, just her own determination to keep going. When the trees eventually started to thin out, it was beginning to get light, though it wasn't light enough for her to see her watch. The hands were too small and the glass smudged with soil. She was beside a narrow country road. Whether it was the road they had come by, she couldn't say.

By this time she was chilled to the bone, her throat was still hurting and the icy air drew the pain down into her lungs. Finally a pair of headlights appeared behind her. The car drove past. Two more cars didn't stop; only the fourth, which was going in the opposite direction, did.

There was a young girl at the wheel, hardly more than eighteen. Marlene Jaeger – a student nurse on her way home in an overheated old car with a blanket on the rear seat. Every time she seemed to get lucky, as if her father were up there somewhere keeping watch over her.

Marlene thought she really ought take her to the hospital, but she refused. "That's not necessary. I've an important appointment. I can't afford to miss it."

Her bruised throat made speaking difficult but her teeth were gradually stopping chattering. "My husband and I had an argument. He threw me out of the car. I fell over a few times in the dark." That explained her muddy clothes and torn stockings but not the marks where Michael had throttled her. Marlene Jaeger gave the collar of her dirty blouse a meaningful look. But she said nothing.

"If you could set me down by a telephone box, help me out with a little change and tell me where we are, I'll be all right."

"If you're saying you're going to ring your husband to get him to pick you up…"

"No, not my husband. A friend."

"Oh, I see," said Marlene Jaeger, as if the penny had dropped. She didn't take her to a telephone box but to her parents' house, where there was a telephone and a hot cup of tea.

She couldn't talk freely, nor could Dieter. Despite that, they understood each other better than during the time when they'd been married. Dieter got Marlene to tell him how to get there and arrived an hour later. He wanted to take her to see a doctor but after some discussion they agreed he would take her home first and ring Wolfgang Blasting. Later on she managed to talk him out of that particular phone call.

She was introduced to Ramie as Nadia Trenkler. Dieter did all the explaining. He was so successful in allaying his wife's suspicions that she offered her a hot bath and a breakfast of chicken soup because swallowing was so difficult. She also provided her with a pair of jeans, a roll-neck sweater, thick woollen socks and a pair of shoes. Nothing fitted, but that didn't matter.

She still felt the icy cold inside her, in fact she was convinced it would never go away. Despite that, she could in a way still understand Michael's reaction. More than once during the last few weeks he'd shown how much Nadia meant to him. But that did nothing to change her feelings. Dieter's ray of sunshine was playing at her feet. And Michael would have killed not only her but her child – and his! She felt she ought to hate him for it, but she couldn't bring herself to.

Dieter couldn't get Ramie to go out shopping, so it was impossible for them to speak openly. Eventually she asked him to drive her home.

"No way," Dieter said.

"You must," she insisted, no longer bothering about Ramie, who was all ears. "I have to get the money, I have to get to Wolfgang, I have to get to the airport. I have to get Zurkeulen off my back at least."

Dieter pointed to the telephone. "Put the meeting off. Ring Herr Blasting and explain the situation."

She didn't think either was a good idea and rang the lab instead. Kemmerling's little laboratory mouse told her Michael was in a meeting. Dieter capitulated. It was only when they were on the autobahn that a problem occurred to him. "You won't get into the house."

"Jo has a key."

But Jo wasn't at home, nor Lilo. Dieter drove to the petrol station, found the address of the Henseler Gallery in the phone book and set off for it. By this time it was close on three o'clock. Time was getting short.

Lilo was delighted at her unexpected appearance in the gallery, though puzzled by her strange get-up. She insisted on showing her a new acquisition and it was several minutes before she realized there was no time for that. Then she handed over her own house key, told her the combination to her alarm system and gave her a general idea of where Jo might keep her house key. She handed over her own car key as well. "But you'll go and get Wolfgang first, darling. You will promise me that, won't you?"

"Of course," she said. "He'll be waiting for me and I'm sure he'll be getting nervous too."

There was no time for Wolfgang. She asked Dieter to go on ahead to the rendezvous and keep Zurkeulen there at all costs. "Drive into his car, if that's the only way. I'll buy you a new one. But for God's sake make it clear to him that I'm on my way with the money."

Lilo's car was considerably more manoeuvrable than Dieter's estate, but not as fast as the Alfa. She had no problem with Jo's own alarm system but the search for the key proved rather more difficult, as she didn't know her way round the house. But she eventually found the little cupboard Lilo had mentioned, next to a workbench in the cellar, and as Lilo had suspected, the key was in the second drawer with his voltage testers.

Four minutes later she was looking at the empty gap between the safe and the housing of the alarm system. And she couldn't even warn Dieter since she didn't know his mobile number. For two, at most three seconds she stood there, as if paralysed. It felt like an eternity. Then she was in the Alfa – the key was on the chest in the coat closet, the car in the otherwise empty garage.

With what she'd learned from Johannes Herzog, she made good progress, despite the heavy traffic. She reached the airport turn-off at seventeen minutes past four. She couldn't drive into the car park, there'd been a collision right in the entrance. Not between Dieter's estate and Zurkeulen's limousine. A Ford Transit had slammed into the back of an ancient Volkswagen Beetle. The two drivers, from all appearances Southern Europeans, were arguing about who was to blame in loud voices and with elaborate gestures, apparently oblivious of the fact that two cars were waiting to get out of the car park. And the drivers in the cars, as well as their passengers, seemed to be trying to outdo each other in a show of patience.

She got out and approached the arguing drivers. "Would you move your cars to the side please, I have to…"

"No you don't," said one of the men and pointed to the Ford Transit. "Get in, Frau Trenkler, and make it quick."

At the same moment the passenger got out of the first waiting car, stretched, as if he was stiff, then came slowly towards her. She recognized Schneider. As he passed he just asked, "Key's in the ignition?" Then he got in the Alfa, reversed a little way and drove off.

She felt herself being pushed vigorously towards the Ford Transit and almost lifted up onto the passenger seat. There was a grey curtain between the front seats and the rear and from somewhere behind it Michael's voice could be heard, almost as clear as if he were in the van.

"It was my wife, for Christ's sake. My wife! Can't you understand? I want to know what you did to her." That was the moment when it was finally over. Zurkeulen might not understand, but she understood – once and for all – that Michael Trenkler could not love her because for him she was a stranger who was to blame for his wife's death. All the energy she'd summoned up went out of her like the air out of a balloon.

The curtain was pushed aside. Wolfgang gave her an astonished smile. "I thought you were in Geneva." With his characteristic grin he surveyed Ramie's pullover and jeans. "Where did you get the fancy dress?" Then he ordered, "Through here before anybody sees you."

The back was full of technical equipment. Apart from Wolfgang, there was another man there, with headphones, sitting at a tape recorder. From somewhere a voice could be heard: "He's getting too close."

Wolfgang picked up a microphone and murmured, "You're in the way, take two steps back. And don't overdo it. Don't make him feel you're about to go for him."

Michael was crying, somewhere among the cars in the huge car park. "That damn Lasko woman fooled us all. Even me! I was in bed with her and I didn't…"

She just sat there feeling the icy cold grip every bone, every nerve. "Where's Herr Lasko?" she whispered. "I sent him on ahead because I…"

"We picked him up," Wolfgang said and told her what had happened so far, while outside Michael continued to try to get Zurkeulen to confess to murder in exchange for the briefcase full of money.

He'd appeared at the Blastings' at the crack of dawn, claiming he'd driven her to the airport. She was to take the first flight to Geneva and stay with her mother for a while. He wanted to be sure she was safe. Zurkeulen knew him, he'd said, he'd hardly be suspicious if he turned up with the money in place of his wife.

He'd given Wolfgang a house key, explaining that he'd already taken the briefcase out of the safe, then driven to the petrol station and on to the lab, where he'd worked until two. After that they'd wired him up.

He must have been convinced she was dead, all he was looking for now was answers. In order to convince Zurkeulen, he kept bringing in the few things she'd managed to tell him.

"My wife," he said, "met the Lasko woman in the summer. At the time she was having a little affair and didn't want me to find out about it. The Lasko woman was just supposed to string me along for a bit. My wife must have told her an awful lot to prepare her for her role. And that damn bitch saw her chance and got together with Hardenberg."

"That's enough," Wolfgang murmured. "Get to the point." With a quick grin he commented, "I always say he talks too much." Bringing his head closer to hers and thus away from the microphone and the other man, he whispered, "If he ever even hints at the little affair to Ilona, I'll wring his neck."

"Where is Frau Lasko?" Zurkeulen asked outside in his usual polite tone.

"Dead," Michael said. "I blew a fuse when I finally realized who she was."

The man at the tape recorder turned to Wolfgang and whispered, "He's doing it beautifully. One confession for another." Wolfgang nodded while Zurkeulen could be heard asking sceptically, "And she told you all that before she died? I'm sorry, Herr Trenkler, but I do have my doubts."

"She didn't tell me of her own free will, if that's what you mean. I had to get pretty rough with her," Michael explained. "And when I hit someone, they stay hit. I don't have to tell you that. Or do you think your thug committed suicide?"

"In that case..." said Zurkeulen, after what seemed like an eternity, even his sigh came clearly over the loudspeakers. "It's all highly regrettable. Your wife would still be in the best of health if she'd told me what Frau Lasko told you."

Wolfgang punched his hand and said, in a jubilant whisper, "We've got him. Now it's all going to come out." The man at the tape recorder adjusted a few controls, the reel continued to revolve, recording steadily.

Zurkeulen described his meetings with Susanne Lasko. He'd first met her at the beginning of August. She'd been recommended by Hardenberg, who didn't have that much to do with the investment of large sums himself. But since Zurkeulen had insured two of his properties through Alfo Investment, Hardenberg knew they were to be sold and knew their value. And Frau Lasko was very competent.

Zurkeulen swore that at their last meeting he'd had no idea it was a different woman he was faced with. He very much regretted what had happened. All he'd wanted was to discuss a small loss with the lady. He'd insisted on seeing some ID because she kept maintaining she was Nadia Trenkler. She'd refused to let him have her handbag, which had led to a tussle with his chauffeur in the course of which she fell in such an unfortunate way that she was beyond help. From that point on his chauffeur had dealt with the matter.

"You bastard," Wolfgang muttered. He turned to the man at the tape recorder and put a hand over the microphone. "It made my stomach heave when I read the autopsy report. They tortured her – with petrol amongst other things. I tell you it was horrible."

A few minutes later the handcuffs were snapped on Zurkeulen's wrists. The driver of the Beetle was cautioning him and reading him his rights, of which he was presumably well aware from past experience. Wolfgang took the briefcase with the money and gave her a victorious wink.

"Where's Herr Lasko?" she asked again.

"We sent him to have a coffee," said Wolfgang. "If he'd heard all that, we'd have had a long article about it in some newspaper next week."

"I'd like a coffee too," she said.

"You get that husband of yours over here." Wolfgang was peering out of the window in the rear door. The Jaguar was parked a long way away, among other cars. "What the hell's he doing over there?"

She didn't want to go, but did anyway. Even from a distance she could see that Michael was resting his head on the steering wheel. As she approached, she saw that his shoulders were twitching. It was several minutes before he realized someone was there. He looked up, stared at her in bewilderment and shook his head, refusing to acknowledge her. But then he did lower the window.

"Do you remember," she said, taking out the ear studs and tossing them into his lap, "what Nadia said when you came back so early from the lab on September the twelfth because Olaf had a virus which might be terminal? 'That's terrible,' she said, 'is there nothing that can be done?' I thought Olaf was one of your colleagues. Do you remember where you sat when you came back late that evening from seeing Kemmerling? You had a piece of toast and a pickled gherkin. First of all you sat on the side of the bath, then on my legs. You were determined to give the tense muscles in the back of Nadia's neck a massage. I didn't want you to. And I certainly didn't want to sleep with you. But she'd made it very clear that I wasn't to do anything to arouse your suspicions. And I'd forgotten to take the tampons out of the cupboard. I'd no idea what having a headache meant to you two."

He lowered his head again and looked down at the rings she dropped, one after the other, to join the ear studs in his lap. First the one with the striking blue stone, then the wedding ring and finally the one he'd put on her finger in Paris.

"And do you remember what you said?" she went on. "'Come on, don't be a prick-tease.' On the Friday afternoon, when Kemmerling stayed in the lab to keep an eye on the technician, then I did want to. By then I'd already fallen in love with you, I think. When she called for me to pick her up here at the airport, I wondered what would happen if I didn't go. I thought if I didn't I'd never see you again."

He raised his head. His shoulders were no longer twitching. He dried his cheeks with the back of his hand. His lips moved, as if he was going to say something. But he put his hand over his mouth, rubbed his face with both hands and shook his head again.

"I did hire the silver Mercedes, that's true, but I only drove it as far as the car park here. She took the Mercedes and I had the Alfa. The first time I was with you, you said you didn't need money to burn. That was the Sunday in August when I had to dismantle the garage door, because I didn't know how the alarm system worked, and when Dettmer then found me in your car with cuts on my fingers. If you don't need her life insurance, then let me keep her name. I don't know if she really wanted me to die, but I do know she's sent me so far up shit creek no one can get me out again. There's another fourteen million lying around somewhere. The other eight men were duped as well. My ex is trying to see to it that they get their money back. I don't want it. But I don't want to have my child in prison. I won't bother you ever again, I promise you that."

Then she went back to the Ford Transit and walked on past it. Wolfgang called after her, "Nadia, wait. Where are you going?" She ignored him. Let Michael give him whatever answer he thought was best.

She quickly found the Alfa. It was in the short-term car park next to Dieter's estate car. Schneider and Dieter were standing there talking. After Schneider had said goodbye, Dieter insisted on escorting her home. It wasn't necessary. Michael didn't arrive at the house while she was there.

She packed some clothes and the things for the baby. The handbag with her ID, driving licence and all the rest she found among the pullovers in the cupboard drawers. She took out the house key and left it in the dressing room. Lilo's key she put in the clothes closet. The Alfa she was going to keep.

For the time being she took a room in a hotel. It was relatively expensive, but that was no problem with Nadia's credit cards. There were no other problems either. No one turned up to arrest her. In the first few days she expected them to. But Michael did nothing to expose her – and nothing to see her again.

342

It was all quite unreal, waking up in the morning in the hotel bed with a mountain of memories of two lives – and not knowing which counted for more, thirty-seven years as Susanne Lasko or a few weeks as Nadia Trenkler. She had breakfast brought to her room. She couldn't face a large breakfast room with unknown faces.

Dieter came several times to report to her. She heard him speaking but what he was saying went straight past her. The part of her that could have paid attention to him was still standing beside the Jaguar waiting for Michael to say, "I'm sorry." Until she'd heard that, she didn't want to hear anything else, she just wanted to be left in peace.

But she wasn't left in peace. Lilo took just a week trace her whereabouts. And Lilo couldn't understand what had happened. No one could. The whole neighbourhood had followed the drama two, now almost three years ago, when Nadia had lost her job with the private bank in Düsseldorf and had started to drink. Then everyone had assumed Michael would pack his bags. That it should come to a final separation now, without anything serious having happened – it just didn't make sense.

The first thing Lilo did was to get her an appointment with her own gynaecologist. She didn't just hear her child's heart beat for the first time, she saw it as well, the tiny creature for whose sake she'd agreed to stand in for Nadia one more time.

Shortly after that, Jo appeared. He had a theory of his own. Since he didn't know which of his next-door neighbours was against children and which for, he presumed Michael was against them and offered to have a serious word with him about his responsibilities. After all, Christmas was coming, the family festival.

"Leave him be," she said. "I think that's for the best."

"Are you going to spend the holiday all alone in the hotel?" Jo asked.

"No, I'm flying to Geneva."

Wolfgang also came once – with a guilty conscience that was the result of his own theory: Michael had been against her playing a part in the attempt to trap Zurkeulen, she had been all for it. Michael thought she wanted to do him a favour, Wolfgang suspected, because of their brief affair.

"But it'll all sort itself out," Wolfgang declared confidently. "I can't understand why he's making such a fuss. He's worse than that time at the swimming pool. D'you remember?"

She didn't, couldn't remember. He grinned. "Christ, I thought he was going to break my neck." Serious once more, he went on, "Well, anyway, everything went smoothly. He'll come to see it was the best solution. Chin up."

It was unsettling. Every day someone could turn up who'd heard from Lilo where she was. Some stranger who wanted give her a few words of comfort. Dieter was trying to find a flat for her, somewhere far away, in Bavaria or Lower Saxony perhaps, since she insisted she didn't want to go to Romania. Lilo also thought staying in a hotel was untenable as a long-term solution. And she was quicker.

Shortly after Christmas Lilo turned up with a big surprise: a large, airy apartment with a roof garden in a quiet neighbourhood on the outskirts of the town. It was more or less the apartment Nadia had promised her. It was impossible to refuse and, anyway, she didn't really want to leave the area. She wanted to be close to Michael, accessible for the moment when he came to see that she wasn't to blame for Nadia's death. Surely he must realize that eventually.

Furnishing the apartment made a pretty deep hole in Nadia Trenkler's accounts. But it filled up again, as if by magic. At some point she intended to get to the bottom of this constantly replenished supply, to make sure she wasn't spending the money of duped investors. Also she was sure Nadia must have invested her own money somewhere, but she didn't get round to looking into it.

Lilo was tireless in her efforts to pull her out of the black hole of depression. She made regular reports on Michael's activities and passed on messages, the meaning of which remained a mystery to Lilo. She was to tell her he'd been to Geneva after the New Year. Her parents had been informed, she didn't need to worry, everything was OK. Nothing was OK! Never again could everything be OK.

"Why did he speak to your parents, darling?" Lilo asked. "You were there yourself over Christmas, weren't you? Could you not bring yourself to tell them? You have hopes that he'll think it over and change his mind, haven't you?"

"Yes," she said.

"Won't you tell me what happened?" Lilo asked. A shake of the head was all that was necessary. Lilo understood that there were things one couldn't talk about and declared, "You've changed a lot." With a hesitant smile, she went on, "Don't get me wrong. I think you've changed for the better. Before I often didn't know where I was with you." Lilo sighed. "Now I don't know where I am with Michael. It's eating away at him. I think he's just waiting for you to take the first step." Then, all eagerness, she said, "I could arrange a chance meeting. What d'you think? He goes to Demetros's almost every evening. Or the two of us could go out for a nice meal together?"

"I don't want to meet him by chance," she said, "and certainly not at Demetros's."

"But you can't shut yourself away for ever," Lilo insisted.

So they went to museums, to the theatre and to a concert – not one by Jacques Niedenhoff, he spent most of the time out of the country. Frederick had told Ilona that Jacques was thinking of giving up residence in Germany – because of the high taxes. Lilo was an inexhaustible source of information and easily fobbed off with an "I'm sorry, but I'd rather not talk about that", on topics where there was nothing she could say.

One Sunday afternoon in March she went with Lilo to a private view in the course of which an embarrassing incident occurred. Professor Danny Kemmerling and his laboratory mouse were there. And Danny Kemmerling felt it incumbent upon himself to give her a sermon about forgiving and forgetting. As he saw it, she had left Michael because of his affair with Beatrice Palewi and that was bringing him close to a breakdown. "I can assure you," he said, "that your husband hasn't seen Frau Palewi for months. She's not with us any more."

He looked at her. She was in the seventh month, highly pregnant. And Danny Kemmerling said, "A true marriage should be able to get over a little affair. Particularly in this situation."

His companion was a few yards away with Lilo and Edgar Henseler, looking at Maiwald's latest picture, which was not at all as severe as Edgar had feared. With a meaningful glance at the young woman, she asked in cool tones, "Does your wife share your opinion on that?"

Following her look, Danny Kemmerling said, "I assume so. It's not something she's had to think about so far."

"That's what I thought," she said. "And I'm convinced you'll get a big surprise if you talk to her openly about it. No wife likes her husband being unfaithful, whatever the situation."

Danny Kemmerling took this as the insinuation it was intended as. His expression hardened as he declared that he wasn't unfaithful to his wife.

Pointing to the little group viewing the new Maiwald, she asked, "So what do you call that?"

For a moment he was speechless. His face flushed. "I'm sorry, Frau Trenkler," he said, "but that is going too far." And with that he turned on his heel and left.

Later on Lilo told her that Danny Kemmerling didn't like being reminded of his first marriage. He had filed for divorce when the doctors told him there was no hope of his first wife's condition ever improving. She'd been in a coma for a long time following a road accident and was now in an expensive nursing home in a state of advanced dementia. Shortly after the divorce came through, Danny Kemmerling had married one of his colleagues. Dr Jutta Kemmerling might look like a teenager, but she was actually in her late thirties.

That was the moment when she was afraid Lilo had realized. But Lilo had never bothered much about Susanne Lasko and was convinced anyway that pregnant women had other things on their mind, especially when their marriage had broken down. Apart from that, she thought Michael had perhaps only told Jo about Kemmerling's first wife and the circumstances of his divorce.

It was the last embarrassing incident. Nor were there any more threatening situations. She had no more contact with Hardenberg. And Wolfgang didn't manage to nail Hardenberg, officially no customers of Alfo Investment had been defrauded out of their money. As Dieter had promised, he made every effort, with Hardenberg's help, to return the money to the other eight investors. And in seven cases he was successful. That in return Heller's murder went unpunished was hardly just, but Dieter saw no way of handing Hardenberg over to the authorities while at the same time protecting Nadia Trenkler.

At the end of April there was €1,600,000 left in a bank in Zurich. 1,300,000 of that had once belonged to a Josef Maringer, the rest was interest. And Josef Maringer no longer needed his money. In the meantime he had died and there were no heirs in sight, though Philip Hardenberg wasn't told that when he transferred the amount to Luxembourg, where Nadia Trenkler had arranged a safe deposit for herself.

Dieter said, "If you don't want the money, then Hardenberg'll get it. We mustn't let that happen. I think you've earned it. At least it would mean you won't have to be worrying about the future."

She wasn't anyway. It was a relatively pleasant life, amusing, varied and yet empty. She learned a lot about art, music, current events. She improved her English talking to Pamela on the phone. On Mondays she had French lessons with a high-school teacher, although she had no idea what the point was. She had no more conversations with Jacques Niedenhoff, nor with the young man with whom Alina passed the time after her separation from Nadia's father.

On Tuesdays and Thursdays she had private piano lessons. Wednesdays was aqua aerobics for pregnant women. Her diary was full. Sometimes she called these activities occupational therapy to stop herself going mad thinking of a man for whom and by whom she'd almost been killed.

She met her mother regularly every second Friday in a café near the old folks' home. Agnes Runge came in a taxi so that Nadia Trenkler didn't have to show herself in a place where people had known Susanne Lasko. These afternoons were times when she allowed herself a few tears. Just tears, no sobs, so her mother wouldn't notice.

For her mother, everything had ended in a straightforward way. Susanne had told Michael the truth and he'd sent her away. But he provided for her generously. And by this time she'd come to see that it was essential Johannes Herzog didn't find out. And, anyway, it wasn't that important for Johannes.

Lilo knew about these afternoon meetings and found it touching that she spent a little time with the old lady and didn't hold the things her daughter had done against her. And the continued contact with Susanne Lasko's ex-husband – in Lilo's eyes Dieter was an interesting person to talk to and Nadia had always had time for people like that.

At the beginning of May Laura Trenkler was born. Everything happened at breakneck speed. She hardly had time for the pain, she just managed to get a taxi and when it was over she didn't know what to do with all the flowers. Even Dieter sent a bouquet. He didn't come himself but rang up to congratulate her and to say that his daughter had a cold and he didn't want to spread the germs.

Lilo and Jo were her first visitors. Jo completed the formalities for her and took a few photos, tears in his eyes. Then Wolfgang came, at first alone, then with Ilona. Ilona told her not to use disposable nappies. She should think of the mountains of rubbish.

She couldn't think of anything any more, only remember – seven years of marriage which for her consisted of a few days and nights in Paris. The rest had just been one long fit of trembling.

Edgar Henseler brought her a bouquet for which there was no vase big enough. Old Barlinkow came specially from Berlin to offer his warmest congratulations and his best wishes for her daughter. Instead of flowers Hannah – she still didn't know her surname, but intended to find out as soon as she could – brought her an amulet, supposedly an Indian good-luck charm.

And then Jutta Kemmerling came. By that time she was back in her apartment. The news of the birth had reached Danny Kemmerling's second wife by a roundabout route: Jo had given Michael one of his photos and Michael had shown it round the lab. "It would be nice," Jutta Kemmerling said, "if you'd let him see his daughter now and then. He won't ask you himself. But it is usual."

"We're not usual," she said. "And I don't think he wants to see me."

She was wrong.

Lilo had found her a home help so that she could take things easy. Lilo was also looking for a babysitter, so she could get out again. And when the bell rang on a Wednesday evening at the end of May, she assumed it would be the art student Lilo had told her to expect. She pressed the buzzer for the outside door then went and waited in the corridor. The light above the lift went on, the lift arrived, the door slid open.

Michael looked almost the same as on the Sunday of her dress rehearsal, wearing jeans and a casual white polo shirt. All she could feel was the thud of her heartbeat. And he didn't know where to look. He looked her in the eye very briefly then approached, head bowed. "May I..." He broke off and gestured helplessly with both hands. "... come in?"

Leaving the door open, she preceded him into the living room and stood in the middle of the floor. He sat down in an armchair, kneading his hands, and asked hesitantly, "Is it really my child?"

"There's been no one else in the last few years."

He bit his lip, nodded thoughtfully and cleared his throat. "I talked to Lasko a few days ago." What he'd talked to Dieter about, he didn't say.

Nor had Dieter mentioned the conversation. Abruptly he asked, "May I see her?"

There was no reason to refuse, but she couldn't go with him. His unexpected appearance had triggered off a whirl of contradictory emotions. After all the months, she thought she'd left the worst behind her. But the only things that had really faded were his hands on her throat and the icy cold.

He stayed in the nursery for almost half an hour. Then he came back – holding the baby. He claimed it had been awake. She didn't believe him for a moment. He sat down in the armchair again, his daughter in his arm.

"If you expect me to apologize, I'm going to have to disappoint you," he said. "I expect an apology from you."

"I've done nothing I have to apologize for."

He gave a harsh laugh and, looking down at the baby, said, "No? And what do you call this here? That was the twelfth of September."

"Or the thirteenth," she said. "Given the way my life's gone, I rather assume it was the Friday. And I've already told you how it came about. If you'd left me alone on the Thursday it would never have happened."

He let that go. Getting worked up, he said, "I'll never understand why she did it. But I would like to know why you agreed to go along with it. What did your think you were doing, getting into bed with a stranger and letting his wife pay you for it? She did pay you, didn't she? How much did she offer?"

"I'm sure I wasn't as expensive as your studies," she said.

With a derisive grin, he declared, "You seem to have learned a lot from her."

"I hadn't any choice. Will you go now, please." She took a step towards him and stretched out her hands for the baby. "Give her to me."

"No!" He shook his head. "First of all I want an answer. If you were there on the twenty-eighth of November, then it was you in the bath on the Friday morning. And I'm sure she didn't pay you to tell me you loved me and to hurt yourself with that confession. In that moment why didn't you tell me who you were?"

"And how would you have taken it – in that moment? D'you think you'd have been over the moon?"

She got no answer to that. "Have you any idea," he asked, "what it feels like to have lived with a stranger, a woman you don't know, and not notice for weeks? And if there hadn't been all that nonsense with Jacques, who knows how long it would have gone on for."

He was too loud, the baby in his arms began to whimper.

"Give her to me," she asked again.

He didn't react, but went on as if he hadn't heard her. "When we came back from Paris, I thought it was the best time we'd ever had together. Everything was different, that was what it was of course. But actually it was the way I'd always wanted things to be with her. I thought she'd finally seen reason. Why didn't you clear off in Paris, as your ex urged you to? Why did you take the risk of staying with me? You didn't do it for the money alone, did you?"

She thought she knew what he wanted to hear. But she'd already told him that. And he hadn't believed her. When she didn't reply, he took a deep breath. "I don't even know what to call you."

"You don't need to rack your brains over that if you go now."

He looked at the moaning infant. Finally he got up and handed her the baby. But he didn't leave, he followed her into the nursery and stood beside the table, watching as she changed its nappy. She decided to leave breast-feeding it until he'd gone. But he still didn't go and she couldn't let her child go hungry because of his obstinacy.

He only left the nursery when she put Laura back in the cradle. She stayed there for a moment, waiting for the front door to open and close. There was silence. When she went back into the living room he was standing by the balcony door, looking out. He must have heard her steps, for he turned round. His voice sounded firm, assured, as if he'd thought out what he was going to say carefully. "I've let you have what you wanted, her name, even her money. In return, I want the child."

"Sorry," she said, "you're not Rumpelstiltskin."

He smiled. "No, but I do have a few cards up my sleeve and I'm not going to be done again and certainly not done out of my daughter. We're not legally divorced. If you want to sue for divorce, I'll fight for custody of the child – and no holds barred. I wouldn't hesitate to cite your drink problem or the reason why you lost your job. There's a whole load of reasons I could give why you're totally unsuited to bringing up a child."

"My drink problem?" She shook her head in disbelief. "I don't believe it. I simply don't believe it. I've never had a drink problem. Are you trying to play the macho man? It would have been better if you'd done that with her. You tried to kill me. How do you think a divorce judge will respond to that?"

He shrugged his shoulders. "I could tell them who you really are. But I don't want to do that. I want to..." He broke off and started again. He didn't know how to put it, he said. It was only the baby that mattered. The baby was very important to him. But it wasn't just that. He wasn't going to say he loved her, because he hated lying. He just wanted her to come back and give him a chance to see if he could love her.

During the past few months he'd had plenty of time to think – about his feelings for Nadia, about the two days in September, the Friday morning in November, the time in Paris, which she hadn't used to make a bid for safety. He didn't want to live with an illusion, just with the woman whom he had thought all the time was Nadia.

THE SINNER

Petra Hammesfahr

Cora Bender killed a man on a sunny summer afternoon by the lake and in full view of her family and friends. Why? What could have caused this quiet, lovable young mother to stab a stranger in the throat, again and again, until she was pulled off his body? For the local police it was an open-and-shut case. Cora confessed; there was no shortage of witnesses. But Police Commissioner Rudolf Grovian refused to close the file and started his own maverick investigation. So begins the slow unravelling of Cora's past, a harrowing descent into a woman's private hell.

Hailed as Germany's Patricia Highsmith for her bittersweet family crime novels where the innocence of childhood collides with horrors enacted by adults, Petra Hammesfahr has written a dark, spellbinding novel which stayed at the top of the bestseller list for fifteen months.

PRAISE FOR PETRA HAMMESFAHR
AND *THE SINNER*

£8.99/$14.95/C$16.50
CRIME PAPERBACK ORIGINAL
ISBN 978-1-904738-25-1
www.bitterlemonpress.com